RECOGNITION

Peter was there when Roger Bacon finally opened his eyes. "You were very ill," he said. "We did our best, but in sooth there was little enough to do but pray."

"I had the death," Roger said tranquilly, "but I slipped away."

Peter's face grew more worried. "I told you you were working too hard. You ought to rest if you can. Is there no place you can go? Some place in the south would be best of all, even if that's barely possible."

It was, of course, wholly possible; for now that he had decided, with an inspiration which had sprouted from the very heart of his delirium, what was to become of him. It seemed so easy now that he knew, beyond all doubt, that he was to make of himself a scientist *instead of* a theologian; he had simply never thought of it in those terms before.

Other Avon Books by
James Blish

AND ALL THE STARS A STAGE
BLACK EASTER
CITIES IN FLIGHT
DAY AFTER JUDGMENT
MISSION TO THE HEART STARS
THE STAR DWELLERS
TITANS' DAUGHTER
VOR

Coming Soon

JACK OF EAGLES

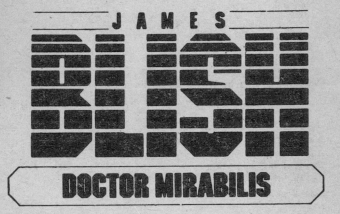

JAMES BLISH

DOCTOR MIRABILIS

AVON
PUBLISHERS OF BARD, CAMELOT, DISCUS AND FLARE BOOKS

For Virginia

Cover illustration by Wayne D. Barlowe

AVON BOOKS
A division of
The Hearst Corporation
959 Eighth Avenue
New York, New York 10019

Copyright ⊚ 1964 by James Blish
Published by arrangement with the estate of James Blish
Library of Congress Catalog Card Number: 81-70572
ISBN: 0-380-60335-7

For information address Richard Curtis Associates, Inc.,
340 East 66th Street, New York, New York 10021

First Avon Printing, August, 1982

AVON TRADEMARK REG. U. S. PAT. OFF. AND IN
OTHER COUNTRIES, MARCA REGISTRADA, HECHO EN
U. S. A.

Printed in the U. S. A.

WFH 10 9 8 7 6 5 4 3 2 1

Truth is the daughter of time.

ROGER BACON

And now through every window came a light into the chamber as of skies paling to the dawn. Yet not wholly so; for never yet came dawn at midnight, nor from all four quarters of the sky at once, nor with such swift strides of increasing light, nor with a light so ghastly. . . . The King cried terribly, "The hour approacheth!"

E. R. EDDISON: The Worm Ouroboros

We are as dwarfs mounted on the shoulders of giants, so that we can see more and farther than they; yet not by virtue of the keenness of our eyesight, nor through the tallness of our stature, but because we are raised and borne aloft upon that giant mass.

BERNARD OF CHARTRES

There are no dead.

MAURICE MAETERLINCK

CONTENTS

ARGUMENT

Forthe, Pylgryme, Forthe!

of how the death came to visit Robert
Grosseteste, and in what mind it found him:
and of a letter from Ilchester to Roger Bacon,
and in what mind it found him: and, how the
Frideswyde Chest was opened

of a meeting with a falconer of fells upon
Salisbury Plain, and the deception practised
upon the knights of Hubert de Burgh by
Wulf the peasant: and what manner of treasure trove Roger Bacon found at Yeo Manse

of the fall of Hubert de Burgh and all his
purposings at Henry the King's hands, and
how Adam Marsh discoursed with the Lady
Eleanor: in which doth appear a clerk before
these courtiers

Of Hem That Yaf Hym Wherwith To Scoleye

How That We Baren Us That Ilke Nyght

DRAMATIS PERSONAE
in order of their appearance

ROGER BACON of Ilchester, clerk.

ADAM MARSH (or, de Marisco) of Wearmouth, Franciscan, lecturer in theology at Oxford until 1250, confessor of Eleanor of Pembroke and later of her husband.

ROBERT GROSSETESTE, Bishop of Lincoln.

WILLIAM BUSSHE of Dorset, Merchant of the Staple.

WULF, a serf of the Bacon estate.

TIBB, a thief.

SIMON DE MONTFORT, Earl of Leicester.

ELEANOR OF PEMBROKE, sister of the King, widow of the Earl of Pembroke, wife to Simon de Montfort.

HENRY III of Winchester, King of England, son of King John.

PETER DES ROCHES, tutor to the King, Bishop of Winchester.

EDMUND RICH of Abingdon, Archbishop of Canterbury (later canonized).

GUY DE FOULQUES, papal legate in England and Cardinal-Bishop of Sabina; from 1265, Pope Clement IV.

PETER DE RIVAULX (or, des Rievaux), nephew to Peter des Roches.

JOHANN BUDRYS of Livonia, clerk.

ALBERTUS called MAGNUS, Dominican, regent master at Paris, sometime Bishop of Ratisbon (later canonized).

RAIMUNDO DEL REY, clerk.

PIERRE DE MARICOURT (Petrus Peregrinus), a noble of Picardy.

JULIAN DE RANDA, clerk.

MATTHEW PARIS, Benedictine, historian to Henry III.

LUCA DI COSMATI, artist.

LORENZA ARNOLFO PICCOLOMINI, Marquis of Modena, and patron of Luca.

OLIVIA PICCOLOMINI, daughter to the Marquis of Modena.

THOMAS BUNGAY, provincial minister to the Franciscans in England 1271-75.

RICHARD RUFUS of Cornwall, regent master in theology at Paris and Oxford.

JOANNES, a clerk, apprenticed to Roger Bacon.

RAYMOND OF LAON, clerk to Guy de Foulques.

SIR WILLIAM BONECOR, emissary of the King to Clement IV.

JEROME DI ASCOLI, minister-general to the Franciscans 1274-89; thereafter Pope Nicholas IV.

OTTO, a gaoler.

ADRIAN, a voice.

RAYMOND DE GAUFREDI, minister-general to the Franciscans from 1289.

Time: 1231-94 A.D.
Place: England, France, Italy

FOREWORD

Though Roger Bacon is generally acknowledged to be one of the great figures in medieval history, and in particular, one of the forerunners of modern science, astonishingly few facts about his life are known. There is a sizable Bacon legend, but of this the historical Bacon was only temporary custodian: the famous story of the brass head, for instance, is an ancient Arabic legend, which first appeared in Europe in the tenth century as a tale about the mighty Gerbert (later Pope Sylvester II) from the potent hand of William of Malmesbury. In Roger Bacon's own time, it was being told about Albertus Magnus. It became attached to Bacon only late in the sixteenth century, via a play called *Friar Bacon and Friar Bungay* by Shakespeare's forgotten rival Robert Greene. (The play itself has been called an attempt to imitate Marlowe's *Doctor Faustus,* but there seems to be good evidence that Greene's work was first; in any event, it is still worth reading.) Since 1589, the brazen head has lived an underground life as the golem, Frankenstein's monster, Karel Capek's robots and their innumerable spawn, and today, perhaps, as Dr. Claude Shannon's mechanical player (after Poe) of indifferent chess. Tomorrow, Dr. Norbert Weiner warns us, it may be outthinking us all—and Dr. Issac Asimov thinks that will probably be a good thing.

The appearance of Roger Bacon as the hero of the Greene play, however, is no accident of legend. The historical Doctor Faustus—a dim figure indeed—became in the same way a vehicle for timeless preoccupations of the human mind, which tell us a great deal about ourselves but almost nothing about Faustus himself. The Bacon legend, which is *not* the subject of this novel, haunted Europe in the same way until the end of the seventeenth century.

What remains behind as reasonably certain knowledge

about Roger Bacon's life would hardly fill a small pamphlet; and the more intensively the man is pursued, the more what was once thought certain about him tends to melt into doubt. What little we know about him personally comes entirely from his own testimony, particularly in the *Opus Tertium*, the *Compendium studii theologiae* and an untitled work, evidently intended as a covering letter for the works for the Pope, which is usually called "the Gasquet fragment." The *Compendium*, as my last chapter indicates, shows clear signs that his memory is failing; and as for the other two, they were intended to impress his patron and hence are not wholly reliable as autobiography, as well as being riddled with contradictions.

Except for an anonymous writer who saw Bacon at a gathering like the one described in Chapter VII, not a single soul in his own lifetime ever managed to mention him by name in a writing which has survived, not even people he obviously knew intimately; and we have the text of only one letter *to* him, that being the mandate of 1266 from Clement IV. A Roger Bacon does appear in one of the footnotes to Matthew Paris' *Chronica majora*, but few modern scholars believe that this anecdote can refer to *the* Roger Bacon. (I disagree, as Chapter III shows, but there is simply no present way to settle this question except by intuition.)

An unknown amount of Bacon's own work is missing, in addition to the fact that not all that is known has yet been published. He mentions two treatises, *De generatione* and *De radii*, which have not yet been found, and the many unpublished unattributed manuscripts of the period in European libraries may include many more. There are no Bacon *incunabula*; the Voynich manuscript, in which W. R. Newbold claimed to have found an elaborate cypher concealing a knowledge of human anatomy which would have been staggering even for Bacon, was once thought to be in his own hand, but modern scholarship has discredited hand and authorship alike (and cyphers, as we have learned painfully from Ignatius Donnelly and his followers, are not reliable clues to the authorship of anything). The only authenticated sample of Bacon's handwriting is that of the corrections—not the text—of the piece of the *Opus Majus* in the Vatican Library.

Finally, just the published body of Bacon's work is so vast—some twenty-two thick volumes, plus smaller pieces—that no one has ever attempted a definitive Collected Works, and the existing partial collections, those of Steele and Brewer, are arranged in no rational order. Furthermore, for the reader who would rather not cope with medieval Latin, only the *Opus Majus* and a few much smaller works have ever been translated, and the translations are long out of print. It is easier to deal with a mountebank like Giambattista della Porta, whose *Natural Magick* can be bought today in a facsimile of the handsome 1658 English printing, boxed; but a universal genius is born mutinous and disorderly, and remains so seven hundred years later.

This is a wholly inviting situation for a novelist, providing only that he has the brass head to believe that he can turn a universal genius into a believable character; but he must not pretend that the book he writes from it is a fictionalized biography. Under the circumstances it would be impossible to write any such work about Roger Bacon. What follows is a fiction. It is as true to Bacon's age as I have been able to make it; there is, at least, no shortage of data about the thirteenth century—the problem is to mine it selectively. Roger Bacon himself, however, is unrecoverable by scholarship alone. The rest is—or should be—a vision.

A word about language:

The reader may wonder why I have resorted here and there to direct quotations in Latin, especially since the characters are speaking Latin a large part of the time and I have been content to give what they say in English. The reason is that these exceptions, these ideas and opinions written down seven centuries ago, might otherwise have been suspected of being a twentieth-century author's interpolations. There is always an English paraphrase close by, but the direct quotations are intended to demonstrate that I have not modernized my central figure, and did not need to do so.

I must, however, admit to one modernization, this being the translation from *De multiplicatione specierum* in Chapter XII. Here it seemed to me that the Aristotelian terminology Bacon uses would be worse than impenetrable to most modern readers. Hence I have followed Sarton and others in converting what Bacon calls "the multiplication of species" (which today suggests that he must have been talking about biology) into "the propagation of action," which shows that his subject is physics. Several other Aristotelian terms, such as "agent" and "patient" have suffered a similar conversion at my hands.

As for the English, I have followed two rules. (1) Where the characters are speaking Middle English, I have used a synthetic speech which roughly preserves Middle English syntax, one of its several glories, but makes little attempt to follow its metrics or its vocabulary (and certainly not its spelling, which was catch-as-catch-can). (2) Where they are speaking French or Latin, which is most of the time, I have used modern English, except to indicate whether the familiar or the polite form of "you" is being employed, a distinction which should cause no one any trouble.

I am greatly indebted to W. O. Hassall of the Bodleian Library, Oxford, for help in locating pertinent manuscripts; to L. Sprague de Camp, whose vast knowledge of the history of technology I mined mercilessly; to Ann Corlett, Algis Budrys, L. D. Cole, Virginia Kidd, Willy Ley and Henry E. Sostman for invaluable criticism and suggestions; and to Kenneth S. White for pushing me into the project in the first place.

JAMES BLISH

Arrowhead,
Milford, Pennsylvania

Implicit prima pars:

FORTHE, PYLGRYME, FORTHE!

I: FOLLY BRIDGE

It was called the fever, or the plague, or the blue-lips, or the cough, but most often simply the death. It had come north across Folly Bridge into Oxford with the first snow, and at first had shown a godly grim decorum, spreading mainly inside the enclave of the Jewerye, so that the mayor and the burgesses of Oxford decided that there was nothing to fear from it.

The astrologers agreed. There was every heavenly sign that the city would be at peace throughout the whole of A.D. 1231. Certainly there would not be another pestilence; and certainly not in October, where Jupiter, Venus and the moon would be in trine before All Hallows' Eve.

Besides, the Jews had excellent physicians, even one or two from Bologna. There was nothing to fear.

Now it is too late to be afraid, Roger thought. The words came to him not as his own thought, however, but like an aphorism which he had only remembered; it was the way he had learned to distinguish the prompting of his self from the general tumult of notions which stormed tormentingly out of his soul the instant he started awake. He stood motionless in the pitch-black, freezing stone corridor, hands folded tensely into each other under the coarse hempen robe he had thrown over his clothing when Adam Marsh had brought the word and called him out, listening; but the self had nothing further to say.

It had said all that was needful. It was too late to fear the death now. Neither the Bolognese Jews nor anyone else had been able to prevent the death. If it was not yet a plague, it had not much further to spread to become one. Half the burgesses were stricken of it already, and the school was dissolved into a shivering huddle of coughing shadows. No classes had met for over a week; no convocations had been called since the death had taken the prior of

Carfax; the halls were silent; the students huddled on their pallets, too sick to care for themselves, or providentially too well to risk breathing the prevalent miasma outside the dormitories. Here, at the Franciscan school, the gloom was absolute, for the death was visiting the lector.

Roger's heart filled; he could feel his knuckles crackling under the robe. Since he could see nothing at all in the damp-ticking black passageway, he could not prevent himself from standing suddenly, also in his shivering shift, by the bedside of his father in the blocky fieldstone house outside Ilchester now abruptly gone, as his father was gone eleven years. *Domine, Domine!* Until that moment he had not loved his father. How little he had been able to anticipate even in his new rough boyhood, five years old and already master of the wide-nostrilled sweaty horses trembling with day-end exhaustion in their stalls, that Christopher Bacon's rude remote justice would some day be replaced by the tradeswine arrogance of Robert Bacon, hardly eight years Roger's senior!

And now Robert Grosseteste was dying, too, only a door away in the timeless darkness. *Justice is Love,* the self whispered suddenly. And he had no answer. The vision of his father's death vanished as suddenly, leaving him empty in snow-covered Oxford, a black mark on a black ground inside a black box. If Robert Grosseteste died, where could Roger go then; what would he do; what would he think? Adam Marsh was well enough, but no man can have three fathers; besides, the gentle Adam lacked both the strength and the desire; he was a brother and would never be more—not a brother such as Robert Bacon, but a brother in love. As a father, he had no vocation.

Adam was with the lector now; had been with him a long time. In a while, perhaps, he would emerge and say: "It is over." There had been no assurance that the lector would be able to see Roger at all; it had been with a shock of guilty delight that Roger had heard that he even wanted to see Roger, but even of that there was no proof. It might only have been an idea of Adam's; he might have been summoned only on a chance.

On the thought, the door opened a little, letting a wedge of smoky orange light into the corridor. That was all. There were no voices, no footsteps. A draught began to

move gently past Roger's face, seeking the smokehole of
the lector's fireplace and discovering to Roger that he was
sweating under his cassock even in this black realm of liquid ice. The light wavered and lost some of its yellowness,
as though a few tapers were nodding and blowing inside
the room. Then a long-fingered hand, deeply chiselled on
the back with shadows between the tendons, took the door
by the latch and pulled it soundlessly to again. Perhaps it
had been only a wind that had opened it to begin with.

But Roger knew the hand. He stood in the blackness and
struggled with a jealousy only a little away from love.
Never mind that Adam Marsh of Wearmouth had come to
him the moment it appeared that the lector might die; he
was only trying to prove to his student how high he stood
in Robert's esteem. Never mind that Adam had recognized
the quick wit of the seventeen-year-old who sat under him
in theology and had won him a place at Robert's lectures to
the Franciscans; Roger could have done the same for himself. Never mind that Adam did seem to stand high in the
esteem of the lector, and in the general esteem of the Order; he was only thirty-one years old and had become a
Franciscan only last year. One Robert Bacon was enough;
Domine, Domine!

But it was not true. *Justice is Love.*

The words drove the jealousy from him, though he
fought sullenly to hold it. There was something about the
self that hated emotion, and particularly the red emotions,
the ones that fogged the eye, inside or out. Why should
Grosseteste have called Roger at all? Roger and the lector
had never even spoken, except once or twice in passing.
Grosseteste had his own favourite students—Adam, obviously, and a frighteningly brilliant lecturer in his mid-
twenties named John of Bandoun—and could hardly be
aware of the deep, irrational awe he had inspired in some
anonymous franklin's son from Ilchester.

Justice is Love, the self said again in its sweet bodiless
voice, and the fury was gone. Suddenly, he was only a man
in a corridor in a hall in a town in a snowfall, his eyes as
empty as embrasures, his head capped like a merlon in
winter with coldness. For an instant he did not even know
his own name; he stood as alone as a planet in the general
dark.

It had been a long day, like all days: the bell in the night, calling him out of bed to church for matins and the lauds, the seven psalms of praise; the Divine Office at prime, six o'clock in the morning, still full darkness and the cold at its bitterest, seven psalms, the litany and the mass with freezing toes; midday mass and then the meal, roots and eggs and water, and the sleep of afternoon—but no sleep for Roger, because of the letter; then the bell again to sing nones at three o'clock; and studies, but again no studies for Roger, because Robert Grosseteste was sick and Adam beside him, and one of the Bolognese, too, especially dispensed to minister to an archdeacon thrice over; then supper, wastelbread, butter and beans, with a little ale (the letter had made him cautious of spending any money on wine, for the first time in his life; besides, it was written in Aelfric, "Wine is not a drink for children or foolish people, but for the old and wise"); then the bell, and compline.

And then the summons from Adam.

He lifted one hand under the robe to finger the bulge of the letter, like a man cautiously investigating a fresh wound. It was a dirty scrap of old vellum, grey with erasures; under its present burden could still be seen the shadows of minuscules which had been the previous writing. These were almost clear at the bottom of the letter and Roger had been able to work out a little of it: ". . . e ministr e omnib fidelib suis Francis e . . ."—possibly a piece of some charter. But this game had run out quickly, and the faint remains of what the palimpsest had carried before it had been pumiced for the charter proved even duller: pieces of a crabbed hymn by some barely literate canon. There was no way to put off thinking about the message on top in new ink.

It was brief and disastrous enough. A villein who Roger did not even remember had thought well enough of him to dictate it to Ilchester's recorder, and had it sent to him by the most reliable means available to a man with neither purse nor freedom: a beggar. It said:

þis daye d Burh hiȝ Menne haþ despiled
Franklin Bacon & putte alle in fleyht to
ferne Strondeȝ Ihab aseyden for Mr
Roher ac hem schal cleym it Aske of þe

Franklin hiȝ serf Wulf at þe Oxen
    Ad majorem gloriae

This, in an oval-rubbed spot in the centre, surrounded by
a haze of extinguished knowledge, or what passed for it.
There was, unhappily, nothing in the least cryptic about
the message. It meant that Roger's home was gone and his
money with it. Somehow the soldiers of the King's justiciar, scouring the country for remaining pockets of baro-
nial resistance, had happened into Ilchester, and had seen
in the substantial heirs of Christopher Bacon, freeman
landholder, some taint of sympathy with the partisans of
the rebel barons, or some stronghold for the mercenaries
who had infected the whole east of England, since the evac-
uation of the French in 1217. The rest had followed inevitably. No matter that Ilchester had always been an
uneventful town, notable for nothing but its Wednesday
market and its authorized fair every twenty-ninth of August; Hubert de Burgh stood accused of the failure of last
year's expedition to the west of France (regardless of the
fact, or, as Adam Marsh had remarked sadly, perhaps because of the fact that the justiciar had advised King Henry
most strongly against any such hunting party); he was out
to prove that French sedition was still eating away at the
body politick, even in a place as unlikely as Ilchester, and
that the King's justiciar was swift and terrible in hawking
it. And so, farewell, suddenly, to the ancient yeoman house
of Bacon, though it had yet to see partisan, baron, Frenchman or mercenary; the serfs would thieve away the har-
vest, and leave the family only exile and poverty. The reference to "ferne Strondes" could only mean exile for Harold, Christopher's brother; he was the last of authority in
the family to remain in Ilchester; not even Hubert de
Burgh could touch Robert Bacon in his factor's fastness in
London.

Very well; and so, good-bye as well to new copies of old
books, to virgin parchment, to clean quills and fresh ink, to
meat and to wine, to warm wool and pliant leather, to a
new growth in widsom under Oxford's once *magister
scholarum* Robert Grosseteste, to a doctorate in theology,
to becoming (*Thou art addled in they wits!* the self cried in
its sweet voice) the world's wonder in moral philosophy.

From now on, he would be poor. Robert Bacon would not help him, that was certain; Robert had been scathing, indeed flyting, of Roger's scholiast bent and his penchant for the Latin language of the papal parasites, and of the money spent to support it—a scorn which had not been much tempered by the fact that Robert had twice been captured by the soldiers of Prince Louis' invading army shortly after the thirteen-year-old Roger had entered Oxford, and had had to ransom himself. By now, Robert thought of Roger as a renegade from the family—and never mind that the still younger Eugene, now fifteen and at the new University of Toulouse, had shown the same scholar's bent without being flyted for it; nor that now in London Robert was farther away from the family than Roger and had even less of the grain on his tongue; still the indictment stuck.

As well it might, the self whispered in the darkness. *Distresseth thou thyself, an thy people be dispersed? Justice is Love.*

And it was true. He was more distressed by the loss of his money and his problematical fame than by the loss of his kin and seat, and more urgent to reclaim whatever effects the unknown Wulf had hidden for him than to succour his sisters, let alone the serfs. Perhaps there was even some money left; Christopher had always been careful to conceal caches of several scores of pounds at a time about the acres during the invasion against just such a catastrophe as this, and did not dream even on the day of his death that his sullen second-born son had found the records of those oubliettes and broken the cypher which told where all but two were buried. Roger had never touched but one, and that one of the two not mentioned in the cypher at all, but deducible by simple geometrical reasoning from the positions of the others; he had lifted a heavy stone and there it was, and he had taken from it one pound, no more, as an honorarium to the power of his boy's reasoning, watched only by three snotty-nosed yearling calves—all of whom had died not long after of the trough fever. It did not seem likely that either a serf or a pack of de Burgh's mailed looters could have had the wit to uncover even the encyphered hideyholes, let alone Roger's deposit-lighter-by-one pound; and at the worst, there was still the undiscovered, unrecorded burial, which by evidence of its highest secrecy, might well be the richest of all—and a problem worthy of a subtle intellectual soul as much for its difficulty as for its treasure-trove.

And after that discovery, there were certain burials and other concealments that he had made—nothing that this Wulf could have known about, but as close to wealth as mark or pound might be in these times. There was, for instance, a flat glass that he had made from a broken windeye in the buttery, with a thin poured lead back in the centre of which he had dug out a peephole; through that chipped spot one might look in a dark room into a cat's eye, reflecting a candle flame into the cat's eye from the glass side—particularly into the eye of massive old Petronius, the black arbiter of the barn rats—and see deep in the lambent slitgated sphere a marvellous golden sparkle, overlaid with dusky red vessels. What might you see inside a man's head with such a tool? He had tried it with the infant Beth, but there had been no light in her eyes that he could see, and besides, his mother had cut the experiment short with a withing. In another pocket in the house he had hidden a small champ of nitre crystals which he had culled with reeking labour from the dungheap; he did not in the least know what they were good for, but anything so precisely formed had to be good for something, like the cylindrical bits of beryl which he had split from a prismatic rock, which laid on a page fattened the strokes and made even dirty minuscules easier to read. Every man has sisters; but how many men have such tools, and such mysteries?

Suddenly he realized that he was trembling. He let go of the letter and clasped his hands back together violently. If there is one thing in the world I will do, he told himself in the tear-freezing darkness. . . . No, if there is one thing in the world I will not do, *Domine, dominus noster,* I will not let go. I will not let go. Thou hast taken away mine house; so be it. But Thou shalt not take away from me what Thou hast given me, which is the lust to know Thy nature.

I shall never let go.

The wind made a sudden sucking sound somewhere in the convent and poured itself up the throat of a chimney with a low brief moan. The corridor lightened slightly, flickeringly. The time had come; Robert Grosseteste's door was open. Adam Marsh was standing in the muddy, wavering light, one long hand crooked, one deep shadow laid along his narrow pointed nose.

"Roger," he said softly. "Roger? Art still there? Ah, I see thee now. Come in most quietly, he is asleep, or so I think. But would talk with thee."

Roger stirred, painfully; his bones were almost frozen. He cleared his throat, but his whisper was still harsh when it came forth:

"Adam, if he is so ill—"

"Certes he is ill, but would see thee all the same. He asked for thee, Roger. Come in quickly, this plaudering lets the chill in, too, and he needs warmth."

Roger moved quickly then, fighting the stiffness, and Adam shut the door behind him with a miraculous soundlessness. If the room had been chilled during their brief exchange, Roger could not detect it; the air seemed almost hot to him, and the heat from the ardent coals in the fireplace beat against his cheeks and made his eyes tighten. Though there were two candles on a lectern against the wall to the left, and two more on an age-blackened, bookheaped table butting a wardrobe just to the right of the door, the room was quite dark all along its peripheries; the light and heat made an island in the centre, between the door and the hearth, where the low narrow bed was drawn up, parallel with the low stone mantel. The bed was deep in disordered robes and blankets.

The matter of the letter and his patrimony fled tracelessly from his mind the moment he saw the massive head of the lector upon the bolster, its bushy grey monk's tonsure in a tangle under a blue woollen skullcap, the veined eyelids closed in deep-shadowed sockets, the skin of the face as tight and semi-transparent as parchment over the magnificent leonine cheekbones. Bending over Robert Grosseteste and listening with cat-still intentness to his breathing was a fierce-looking swarthy man in mouse-coloured breeches and a saffron tunic; the ear that was tipped down to the lector was bare, but from the other a gold earring lay along the cord of his neck. As Roger made an involuntary half-step forward, the swarthy man held up one palm with all the command of a lord.

"Very well," the swarthy man said. "A will stay on live, an his stars permit it. But these are mischancy times. Give him of the electuary when a wakens."

"What is it he hath with him?" Adam said with an equal intensity.

"Not the consumption," the Jew said. "Beyond that I am as ignorant as any man. If there's a crisis, call me no more; I have done what I could."

"And for that all thanks," Adam said, "and my purse. Would God might send thee His grace as well as His wisdom."

The physician straightened, his eyes burning sombrely. "Keep thy purse," he said between startlingly white teeth. The purse struck the stone floor almost at Roger's feet and burst, scattering coins among the rushes and the alder leaves spread to trap fleas. "Thou payest me ill enough already with thy blessing. I spit on thee."

For a moment it seemed to Roger that he might actually do just that, but instead, he strode past them both with an odd, stoop-shouldered, loping gait and was gone. Adam stared after him; he seemed stunned.

"What did I say?" the Franciscan murmured.

"What matter?" Roger said in a hoarse whisper. He was having difficulty in keeping himself from tallying the spatter of coins in the rushes; he felt as though the parchment in his pocket had suddenly been set afire. " 'Tis but a Jew."

"As were three of the nine worthies of the world," Adam said gently, "and among Christians there were eke but three, as among the paynims. Since Our Lord was a Jew as well, that giveth the Jews somewhat the advantage."

Roger shrugged convulsively. This was an ill time, it seemed to him, to be resurrecting the Nine Worthies.

"Thou'dst talk nonsense on the day of wrath could it be mathematical nonsense, Master Marsh," he said edgily. The words, as they came out, appalled him; suddenly, it seemed as though he were giving voice to the self for the first time in all his guarded life—here in the presence of an undoubted elected saint, and of the angel of death. But it could hardly be unsaid. "Forgive me; Christ is as Christian a worthy as He was a Jew, it seemeth me. And meseemeth the *Capito* yonder as worthy a Christian as

Godfrey of Bouillon, and leader of as worthy a crusade. I count ignorance as deadly as the paynim."

Adams stared at Roger a little while as though he had seen the youngster for almost the first time. After a few moments, Roger was forced to drop his eyes, but that was no better, for that brought him back into encounter with the money on the floor.

"A dangerous notion, and a bad piece of logic," Adam said at last in a strange voice. "Thou art an ill-tempered youngster, Roger. Nevertheless, thou remindest me that our matter here is with the lector, not disputation; which is a point which pierceth, be it never so poorly thrust. Let neither of us raise our voices again here."

"So be it," Roger muttered. There was a long and smothering silence, during which Roger began to hear the slightly ragged, slightly too rapid breathing of Robert Grosseteste, as though his lungs were being squeezed by a marching piper of the Scots to keep him harrowing the air. As time stretched out under Adam's level eyes, the pace of the breathing increased; and then, with a start, the lector coughed rackingly and jerked his great head up.

"That shall I do," he said in a thick, strangled voice. His head moved uncertainly and for a moment his eyes rested on Roger without seeming to see him. Adam stepped forward and Grosseteste's head turned once more, but his eyes were still glazed; two hectic fever-spots began to burn on his cheeks, as though they had been rubbed with snow. Seeing the great head lolling thus frighteningly brought home to Roger as nothing else had done the precariousness of the lector's future from moment to moment; he was, after all, fifty-seven years old and the uprightness of his life had not prevented it from being most active and taxing. He had been the chancellor of the University until 1229, when he had resigned the post to give the lectures to the Franciscans, and in the short course of Roger's own lifetime he had been archdeacon of Chester, Northampton and Leicester, one after the other. No man in orders had ever been more attentive to the needs of his parishes; no member of the Faculty of Theology more assiduous of the needs of the whole University and all three thousand of its students; no scholar more careful to build the massive learning which alone justifies a master to lecture before the young. Were God to terminate his life in the next instant, no man could call it anything but long, full and rich in works—and the death had been laying an especial hand on the old.

Adam Marsh, murmuring something indistinguishable, was kneeling beside the bed, holding an enamelled Syran wine glass to Grosseteste's lips. The lector drank with difficulty, made a fearful face and then lay back among the blankets with a shuddering sigh. The quiet seeped back into the room, which was becoming hotter and stuffier with every instant; nevertheless, the lector's breathing was becoming a little easier, and he seemed now to be relaxed without either trembling from weakness or looking flaccid with morbidity. The honey vehicle of the Jew's electuary obviously had not much sweetened the dose, but the active principle of the slow-flowing mass was quick to take effect. Mandragora? No, that would have put the lector back to sleep, whereas he was obviously not under any narcotic, but simply more composed, less desperately distracted by the failure of his flesh. He lay staring at the dark flickering ceiling for a long time.

"Adam," he said at last. "I have been charged."

"Rest thee and let it wait," Adam Marsh said softly.

"Nay, the time is too short. I have been given a charge and will keep it, an I live. It came to me while I slept, and from God as I no doubt. And it concerneth thee, Adam."

The Franciscan gathered his cassock up and sat down cross-legged amidst the rushes and alder leaves. "Say on," he said resignedly. Roger was startled at the overtone of sadness in his voice.

Grosseteste heard it too. Still looking up into the shadows, he said quietly: "Thou may'st not refuse preferment all thy life, Adam. Offices are repugnant to thee, as I know well. But should God take me, thou shouldst become first in the Order in the realm; dost think Hubert de Burgh's countess ward hath sought thy counsel to no holy purpose?"

Roger looked up sharply, but at once he realized that Grosseteste had intended no reference to his own cloudy troubles in Ilchester. There was as yet no indication that the lector even recognized his presence. Hubert de Burgh was the King's justiciar, a public figure—it were folly to suppose that any reference to him was *ipso facto* a reference to a student at Oxford only two years come of age, even were that student Roger Bacon his unique and universe-pivot self.

"God will leave thee with us," Adam Marsh said. "Thou'lt not die. This I know."

"But there's no escape there for thee," Grosseteste said, with the faintest of ironies in his voice. "I have been charged, as I rede thee. And I live, I must resign my benefices and preferments, and devote myself to piety and contemplation, as befitteth one brought to the very verge of judgment. I shall keep only the prebend in Lincoln; that will suffice. Therefore, live or die Robert Grosseteste, thou must take responsibilities, Adam, and offices eke if it thee requireth. There can be no more exits for thee from these matters."

"As God willeth," Adam said.

"As God would have me bequeath it thee, Adam," Grosseteste said in an iron voice. "Shirk not, nor say me nay what I have charged thee." His head turned on the bolster and Roger flinched from those driving grey eyes, though they were not bent on him at all. In his heart a certainty that he should be present at this recondite deathbed quarrel not at all fought breast to breast with a self-urged demand to speak and settle it, and with the simple alarm of the vegetative soul at being in the presence of death at all, and with the immortal soul's urgency to bear witness in the presence of God, and with the intellectual soul's pride of proof of what the *anima* was well content to believe and demand that all else be taken on faith as well—faith being at the heart of things.

It seemed unjust that all the natures of man should already be at war within him, but it was not a surprise to him any more to find himself the ground of such a battle—nor to find the hailing arrows of the self penetrating every link and joint of the other armies to slaughters, routs and senseless strewn bleeding heaps of mail which had once been proud-mounted and pennon-bearing arguments. The self was Frankish; the last arrow always was his, and like the shaft which had ended Harold at Hastings, it went to the brain. Roger said:

"Master Grosseteste. . . ."

The lector did not reply, but after a while, he shifted his glance. Instantly, Roger was ashamed to have spoken at all; but the self was not abashed.

"Thou shouldst redeem thy chancellorship here in Oxford," Roger heard himself saying. "Piety without contemplation is but an exercise, and contemplation without learning is an empty jug. Thou art the only master who ever lectured on perspective here; yet, surely there is more to know in that subject alone. And we are much in need of masters in Aristotle here, the more so that his books of nature and the *Metaphysics* are banned in Paris."

"Banned in Paris?" Adam said. "That's but a farthing of the whole. The University itself is closed entire these two years past. Perhaps half our scholars are come from there, on the King's direct promise of their safety."

"I wis, I wis," Grosseteste said. " 'Tis common knowledge."

"But not the whole," Roger said with helpless boldness. "I've myself seen a letter from Toulouse—I've a brother there—'ticing scholars to lectures on the *libri naturales* because of the ban on them in Paris. Doubt not that we have many such scholars here to hear such lectures, on the same account. And we be poor in them lately."

This, as Roger knew well enough, was inarguable, though that alone was a poor reason for his breaching the decorum of a sick-room with disputation. It had been Edmund Rich of Abingdon who had been the first to lecture at Oxford on the *Elenchi*, but he had said his last word on the subject of Aristotelian logic when Roger had been six years old; today, the saintly old man lectured only in courses of theology far too advanced for Roger to attend. Master Hugo still continued to drone on about the *Posteriores*, his own pioneer subject from Aristotle, but nobody would learn much logic from him any more—he had gone frozen in his brain, as often seemed to happen even to doctors when very old (*It need never happen,* the self whispered, with sudden, distracting irrelevance). As for John Blund, who taught the books of nature, he appeared to think of nature only as a source of examples for sermons, bestiaries and cautionary tales. Beyond these three, the only Aristotelians at Oxford today were Robert

Grosseteste, Adam Marsh . . . and Roger Bacon, at least in one pair of eyes.

Whether or not that seed had been planted in Grosseteste's mind could not yet be riddled. The sick man continued to look at Roger with that upsettingly penetrating speculative gaze.

"Paris will be opened again ere long," he said at last. "His Eminence hath been bending many efforts to that issue, and indeed, can hardly fail, unless the struggle with the Emperor hath sapped his ancient strength entire. Yet, meseemeth that we still have here some advantage. Aristotle on dreams is galling hard for a schoolman with's eyes closed to experience and nature; should see dogs dream of rabbits and think thrice, but dogs are naught to bishops; would only ban nuns from keeping them, which is impossible; women are women, *quod erat demonstrandum est.*"

He sighed and looked back at the vault. For a moment, Roger was sure that he was asleep. Then he sighed again and said:

"I am astray. Nay, I see the road again. There'll be no lectures from Aristotle at Paris, not in my lifetime. Dogs are ne to the purpose; I was wandering. But on th' eternalie of the world, there shalt crack their brains for years to come. And eke on motion—there's a potent farrower of heresies undreamed. And light—there's heresy upon heresy in the *Perspectiva*, given a sciolast to seek them instead of using his eyes, and the Arabs to confound dogma at every stand. Boy, how old art thou?"

Roger came back to consciousness with a terrible start. The vitiated air and the lector's wandering had conspired to throw him into a standing slumber full of weary portents, all charged with dread, all fled of meaning now. He said:

"Seventeen."

"Thou hast two years before thee to become a Bachelor in thy faculty, and then two more years to thy Master's degree. Thou'rt to undertake explication of the texts thou invokest, and in disputation thou'rt a child, as is plain to hear. And yet, wouldst teach Aristotle at Oxford?"

To begin with, the self said. No response could have been

further from Roger's desire; he was in full confusion and
retreat; the lector had found out not only his ambition, but
the mean and inept method he had come here to use, the
practice of trickery at the deathbed of a holy man. Yet,
somehow he must have said it aloud, word for word at the
prompting of the self, without even hearing it. He did not
know he had said anything until he heard Adam Marsh
laugh.

"To begin with?" the Franciscan said. "Thou'rt frantic,
Roger. Seek ye the doctorate in the sacred college? Dost
know that will take thee sixteen full years after thou hast
thy secular mastership? Canst thou do all that from the
Frideswyde chest? And from such poor beginnings in
humility?"

"What's this?" Grosseteste said. He pushed himself
painfully back on to his elbow and stared at Adam. "Hath
the boy need of the chest? An 'tis so, thou dost ill to mock
it. Tell me the truth of this matter, Adam. If 'tis true, wast
ill concealed; much rides on this, as thou shouldst know all
too well."

Adam looked down at the floor in his turn. Roger was as
much astonished at his abasement and at the unforgiving
condemnation in Grosseteste's tone as he was at the revelation that Adam knew about the letter.

"His family is suddenly afflicted," Adam said in a low
voice. "He hath had a patrimony, but witteth not whether
he hath it still. Whether or ne he needeth the chest I cannot say; ne no more can he."

And to be sure he could not. The chest in the priory
church at St. Frideswyde, in whose dissolved nunnery and
in that of Oseney Abbey Oxford had been founded more
than a century ago, was a benefaction long established to
help poor students; but was he *that* poor already? It was
hardly likely; in extremis, he could always sell part of his
library; but no, in the ensuing eighteen years with which
Adam had mocked him, he would have to add to his manuscripts, and most expensively; he could not take from Peter
to pay Paul. But did that bring him to the Frideswyde
chest? It was impossible to know. It depended, he realized
suddenly, on the peasant Wulf—and on the astuteness of
the justiciar's raiders. And to go all that long distance
home to find out—seventy-five miles as the crow flies, and

not by crow either, but on the back of the best horse he could hire, and that probably no courser's prancing jack—he would need now to know just how much pocket money he had left, a thing he had never counted before in his life.

"How knewest thou this, Adam?" Grosseteste said. Roger looked gratefully toward him. It had been the very question he had wanted to ask, but could not.

" 'Tis common fame in the Faculty of Art," Adam said. "The word was brought by a beggar who knew a little his alphabetum—enough, certes, to riddle out the pith of it. I have told thee before that Roger's not held high among his peers; hath a high opinion of himself, and no will to conceal it. There are those who have hoped him some such misprision, and be not slow to spread the tidings."

"For which act their souls will suffer grievously, an they bring it not to their next confessions," Grosseteste said heavily. He was interrupted by a seizure of hacking, raw-edged coughs. Adam bent over him but was waved off. After a while, the lector seemed to have recovered, though his breathing was still alarmingly dry and rapid. Again, looking at the ceiling, he said:

"The common rout customarily hateth and distrusteth the superior soul; 'tis a sign to watch for. Boy, thou shalt have thy wish, and thou performst all thy tasks as faithfully as thou shouldst; and eke much more that thou dreamest not of now—though I see that no man may hazard a tithe of thy dreaming. First, thou must go home and find all the truth of this beggar's message, and succour thy family an thou canst. The Frideswyde chest shall be opened for thee, I shall see on't. Leave thy books in Oxford and all else but very necessaries; and when thy business in the south is done, return here incontinently and take thy degree. I shall promise thee no more but this: make Oxford and Aristotle thy washing-pot, and thou shalt cast thy shoe over many a farther league ere this night's intelligence hath its full issue, an it be the will of God."

His voice died away in a whisper, and his eyes closed. For a long passage of sand in the glass, neither Adam nor Roger moved or spoke; but at last it became evident that the lector was asleep. Adam took Roger by the elbow and led him, tiptoeing, to the door.

"Thou'rt fortunate," Adam murmured in his ear. "Visit me tomorrow after sext, when we'll conspire how to see't brought about. Now thou must go."

"I am most deeply—"

"Hush, no more. It is he, not I, who hath done it—and more than thou wittest, as he said. Bear in mind that he may yet die; I would not have had thee here so early, but that he would have it so. Go, thou, speedily."

Bowing his head, Roger went out. The door closed behind him with that same magical soundlessness. The coldness in the black corridor cut like knives, but he hardly marked it for the brand that was burning within his breast.

II: NORTHOVER

It was more than hard for Roger to leave behind him, over Folly Bridge, those grammars of Priscian and Donatus, together with the *Barbarismus* of Donatus and Boethius' *Topics,* which were his texts in rhetoric; and the *Isagoge* of Porphyry, that great hymn and harmony of logic—all the beloved books of his trivium years, all so essential, all so expensive of copyists and of virgin parchment. It was even a worse wrench to have to leave in Adam Marsh's care his precious works of Aristotle: the *Logica antiqua* in the eloquent translation of Boethius, the *Logica nova* in the new, zigzag, fantastical translations from Avicenna with the Arab's heretical commentaries, the *libri naturales* from the hand of Oxford's own John Blund, who taught them (as befitted such an idiot as Blund) as a dialectical adjunct to the trivium, rather than as a part of metaphysics in the quadrivium where they plainly belonged. (But that was hardly unusual, Roger reflected on the back of his placid horse. Had he his own way, the whole subject of rhetoric would be subsumed under logic.) But there was no help for it: the books had to be left behind, and that was that.

Nevertheless, he had his copy of the *Metaphysics* in his

saddlebag as he left Oxford. Nothing in the world could persuade him to leave it behind. It had been the key which had let him into his still unfinished quadrivium years with an understanding of the four subjects—arithmetic, geometry, astronomy, music—so much in advance of his masters as to excite his vocal and injudicious contempt (injudicious only because vocal, for Roger knew not a single student who was being taught as much Aristotle as he wanted; the masters were far behind the scholars there, and getting farther every day). Of course Aristotle was of no special value on music—Boethius was still the best authority there, once he left off reprising his descants on the consolations of philosophy, a subject upon which he apparently had taken pains to become the dullest man in the world—but as a systematic summary of the world of experience in every other category, the *Metaphysics* was unique. Roger had copied it himself to be sure of having every word right; it was worth more than diamonds, which would have taken up far less space in the saddlebag, but which dissolve in goat's blood. Nothing would ever dissolve the *Metaphysics* but a human mind, and that not soon.

The horse was as cautious an idiot as John Blund, but in two or three days, it got him from inn to inn on to the marches of Salisbury Plain, stopping at every roadside ditch to crop the watercress. It had seemed the strongest and healthiest animal the courser had had for the money—six whole pounds—but it had never entered Roger's mind to suspect that it might have been *overfed;* yet, it put its nose into the sweet herbs like serfs putting their elbows on table, full and waxing lazy as freemen, and as disputatious. At the last inn before Salisbury, he saved the price of the beast's hay; the next morning it suddenly discovered that it knew how to trot.

This far from satisfied Roger's passionate urgency, for he had been unable to get away from the Great Hall for nearly a month, what with duties, observances and arrangements; but he had a three days' journey ahead of him, and he knew better than to force the animal. He had had a fair dawn to start in, warm for November, so that the snow was going, and the road was soon to be a motionless river of mud; but this early in the day the earth was still frozen, and the high sky was an intense, almost Venetian blue without a finger of cloud. Before him stretched the reddish, chalky-loamed downs in a broad undulating sweep, littered by the thousands with those huge blocks called sarsen stones or grey wethers (and to be sure they did look a little like a motionless flock of sheep from a distance) which had been used by the unknown builders of the enigmatic and faintly sinister structures at Stonehenge and Avebury. Had Merlin truly been their architect, as one of the *romans* would have it—and by what magic had he moved such enormous stones, some of them as long as twenty feet and as big around as forty feet? There was another *roman* which called the great circle at Avebury a monument to the last of the twelve Arthurian battles, in which case Merlin could hardly have been involved, having been by that time himself ensorcelled by Vivien—had there ever been any such magician, a question which, like that about the stones, did not strike Roger as very profitable. Still, the stones *had* been moved, some of them over long distances, so it was plain to see that there must be at least *a* method—whether it had been Merlin's or not—and that was discoverable.

The horse tired and began to amble again, so that before noon by Roger's stomach—which reminded his brain that today was the eleventh of November, and the eleventh of November was Martinmas, and Martinmas was the time to hang up salt meat for the winter, and there was salt meat in his saddlebag, and he was hungry—he was beginning to fear that he would have to spend the night out alone on the Plain. There was a good deal of danger in that, for the Plain was bloody ground, a favourite spot for pitched battles and for thieves alike.

Nevertheless, Roger had to face the prospect. From this point in the road—little more than a track, meandering around the hills, following the contours of the land—there was no inn or habitation in sight, and none, very likely, this far out. It was, of course, perfectly possible that he had got lost.

Abruptly, his eye was distracted by a flurry of movement ahead: straight out from behind the next wave of low hills something small, dark and compact went hurtling into the blue sky like an arrow. It was a hawk. Roger watched it soar with astonishment and increased disquiet, for he could not but regard it as ominous. No such bird would be hunting in the middle of the Plain at this time of year—it would be an unusual sight at any season—and why would a human hunter be hawking in such cheerless, unfruitful country?

But hunter it was, human or devil; he topped the rise now on his horse, a tall burly figure, bearded and cloaked, and pulled to a stop while he was joined by two more riders. The hawk wheeled high above them, screaming disconsolately. The three, plainly regarding Roger where he had halted on the ancient, pre-Roman trackway, talked among themselves, leaning in their gear. After a while, the tallest of them raised his left hand as if in salute; cautiously—it could not but pay to offer friendship, or at least neutrality, especially as he was outnumbered—Roger saluted back, and immediately felt like a fool, for beyond him the hawk screamed again, stooped and came down, sculling to a perch on the gauntleted wrist with a noble display of wingspread.

Roger lowered his arm and loosened his sword. Though, as a clerk, he was under the protection of the Church, he was not naïve enough to expect this to be respected by a pack of highwaymen. Furthermore, as a clerk he had a right to the blade, and as a scholar, he was as expert with it as the next; the students were a squalling, brawling lot, very likely to summarize disputations with blood, and when one was not defending one's self against some such "argument," there were the burghers of Oxford to be on guard against—there had been four outright riots between the scholars and the townsmen in Roger's time, in two of which he had had to slash his way out without wasting an instant on ethical or moral niceties.

It certainly would not do to get killed now, with such great prospects a-dangle in the near future like the grapes of Tantalus, though rather more indefinite. Miraculously, Robert Grosseteste had cleaved to his life—or had been so cleaving still when Roger had left the Great Hall. He was still gravely ill, to be sure, and unable to see anyone except his physicians, and Adam Marsh his confessor, but the crisis seemed to be over, and Adam had estimated cautiously that three months of pottages, gruels and broths would restore him to something like his old strength. The death

seemed to be generally on the wane; lectures had been resumed at the University, and trade in town was almost
back to normal. The burghers buried their dead and
agreed solemnly that it had not been a pestilence after all,
but only a narrow escape from one.

The party to the south was moving down the hill toward
Roger now, and with every moment seemed to be growing
larger; following the three leading horses came a train of
pack-animals, heavily laden, two by two over the brow of
the hill. Suddenly Roger realized what it was that he was
seeing, and with a sigh of relief allowed his sword to settle
again.

The big man was obviously a wool merchant, his two
companions prentices, chivvying a purchase of fells and
hides over the downs. And in fact Roger knew the man;
had he not been now close enough to recognize, the hawk
should have given him the clue, for there was only one
such merchant customarily buying in Dorset and
Somersetshire who went about with a peregrine falcon on
his wrist: William Busshe. The falcon's name was Madge,
and Roger even knew that the horse was called Bucepha-
lus after the legendary animal of Alexander the Great, but
was always addressed as "Bayard"; for he had watched
this same man bargaining for the spring clip and the fall
hides for ten years before leaving Oxford, haggling solemnly with his father until Christopher's death, and
thereafter, first with Robert and then with Harold.

Busshe recognized Roger simultaneously and pulled to a
second time, his shaggy eyebrows rising almost into his
Flemish-style beaver hat. Wearing that expression, he
looked almost like a sheep himself, despite his forked
brown beard and the fact that his face was, of course, not
black. His vair-collared cloak spread like Madge's wings
as he put his hands on his hips. Feeling the reins on his
neck, the big bay promptly began to graze, and Roger had
to hold John Blund's head up sharply to keep him from following Bayard's example.

"How now, young Roger," Busshe said in his heavy, deliberate voice. "Little I expected to encounter thee on this
dreary moor, and in sooth, I wis not whether't be well met
or ill with us."

"No more wis I," Roger said, with some return of his uneasiness. "Meseemeth 'tis early for thee to be faring north with sealed bales, this being but Martinmas. Someone hath slaughtered early, and I greatly fear that 'tis Yeo Manse hath done it."

"Thou wert ever a gimlet-eyed youngster," Busshe said. "Thou hast seen to the heart of the matter. There's a knight of the justiciar sitteth as lord in thy cot, hath ordered the slaughter a week ere we had arrived, would sell me the fells at half the prices I'd contracted for with Franklin Harold these eighteen months gone. And so much and no more did I pay him, seeing that the slaughtering had been hastily done to fill's purse quickly, and the wool thus not of the first quality."

Roger felt a brief flash of anger, but after a moment, he realized that it should not be Busshe at whom it was directed. He was doubtless telling the exact truth—after all, he had no part in this quarrel—nor could it matter in the least which price he had paid, since none of it could go to the family under the circumstances. If Busshe had cheated the justiciar's equerry out of his very shirt (though nothing could be more unlike Busshe), Roger ought indeed to be pleased. But it was hard to think of a year's flock spoiled and knocked down for the enrichment of some marauding noble in de Burgh's service without feeling a general anger at everyone concerned, even the silent prentices who were watching him with evident sympathy.

"Then are we much despoiled?" Roger said after a while.

"Nay, this knight, a highteth Will of Howlake, hath far too stern a hand; a hath kept the serfs hard at it and much increased the rents and the boon work. All thy kin are gone, but for thy sisters, no man knoweth where. How farest thou?"

"To the manse, to retrieve what I may," Roger said, preoccupied. "And my sisters?"

"In the women's houses, where, by order of Franklin Harold's steward, they be so craftily clothed, this Will of Howlake knoweth them not from villeins' women."

"I thank God for't." Indeed, the whole situation as Busshe outlined it seemed far from the worst that Roger had imagined. Though he had had no experience of such an occupation as Yeo Manse was undergoing now, the pattern had been familiar for centuries, and Will of Howlake's behaviour did not sound like that of a man who expected to remain lord of the property for long. He was wringing the good out of it with the stringency of a man who expects recall, and so was adding to his personal store, as well as to that of Hubert de Burgh, by as many marks a day as the manse could possibly be made to yield. A brief cruel plundering of that kind had proven the ruination of many a holding—lords who expected to be awarded the property were kinder to it—but the orchards and fields and gardens of Yeo Manse were extensive, and Roger did not doubt that they would survive such treatment, were it only not much prolonged. It meant that the serfs and even the stewards would be despitefully used while it lasted—but their days were miserable enough even in normal times—their reward only in heaven, never in this world.

"Thou'rt ill advised to go hither," Busshe said in a troubled voice. "Howlake is wroth at having missed taking every man in the family; an thou becomest known to him, wilt go ill with thee. And thy fat gelding there wheezeth like a monk with the asthmaticks—'tis plain to see a's all out of the habit of work."

Madge stirred her wings under the cloak, and Busshe lifted his left arm to the sky again. Reluctantly the red peregrine climbed on the air; being recently fed from Busshe's own hand, she wanted only to sleep, or at least to perch quietly and pursue some single savage thought, but hawks had to be exercised or they would not hunt—indeed, would forget even how to come home. Busshe put his hand back on his hip again, and Madge began to circle at her pitch, crying Kyaa! Kyaa!

"Come thou with us till yon Howlake's outworn his commission," Busshe said. "We're to Northleach to cast a sort of fell and fifty tods of Cotswold wool, dear though it be at eleven shillings; thence to our offices in London for th' assizes at the Leadenhall, and to pack sarplers for shipboard. Our quarters be in the Mart Lane, not over-far from where thy brother Robert doth deal in Egypt's cotton and I wis not what else. An 'tis money thou seekest, belike a will succour thee. Mene-whyles we'll put thee on a proper horse, and give yon hay-bottle bales to carry; and thou'lt add thy blade to ours 'gainst thieves or Lombards, as is equitable."

It was a generous offer, and for a moment Roger was tempted to accept it; he did not underestimate the risks he was taking. But it was not, after all, money that he was primarily hoping to recover, and he knew besides how little likely he was to be given any money to go back to Oxford from Robert Bacon's hands; then he would be stranded in London, with no possible course but to ship with Busshe's wool to Flanders and try his luck in Paris at the dormant University. That was out of the question; he was not ready for that by years.

"Nay, I cannot," he said. "God's blessing on thee, William Busshe, but I'm bidden to Ilchester, thence to Oxford, and will abide the course. I'll recall thy kindness in my prayers."

"As it pleaseth thee," Busshe said. "Fare thee well, then." He called Madge home and hooded and jessed her; and in a while, the last of the procession had vanished to the north.

Gloomily, Roger got John Blund into motion, more than half convinced that his refusal had been the worst kind of folly. He was not even much cheered by the sight of a distant inn from the top of the next rise, nor finding, as he drew closer, that the "bush" or sign was up on the ale-stake, meaning "open for business." Good wine needs no bush, but he was in no position to pay for good wine, nor bad, either. And there could hardly be any money for him at Yeo Manse; he was making this wittold's pilgrimage for the sake of nothing but a few childish trinkets. . . .

A few toys, and an *ignis fatuus,* a will-o'-the-wisp drifting far in the future, conjured into being by a Greek dead fourteen weary centuries already.

Yeo Manse was not, properly speaking, in Ilchester; legally, it was in the parish of Northover, on the other side of the river, connected with Ilchester by a low stone bridge. Northover was, however, nothing notable as a town, while Ilchester stood athwart Fosse Way, a major road through the district ever since the Romans had built it, and the Bacons had seen the advantages which would accrue from identifying with Ilchester quite early on—long before most of the other local franklins had, in fact. The parish church of St. Mary had been established by Christopher Bacon's grandfather as a chantry where masses were to be sung for

his soul by a single priest; later, Christopher's father and
two other freeman landholders had contributed the silver
and the boon work which had raised the squat octagonal
tower, so oddly pagan and brooding for a Christian temple,
and since that time, all the Bacons who had died at home
had been buried there.

How the town had prospered since was clearly visible to
Roger from where he had paused in the early morning
light just over the rim of the valley. The chessboard of orchards and pastures was sere and without motion in the
cold of Autumn-Month, but from the clustered houses and
shops south of the Yeo, there rose many slow-writhing
lines of hazy white wood-smoke; and the bare trees of the
churchyard could not conceal the elegance of St. Mary,
with its new (no older than Roger!) horizontal building
abutting the octagonal tower, which had piers formed of
mouldings in stone at doors, windows and arcades.
Ilchester was a borough of substance now: it even had bail-
iffs, though only as of last year.

What of substance now remained for Roger of Yeo
Manse was the question. Ilchester itself did not, from this
distance, look at all disturbed by the incursion of the
King's justiciar, but that meant only that de Burgh's
knights had not burned anything down—for which, of
course, one should thank God, but not too hastily, for there
were worse depredations possible which would still leave
behind just so superficially peaceful a scene as this. The
problem now was to skirt Yeo Manse closely enough to as-
sess how it had fared, and thence into Northover to find
that inn called the Oxen by the serf Wulf (there were four
or five inns by that name in Ilchester, at least two in
Northover to Roger's knowledge) without being recognized
for what he was by some soldier of Will of Howlake. To do
so without being seen by some such man was out of the
question, but Roger was reasonably sure he could pass any
casual inspection—after all, his breeches and coarse sur-
coat were just like those of a thousand other young men
from the anonymous poor, except that they were slightly
less threadbare. Unless he was incautious in his curiosity
about the manse, he would probably not be picked up at
all; and even if he were seized and searched thoroughly
enough to turn up the manuscript in his gear, he could

feign to be a goliard—one of the many raggle-taggle vaga-
bond scholars who, eager enough for learning but utterly
impatient of university routines, wandered from teacher
to teacher and monastery to monastery, themselves teaching or writing anew the text of one or another of the Miracle plays in return for their instruction and keep. He would
get by with such a deception if he had to practise it. The
danger did not lie there. It lay in the good possibility that
someone in Northover, someone who belonged there,
would recognize him under the eye of someone of Howlake
or de Burgh, and speak too soon and too loudly.

He dug one heel into John Blund; the horse moved reluctantly, and just as reluctantly Roger gave it its head, for
the side here, though only half as steep as a roof, offered no
road—he had quitted that before topping the crest out of el-
ementary caution—but instead slippery out-croppings of
rock and moss, giving way farther down to a tumble of rubble, like a talus-slope at the foot of a cliff, full of incipient
shifts and slides and glistening menacingly with frost. No
man could presume to guide a horse over such ground, but
instead, must let him put each of his four feet where he
chose and as delicately as he could manage, until he
showed himself willing to resume his gait.

And, in fact, to Roger's faint surprise, John Blund managed the sliding course without even a serious stumble,
though there was one rock-tumble moment when he
seemed certain to break a foreleg, and probably to pash his
own and Roger's brains out as well. It was over in half the
time it would have taken to say a pater noster, however
(and in actuality, it had doubtless taken no more than ten
pulsebeats); and then the horse was clump-clumping
across rimed brown grass in a complacent trot he had decided to undertake all on his own. Roger found himself
grinning. A lifetime of intimacy with horses had convinced
him that nothing else on four legs can be so stupid, but so
frequently and humanly overwhelmed by its own good
opinion of itself.

He had, as well, good reason to be pleased with himself,
for as he resumed the reins, he found himself and John
Blund crossing a frozen ditch into a broad ploughland
which he recognized at once as bordering on the west vine-
yard of Yeo Manse. He could hardly have arrived at a safer

quarter of the estate, this time of year, for, to begin with, it
had always been the poorest cot in its *fisc*, secondly, the
most remote from the seigniorial manse and hence from
Will of Howlake, thirdly, the cot (if Roger's memory, dim
here, could be trusted) of the serf Wulf (who could be presumed to be haunting some tavern in Northover to the detriment of his week work), and finally (though this, at least,
could be laid to no foreplanning on Roger's part) today was
obviously a boon-work day: for on the other side of the
vineyards, where the little group of sod houses belonging
to this and three other cots were huddled, Roger could see
a group of small hunched figures assembling, most of
them carrying axes, mattocks and adzes—a wood-cutting
gang—and hear the shouts of a dean, one of Tom the steward's overseers, distant but clear. Shortly they would be
moving off to give their one day's work out of the week at
the big house; in fact, they were moving away from him already. Thinly over the motionless fields a hoarse baritone
voice began bawling:

> *Bytuene Mershe and Averil*
>   *When spray biginneth to springe,*
> *The lutel foul hath hire wyl*
>   *On hyre lud to synge. . . .*

but the lyric, so plainly of spring and the gentry, came
stiffly from amidst the rime-caked villein's beard on to the
November air and began to fade:

> *Ich libbe in love-longinge*
> *For semlokest of alle thynge,*
> *He may me blisse bringe,*
> *Icham in hire baundoun. . . .*

and yet, just as the hewing party was almost gone entirely
to Roger's sight, other voices, equally unmusical, began to
float back the round:

> *An Hendy hap ichabbe yhent,*
> *Ichot from hevene it is me sent,*
> *From alle wymmen mi love is lent*
> *Ant lyht on Alysoun! . . .*

lyht on Alysoun! . . .
    on Alysoun!

Alysoun, said the Yeo Valley. *Alysoun . . . soun . . . soun. . . .*

Heaving his huge keg of a chest up and down, the horse blew solemnly between his thick mobile lips, and Roger, too, resumed breathing with a subdued start. What was left behind of the world was essence, without sound, motion or life, keeping its slight claim to be real in the rank order of the generation of forms only because it was—least close of all secondary qualities to the primary and real—still bitterly cold. In contemplation of these things as they always had been, it was impossible to believe that Yeo Manse had changed or could change in th'eternalie of the world. Though Heraclitus had never been able to put his foot twice into the same river, he had never been in any doubt about which was river and which was foot (one was cold, one got cold; but how in memory could he trust the order of these events, one being—secondary—used to judge the primary other?); everything changed, but only to remain more and more perfectly the same, like the River Meander which cut new banks and channels every year to maintain that clear, fixed, Platonic word of which the river in flux could never be more than a shadow.

But the shadowy solid horse beneath him, still sweaty after its delicate slide into the valley, trembled and reminded him that this was no ultimate Horse he was riding, he himself no Idea of Man, and Yeo Manse no shadow of some ultimate Estate; they all had names, and things with names pass away. He would have to give this horse-with-a-name (though it be John Blund, or just "you hay-bottle") a rub before very long or it would come down with the glanders—and though there might be some ultimate Glanders in Plato's cave, when one hitched it to a horse with a name, one had a sick horse, which was a good deal more serious in this world than any coupling of Sickness with Horseness; and the Heraclitean river—not the Yeo, but a much more drastic Meander—flowed in an underground torrent beneath Yeo Manse, too, as under all things else.

As that river flowed on inexorably, the morning grew

older . . . it must be well after eight already . . . but for a
while Roger found himself unable to move on, urgent
though his errand was, and more urgent though the danger grew with each increment of delay. These ditch-
guarded pasturelands deep in long brown grass, the vine-
yard surrounded with its fence woven on close-set stakes,
the ploughlands lying humped and frozen in the heatless
sunlight, the owl-haunted timber stands, the willow plan-
tation where withies and barrel-hoops were cut, the pali-
saded orchards where every tree was a boy's lesson in
climbing for the daylight and a well of sharp cider and
perry for the evening meal; the voice of the serfs, the
shapes of the hills, the blue bend of the sky over the
wrinkling Yeo . . . these were all his home, now most
strangely and heart-breakingly hostile in its absolute,
changeless stillness. It had been with bitterness and defiance toward Robert, and an unbrookable, long-swelling
passion to be free of Yeo Manse once and for all, that he
had left this place to become a clerk, but never with any
thought that it would itself reject him in its turn. No, Yeo
Manse had borne the Bacons on its breast for centuries,
and would always lie awaiting his return, should he deign
to make it. . . .

His shadow, wedded to that of John Blund, slowly lost
stature on the earth beneath him. His breast hollow with
sullen, helpless loneliness, he turned the horse's head
northward. There was nothing more to be learned here; it
was all exactly as it had always been . . . except that it was
suddenly an alien land.

We shall not all die, the self murmured; *but we shall all
be changed.*

"Us be an old man, Meister," Wulf said. "Old and cleft a
bit, as it mote be said, and most deaf and blind eke, as mote
be said, and good for naught. But us remembered thee."

Old the man was, without doubt nearly eighty, his hairs
white, his teeth gone but for a few brown tusks, his skin
the texture and colour of bad leather. Even across the
splintery trestle table in the Oxen, he stank most mark-
edly, a mixture of sod, sweat and a sour and precarious di-
gestion; yet, curiously, his homespun was sturdy and almost clean, and his filthy ankles rose out of crude but

strongly stitched slippers of hide so well and recently
cured that the pointed toes still protruded straight
ahead—in proud contrast to the points of Roger's own
shoes, which tended to fold under the balls of his feet every
third or fourth step.

"How didst thou know me?" Roger said, shifting his
stone mug on the planking. "And how canst thou lurk here
away from the manse, morning as well as night? Inns are
not for serfs, even such a one as this."

The old man smiled dimly, as though recalling some exercise of craft half a century bygonnen. "Us knew thee,
Meister," he said. The gnarled hand closed about a leather
tankard but did not lift it. "Us saw thee and followed thee
when thou wert but a new lamb. Nay, a badger, thou wert,
with a girt chest and shoulders, and always at digging and
burying. Wold Wulf was proper crofter then with's boy to
lead the oxen, twice as old as thou art and with boys of his
own now, Meister; and us good for naught in these years,
as mote be said, but for to hold the cot till us be called. Us
be'ent missed now that oor son's a man grown and ploughs
and has childer. Nay, wold Wulf may go where us will, as
mote be said, and there's an end to it, Meister."

Roger frowned, unable to press the question further, but
remaining as puzzled as before. Of course the grandfather
of a serf's family would not be missed from the work
—he had understood that much of the mystery of the
unremembered Wulf the moment he had been confronted
by this snaggly sour-breathed ruin; but when his query to
the suspicious host had flushed Wulf at last, the old man
had been brought from the back of the inn, still wearing a
nightcap in the midst of the day, so that it had been made
most clear that he was living at the Oxen, which was impossible for a serf, though he be the grandsire of all the
serfs that ever were.

The old man seemed to have forgotten that that question, too, had been asked him. He stared with his white-
filmed blue eyes at the fire, over which a soup of some
kind—from which a faint additional odour of hot mutton
fat attested to the early kill at Yeo Manse, for under normal circumstances, no mutton could yet have reached so
mean an inn as this—was seething in a huge black kettle
hanging from an iron chain.

"Us were a sheep herd, then," he said abruptly. "Us took they sheep to the uplands for pasture, with Hob that was wold Wulf 's dog that died afore thee'd remember him, Meister, and wold Wulf 's boy that keeps the cot now to carry the hurdles. And Tom the steward, that was no older than Wulf 's boy, he told us to mind thee when thee wandered, Meister, as wander thee did till us was blue out of breath. A-diggin' up and a-buryin' thee was, and in and out of rafters and trees—"

"Go thou to the point, old man," Roger said, gripping the edge of the table fiercely with both hands. Yet he was sure that he already knew what the answer was to be. "Why didst thou write to me? What hast thou for me?"

"Us shall show thee, Meister," Wulf said with a secret smile. "Us can't show thee here, but us has it all, fear thee not. Us took it all, and more. Us made proper fools of they King's men. Us took away thy diggings, and put thy buryings in they ilke holes."

"*What dost thou mean?*"

"Nay, Meister, glare not so at wold Wulf," the serf said, beginning to snivel. "They was but bits of trash, as mote be said, like boys ud bury—"

Roger fought back his temper, as best he could. There would be no point in so alarming the old man that he became incoherent.

"Tell me what thou hast done," he said, with a gentleness he was still far from feeling. "And hew to it quickly and directly."

"Aye, that be what us was doing, Meister, an thee'll let us. Meister Christopher that was thy father was a gentryman, could read and cypher, and yonder King's men be gentry, too, as mote be said. Wold Wulf ud not want his hands snipped off for thieving—or drawn and quartered like a common traitor, they being King's men. Us thought better to leave summat in they holes, an they King's men find some writing of Meister Christopher to riddle where they holes be duggen. So us put matter into 'em from thy boy's holes, that thee made when thee was a-writing precious little, Meister Roger. All the rest us has here."

The old man looked filmily at him with a mixture of hope and senile cunning, slightly tinged with reproach.

"All?" Roger said.

"Nay, not all, Meister," Wulf said. "Thee knows a poor serf's let into no inn free, nay, nor wears new shoes neither—us be not so blind us can still see thee a-looking at oor poor feet. But us be eating of naught but millet porridge and a mite of dredge-corn; thilke ale thee did buy us, and the first wold Wulf's tasted since us runned away. But all the rest, us has, Meister."

"I thank God thou didst not run clean away," Roger said grudgingly.

"Where ud us rinnen, Meister? Us be full of pain in the bones and good for naught, as mote be said. Here's a safe enough cozy for wold Wulf that's as near to his Maker as may be, and knew thee'd nowt but leave us silver penny to buy a herring with till us be called."

"Show me what thou hast."

"This way." The old man got up stiffly and led the way toward the kitchen. On the other side, he admitted Roger into a narrow room so hot, airless and foul even in this weather that Roger could hardly drive himself further once the door was opened. The door itself was fastened with nothing but a staple.

"Thine host hath doubtless stolen it all in thine absence," he muttered, trying to hold his breath and breathe at the same time.

"Nay, Meister," Wulf said absently. "He's wold Wulf's nephew-in-law—no slyer ever put green vitriol in vinegar, but won't steal from us till us be dead. Here, now—"

He rummaged in a heap of filthy straw while Roger accustomed his eyesight to the dimness. There was literally nothing else in the room but a low, broad three-legged stool and an anonymous heap of rags.

Then, grunting, the old man had bauled from the straw a purse of rawhide almost twice as big as his head. "Here it be," he said, setting it on the stool. "Us saved it all for thee, Meister Roger."

Roger pulled open the mouth of the bag and plunged a hand in, his fingers closing convulsively in the cold, liquid mass of coins. He carried the handful to the door, which he opened slightly to let in a little more light.

The coins were in little the hoard of well more than a lifetime. Anyone looking at them could have told at once that the Bacons were wool-sellers, for nearly every coin of

commerce rested in Roger's fist: English pennies and
ryalls, new and old shields of France (the old worth something in exchange if they were real, the new clipped even if
genuine), the golden Lewe of France, the Hettinus groat of
Westphalia (debased), the Limburg groat (debased), the
Milan groat (debased), the Nimueguen groat (debased), the
gulden of Gueldres (much debased), the postlates, davids,
florins and falewes of the bishoprics of half of Latin Christendom (debased beyond all reason). Obviously Wulf's
host (and nephew) had much depleted the real value of the
hoard by taking from the serf nothing but English money,
but this handful of dubious riches could not be blamed on
Wulf and the innkeeper alone: Christopher Bacon should
have had better sense than to bury foreign coins, or for
that matter, to have taken them in payment from William
Busshe or anyone else. Probably he had never had any reason to suspect even the existence of the intricacies of foreign exchange, being naught but a farmer all his life long;
to him these clipped and adulterated coins with their ex-
otic designs and legends must have seemed mysteriously
more valuable than the mere pennies paid him year after
year by his tenants—why else would he have gone to the
trouble of burying them?

Yet Roger was little inclined to absolve his father for
that, let alone Wulf and his nephew. What he held in his
hand was all that remained of his patrimony—that and the
rest of the trash in the purse—and though it would be impossible to judge what it all amounted to until he had a
chance to count it through somewhere in safety, it was
clearly far from any sum sufficient for his needs. And for
this, this ignorant, smelly old man had buried Roger's
rhombs and his glass and his time-costly measuring tools
for the discovery of a pack of raiders!

He swung away from the door in a fury of frustration
and hurled the coins at the wall. Wulf dodged clumsily
away from the sudden motion, but in a moment he was
standing again as straight as his old man's back could
stiffen.

"Thee must be more quiet, Meister," he said. "Else thee
will properly lose all."

"Thinkest thou I have aught to lose, old man?" Roger
said between his teeth. He strode to the stool and jerked
the drawstring of the purse tight savagely. "Nevertheless,

I thank thee for thy cunning, stupid drudge though thou be'st. Dost think Will of Howlake will never hear of thee, dwelling here like a freeman after eight decades as a serf? Thinkest thou he'll not dispatch his men to seek thee out, and ask thee whence thy sudden riches came? Thou shouldst have run till thy bones broke with thy weight, wold Wulf; for traitor they will adjudge thee, and draw out thy bowels, and pull the rest of thy corse asunder 'twixt four horses!"

"Aye, us, thought it mote be so," Wulf said, "And thee wilt leave us nothing, Meister, but they orts there that thee flung away?"

Roger opened the door and turned back to stare at the serf for the last time. "Certes, I'll leave thee more," he said savagely. "Dig thou for that boy's trash that thou stol'st, and give that to thy nephew-in-law for thy meat!"

But the old man no longer seemed to be listening, as though he had known what the answer must be. He was on his knees, patiently picking over the filthy straw for the discarded, debased, fugitively glittering coins.

It had been no part of Roger's intention to strike out for Oxford again without so much as a night's rest, nor with the same horse, either, but the dead weight of the knobby purse impelled him to triple caution; now, surely he dared not risk search, let alone recognition. He risked only a long meal for himself and John Blund and then struck out during the afternoon sleep, not daring to hurry while he was still anywhere in the valley, but thereafter driving the horse at a merciless gallop until it began to sob and heave.

In a small, forest-bordered meadow, which did not look tended enough to belong to any farm, he dismounted and tethered the horse after watering it from a tiny stream, little more than a runnel. Here he risked a fitful nap, standing with his back against a tree and with his hand on his sword. He had intended no more than an hour, but somehow he fell asleep even in this position and dreamed that a ring of bowmen with the heads of foxes had tied him there and were stuffing eleven pounds three and a half shillings Fleming into his mouth one red-hot penny at a time.

He awoke with a start which nearly toppled him—for his knees, which had bent somewhat, ached horribly, and he

was stiff throughout his body with cold—to find the sun almost touching the hills to the south-west, and someone on
horseback sitting above him hardly more than ten paces
away.

He had the sword only half out, with a creakingly ugly
motion which would not have been fast enough to discour-
age a boy with a quarter-staff, when the fox-head dissolved
back into the nullity of dream and he saw that, in fact, the
rider was a girl. Furthermore she was smirking at him
with an infuriating disrespect.

"Well then," she said, "tha be well overtook, by Goddes
bones. Art going to run a poor maid clean through the
butter-milk? Tha'll first needs be friendlier with thy girt
feet, boy."

Roger ground his teeth in exasperation and forced his
aching muscles to pull him into a more human stance. He
looked about for John Blund and found him, munching
brittle grass with his eyes half closed, which made him
look at once maidenly and vacuous—an expression which,
for some reason, infuriated Roger all the more.

"And who beest thou, lip-kin?" he said, glaring up at the
girl. She was, he saw now, probably about fifteen: a good,
bouncing year for a peasant girl, though she did not talk
quite like a serf's daughter, despite her West Midlands di-
alect. The horse, a small sturdy cob, was not any serf's
draft animal either. Her hair was cut short—which was
good sense for peasant girls looking to provide as few hand-
holds for rapists as possible—but the stray curls of it that
came out from under her black woolen wimple were little
flames of dull gold. He felt his glare dimming a little, entirely against his intention.

"Tha can call me Tibb, an I let thee," she said. "Tha'lt
better clamber on thy bulgy-eyed dray there, afore some
coney kicks tha in thy ribs. An tha'rt faring somewheres,
at least I know the roads."

This sounded like the best advice, unpalatably though
the spoon was being proffered. He picked his way cautiously to John Blund and untied him from his stump.

"Whither farest thou, then?"

"Nowheres that tha'd know, by the looks of tha," she
said, swinging her own horse around. "I'm to my uncle's
inn, with whey and buttermilk—didst think I was jesting?
Well, certes I was then—from Northover parish. An tha

hast money, tha canst find lodging there; otherwise, tha'lt find it a cold night outside our very door."

"Thou dost not sound so cold in the heart," Roger said.

"Softly thee, boy. I've a needle in my girdle, shouldst tha need stitching." She looked back at him, still smiling. "Tha canst not draw before me; that tha's shown every owlet in Rowan Wood already."

"I molest no one," Roger said stiffly, "ne childer nor animals."

"There's a light oath," Tibb said. "Naytheless, ride closer then, and work the cement out of thy sword-elbow. I was fond to stop for thee, this is a bad hour; canst tha strike if we be beset?"

"Fast enough," Roger said. "No man becomes a master by his wits alone."

This outrageous lie passed between his teeth before he was quite aware of it; yet he was disinclined to correct it. The day, in particular, and the journey, in general, had cast a false air around everything, and around his own bitterment, a tatterdemalion motley.

"I guessed tha clad too fair to be but clerk," Tibb said. They were riding abreast now. "Art tha a Grey Friar?"

"Nay, that's to come, an God willeth." Was that the indirigible self again? He had never thought of such a thing before. But what else could have spoken this? It was hardly possible that any mood inspired by a dirty blonde peasant girl should suggest his becoming a mendicant.

"What dost tha teach?"

The lie was becoming exceedingly complicated, but it was too old now to bury. "Logic," he said. "Have we a long ride further?"

"Nay, not in full day. But these shadows are mischancy; 'ware sink-holes" Almost on the word, the cob stumbled and righted itself with a muted nicker of alarm, and Roger grasped the girl's hand.

" 'Twas nothing," Tibb said; but she made no move to free herself. They rode side by side for a silent while. The sun was almost gone, though the sky was still half bright.

"Tha'rt a strange twosome, as crossed as herring-bones," Tibb said. "A ninny scholar, a sleepy swordsman, a well-clad clerk. And a boy man."

"I am indebted to thee," Roger said shortly. "Mock on."

"I may, an it pleaseth me. Ah, go up!"

The sharp change in her voice made Roger sit bolt upright in the saddle.

"Here—what's amiss?"

"I shan't tell tha. Yes, I shall, it'll give tha thy turn for mockery. My garter's fallen untied, ne more, and I'll lose it ere we see home."

Roger looked away at the deepening twilight until he got his breath back. "Small ills, small remedies," he said. "I'll take it up for thee."

"Not here," Tibb said tranquilly. "The Plain's just ahead. I'd not see myself surprised out of these gullies—there are knives abroad here. Tha shouldst know that much."

She was not content until they were on the flat top of a rise some five minutes' ride on to the Plain, and it was almost dark. Then, without a word, she slid rather ungracefully off the cob and sat down on the hard earth.

She was most matter of fact in allowing her garter to be tied; and in allowing him to find deeper in her skirt a fold which needed some stitching beyond the repair of any needle she might have had with her (nor did he detect any such bodkin as she had threatened him with; only a button which gave but would never fasten). By the time all the repairs were made—it was far from the first time she had employed such a tailor, that was plain—the night was pitch black and Roger was as sweating cold as he had ever been in his life.

Tibb tucked one leg under the other and stood up, helping him to his feet. "Tha'rt a wolf cub," she said. "A fierce beginner. Tha hadst best kiss me afore I kick thee."

He took her around the waist, which was surprisingly small for so broad a belly and bosom, and kissed her, but this only made her laugh. "I thank thee," she said. "Let's mount; there's still another ride to take."

He groped his way on to John Blund and followed the sound of the cob's hooves, not sure whether to be alarmed or assuaged, and too sleepy to be sure he should care.

"Thou'rt no beginner, Tibb," he said. "Thou'st churned thy buttermilk to whey before this nightfall."

"Tha'rt being over-nice for a lover," Tibb's voice drifted

back to him. "Tha meanest maidenhead, tha shouldst say so. 'Twas only a trouble to me in the bed; waxed cold, waxed hot; and in smalwe stead it stood me. That which will away is very hard to hold."

And then, eerily in the cold night, she began to sing in a piping, clear, sweetly tuneful voice:

> "Ye mayds, ye wyfs and witwes
> That doe now her my Songe
> Doth younge man put kyndnesse
> Pray tak it short ne lange
> Fer theyr be nat sich comfortal
> Lyk lainnage wyth a Man
>   To cum Downe a downe,
>   To cum Downe,
>   Down a down a ."

The plaintive song died echolessly; and after a while, a tiny spark of light rose from behind an invisible hill some inch or miles ahead.

"There, 'tis home. Ready thy purse, sweet goliard."

He heeled the exhausted horse forward and caught her about the waist.

"Sweet Tibb, I was too soon for thee—"

"Nay, boy. Go up. Get thyself a bed. Mayhap I'll come to thee. Go now."

"Thine oath, Tibb?"

"No oath from me—ne to no man without bed to raise horn in. Go up, and then I'll think more on it."

"Thou art an ungrateful whore."

"Tha'rt a foraging pinchpenny. And I love thee. Let me, now. Go put thy bone to bed and mayhap I'll cast thy dice for thee once more—ne more will I promise. Be off, coneysnare."

Grumbling, he helped her to dismount, and took both horses around to the back, where a mute and scrofulous dwarf, apparently recognizing Tibb's cob, took them both without demur and began to unload the cob of its leather bottles. The inn struck him no less grimly than the mute; mostly without light and full of sprawling men who watched Roger, scratching in their patches, from under

brows as dense as thorn-bushes, while Tibb's uncle bit
with an appalling yellow canine into the Philippe d'or
Roger proffered for his pallet.

Tibb came back to him some time before dawn, but she
had company. No sooner had she thrown her leg over him
and welcomed him home than the room was full of creep-
ing bravoes. She fought hard to hold him down when he
snatched up his sword, but evidently she had under-valued
his devotion to the purse: he shucked her with one great
seizure of his back-muscles; and when she sprang to block
the door while they slashed at the rest of the blackness toward him, he spilled her decoy's ouns into her polluted
shift with a single cut and escaped into the morning over
her, the purse slung over his shoulder and pounding
against his spine, as he ran for the stables and John Blund.

III: BEAUMONT

It fell by the stars that, early in 1233, the Henry called
Winchester who was Henry the Third, eldest son by
Isabella of Angoulême of that murderous, incompetent
and yet princely-hearted usurper King John, moved his
royal person and his court into his father's birthplace, for
the hunting; which was published abroad. This place was
Beaumont Palace, without the earthenworks and timber
of the north wall of Oxford town, overlooking Osney and
Port Meadow. There were boars and stags in the King's
woods there, but more was intended than hunting.
Beaumont was but four years seized back by Hubert de
Burgh from a traitor to the French—one whose large bones
had been burned, and his knuckles, spine, fingers and toes
scattered like dice, every last die unshriven for the
Resurrection.

It was by this proximity to Oxford that Adam Marsh—in
default of Robert Grosseteste, who was in retirement in
service of his God and naught else—was found at
Beaumont with many others of church, university and
town on the night of the King's third coming of age, that

being the feast of St. John; and having the skill to speak
Romance of both the Norman and the Iberian kind, was
taken up into a history totally undesired by him; as
follows:

That Henry III was of age could hardly be doubted, he
being now twenty-nine years old and having been declared
of age twice before: first by Pope Honorius III in 1223, at
the instigation of Hubert de Burgh, to justify the resumption of all the castles, sheriffdoms and demesnes granted
since Henry's accession; and again in 1227, when Hubert
himself declared the King of age—as by then he had become enpowered to do, having gradually married his way,
one marriage after another to the number of four, to the
tacit mastery of the regency left vacant by the death of
William earl-Marshal of Pembroke in 1219. That everyone
sufficiently understood the lesson had been well enough
attested by the sudden self-exile of Peter des Roches, the
Poitevin Bishop of Winchester, Henry's tutor and Hubert's
most bitter enemy. Should anyone be so blind as to miss
the import, however, Henry was pleased to allow Hubert
his homage for the title of Earl of Kent.

Ask for this hero now and find him justiciar of Ireland,
the meanest royal grant in all Christendom; for tonight
Henry, pale as whey and speaking out of the side of his
narrow mouth so quietly as to terrify the most loyal and
most noble subject of the crown, was celebrating with wine
and flesh his third coming of age, the repudiation of
Hubert de Burgh. The great soldier who had refused King
John the blinding of the captive Arthur of Brittany, and
yet had stood fast by John when some other hand of John
threw that young owner of John's crown into the Seine;
who had adhered to John even after the barons had enforced on the King the Great Charter; the admiral who had
sunk Eustace the Monk and all his pirates' fleet in the
straits and thus cut off Dauphin Louis' last hope of holding
any part of England; and scourge of all earls who would
take from the King's hand what was divinely and right-
fully the King's—that great soldier and administrator was
tonight to be cast down.

Nothing of this was apparent to Roger, who was too surprised to find himself Adam's familiar (chosen, Roger supposed shrewdly, to express Adam's forbidden rebellion

against so worldly a commission—and because Roger could
not only speak fair French, but also, being recently come
into more than two thousand pounds, could clothe himself
for such a function) and too confused by the rebounding
noise, the flare and smoke of the torches, and the press and
stink of so many elegants and their scarcely less elegant
cup-bearers in Beaumont's great hall. Even the dogs, of
which there were a great many, seemed surer of foot and
favour in this roaring cave than Roger was; he recognized
no one but the King himself, and the King only by his
expression—that half-lidded, pale, incontinent cast of the
young man to whom alone is given the power to slay any
person on whom he looks, and needs only to be jostled in
the press to put that power to the proof.

Adam, however, was not so easily confused. "Stay
close," he said at once to Roger in his smooth Frankish.
"Here's a fine display of Latins; there's des Roches
back—and there's his nephew, Peter des Rievaux; and
there's Simon IV's son of Montfort. . . . There's Poitevins
wherever you look; a fair *auto da fe* on Hubert! Would God
we'd kept home."

He darted suddenly sidewise into the milling army of
courtiers and servants; Roger, concerned to begin the evening, at the very least, with obedience to Adam's command
to "stay close," was nearly brained by a boar's head on a
vast dish of pewter which came sculling between himself
and the Franciscan as he tried to follow. When he caught
up with Adam again, he was earnestly in conversation
with that hawk-beautiful young Frenchman he had just
previously identified as Simon de Montfort.

"I think my suit goes well enough, I thank God," Simon
was saying. "It's no easy matter to find one's self an alien
in a land one has always thought of as one's own; but this
is a time of overturns. In the meantime, four hundred
marks a year is what the King hath settled on me, and four
hundred marks is perforce what I must suffer."

"No news of Amaury?"

"Ah, there's the heart of it," Simon said ruefully. "He's
constable of France now; why should he want an earldom,
too? Yet, well I know that it is not Leicester itself he cov-
ets, but only for that brotherly rivalry we bore each other
from the cradle—there's the scar for it, and he hath a like.

Were Amaury to give place, I'm the next surviving, and should do homage for the honour of my father's shire instant upon the news." He smiled suddenly. "And, certes, also upon the look in the King's eye, to manoeuvre for the weather-gage."

He turned his head suddenly toward Roger, his smile still present but no longer ironic, like a man who hopes for but knows better than to expect a pleasure. "And who's this, Adam? I've not see him before, I know."

"True," Adam said. "He's called Roger Bacon, of a franklin's family in Ilchester; a scholar with us. The Bacons suffered somewhat at Hubert's hands, yet not so much as they might have, it appears."

"Grow thou in learning," Simon said in English, searching Roger's face with alarmingly penetrating eyes. Then, in French again: "Yes— what think you of these proceedings, most Christian Adam? I doubt not that our Hubert's been extortionate, else how would any armed man hold troops together? Territory's to be lived on, and to be just with later, if time permit; and Hubert's an old soldier, thereby rich, in the natural order of things. Is the Crown so poor it must bite coins out of its own swords?" He gestured at the pack around them. "It has not that appearance—though I speak from four hundred marks' pension, as I grant."

"And from overlong from these shores as well, I fear me," Adam said. "The docket is far more grave than that, and far graver the exactions for it. Last year, a huge pack of robbers took from the granaries the harvested corn of the Roman clergy, throughout most of England. The corn was sold and the money vanished—much, it appears, as largesse to the poor. It's said this was more of Robin of Sherwood's doings; the harpers will not let that poor highwayman rest at his crossroads. But your friend Bishop Peter of Winchester—"

"Not so," Simon said, in a voice so quiet that only Adam and Roger could have heard his words. "Pray exercise better taste in friends in my behalf, Adam."

"I'm glad to hear you say so. Nevertheless, Peter des Roches alleged to have captured certain of the robbers, and made them to confess that they had warrants from Hubert, and from the King, too, given them from Hubert's own hand. Witnesses there were none, but at the end of July, Henry dismissed Hubert in favour of Stephen de Segrave—and then came this enormous letter in charges and demands: that Hubert account for the estates of Penbroke and Strigul—"

"Then the second earl is now dead as well?"

"Yes, two years ago; there's another Marshal, Richard, but not of age yet. Also, Hubert was to account for all liberties, losses, taxes of the fifteenth and sixteenth part, castles and preserves withheld and restored—I cannot begin to summarize it. Following these, charges of treason, of conspiring the people to riot against the Latin emissaries of His Holiness, of seeking to become such a hero in the sight of the mob as Robin Wood was against King John, and more, and still more; so that Hubert fled his kinsmen in Ireland and took refuge in sanctuary at Bury St. Edmunds. Whence, however, the King had him dragged, naked."

"Ah no. Can there be more? This to Hubert? Would God allow?"

"God thinks continually on all our sins, and waits," Adam said sombrely. "And there's little more. They essayed to fetter him, but some common smith refused, saying he would put no irons on the man who restored England to the English—with your pardon, Simon. Hence, they closed Hubert in the Tower, till Bishop Robin of London heard how sanctuary had been breached, and as good as ordered the King to return him to Bury St. Edmunds. Where he is now; and that is all."

"I'd credit it from none but you," Simon said. "Had he no defences?"

"One bad, one worse. He would have it that a charter from King John exempted him in perpetuity from any examination of his accounts—which means only that he was guilty of embezzlement, the privilege all soldiers claim, my lord, as I have just heard it from your lips. Upon this, Peter des Roches, of course, ruled that the charter died with King John—and then, by ill luck, Henry asked Hubert to produce revenues from a place called Yeo Manse, that was this my familiar's property till Hubert took it; and there were none at all—not a groat, nor a broken brass penny for the Crown: a singular accident, but

had it not come thus about, the King would have found
something as suitable; Henry means to crush Hubert
entire."

"I heard," Simon said thoughtfully, "that the King near
stabbed him at Portsmouth four years ago—solely for want
of ships to send against the French provinces."

"That is true," Adam said, "I was there. Henry was mad
as wolves."

"Well," Simon said. "I must think on this. Pray for me,
most Christian Adam, for I need this King."

"Certes, and he needs you. Only keep my counsel—"

"That I'll not swear, for you know I shall." Simon bowed
briefly to the stunned Roger and vanished into the crowd
with a grace not even Adam could have equalled.

"Is it true—" Roger began, inadvertently in English.

" 'Tis true entire—and forget thou every word. Thy bag
of coins is Henry's, should he or any of his o'erhear thee.
And speak no more English, or thou'lt be taken as a spy of
Hubert's, aye, and so shall I."

"But this de Montfort—"

"Trust him; and hush, thou'rt being far too far a
plauderer for the role I cast thee in. I brought thee here to
listen; listen thou!"

"Yes," Roger said, "but, Adam—"

Adam ducked his head in a brief nod of satisfaction and
began to worm his way through the gathering once more.
He had only just disappeared again, however, when a blast
of sackbuts and clarions froze the whole small cave world
upon the instant. King Henry, having finished with
feasting, was ready to begin those ceremonies by which,
could he but keep his head sufficiently cool, he would complete the severance of his right arm.

Knowing well enough what course the King's evenings
of state took by ordinary, and how to clock them by the
clepsydra of the wine in Henry's glass, Adam Marsh escaped by first intention the theatre of this proposed ampu-
tation before the heralds of it had properly tautened their
lips against their instruments. This he did with some misgivings, especially on behalf of Roger Bacon left behind in
the flickering underwater darkness of the feast-hall
among many fish all strange to him and not a few danger-

ous, too; but Adam was impelled, for he had already spied escaping before him with her ladies the King's sister, Eleanor of Pembroke, whose confessor he was, and whom he followed forthwith in the utmost disquiet.

He knew well enough where to find the Lady Eleanor where else she might have gone in drafty Beaumont; but once out of the hall he did not hurry, walking instead as gravely as he might in his youth through the barrel-vaulted corridors with their smoke-blackened hangings, appearing not to notice the gleam of the occasional torches against the chain-mail of the King's sentries standing in their niches like statues of saints militant. It was his duty not to alarm his penitent—she who had so much to alarm her already, though but barely turned twenty-four: not only sister of this royally incontinent King, but widow scarce two years of the son of William earl-Marshal of the realm, once holder of those Pembroke estates (which she could never convey) for the stewardship of which Hubert de Burgh had failed to account. Small marvel that she had found herself unable to stand placidly at her brother's side while he trumpeted wrath on the beloved stern guardian of her bridal fief, the green pleasaunces of which—now nothing to Henry but money, and the heady possibility of blood—encompassed as well all the garden-ensorcelled girlhood she would ever be able to remember.

Adam was not challenged as he crossed into Eleanor's apartments in the left wing of the castle, but he was recognized quickly and embarrassingly by her tiring-maid, a fresh girl of eighteen attached to Eleanor's service as a courtesy by the Bigods, her dead husband's claiming relatives; a girl all too plainly bemused enough by Adam to see in him her Peter Abelard, and herself an Héloïse; but Eleanor was not there. She would, therefore, be in the chapel which her brother had made for her, which was at some distance from the apartments; but there was a passage that Adam knew of, which perhaps King John had known but Henry did not, which led quite directly to the priest's hole in the chapel from nearby, through the walls. It had been Eleanor who had shown it to him, for it debouched into her most private chamber, disguised as the monstrous black oak door of a wardrobe; and he took the route at once, shutting his Héloïse manquée out first (and not without a shudder) with, "I will wait here."

She was waiting for him as he settled into the stone-cold niche. Though the chapel was dark except for two tapers burning before the altar, that was enough to figure for him the marvellous bent head in profile through the confessional window—once, no doubt, a full door to be used in passage to whispers and confessions in composition, not absolution, of sin. *Dona nobis pacem*, Héloïse-and-Abelard. . . .

"Father . . . I was waiting. You said . . . ?"

"I was catching my breath, my lady. It's a long clamber here. And we'll needs to be quick; I've a scholar above, promising, but too green in the vintage to leave abroad among so many Latins; and thy brother will call on me ere this work of his be done. And very ill it is, too."

"Certes, but rest thee a moment, Father, all the same," she said in a low voice—hardly more than a whisper but for the music in it. "Please, my need is greater. I'm afraid, I am most afraid."

He saw her head turn toward him with this, and even in the two-starred darkness, he was momentarily riven of all his good advice by such fairness, less than half seen though it was. Judging both by images and by such members of the line as Adam had seen, the Plantagenets had always been notable for personal beauty—at least from Coeur-de-lion on—but Eleanor, of the high brow and wide green eyes, was to Adam that trial of his vocation which is greater than all the trials to which the princes of the world are subject, since to them it need be no trial at all.

"You have more reason to fear in this cubby than you would in the hall," he said. "In seclusion, you appear most pointedly to be taking Hubert's part. Your brother will be all the less likely to privilege you at Pembroke if you so humiliate him—as all will see it, not just the King."

"Then, shall I stay and weep in their very faces, while they cast my uncle down? I have infuriated Henry with far smaller shows."

"But that's a woman's role," Adam said patiently. "To weep shows the kindness in your heart, even toward a miscreant. But to be absent—that might mean complicity. Besides, my lady, Henry's mind will dwell not long on Hubert now, for he'll find matters far more quick to spark his tinder than your uncle is, before this feast is over. Therefore, I pray you, be present at the Hubert part, so's not to be marked partisan while that runs its course; and should you weep, it will yet be forgotten when Henry weeps, as he's sure to do, aye, and gnash teeth, too."

"You choose odd words to calm me, Father," she said; but there was a slight trace of amusement in her voice. "Must you be so ominous?"

"By no means, my lady. That was not my purport. I mean only that the defiance of the barons is a greater thing to the King than his sudden hatred of Hubert, and will so seem to him when he thinks on it a little further. And if you follow me, my lady, your brother's every outcry against these rebel earls may yet be a golden note in the ladders of your ears, and of your fortunes, too; for there's one with us in Beaumont tonight who cannot but rise in the pan as the barons go down—and would, I doubt not, count it his deepest desire to bear you with him."

She laughed suddenly in the dark chapel, setting echoes afire. "Father, how secular the errands that you scurry on! Has this unknown sent you with this Cupid's message? Or hope you to be my brother's Vulcan, to catch the unknown and Eleanor in the same net?"

"Neither, my lady," Adam said, his throat a little thickened. "I come on my own recognisance; and depart the same as I came in."

"Swef, swef, douce Pere. I was mocking. I know not how I'd have lived without you since my noble lord went thither. I will go now, borne on as much as bearing your advice. Bless me."

He did so; and with a rustle, she was gone, leaving him staring at the two far-away candles, now guttering so low that the images in the chapel no longer seemed to have any heads, and nothing was left of the Christ above the altar but two feet and a nail. Still he waited, until she should have time to pass around her apartment by the long route and resume her place near her brother's chair. As he waited, he slowly turned cold again, and one of the tapers burned blue and went out.

Thanks to this necessary wait, even the short route back through the walls and the wardrobe did not bring him back to the hall until much of the fury there had worn itself thin. He arrived only just in time to hear, but too late to prevent, Roger Bacon giving advice to the King.

Which had been no intention of Roger's, ne as he would have seen it earlier even the part of sanity; nor could he have said afterwards which of many small steps might have taken him otherwhere than to that brink, however he might have turned (but did not turn) each one. The hubbub after the sennets died soon under the King's ophidian eyes. In the smoky silence the white-faced Henry curled his hands around the lion-paws of his chair and said:

"Sound again for my servant Hubert de Burgh."

The heralds lifted their pennoned instruments and sounded the hoarse Plantagenet battle-view halloo which, the singers said, had been Blondel's first notes to Coeur-de-Lion imprisoned: but nothing happened. The dark hall became deathly quiet. A white-lipped look from Henry set the heralds to sounding once more, and then again, but no one appeared, no one even stirred. At long last, Peter des Roches leaned in his rich bishop's brocade to the King's ear, his ringed fingers shielding his mouth. Henry, very pale, listened without expression, and finally nodded once, sitting back in his chair.

"I have treason all about me, gentleman and ladies," the King said quietly. "My justiciar that was answers me not, and no one stands forth in his stead. My barons and my earls that I called to this feast are not here. They say they fear treachery, that sit in their fastnesses and treason plot against their King."

He snatched up his goblet suddenly and drank with a kind of desperate greediness quite unrelated to thirst. Then the goblet hit the table with a noise like the fall of a hammer, and Henry's eyes were roving over his audience like the eyes of an executioner.

"Where are my earls, where are the barons of England?" he said hoarsely. "Let us have passed here a decree which will tell them who is their King. Here we have a sufficient gathering of nobles, as the Great Charter insists. Give me that order—an order to compel, by England and St. George."

He swung on the Bishop.

"Be better advised, an it please you, my lord King," Peter des Roches said softly, folding his plump white hands together. "These barons have defied you already, and by special messengers. No new demand will win aught more for the Crown. Seek to summon them instead; sound for them, as you sounded for Hubert de Burgh, and prove will they respond."

"There's none of them here to hear," Henry said. "Why sound sennets to absent ears? They fear me, and that's the end of it. I want an instrument that brings obedience, not a noise that won't be heard outside Beaumont."

His eyes lit on Simon de Montfort, "Montfort, what say you? Is the throne of England to woo those rebels back with music? Or shall we have our decree as we have demanded it? Advise me; I am weary of these counsels of caution from all these mitred heads."

"Sound, my lord King," Simon said. "Indeed, sound thrice, for the hearing of these the barons' messengers. And let them bear back your summons. If your nobles fail to answer your triple summons, they will be as little likely to honour a decree passed for you by the Frenchmen they hate and mistrust."

"Guard thy tongue, Montfort. Thou'rt in my court by sufferance. If your next word is in praise of Hubert—"

"And so it would have been, my lord King," Simon said steadily from his place below the Bishop. "The barons trust Hubert; they do not trust me. They do not know even who I am. Nor do they trust any Poitevin."

"You bewray your suit for Leicester, Montfort—"

"You asked me to speak, my lord King," Simon said. "Had I told you only what you wished to hear, I'd better been silent. If that only's what you will from me, then away Leicester; I'll not so traduce my Crown to win a fief, nay, not now nor ever; my head's thy forfeit for it, my lord King—today, tomorrow, forever."

"Stop, that's more promise than I've asked thee for," the King said. "Press me not so closely, Montfort; when I want your head, I'll ask it. Why can nobody advise me without throwing his life at me? When did I ever ask that for the price of oats? Witness all here that I am not, not, not my bloody father!"

No one answered. Henry calmed himself with a deep draught of the green wine. Then he began looking through the press again, his shoulders hunched; but was distracted by the return to his table of the lady who had been pointed out to Roger as the King's sister, with several of her household. The King stared at her, frowning, and looking for a moment a little confused, and then back at the lower tables.

"Is there no one here to profess the word of God?" the King said, beginning suddenly to smile. "Who reads for England at the King's feast? Where is the Church in this my hour of extremity? A word, a word! Where are my Oxford scholars? Where's the great Grosseteste? Where is my sister's confessor; where's that subtle boy Adam de Marisco?" He was standing now, his hand rolling back and forth on its knuckles on the table before him, like a battering-ball encrusted with jewels.

And then he saw Roger. "Now there's one," he said. "Rise, scholar of Oxenford, and profess the word of God. Read to your King, as you were summoned to do. Your head is safe; I swear, I am not blood-thirsty. Rise, and rede me."

Everyone turned to look. There was no way out. Roger rose, his shanks as shaky as reeds.

"Good, he rises," the King said. "Now speak. What says my English church? Has it anything to say to me? Speak."

"My lord King," Roger said.

"I hear you, friar. Say on."

"My lord King . . . I am not in orders. I am only a poor student."

"Speak," Henry said. "Advise me."

"My lord King. . . . Then I will ask you: What is most dangerous to sailors? What fear they most?"

"A riddle?" Henry the Sailor said, smiling. "Very well. I know not. Those whose business is on the wide waters know best, not I. What's the answer, sweet scholar?"

"My lord King, I will tell thee," Roger said. "The answer is: Stones and rocks."

The King frowned. "Oh? Dost thou make game of thy King, friar? Or. . . . Aha *Petrae et rupes!* Your Grace, he means you; what think you of that? Shall I then be quit of you again?"

It was plain that Henry was joking, after his fashion, but Peter des Roches, who obviously had read Roger's meaning instantly and had been staring at the tonsured clerk like a man attempting to memorize a text, could manage only a rather grim smile. The moment the Bishop's gaze turned, Roger sat down.

"Henry is King," the Bishop said, "and will do what he will do. Meanwhiles, my lord, I judge Montfort's words not ill advice."

"What Satan's imp made thee say that?" Adam Marsh's voice hissed suddenly in Roger's ear, making him jump in his chair. "Dost not know Henry's calling 'the Sailor' only on de Burgh's account, since the sinking of Eustace in the straits?"

"He called on me," Roger said sullenly. "He called you first, and you not here to hear it."

"Couldst not praise piety, or say aught else equally harmless? The giving of advice to this King is a career likely to end suddenly."

"Then example me, Adam," Roger said, a little grimly. "He's looking at thee now."

"What say you, Marisco?" Henry said. "Reserve not thy wisdom for women and clerks. Shall we follow Montfort in this?"

"My lord King," Adam said steadily, "I was not here when Montfort spoke, and know not the import of his proposal. But well I know him to be wiser for his years than was even his father; I can say no more to the point."

"And enough!" Henry said. "Conspiracies within conspiracies! Nevertheless, we will be governed once more, and only once more. Segrave, your Grace, Montfort, Rievaux, let it be heard that we summon the barons of England thrice, to see whether they will come or no. They are called to attend us at Westminister—we will set them July eleventh, that no man may say he has failed to receive our letters. There we will fairly hear their suits, and fairly consult with them on their problems. What think ye, my lords?"

"That is kingly done," Peter des Roches said; but he

seemed a little uneasy, and Roger, regarding him covertly, was reminded that John Blund—the man, not the horse—had been raised this year and cast down as Archbishop of Canterbury in a single six-month.

But that was no concern of his.

IV: WESTMINSTER

How to live to very old, Roger wrote scratchily with the goose quill, *and enjoy it.* At this point a lump in the ink blocked the quill and he had to stop to clear it; but that done, he was able to sand his title and regard it critically.

He did not like it. It promised too much, especially from the pen of a man in his early twenties; and never mind that that was at Providence's gate, whence had come the commission. Better to say: how to postpone the accidents of age, and preserve the senses. No, still better to omit "how"; say, *Liber de retardatione accidentium senectutis, et de sensibus conservandis.* That needed nothing more than a dedication; he dipped the quill and added, *ad suasionem duorum sapientum, scilicet Johannis Castellionati et Phillipi cancellarii Parisiensis.*

Nobody would be likely to question that since it was perfectly true—and yet, he was as instantly stabbed by the conviction that it was not true in the eyes of Veritie. Philip the Chancellor had invited somebody of Oxford to write a work on the postponing of old age, and with the suggestion that, were it to prove worthy, it might be sent to the Pope; but 'somebody' was not the same as "Roger Bacon." The assignment of the task to Roger had been wholly the doing of Grosseteste.

The pinprick of his thought brought with it again the desolate realization of how much had changed in Roger's world, as it had in the world at large, since that moment of incredulous triumph five years ago when he had counted over the gold and the trash in Wulf's bag in this very room, laboriously allowed for the rates of exchange on every piece and found himself the possessor of close to two thousand pounds; and the realization, too, that the decision the changes were forcing on him could not be delayed much longer.

He had told no one of the sum he had recovered, not even Adam; word of that kind travelled too swiftly, and he had been grimly determined to hold every coin until the moment when circumstances absolutely forced it out of his grasp. Adam, to be sure, knew the general outcome, but he did not press Roger for details once he had satisfied himself that Roger was no longer in any danger and could, when Adam needed him, make himself presentable at court. What Grosseteste knew or thought about the matter was unknown to Roger, and now doubtless would always remain so. The rest of Oxford saw only that Roger continued to live frugally, or perhaps even a little more frugally than he had immediately after learning of the disaster at Yeo Manse, and that he had become almost completely solitary; any rumours that might have circulated of his recovery of funds—and there were, of course, bound to be many of these—died quietly away in the face of these obvious misleading facts.

What the situation was now at Yeo Manse he did not know and was afraid to inquire. Will of Howlake was, of course, long gone, withdrawn to serve the more immediate needs of his desperately besieged lord; but if Harold had returned to the manse—or if he had, whether he knew anything of the depredation of his brother's buried hoard—Roger had heard no word of it. A letter from Toulouse a year ago had shown Eugene equally ignorant, as was expectable; even had Harold repossessed the property, he was an indifferent correspondent. With this blank spot in his mind where Ilchester should be, Roger was uneasily content; the last word he wanted to hear was some news which would force him—or make him feel that he ought—to return any part of the money.

He laid down the quill on the lectern and stared blindly out of the single small window, now blazoned with yellow fire from the westering July sun. Near by was the stack of new parchment awaiting his fair copy of the book, not a sheet of it more than close calculation had shown him he would need, but still representing an expenditure which

would have startled any of his fellow-clerks out of their illusions about "poor Roger Bacon"; next to it, the heap of
tattered and smudgy palimpsests which was his draft, his
maiden experience as a writer, more than fifteen thousand
words put down with pain less than a thousand at a time,
with every day's end a new problem in resisting the temptation to write "finis" during the first half of the task—and
then, suddenly, the luminous moment when task trans-
forms itself into mystical experience, whereafter the temptation is to turn the illumination to an orgy and never stop
at all.

But he was unable to go back to his fair copy now, inviting though all that virgin parchment was, and imperative
though it was to have the work ready to be sent to Paris before this month was over. Instead, he moved suddenly to
sponge off the face of the sheet which had carried his outline for the work; and on this, while Oxford slept the midday sleep outside his hot, still cell, he began slowly to write
down a letter to himself, beginning.

i: Robt Grosseteste has left Oxenford.

He had only slowly become aware of what it was
Grosseteste had been about during his long meditative
convalescence, and had been even slower to connect it with
those few words of mysterious promise spoken to him by
the lector during the winter of the death. Doubtless Adam
had known all about it, but he had said nothing; in the
meantime, Roger had been left tacitly to understand that
his new privilege as a teacher of Aristotle—now much
threatened by the arrival of Richard Fishacre, a
frighteningly learned master who had brought with him a
new translation by Michael Scot, with commentaries by
Averroes—was the whole sense to be read in that sickbed
adumbration. It had certainly seemed sufficient at the
time; to Roger's elation, he had become the first man ever
to teach at Oxford before entering upon his secular mastership in the Faculty of Arts; and he had made much of the
opportunity, so that after the passage of less than two
years the students crowded into his classes (some of them,
no doubt, there simply to hear him say something outrageous, as under the prompting of the self he occasionally,
helplessly did, but most to hear the new knowledge dis-

coursed by the only regent master in Oxford who had it at his fingertips.)

All of which had been so enormously satisfying that he had neglected to think, until last year, of where he might hope to go next, even putting off as of no special urgency the question of whether or not to read for the Faculty of Theology. Certainly it had never entered his head that the now inaccessible Grosseteste might have been engaged in politicking, even of a peculiar and limited kind; Adam Marsh, yes—though Adam appeared to hate any involvement with the powerful, there was something in his nature which drew the powerful to him with almost the force of love—but certainly never the lector. Besides, Roger had been too busy; preparing his lectures, gratifying though it was, multiplied the difficulty of becoming Master of Arts, which, in these last two years, involved the explication of exceedingly difficult texts and rigorous practical training in disputation; and his unwelcome, unavoidable involvement in Adam's outside affairs had further deprived him of contemplation when—as he now saw, but perhaps too late—he had stood most in need of it.

And then, after a lapse of years, Grosseteste again called Roger and Adam Marsh to his study and unleashed his levin.

"Roger, I've seen too little of thee," he said without preamble, "but thou wilt understand when I tell thee that I mean now to assume the bishopric of Lincoln, which Adam and the King alike have been urging on me. Hence, I must leave Oxford; the next lector to the Franciscans will be magister Hugo, as Adam knows; thou wilt approve, Roger, I ne mislike."

"Yes," Roger said faintly, stunned.

"Good. Now I must tell thee what work I've been about since Adam first brought thee to me as a stripling. I've said naught of it before, it being mischancy and far too far in the balance; but the finger of God hath been on me since mine illness, o happy accident! and now it must all be broached, and brought into flower. I've been conspiring all these years with Philip the Chancellor to bring about the restoration of the University of Paris, and in particular, to see that blind prohibition of Aristotle rescinded there. In large, we've succeeded; but who'll teach Aristotle in Paris now? There they've no students grown in him, let alone a master. Yet we have such a master to send them, Roger. Wilt thou go?"

Roger could say nothing at all; he felt as taken up out of his waters as a little fish in a net; yet, at the same time, the brand was alight again in his breast as burningly as ever in his life, and more, more.

"That's early asked, Capito," Adam said, eyeing Roger with what seemed to be amusement. "Let be a while; I ken our Roger better thilke days, and the dose is heavy."

"I wis it well," Grosseteste said, nodding gravely. "Say on, then; wilt have it so, Roger?"

"Please," Roger said. "I'm lost as lost may be."

"Spoken like a Platonist," Adam said, still with that slight gleam of amusement. "Knowest thou then, Roger: Philip the Chancellor would have us provide him a book from Aristotle, new-written, which he might send the Pope as evidence of the uses of learning; the subject to be the postponement of old age. We've promised him just such a work, but are in some straits as to who shall have the writing of it. We are too busy both to compose any such book in a useful period of time, nor are we as perfect Aristotelians as we'd like. John Blund is gone from us, poor wight, and our saintly Edmund Rich is Archbishop of Canterbury in his stead. There's to come to us next year a great master named Richard Fishacre, but alack, that's next year and not now. Whom have we but thee?"

Whom indeed?—Roger's own silent argument at the sickbed now turned upon him.

"Which should be naught but to thy liking, Roger, an I read thee right," Grosseteste added. "There's scholarship in thy blood, as is plain to see, not only in thee, but eke in our Dominican frater Robert."

"The eminent Robert's no kin of mine," Roger said, for sheer want of knowing what else to say; he a little welcomed the diversion. "The name is very common, Master, I've a brother Robert, 'tis true, but he's no scholar; my younger brother Eugene may become a scholar in time, by God's will."

"Well enough; but not to the point," Adam said. "Wilt thou undertake the book? Thou canst make free of my library, and Master Grosseteste's, where there's sure to be

much thou might simply copy for better speed; yet, harm
there'd be none were it to be a work of some substance in
the art of medicine, for Gregory's much enfeebled as thou
knowst, and the next Pope may be hardly so great a friend
of universities."

"That being so," Roger said, "why not thy Dominican
physician, Master Grosseteste? I know naught of medicine—"

"And John de St. Giles knows naught of Aristotle,"
Grosseteste said, "and being rusty in disputation, writes
but slowly and that with a club foot. Nay, Roger, Adam is
right; thou canst consult with John to thy profit, I ne
doubt, but thou art the man an thou'lt grasp the nettle.
The burden's great, I grant thee, but why else did the lord
God give shoulders to His children?"

"I know not," Roger said. "But thus I'll answer you, my
Masters: certes, I'll write you your book, but Paris is a second question which I must abide. In all this time I've
thought myself to be reading, when the time came, for a
doctorate in theology, as is small secret anywhere in Oxford. Moreover, I've much in mind to study in the natural
sciences, and where in Paris would I find. . . ."

Here he faltered and found himself unable to continue.
Grosseteste would soon leave Oxford to be charged with
the largest diocese in England, reaching from the Humber
to the Thames. Where in the world would Roger find another master in those science, even at Oxford? It was not a
subject that interested Adam greatly, despite the younger
man's mathematical bent.

"But to what purpose, Roger?" Grosseteste said. " 'Tis
always and only the end in view which doth condemn or
purify. True that the arts help purge us of error and guide
to perfection *mentis aspectus et affectus*; yet belike are they
that well of water dug by Isaac called *Esdon*, signifying
contention. But the *scientiae lucrativae*, as medicine, the
two laws, alchemy—they signify enmity, *puteus, qui
vocatur Satan, quod est nomen diaboli.*"

"From thee this is a hard saying," Roger said, "that art
first in all the world in the *libri naturales.*"

"But the purpose, Roger! Dost thou wish to preach, then
the sciences be well enough, after thou art become a theologian; but thou knowest well that many learned men wis

not how to preach ne wish to; they whore after such sciences as will add to their riches or repute; one studying medicine to cure the sick and be made wealthy, or raise the dead and be called a magician; another alchemy, to make heavenly what's naturally impure, yet without a dram of piety; another music, to cast out demons; another wonders, such as stars, winds, lightning, beasts, stones, trees, and all else that appeareth wonderful to men's gaze. Yet, theology is first among all studies, through which a man might know all such marvels better and more notably—not for vain glory and worldly wealth, but for the salvation of souls."

"Master Grosseteste, well I ween all knowledge to be theology's handmaiden," Roger said haltingly. "Nor do I run after knowledge for greed or pomposity, but out of the lust to know, which I count holy. Even in the Proverbs be we commanded to love wisdom for its own sake; for whatever is natural to man, whatever becoming, whatever useful, whatever magnificent, including the knowledge of God, is altogether worthy to be known, *integritas eorum quae ad sapientiam completam requiruntur.* No more can I answer thee."

For a moment, Grosseteste seemed taken aback; then he smiled gently. "Which will suffice for the present," he said. "We'll not compel thee to Paris, Roger, an it be not thy will and desire. Only be not hasty-firm in thy choice, which thou mayst repent no matter how it goeth. Enough for now that thou'lt give us a book for Philip de Greve—"

"How long a book?" Roger said with new, sudden misgiving.

"How long is a book?" Adam asked reasonably. "No longer than the subject; that's all that's proper. Put down what's known of the postponement of old age—which is next to nothing, surely—and such conjectures as thou thinkest worthy so to dignify. A fair summary of Aristotle on thilke subject will be thy meat, and all else be subject to thy discretion."

"There be books of Scripture a copyist with a fine hand might encompass with a single sheet," Grosseteste said. "Should what thou'lt add to Aristotle be no more than that, none could think ill of thee on that account; though I hope that thine ambition will let itself be bolder."

And deep in Roger's heart came again the voiceless whisper of the self: *Thou kennst me over-well, Seynt Robert.*

And there it was, awaiting the copyist whiling his day's pittance of working time on a letter to himself: Greece, Rome, Chaldea, Arabia, Zion; fire, air, earth, water; Aristotle, Galen, Avicenna, Rhazes, Haly Regalis, Isaac, Ahmed, Haly super Tegni, Damascenius; cold, heat, moisture, dryness; aloes, balsam of Gilcad and Engedi, basil, wild cabbage, calamint, camomile, wild carrot, cassia, the greater celandine, cinnamon, saffron, dittany, elder, fennel, fumitory, hellebore, hound's tongue, mace, marjoram, myrobalan, olea, penny-royal, pomegranate, radish, rhubarb; blood, phelgm, yellow bile, black bile; the seven *occulta,* ambergris of the whale, the pearls of Paracelsus, the skin of vipers, the long-lived anthros or rosemary, Galen's body heat of the healthy animal (whether child or fat puppy), the bone which forms in the stag's heart, the fat underflesh of dragons; and the precious incorruptible underground sunlight of gold, that *aurum potabile* which being itself perfect induceth perfection in the living frame. . . .

The copyist looked away; the quill scratched; the letters flowed slowly and formed in small clots:

ii: Marisco will have us alle politick'g, scilicet the Capito & that Roher call'd Bachon, inside a xii-month.

This was not a new thought, for he had scarcely escaped from within the breastwork and bastion of Westminster Hall that furious April of 1235, more than a year ago, before the self was whispering it; yet, he was no more comfortable with it now than he had ever been.

At first he had thought he had been reprieved. He had expected to be haled by Adam *ex studio* to the King's proclaimed parliament with his surly barons; and though he had never before been to London, the prospect did not gratrify him—one exchange with Henry had been more than enough for Roger. But for reasons unknown, Adam went alone to the 1234 meeting, which apparently had proven as unproductive of earls and barons as had the Oxford conclave.

Not long after that began the rebellion of Richard earl-Marshal. There was hardly a sign of it in Oxford, where nothing of moment was going on but the establishment by the King of a hospital for pilgrims and the sick, near the bridge; but the roads became less safe than ever, and in the north and in Ireland the whole countryside was said to be smoking with pillage and slaughter. At the beginning of November the whole of England was assaulted by thunderstorms more clamorous and violent than any man could remember, so that the serfs began again to mutter that old saw, "Weep not for death of husband or childer, but rather for the thunder"; and on St. Catherine's Day, November twenty-fifth, the King's forces met Richard's before Monmouth in a battle that left the earth deep in slaughtered foreigners, yet gained the earl-Marshal nothing except to preserve him a while. There was another such blood-letting on Christmas Day, equally indecisive; and the word from elsewhere in the kingdom was that the holdings and estates of the rebels were being vengefully put to the torch and their people cut down, freemen and serfs alike, by French-speaking bands with letters from Henry. It was not a good season for pilgrimages.

Yet by March, Adam had brought Roger warning to prepare to attend at Westminister, where the King on the ninth of April would at long last have the assemblage of his full court, saving only those who still cleaved to the earl-Marshal and to de Burgh. The meeting had evidently been arranged by Edmund Rich, perhaps the only man in England still fully trusted by both sides. Roger was not overjoyed, nor did the possibility of seeing his London brother after the meeting was over tempt him even slightly; but Grosseteste would be there, since he was soon to be elevated to the bishopric, vacated by Edmund a year before; and Adam would nave no other familiar with him but Roger, which ended any argument Roger was empowered to offer to the contrary.

The trip to London was long, and Adam had seemed both elated and secretive about some matter which, since he could not penetrate it, soon had Roger miserable with mixed curiosity and boredom; attempts to produce conversation on any other subject ran up against the blank wall of Adam's preoccupation:

"Adam, what thinkest thou of the *intellectus agens?* Of the nature of it?"

"Hmmm? Why, 'tis the raven of Elias."

"But the raven was not *of* Elias himself. What is the signification? That the active intellect is more of God than of man?"

"No, not exactly." And that was all. Or:

"Whom shall we see at Westminster? Hath thy friend de Montfort been confirmed in the earldom of Leicester?"

"Yes, two years ago. Nay, not properly confirmed, but the land and appurtenances of his father were conveyed to him."

"Then we shall see him?"

"Nay, an God willeth. He's abroad, I trust, or else will need to be."

Obviously nothing was to be learned from such scraps of enigmas, and Roger had retreated, at first sullenly, then with an increasing preoccupation of his own, into the interior composition of the *Liber de retardatione,* about the possibility of which he was then only beginning to become aroused; and so they jogged the rest of the way in a mutual silence, broken only by the commonplaces of journeying, of which Adam seemed wholly unaware and to which Roger eventually became quite accustomed.

London itself had proven to be overwhelmingly like a gigantic Ilchester in the midst of a perpetual market day, a seemingly endless labyrinth of narrow streets and alleys choked with stinking ordure and with stinking people. The rain, which fell every day and night that Roger was in London, did not the slightest good, for it was accompanied by no slightest breath of April breeze; the stench simply rose a little distance and then hung in the fog, refusing to disperse, while below on the cobbles, the sludge thrown down from the second-storey windows was spattered impartially upon walls and pedestrians alike by every passing horseman. Like sin, such filth was the common situation of humanity, but Roger had never before encountered either in so sensible a concentration.

It was better as they approached the Hall, which stood directly along the Thames; for though the river itself sublimed into the air the miasma of the grandest Cloaca Maxima of them all, here at least the air could distinctly be felt to be in motion. Nevertheless, by the time he and Adam were left alone in their separate cells in the palace, Roger was more than ready for the spring bath with which he had already planned to conclude the long trip.

What he had expected to follow upon their arrival he could not have said, but in fact, there was nothing of any moment. They had reached the Hall early in the afternoon, and Roger spent the rest of daylight prowling his cell. Occasionally, a distant sennet announced the arrival of one of the barons and his suite; on each such occasion, Roger halted his pacing and looked out his one window, but for the most part there was nothing to see but fog; when, once or twice, the fog lifted slightly, nothing but the river. The day, a dim and depressing one even at high noon, died early, obviously of suffocation. A man came with a lit rush and touched it to two lapers beside Roger's low wooden bed—even inside the cell the air was so moist that both flames showed haloes only five paces away—and then there was another long wait. Part of this he was able to fill as a matter of course with the prayers appropriate for the hours; but he was able to go no further with the book on old age without writing materials, and perhaps could have accomplished as little with them, for he discovered that away from his references he could not call a single quotation to mind with surety—either something had abruptly gone wrong with his memory or (the self suggested with its usual exacerbating abruptness) his memory had never had the true scholar's infinite retentiveness for the letter of the text. The simple attempt to choose the least unattractive of these two new appearances made him feel slightly motion-sick, like a child taken trotting for the first time; and as the hours lengthened, the giddiness seeped down into his knees and began to transform itself implacably into panic.

Someone knocked. After his first start, Roger jerked open the door with a great surge of relief travelling through his muscles. Anything that would serve to take him out of this prison-yard circling had to be welcome.

It was Adam. "Eheu," he said, twitching his long nose. "*Stercor stercoraris!* I was about to ask thee if thou'd supped, but that could no man in this chamber-pot. Ho, Roger, ware the candles—"

Roger missed the candles, but he did not miss the bed,

though he tried. He gasped and glared at Adam.

"God pardon me, and do thou, too," Adam said, instantly repentant. "Here, let's sponge thee off and get fresh linen—hold off, thou'rt but making it more hopeless—and then we'll have thee changed to higher quarters. Stay'st thou here and thou'lt suffocate; look how blue yonder candles burn; 'tis like the vault of a sewer."

He helped Roger to strip, steadying him, and bathed him again.

"Full many a rogue's died from taking such a refuge," he said, wrapping the still-damp surplice over the warm dry shift he had removed from his own back. "There's a foulness collects over still sewage that kills even rats. I myself have seen spectral fires burning over cesspool-heads, in the midst of nights; demons, belike, come to breathe what's closest on earth to their air in hell."

"How can a demon leave hell by first intention?" Roger asked, staring with fascination at the nearest candle-flame. It was undeniably mantled with blue, but not the blue of incipient guttering-out; the flame itself was as tall as ever.

"Ah, Roger, as to that, no demon's ever left hell, nor ever can; yet, they appear. Don thy shoes, Roger. Did not the prophet Elijah appear before all during Passover to tell of the coming of our Lord? Yet left not that place where he abode? These things lie in Nature, or in Miracle; as to the latter, the Angel of Death is everywhere, and yet always in heaven; as to the former, the sun is in heaven, but his light is ubiquitous and all-pervasive—thus speaks one who comments on the Haggadah, with wisdom as I ne doubt. What doest thou? Save the linens, the King's household will wash them!"

Roger carefully finished stuffing the window with the sticky bedding and clothing, adding straw judiciously here and there. "Peace, Adam, I mean not to throw them to the Thames. Mayhap I'll trap a rat, should thilke chamber be such a death-cell as thou foresee'st."

"But to what purpose?"

"None. To see an it will happen. Now I am ready. Whither away?"

Adam shook his head. "Thou'rt mad as Henry. Well then, away; I have in mind that we should while away our

time with certain persons close to the King; whereby all
may gain, be we politick enough. There, close thy door and
let thy miasma collect, if that's to be the boy's bird egg,
and take a breath. Now forward, for we're already much
delayed."

The air in the corridor was to be sure so much better
than anything Roger had breathed in the last few hours
that it made him dizzy all over again; he had to steady
himself against the wall for a moment. While he waited,
another notion came into his floating, nearly detached
head.

"How didst thou read in this infidel text, Adam? Have
you Hebrew?"

But it was too late; the preoccupied, eager, secretive
Adam of the transit to London was back with Roger now.
"But little," the Franciscan said. "Come now, for tomorrow is Henry's day; tonight we must put his house in order,
though he wis it never. . . . But first to sup in my chambers, where thou'lt learn ease a while; for truly I ne'er before saw clerk nor Emperor with so wild an eye. When thou
opened to me first tonight, thy left eye was stuck shut, and
thou didst know it not, nor when it opened; as a two-eyed
Polyphemus I can conduct thee nowhere."

"I'll see, an there be light. Go on."

But, in fact, he saw little; or rather, saw as much as
usual, some of it doubtless of pith and moment, but without understanding. To begin with, he remained more light-
headed from the miasma than he realized until too late.
The meal with Adam gave him little to occupy his intellect, Adam waxing more secretive and preoccupied by the
moment; and the meal being accompanied through some
whim of the King's with an excellent Spanish sack, and
Roger having scarcely tasted wine of any quality since
that crucial Fall of 1231, he left Adam's table in a mixture
of befuddlements.

Then, Roger was reasonably sure, they had gone to the
apartments of someone who could only be the King's sister
Eleanor, where Adam had disappeared for what seemed in
retrospect like a long time, but might have been shorter
than a low mass, considering all the poisons—material and
spiritual—adrift in Roger's brain. There was perhaps nothing very unusual about this, since everyone knew that

Adam was Eleanor's confessor—and yet, Adam beforehand
had been so full of conspirator's airs about it that even a
clear head might not have known what to think. The
apartments themselves were sumptuous, far more so than
any possible apartments at Beaumont, which, after all,
was closer to being a castle than a palace, but Roger was in
no position to enjoy their richness even had he had a taste
for such things; for it shortly became plain to him that his
role, as Adam had intended it, was to be a lure for a brash
tiring-wench named Judy who otherwise would have been
an inconvenience to the Lady Eleanor and the Franciscan.

Thus the visit to Eleanor's rooms was long, uncomfort-
able and mysterious, and if the King's household was in
any way set more in order thereby, Roger did not come
within bowshot of knowing how or why that night. Adam
looked stern when he emerged at long last, and he left behind him the sound of suppressed weeping—but perhaps
tears were the customary cost of settling a Crown more
firmly. If so, Roger was grimly happy to remain a perpetual antechamberer in such matters.

Yet, he was at the same time in a fury with Adam, and
promptly turned on him a denunciation so stammering
and disconnected that he scarce understood two words of it
himself.

"Eh?" Adam said. "Master thyself, Roger, I pray thee.
What's this? There's no harm in Judy for thee, be thou
only on thy guard as becomes a churchman—"

"That—that's naught to the purpose. Deny thou if thou
canst that thou intendedst naught else but to throw us together, for thine own easement? I'd have thee know that
I'm no brawling clerk. I'll have no more to do with women,
ne ladies nor tiring-maids nor whores, attendest thou me?
How dost thy conscience rest to have led thy fellow in
Christ into such a test?"

"Swef, swef," Adam said. " 'Twas not meant to be a test,
Roger, only a diversion; whyfor so savage? A peasant girl
is not a pestilence."

"Devils live in them," Roger said, the sullen fumes in
his head seeming to issue forth in wreaths with the words.
"They are all thieves and whores, to the Last Judgment."

"No Christian may declare another eternally damned
except on pain of sin," Adam said. "How wilt thou preach,

and yet have naught to do wth women? They are the half of mankind."

"Nor will I preach, be that the price of it, whatsoe'er the *Capito* would have me do. Better to teach than to go down among these placket-pickers."

"A grave matter to be making puns upon," Adam said, looking at him speculatively. "Then thou hast decided for Paris, Roger?"

"Mayhap," Roger said. "Another trap, Adam? Is this then the corner that thou meanest to drive me into? Take care, I may bite thee!"

"Thou'rt ill," Adam said. "I was mistaken to take thee at all. Thou'rt so disputatious at thy worst, Roger, I'm forever mistaking it for thy best. Go thou to bed; I'll manage without thee; there's still more to undertake, but needs a brow as cool as stone, else better not to undertake it at all. Dost remember the way?"

"Better than thou. Go to; I've had enough."

Adam nodded curtly and turned off through a door which Roger had not even noticed, leaving him alone and suddenly much more befuddled and afloat than he had realized. He had, he understood with the awful clarity of the drunken man, just created a disaster for himself, though how it had come to this ened he could not riddle. Nay, he had not created it entire by himself; Adam had been as much to blame as he And now the Franciscan was gone, with a brusque order to Roger to return to his room, his promise to find Roger something better than that sink-hole quite forgotten in his passion to play with the lives of more important people.

So mote it be, the self whispered icily inside Roger's swimming head. *Time will discover who these self-same worthies are.* Snatching a torch from a bracket, Roger blazed his uneven way back to his room, at the head of a comet of smoke and sparks. He butted the door open blindly and thrust the torch inside.

The whole room turned into a solid block of blinding yellow flame. The door slammed against his forehead. The slam was like a summary of all the thunderclaps since creation. The floor shuddered with it, the very palace seemed to rock.

He did not know that he had fallen until the back of his

head struck the stone. The shock was stunning. When he was able to see and think again, he was as sober as though all the wine had been bled out of him by some miraculous barber. He was slumped against the opposite wall, every bone aching. In the distance, he could hear shouts and the sound of running.

It was impossible to imagine entering that room again, much less striking a light there. A demon had come to breathe the poisoned air in very truth. But the sound of running was coming nearer—and tomorrow was the day of all days for King Henry; he would be sure to take such a blast as the worst kind of an omen. Suppose he were to discover that it had taken place in the room of that same man who had flung "stones and rocks" in his face at Oxford? Men had been burned as sorcerers for less.

Someone in mail ran by him in the blackness, clinking and wheezing, and trod without noticing it on Roger's outturned ankle. Biting his tongue to keep silence, Roger wormed his way up against the wall to a sitting position, drew his knees into his chest, and drove himself to his feet. The runner went on. Calling upon God in his heart, Roger crossed to the door and pushed it. It opened at once.

The air in the room smelt burnt, but no longer foul; perhaps the demon had gone. Holding that thought high, Roger groped across the room to where he had last seen his box. It was there, and in it the two flints, a bit of tinder, the stub of a candle. It was hard to strike a light with hands that shook so, but he got one after only five tries.

In the weak light, the room seemed utterly undisturbed. No: the plug of wet bedding at the window was gone, doutless destroyed by the flight of the demon. The tapers that had been brought earlier had been blown out, but not toppled, and he lit them from his stub.

The air was flocculent with fine fingerlings of falling soot. When his hand came trembling away from his cold wet brow, it was smeared greasily with the stuff, as though it had been settling on him for hours. Also, there were splinters in his face—a sizeable number. He closed one eye, then the other; no, they had missed his eyes; but they were beginning to hurt. And he did not dare call for a surgeon, nor take a needle to them himself—such wounds would be marked at tomorrow's convocation; better to appear tomorrow with a puffy face and let it be ascribed to excess. Adam himself might be the first to so interpret it, if perhaps not the first to speak it out. The soot could be wiped off somehow.

The hubbub was farther away now, and sounded as baffled as it was angry. The immediate danger seemed to have passed. As for tomorrow that would take care of itself.

But how under God had it happened? Surely demons did not come to live in poor students' rooms simply because they liked the air there; after tomorrow, someone else might sleep here, and become slowly surrounded by the same miasma, and become as sick. And suffer the same lightning? Perhaps, if he sealed the room . . . and thrust a torch in it after. . . . Clearly there was some connection, but Roger could not gasp it. Abruptly he was felled by exhaustion as though by a hammer. He barely had time to shed himself of his coat before sleep claimed him on his straw, leaving all the candles still burning.

That Henry had been shaken in his Hall was at once to be seen in the High Chamber that merciless April morning, for he came before his earls and his barons, his Poitevins and their relatives in search of preferment, and before Edmund Rich and his bishops with the face of a man who has slept not at all, but wrestled the whole night long with terror and a bad conscience. He seated himself without a word and regarded all before him with alarmingly bloodshot eyes.

Roger, less than nothing among all these high counsels, was not noticed at all, except by Adam, who shot him one startled glance and a half-smile of commiseration, and as promptly seemed to forget that he existed. With Edmund was Grosseteste, magnificent and strange, not yet consecrated but full of works, and often consulted by the bishops around Edmund; and at Grosseteste's elbow was Adam. Among the barons Roger recognized Simon de Montfort, somehow no longer beautiful but as sternly handsome as a shaft of granite, yet oddly ill at ease, as though he found himself torn between the earls and the Frenchmen who were his countrymen. If de Montfort looked ill at ease, however, Peter des Roches looked positively ill; his plump face was like whey.

The King continued to say nothing at all. At last, however, a herald ventured to offer him the mace. He took it without seeming to notice what it was; his eyes shot open in alarm when he heard the trumpets.

"Eh?" he said hoarsely. "Well then. Speak, someone."

"I will speak, my lord King," Edmund Rich said. His voice was quiet, but it filled the Chamber. "We are here that thy kingdom be no more dismembered. These thine earls and barons have gathered with us under the protection of Christ the Almighty King and His vicar on earth, under whose sign and seal thine earthly kingship has its patent, and under none other."

"Go on," Henry said.

"Aye, that we will. My lord King, didst hear the earthquake eat at thy kingship only last night? What dost thou say to this? Shall these ancient stones quiver, and thine heart be unmoved?"

"We called you, as we called you all oft before, to seek composition," Henry said with a whisper of the old arrogance. "We have never sought else. Therefore, say forth, and affright us not with thunders."

The words were brave, but the tune was almost humble. Here is a king, Roger thought, with a heart of wax.

"There is no way but this," Edmund said. "Thou shalt repair thine errors, my lord King, or thou shalt be excommunicated. The church hath protected thee long and long, since thou wert in swaddling clothes. It will withdraw that protection momently. Act now. Begin with these Poitevins, who have leeched at thee and thy kingship long enough."

The King turned suddenly to look at Grosseteste. Adam whispered into Grosseteste's ear; the great head nodded slowly. The King clenched his hands and looked away again, and his eyes lighted on Peter des Roches. For a long moment these two stared at each other in a passage at arms which was as silent and furious as an embrace.

"Thou," Henry said, "thou adder in our ear."

"My lord King, consider—"

"Speak no more, thou compromiseth thine holy mission," Henry said, his voice beginning to rise. "We command thee. Obey."

Des Roches looked at the flagstones.

"Go thou back to thy bishopric and attend to the cure of souls, as God permits thee. And thenceforth, on no account, meddle with the affairs of this our kingdom."

Henry's head jerked sidewise. "Peter de Rivaulx."

"My lord King."

"We command thee without fail to give up our royal castles to us, to render us an account of our royal monies, and immediately to leave our court."

"My lord King, it shall be so. Only a few days for the accounting—"

"Leave our court!" Henry said, lurching to his feet. "By Goddes bones, wert thou not beneficed and admitted to the rights of the clergy, we should order thine eyen twie enriven from thy skull, thou that stolst from us the loyalties of our earls, and whispered blood, blood, blood in our ear all the nights and days! Out, out!"

Rivaulx knew his king; he picked up his skirts and ran. Peter des Roches hung back, ashen but clinging to some last unimaginable shred of dignity, but most of the Poitevins were swirling after Rivaulx, trying to sneer into the blackly triumphant faces of the barons.

"Go not without our charge, pack-rats," Henry shouted after them, brandishing the mace. "You are expelled one and all, from our court and from our country and from the charge of our estates. Go you away to your own burrows, and never show your faces before us again, else we shall use your skulls as bowls."

The last pair of Poitevin heels scuttered out of sight like magic. Roger had to press his hand over his splinter-stitched lips until the pain came to keep from bursting into laughter. The King, his chest heaving, looked over the rest of the Chamber and saw nothing but solemn approval. After a while, he sat down, and settled his trembling body forward in an attitude of command.

"First things first," he said, in a voice that shook only a little. "And now, Archbishop Rich, let us compose our kingdom as well as may be. Wilt thou to Wales? We'd have Richard earl-Marshal back, an it could be brought about; let us all make peace, by Goddes bones."

Edmund Rich bore toward Henry the look of an eternal judge. "How can that be, my lord King?" he said, in a voice as unforgiving as riven stone. "Dost thou believe I can undo all thy treacheries with Richard Marshal?"

"Then take with thee whomsoe'er thou willst. Whoso'er is highest in probity in thine eyes, and in Marshal's. We see with thee the Bishop of Chester, and eke the Bishop of Rochester. That should be a deputation worthy of trust. What think my barons of this?"

There was a short consultation. Then de Montfort stepped forward.

"Thou, Simon? Art so quickly leading earl of the realm? We like this not."

"Nay, my lord King. I am the least, and therefore can speak for all, rather than for myself alone. And this is our rede: An thou become reconciled with Richard, we shall be reconciled with thee."

"We have made you concessions enough," Henry said, rolling the rings of his knuckles back and forth along the arm of his throne. "But we shall abide you. Richard Marshal shall live and live in our honour, will he desire it. Enough. We are ill. We thank you for your graciousness. This convocation is ended."

He relinquished the mace and stepped unsteadily down. The sackbuts sounded while he walked behind the throne and went out through the same small door he had come in. Under the vair of his cloak, Roger saw, the shanks of the beautiful Plantagenet legs were as thin as rushes.

What remained of the convocation began to move and break into groups, with a general murmur of bemused and cautious self-congratulation. The Bishops of Chester and Rochester edged through the muggy press toward Edmund Rich—obviously the Welsh adventure was going to require planning of the most mischancy kind—but Rich was already deeply in converse with the Oxford group, in which Roger found himself included without protest, and the two appointed bishops hung back deferentially until this conference should be through. No such considerations restrained Simon de Montfort, who found his way directly to Adam.

"What news?" he said, drawing the Franciscan a little aside. "No, no, Roger, ye needn't withdraw, I remember

thee well; 'stones and rocks'; the best advice our Henry
ever had. Well, dear Adam?"

"She is willing," Adam said, with a glance over his
shoulder at Grosseteste. The master appeared to be out of
earshot. "I had no easy road in my suasions, but she sees
that 'tis the only way out of her present dilemma. She's affrighted of thee a little, which I assured her was unfounded
quite. The rest, Simon, thou must do thyself; this present
marriage of thine is without my demesne."

"Well I ken it," Montfort said. "I have work in progress
to dissolve it. It may be that I shall have to go to the Holy
See; if so, very well, I shall. What thinkest thou of today's
bit of business?"

"I mislike it. Doubtless the earl-Marshal will trust the
Archbishop; but can he trust the King?"

"I greatly fear that he may," Montfort said grimly.
"Though certes Henry means what he says, he has the
Plantagenet bias for tortuous dealings. Roger, we are well
met today; there is one here, Guy de Foulques, the papal
legate, who hath heard of our Oxford scholars' studies in
the natural sciences; and I have told him of the book thou
art writing, as Adam told it me. Thou shouldst talk with
him a while, an Adam can let thee; for if thy book be well
received de Foulques may ask thee for more at some later
date."

"My lord," Roger said. "Gladly. Though I am exceeding
poor in knowledge of the sciences as yet. I am astonished
that thou know'st my passion so well, when as yet it be no
more than that."

"Simon never forgets a face or a fact," Adam said with a
half smile. "He is my perpetual despair. By all means,
take him with thee, Simon, for there are still some favours
to be curried ere the other matter is made certain."

"Come then, Roger."

How much had been done an undone since then! There
had been as much promise, precisely, in the meeting with
Guy de Foulques as Montfort had foreshadowed, but that
promise depended upon the completion of the present
book, which lay neglected still. That the marriage of the
King's sister to Simon de Montfort would be celebrated
was now certain—for that had been the meaning behind

Adam's high manoeuvring, that, and that Adam would become spiritual adviser to both the earl and his countess thereafter; which meant that both Adam and Grosseteste would inevitably become court personages, and Roger, too, if he remained, if only through Adam's inexplicable delight in involving Roger in these matters, and the earl's incredible desire to do everyone he knew a service (which, thanks to the earl's miraculous memory, seemed to include everyone he had ever met). As for Henry, his court remained the same as it had always been, an incredibly complex little society in which affairs managed to go backwards and forwards at the same time: Richard earl-Marshal had sensibly refused the King's peace offer even when it had been delivered by three bishops, but had later been taken prisoner by a set of treacheries so involved that even Henry's worst enemies suspected that he could have had no hand in some of them, and had died of his wounds on Palm Sunday; yet Hubert de Burgh and the nobles had, nevertheless, become reconciled with Henry the day before the Sunday preceding the Ascension, though there was not a baron to be found who did not believe the earl-Marshal a martyr—all in all, no court to leave a sane man time or sanity for any study of the sciences. Oxford would be no better now, not with Adam utterly taken up in de Montfort's affairs, Grosseteste consecrated by Edmund Rich at Reading the next June, and now Richard Fishacre steadily cutting into Roger's ephemeral reputation as resident master in Aristotle.

The sun was almost down, and the treatise on old age still resting unfinished. The letter to himself was unfinished as well; it would never be done; it was slowly winding itself into a Gordian knot which would make a decision impossible, rather than offering him through the sternest of logic any decision upon which he could depend. Nothing remained now but what he wanted to do, for the letter to himself made nothing clear about the logic of events, except that there was no logic to them except in the mind of God.

Well, then, Paris.

That road, too, had seemed impossible, without spending almost the whole of his hoard. He had driven himself to see his brother Robert before leaving London, but that had been as profitless a meeting as he had known it would be *ab initio*: where Robert had been without sympathy for Roger's clerkship at Oxford, and contemptuous of Eugene's at Toulouse, the idea of expending good pounds to send Roger from Oxford to Paris had provoked him to gross and intolerable laughter. They had parted in a blizzard of enmity; Robert's last words were a flat order to return to Ilchester to put the estate in order, or be disowned the moment that Robert could legally consider Harold Bacon dead. Roger could only turn his back and exclude Robert forever from his memory; *and from rumour*, the self told him with icy satisfaction, *to the end of time.*

Nevertheless, it could be done, and without too much diminishing the bag of money. It was only July; by swinking, he could complete his secular mastership by the end of summer. Between then and Martinmas would leave him enough time to complete the book for Philip the Chancellor, and give him in addition a little time to work on something to satisfy Guy de Foulques; perhaps something on light, a subject about which Grosseteste had written extensively already, so that Roger would again have a library upon which to base his first draft.

And Martinmas was slaughtering time. Soon thereafter, in the winter storms, William Busshe would be leaving one or another of the Cinque Ports with his sarplers and fells for Wissant. With him would be one Roger Bacon, lately of Oxenford, master in Aristotle to come to the hundred colleges of the University of Paris, under the aegis of Robert Grosseteste, scholar to all the world.

He sponged out the letter to himself in the last light of the day. Tomorrow he would write again, but to another self: Magister Roger, whose works were writ for popes.

Explicit prima pars.

Sequitur pars secunda:

TO FERNE HALWES

V: STRAW STREET

There might have been a time, in Roger's mind belonging
so safely to history that it might have happened on the
moon, when William Busshe had been young. Busshe himself remembered it well: then he had sailed out of
Maidstone and across the Channel in a barge—of necessity, to begin with, since she had been his first vessel, and
secondly because nothing larger could have passed under
Aylesford Bridge. She had displaced twenty-two tons, and
had cost him exactly three pounds; not quite a fair price,
but a good enough transaction for a youngster, especially
one who meant to do his own sailing, as well as his own
trading in the Staple.

The barge had been called the *Maudelayne Busshe,* after
his mother, but now was the *Maudelayne* only, as a more
considerable enterprise better meriting the protection of
heaven. She was five times the displacement of her original; about four times the price, neither a bargain nor an
extortion; sailing out of the Hull with a crew of nine (not
counting her master, still Busshe himself, and the boat-
swain and cook); loaded with packs of fells (four hundred to
the pack, eighteen packs in all, some forward of the mast
under hatches, some in the stern sheets, the summer fells
marked X and the winter fells O in red chalk—but not all
Busshe wool, for he knew better than to ship his whole con-
signment in one bottom, his though she be; and besides, on
the wide waters he was a master, not a merchant, and
there was a profit to be taken in shipping the sarplers of
other traders); loaded also with bows and quarrels for
every man, boarding hooks, pikes, pitch and a barrel of
darts, in case of Scotsmen, Lombards or other pirates; with
salt fish, onions, bread and beer in case of being blown far
off course; and, this time out of the glowing, wrinkling bay,
in honour of a promise, with Roger Bacon.

Of that choppy black howling crossing Busshe was to say thereafter that even the rats were sick, and his sailormen that none but a saint, a devil or William Busshe could have forborne to cast his wool overboard for the saving of his life. This, however, was the turn of the dice that a man chanced when he shipped with Busshe, for it was known that no storm had ever wrested a single sack from him since the day he had burned his whole cargo under the hatches rather than let it go to two close-pressing Lombard corsairs (the stench had been ferocious, and the Lombards, quite without Busshe's anticipating any such outcome, had lost him in the huge pall of greasy black smoke which had lain in the wake of the *Maudelayne*); most of his crew, all the same, had been with him for fifteen years.

As for the supercargo, it took Roger three days, in the house of Busshe's host in Wissant, to stop the earth from swinging under him and to look without horror at his own face on the surface of a broth. It was only then that he discovered he was in Busshe's customary bed, wide and deep, with a fine mattress and two linens and the richest of coverings.

"Never mind. I've slept in that bed these dozen years, I've naught to suffer for a night out of it. Eat."

"Yes. But, William . . . was I . . . meseemeth I was dying, or so praydeth I. But do storms . . . doth the sea always. . . . I would say, did I commend me to God for a trifle?"

"Nay. 'Tis not always thus. But it's never a trifle. To say sooth, young Roger, we 'scaped narwe. But rest thee, and sup, for that's a voyage past."

Roger shuddered and tried the broth. His shame was promptly overcome by the marvellous discovery that he was hungry. Only toward the last swallows did he remember what he ought to have been thinking of from the first.

"William—my chest? My books?"

"Yonder. Dost think, young Roger, that William Busshe would save a fell and drown a book? Merchant I be, but nat so ill a man as that."

"God's blessing on thee," Roger said with a great puff of a sigh. "And on thine hosts, now that I reflect on't. I'm a trial to all, I fear me."

Busshe smiled. " 'Tis an old song in Wissant. Half the

populace is just in from the keys, and the half of that abed
with the sea-sickness, at least as the winter draws in. I am
just up of it myself. Nay, I meant not to 'stonish thee; I'm
oft fearful seasick; so be we all from time to time. 'Tis the
Channel—no lilypond when the wind's from the north."

"God preserve me from it till I die. Why persisteth thou,
William? Dost *like* being seasick?"

"Nay, there's a fool's question. 'Tis what I do, ne more,
and it bringeth me money, on which I am most fond. Were I
not William Busshe, by God's hand, might I be fond on
something quite other; but there, I'm not; and thilke
other'd be the selfsame drink, half honey, half aloes. It is
so decreed, and therefore are we bidden to use one another
kindly, lest the bitter half make us doubt even the love of
God."

"Nay, never! Forgive me, but thou art wrong entire.
There cannot be a dewdrop of that doubt in a Christian
heart—least of all thine."

"Wait," William Busshe said heavily. "It will assault
thee, in due course, thouten thou beest heavy with saint-
hood, young Roger. Then wilt thou need the love of man. If
thou canst find none better, pray for me then; or for some
beggar; only thus is the cup passed. But enough, enough.
How wilt thou go to Paris?"

"Oh," Roger said, "somehow." He was not ready to
think of travelling again yet; instead, there hovered in his
memory, from Hroswitha's *Abraham*—how oddly Terence-
like a comedy to come from the pen of a nun in the convent
of Grandesheim!—the speech of the anchorite to his more-
than-Alexandrian sinner: *Who despairs of God sins mortally.* Busshe did not have the look of a man in pain of
mortal sin; yet he had not only accepted the error but was
counselling it, which made him at the least an abettor of
heresy.

If William Busshe were an evil man, how then could a
good man be known? For a moment Roger felt as though
the seasickness were returning, but it passed; it passed.
The question, unanswered, remained.

By the river on the left bank the water in the evening
whistled like sleepy blackbirds: *Vidi . . . viridi . . .
Phyllidem sub tilia . . .* ; or with a brief flourish of breeze

would start up a lisping distant nightingale, *Veni . . . veni . . . venias . . . ne me more facias. . . . Hyrca, hyrca, nazaza, trillirivos! . . .* Across the Seine, the Île de la Cité gradually lost reality, and Notre-Dame with it, almost as though one could see the cathedral schools falling silent with the night; the stews about the cathedral would be noisy till dawn, but they were too tangled to allow much light to escape across the river. Candles still burned visibly in rooms here and there on the Petit-Pont, little stars votive to the philosophers who lived there, the rising Parvipontani; on the water, Roger thought, they looked like real stars, except for their yellowness. Would they seed jewels into the mud of the river, as the real stars gave birth to jewels in the hot press of the deep earth? Probably not. It was by no means certain that real stars were so potent, though the best authorities maintained it to be true. How, after all, would one test such a notion, the deep earth being so furiously hot and so close to hell, as one could see readily in the volcanoes of Greece and Italy, the *mofettes* of Eifel, the hot springs of Baden? And of what use would the answer be, except to defraud further such princes as were already fond on alchemy? None, almost surely—unless one appeal to Cato, who said that to know anything is praiseworthy.

But Cato was only another authority. Suppose him to have been wrong; how would one test that?

Roger sighed and got up. His walk had been a failure: none of these questions would be of any use to him in Paris, even should he by some miracle be given the answers to all of them. Besides, the plain fact was that he was hungry, which made coherent argument hard come by, even with himself.

Behind him he could hear the early-evening noise of the Latin's quarter, not very Latin now since the English nation had moved its drinking headquarters to the Two Swords in the rue S.-Jacques. The move seemed more than likely to lead to trouble, though of trouble of that kind there was already more than enough.

Roger picked his way carefully. There was still some warm light, but it was deceptive, and the pavements of Paris had been very little repaired since the Romans first built them; in fact there was a doggerel verse going around

among the students which derived Lutetia, the Latin
name for Paris, from *lutum*—mud. Latrines generally gave
into the sewers, which were not sewers at all in the Roman
sense, but only open channels in the middle of the street;
and though carts were not allowed in town—because their
nail-studded wheels further pulverized the Roman paving-
stones, and made new ruts in the mud to divert the
sewage—horses were, which piled up more soil than an
army of the blessed scavengers, the belled pigs of St.
Anthony, could cope with were every day a night and
every night an eternity. Even during the day one could not
walk in Paris at all without high, heavy, thickly-soled
shoes, intolerably expensive though they were for students. To walk at night one had to be rich, for though there
was some light from the windows of houses, the streets
themselves were not lit, so that one could not take three
steps in the dark without turning into a dung-beetle unless
one could afford a linkboy.

The English were hard at it as he passed the Two
Swords; evidently they had taken in fees from new members or new officers, and were now engaged in drinking up
the surplus. At the moment the singing was being done by
the Germans, in their own language, but obviously in honour of their English co-Nationals, since the song was about
the "Chünegin von Engellant"—not Henry's new queen,
probably, but instead Eleanor of Aquitaine the long-
mourned.

Later in the evening this wine-warmed fellowship would
begin to evaporate into slandering all the other nations,
beginning, in the natural order of things, with the
French—who were puffed with pride, everybody knew
that, and dressed themselves like women—and their sub-
stituent countries: the vulgar, stupid Burgundians; the fickle Bretons who had killed the Great King, Arthur; the
grasping, vicious and cowardly Lombards; the Romans
with their noisy slander and their silent seditions; the
cruel and harsh Sicilians. Since there was a grain of
truth—or at least a grape—in all this, the game once
started quickly became a contest in the kind of student
malice they had all learned from Buoncompagno. The Nor-
mans, a whole nation in themselves, generally were dismissed as being no more vain than the French, but much

more boastful. The Picards, too, usually won free with no
more than a few elaborate but barbless quills; but their
sustituent Flemish were proclaimed to be fickle, gluttonous,
lazy, and so soft they would dent like butter; while the
Brabantians were at the least rapists, robbers, pirates and
murderers who could not even compose a neck-verse for
the saving of their lives.

At the best, by morning the Germans would be accusing
their friends the English of being drunkards, and challenging
them to heist their cloaks and show their tails; the
English would countercharge gluttony, obscenity and berserker
fury; pots would be thrown, and all would retire to
nurse their noddles and wish they had studied canon law,
the lectures on which did not begin until mid-morning—
every other course in Paris began at six. At worst, someone
would suggest that the insults be taken down the street
and shouted in the windows at the Sign of Our Lady where
the French Nation met, or perhaps the French would conceive
this notion first; in which instance there would be before
morning several clearks who would copy out no more
letters home begging for money or a new shirt, and several
masters who would dispute no more—and never mind that
Paris sternly forbade the carrying of arms by scholars.

As Roger passed by, however, the Two Swords fell
unwontedly quiet. After a moment he could hear a single
counter-tenor voice, as pure as any he had ever heard in
this life:

"Ich sih die liehte heide
in gruner varwe stan.
Dar suln wir alle gehen,
die sumerzit enphahen. . . ."

and to his own astonishment felt the tears start into his
eyes, little though he knew the language. Alarmed, he
walked faster.

Elsewhere the street was in its more usual state of evening
irreverence. Overheard in one of the hostels, a poor
thing which would have held no more than ten fellows and
a master as poor as they, the dice were already rattling, for
there were three baskets of waffles or rissoles hanging out
the window, and some lucky *socium* of the college had also

thrown himself a sausage: there it dangled, with two cats
hopelessly a-siege of it in the street, their spines stretched
like mandolins, their fretted noses bumping speculatively
against the empty burdened air. Roger's belly twinged in
sympathy, and he bought from the next *pâtissier* he saw in
the street an eel pie which filled all the rest of his walk
with a marvellous vapour of garlic and pepper; and then,
belatedly remembering patient John his companion in the
room on the rue de Fouarre, from another pastryman a
tart filled with cheese and eggs. Since he was already
carrying another heavy bundle, he had to juggle them all
before he could resume walking; and then, the two cats
who had before been observing the Constellation of the
Sausage (or two exactly like them) were following him instead. Behind him the sounds of the English Nation died
away, but there was no less music for that; it was everywhere in the transparent Paris evening, now and forever-
more, world without end.

It had been a cold rancid meat indeed to devour that he
had been forced, that first spring in 1237, to matriculate at
Paris as no more than a mere yellowbeak, despite
Grosseteste's cachet and the existing invitation; but the
charter of 1231 was explicit about the matter: there were
three years of additional studies which Roger must undertake before he could be allowed to lecture on Aristotle or
even any lesser subject. And worse: by the time he arrived
in Paris, Philip the Chancellor had died, breaking the link
which might have brought Roger's book on old age to the
attention of the Pope. Three years the book had rested in
Roger's box, and three years had he ground away at the
corn of knowledge as it was milled in Paris, until the hull
of his ambition was almost worn away into dust. But it had
not been all chaff: as a non-regent master he was neither
expected to join a Nation nor maintain rooms for teaching;
the former had spared him the ritual dehorning, confession and degrading penitence the Germans invariably imposed upon new English Nationals, while the latter had
spared him his purse. In nights as white as Virgil ever
knew, he had ground his teeth to be no more than another
master of arts in young and strenuous Paris, a valley
seething with the ferments of Franciscans versus Domini-

cans, Alexander of Hales versus Thomas Aquinas, Nominalists versus realists, while Roger Bacon swinked away unknown, his lectureship still to come. But his examination before the new chancellor was fixed, at last, for the day after tomorrow; and he was prepared, aye, prepared with a thoroughness he had earlier never even imagined that he would need—prepared to take examination in full university if the chancellor so ruled, and the hot cheeks thereafter would not be Roger Bacon's!

It was a long climb to his room—four flights of black and ancient stairs. They invariably left him a puffing and helpless target for the sallies of his room-mate, unable to give back in kind for minutes at a time. The two-headed Livonian youngster—unlike Roger, a true yellowbeaked freshman without a degree to scribble after his name—seemed to be in an unusually pensive mood tonight, however, for all he said was:

"How was the walk?"

"Well enough," Roger said, putting his bundles down on his bed.

"Is the Seine full of philosophy tonight?"

"Alas, no. Only water."

"A pity." Then they were both silent. They had spoken as always in Latin—not only because it was the rule, with informers or "wolves" everywhere to turn one in to the university if one didn't, for a portion of the fine; but because Roger did not understand a word of John's language, nor did John any other that Roger knew. John, who was standing at the desk, had already looked back down at his book, as if his mind had never really been drawn away from it. In the light of the single candle his face seemed oddly old; but after a moment his nostrils began to twitch.

"Aha," he said with satisfaction. "The magician has waved his wand again. What have we here?"

"An eel pie—"

"Fie, Roger!"

"—and a cheese omelette pastry. Judging from the pepper, they may both be a little fleshy."

"That's what pepper is for; who sees fresh meat in the city? Ah, this is good, very good. The song's right:

> *Bad people, good town*
> *Where a ha'penny buys a bun.*

Non vix a triginta ha'pennies had gone into those pastries, but Roger as usual said nothing. In these years a peculiar horror of being thought generous had begun to colour his already well-set secrecy about his money; he could not afford to seem to eat or live better than John, yet he was constantly being tempted into such extravagances as this. The deceits he had worked out to justify them would have done credit to a poet.

"There's else for you in the other bundle," Roger said. "I found you your *Ars dictaminis*, though why you need it I can't think. You write as well as any student I ever knew."

"Thank you," John said, lifting the book with gentle hands. "The very book, and not much scuffed, either. How did you do it?"

He had done it simply by going to the bookstalls of the Little Notre-Dame, but he said: "The man who had it owed me a favour. I'll not be able to do it twice. Better not put it up to Decius again."

"Aha, you remind me, I have somewhat for you, too," John said triumphantly. "Look: a quart of wine."

"Now you are the magician. Where'd you get it?"

"Well," John said, "you see, dice aren't as bad as you paint them. Yesterday while you were in class four of us were playing and I lost. (This is a complicated story, Roger, I warn you.) I hated to drop out, because I was playing with those three from across the street, the Picards who live in the garret and have one gown for the three of them to go to lectures in. Then in came the cat from the same place, the one that belongs to the landlord, so I said, 'Look, here's a fellow that eats regularly and never pays a penny; let's make him play.'"

"Where on earth do you find these wild notions?"

"They come to me," John said modestly. "Well, so I folded the cat around the dice, as it were—you understand, with all four paws over them. I shook him a bit—the fat thing didn't even meow—and threw, and he lost."

"*He lost?*"

"He threw the dice, didn't he? So I wrote a little note to the landlord, explaining that the cat had lost a quart of wine and hadn't paid up, and if he didn't pay up in due course we'd have to collect his pelt instead. (Cats make good gloves, did you know that, Roger?) I tied the note around his neck. Well, the Picards went home and I didn't think any more about it until this afternoon when the cat came back; and he had the money around his neck."

Roger stared.

"He did, Roger, I swear. And there was a letter from the landlord, asking us please not to make the cat play any more, because he's so old that his eyesight is poor, so he can't count his throw. And here it is."

"The note?" Roger said. "Or the cat?"

"No," John said innocently, "the wine. I seem to have mislaid the note."

"You have swept the field," Roger said, laughing in spite of himself. "If there were a doctorate of lies, I'd vest you in it and then disband the faculty. Well, then, let's have a toast to Decius."

"With a whole quart of wine we could have a mass to Decius—but then we'd have to have those thirsty Picards in for servers," John said. "Well, then, away with it: To the dice! Ah. Roger, Albertus Magnus is your first master, isn't he?"

"Yes," Roger said shortly. He had not been getting along well with Albert of late. Perhaps he had been winning too many arguments.

"Are you ready for examination?"

"I'm sure of it," Roger said. "I selected the *De plantis* as a text. I know it by rote."

"Dangerous; Albert knows his vegetables even better than Aristotle. Speaking of which, how about the dinner?"

"What dinner?"

"Dear God, Roger, three years in Paris and you don't know how these things are won? You don't consort enough with students, like me. Well, Albert will set what other masters will attend, of course. How many would that be?"

"John, please begin again. What are we talking about?"

"We are talking," John said sternly, "about your preexamination dinner, which you will pay for. A few florins go a long way in these matters. If you can afford it, buy them all a free bath beforehand, too. Nay, look not anxiously at your box, Roger. I know you have money, you have only been pretending to be as poor as I. You've been buying me books and wine and food, and I am not a stupid man; I've known it the better part of two years. I've given back as good as I could, and now let me advise you, take some money out and spend it openly on a banquet. The masters expect it. And I beg you, count your money ere we part, so you'll know I've touched not a coin, nay, never even looked into your chest."

Roger swallowed. "Are we parting? I'd hoped not. But I'm the stupid one, it appears."

"Who knows?" John said. For a moment he wore the same abstracted look Roger had surprised on his face earlier in the evening. In this world everything happens suddenly. But will you take my advice?"

"I'll think about it," Roger said. "But I'm not much moved to do it. I know my book, and can dispute. That ought to be sufficient."

"Ought to be is not is. Well, never mind. You'll dispute with Albert? There's pride for you!"

"Nay, he surely won't examine me. I am not his favourite student; I argue more than he likes, I think. I expect the Chancellor."

"Why in heaven's name? He *never* comes to examinations any more. Or do you mean Gautier de Chateau-Thierry? He never comes to examinations either—you know as well as I do that he's hardly a year into his duties, he pays as little attention as possible to the university. Or are you the son of some great lord?"

"No," Roger said, and hesitated; and at this moment the self cried soundlessly to him, *Speak!* so that he nearly started. "The university invited me. I am supposed to teach here, after my inception. I don't think I can banquet my way into such a post. They will ask me hard questions and insist that I be letter-perfect in them. Nothing else would be fair."

"Aha. Yes, fair. Well . . . perhaps so. Too bad; some of those fellows havn't had a bath since Gerbert rode the eagle. When I study under you, Roger, I will buy *you* a bath and a banquet, if I have to borrow the money from my sister. By that time you may be as dirty as Thomas Aquinas himself—layers and layers of accumulated dignity."

"And when did you last bathe, Daun Buranus?"

"Students aren't allowed to frequent public baths," John said, regarding his bowl of wine critically. "So you must not tempt me, Roger. So you're to be a regent master. And all the time I thought you were just a harmless black magician, too backward on his grimoires to be admitted to a coven. Think how my soul's been in peril."

"The more so if you wait long enough to study under me. By then you'll be far away, and holy."

"Perhaps," John said. "But perhaps not. I've no great stomach for a mission in pagan Livonia. I was thinking before you came in tonight, I might make a good graduate beggar. I know all the degrees of staleness that bread can go through and still be bread, and every tune that King Borborygmi sings. And the truth is, I'd rather study than preach."

And I, the self said piercingly.

"Well then. It's not so difficult to become a *vagus* without losing one's tonsure, bulls or no bulls, if one does it in the name of learning. I've near completed the trivium, and shall have my secular mastership; and thence I might go to Montpellier, if you like, and become a physician; and still my bolt's not shot, I could spend seven whole years more at Bologna and become a doctor of law. And it might take me two or three years just to get from one school to another, if I sang well along the roads."

"Doctor of civil law?"

"To be sure; canon law's not for the roads. As is only just: if your clerk's to claim the privileges of the altar, then he should stay close to it. But who knows? To become a doctor of *both* laws might keep me another seven years *in studio*; that would put another face on it."

"You have more faces than Janus, but still. . . . It's not an ill way to learn. I've hardly decided myself what I'll do. I've no gift for the road, that much I know."

"It's probably more curse than gift," John said. "But both are callings—if I have the word right. In my country we have only one word for all three, and you use it on pigs. A sad condition for a language to be in. And look you, alas! The wine's gone."

That was just in time, for the taper was almost gone, too. The murmurous night world around them had suddenly become very fuzzy in all its categories. They shook their heads over the empty quart, frugally blew out the candle-stump, and let time swallow the dregs of the day.

In the early morning, John was gone, his few possessions with him; nothing remained but a small book bound in black, placed on the lectern where Roger would see it. No other trace of the life they had led together, as warmly uncommunicative as cat and puppy, existed now in the room but a memory of the plans John had hinted at while the candle fickered; and these rang hollow at dawn. Had the Livonian youngster really stolen away, even before his inception, to join the *Ordo Vagorum?* Nothing was left to say aye or nay.

On the morning of his examination, Roger looked down at the empty pallet for a long time, as a man looks who would part with his first friend, and cannot; while the light grew pitilessly, and the time drew nigh.

And then, as always, someone was singing, and the song came floating through the window like eiderdown:

> *"Li tens s'en veit,*
> *Et je ei riens fait;*
> *Li tens revient,*
> *Et je ne fais riens. . . ."*

Enough; that was how it was. He looked at the book on the lectern, but he did not need the self to tell him that he did not dare open it now. After the song had come cock-crow; and after cockcrow, bells. He donned his gown and left.

"Sit thema," Albertus Magnus said, but he was drowned out. The hall had been filling for nearly an hour, as the word got around that Albert was examining a student, and that the student had answered eight questions out of eight on his book. But the noise and the movement in the hall failed to divert Albert's hooded eyes. He stood before the leaves of his manuscript, as blocky and immovable as a sarsen stone in his stiff black master's robes, and watched Roger where he stood sweating ice in the dock. It was intensely hot.

"Sit thema," Albert said again with his glacial patience:

"Queritur quomodo materia est una, an numero vel genere vel specie."

It was a little quieter now, and Roger needed the quiet. There was something like Nemesis in Albert's heavy-lidded regard; nothing, that look seemed to say, could come from this disputation to Roger but disgrace. Had his contentiousness really inflamed the German that far? Never mind, it was too late; the question, the question!

It was frightening enough. The doctrine with which Albert had presented him was the first of the questions which had led the teaching of Aristotle to be forbidden until now. It was the essence of the heresy of David of Dinant, unless it could be answered; matter cannot be one in number and the same throughout the Creation, else there is no need even for God. But did Albert want him to argue it from Aristotle, *per se et per accidens,* and thus show himself to be too good an Aristotelian to be immune to the heresy? Or did he mean to force Roger into making a ruling of his own, independent of authority, and thus diminish his standing as a lecturer-to-come on Aristotle? It was not a question of knowing what *the* answer was; to any Aristotelian that was perfectly clear: matter, being imperfect, incomplete and ignoble, cannot be one; but instead, a question of knowing the dangers inherent in the problem. There was no doubt that Aristotle sometimes gave the wrong answers, but he never failed to ask the right questions, and this one was fearsome; did Albert really want to hear Roger argue it?

"The universal forms are not one in number," Roger said at last, in a dead silence. "They are multiplied as particular forms are received. Even were primal matter one in number, it cannot remain so: *sic non est una numero, tamen est numerositate essentie."*

The whole hall was holding its breath. Albert's expression did not change; he simply turned a page; but that was enough. Someone in the corner of Roger's eye rose and pushed excitedly out into the streets.

"Sit thema," Albert said: *"Queritur diversas substantias et animam in corpore hominis esse, qui adducantes Aristoteles viditur dicere in sexto-decimo librorum suorum de animalibus."*

The eyes looked at Roger as though seeing inside his flesh to the very selfsame self; and thilke self set up such a sweet silent storm of rage that Roger shrank away from it, dazed and shocked. He had never doubted until now that the thing with the bodiless voice belonged to him in some way, even spoke for desires he was not yet ready to acknowledge, perhaps in the long run to his greater good; but this dizzying fury!—the voice might have been a demon's. He felt himself turning pale, and closed his eyes for a moment. When he was able to open them again, a small group of medical students in the forefront of his vision was whispering together interestedly.

He set his teeth and said to the self, *Silentium!* The storm in his blood did not stop, but it abated a little; enough for Roger to reset his jaw into the substance of Albert's question. There was now no doubt in his mind but that Albert meant to take him step by step through every opinion of Aristotle which had once been, and again might be, a breeder of heresy. Now in particular he was demanding knowledge of the selves and the souls that Aristotle had detected deep inside every man: the active intellect which reasons; the non-reasoning intellect which bears like scars the wounds of experience, and which can prevent the *intellectus agens* from talking or even thinking about a painful subject; the entelechy or vegetative self, which does not think at all, but can compel a man to breathe even when he is determined to yield up all that, and to digest even an eel pie, or heal over a hopelessly running sore; and all those others—the ones that think; the ones that perceive; the ones that desire. Were all these one soul, or was a separate soul required for each?

Aristotle himself was of no help here, as was the case with all the great potential heresies. He had simply looked into the mind of man and reported it a single substance multiplied by secondary virtues, some more perfect than others, as Averroes agreed; but he had never ruled on the question of separate substantial forms. Yet for one entrusted with the care and cure of souls, everything depended upon whether the sinner were single and indivisible, or in himself a little Hell and Heaven of warring factions, all originally from God, all at odds now.

As thou knowest, the self said in a tiny whisper in one

ear, indefeasible and terrifying. In this extremity, Roger remembered the teachings of Richard Fishacre, of whom he had been so jealous just before leaving Oxford, and put out his hand to them as a man drowning to a battered log.

"A Christian may hold three views on this matter," Roger said, and then had to clear his throat. "*Estimant enim aliqui, quod vegetabilis et sensibilis et rationalis sunt una et eadem forma, et variantur tantum secundum operationem.*"

"*Et?*" Albertus Magnus said.

"*Alii posuerunt quod in homine est anima unica forma numero.*"

"*Et?*"

"*Tertii ponunt quod sunt tres formae et tria haec aliquid in hominibus a quibus sunt istae tres operationes—*"

"*—cui plena contradicit Magister Augustinus,*" Albert said, in a voice as quiet as rats scampering up a hawser. Roger could hear the intake of breath all over the hall. "*Et?*"

"*Diffinere non audeo,*" Roger said stonily.

For a moment Albert stared at him in stunned disbelief. "Thou art not permitted to entertain no opinion of thine own on such high matters, youngling," he said at last. His voice was still very quiet, but it was as wounding as sleet. "Answer thou me, or stand down."

"Corruption shall put on incorruption," Roger said. "As it is given. Thus is the soul of man a composite substance, composed of a sensitive soul and a vegetative soul, alike corruptible, and the intellectual soul which is incorruptible; yet from each of these is made by God one soul *secundum subjectum,* summarized in perfection as Aristotle teaches; one, composite and perfect; diverse and simple; matter and form, natural and derived from nature, but perfect in its unity before God, whence it came."

"Ah," the hall said, generally. Albert flicked the massed benches a glance of subdued scorn, but there was obviously no more to be pursued down this road. The self—whatever it was in the eyes of God—had built around Roger such fortifications as would not be breached in an afternoon, nor in a year. For the first time in all Roger's experience, it seemed to be singing; and to his horror, it could not carry any tune, but whined away like a wheel of wet slate cutting a green log. Its ordeal over, it had abandoned Roger's body, which promptly began to tremble like an aspen leaf; yet his ordeal was still young.

The ordeal was, however, curiously slow to resume. Albert turned a page, and then another, and then seemed to become preoccupied with his clothing: first adjusting his bishop's mitre forward until it made five distinct furrows in his rather sloping brow; then folding his robe carefully over his left arm before leaning upon that forearm on the open book. Suddenly he looked up again at Roger, but only to ask him a wholly simple double question as to whether or not all motion was animal motion, and if so whether or not the heaven had life. The very simplicity of the query baffled Roger, the more especially since it was fully dealt with in the *De plantis,* and the examination on that book was over; had Albert reverted to it to gain thinking time? If so, best not to give him the satisfaction or the opportunity. Roger disposed of the double question with two quick denials. "In addition," he said, "the text makes it clear that Aristotle is here citing other writers' arguments; hence it would be wrong to maintain that his statements on this subject are authoritative."

But Roger had underestimated his opponent; rapid as Roger's answer had been, the next question followed even faster, and the next, and the next. Was substantial form arisen out of nature *per generationem,* or induced by special creation? How shall we interpret Aristotle's position that dreams are never sent from God and cannot be interpreted? Are the movers of the inferior orbs continuous with the First Cause, and if so were they needed to implement Creation, to produce their own inferiors, or to operate these inferiors after the Creation?

They were not, it was true, particularly hard questions, and Roger was slow to realize why Albert was requiring that they be answered under so much pressure. When in the middle of his argument on medium and motion the self suddenly presented him with the key to the riddle, he was furious all over again. Every hailstone in this storm of questions was derived directly from the thousand-and-one objections to Aristotle's teachings embodied in the writings of William of Auvergne, Bishop of Paris, upon whose review of the written record of this examination Roger's appointment would finally depend. Albert was rushing him in hope of provoking a slip or a potential heresy, since he could hardly have supposed that Roger would have come to the examination unaware of the Bishop's mountain of quibbles. Evidently the book before Albert was a compendium, including at the very least the *De universo*, the *De legibus* and the *De anima*.

The hall—now so packed that you could not have thrown a melon without striking a student or a master—was utterly silent, and the massed faces turned from one man to the other as though following a tossed ball. Probably not one man in ten was able to follow the argument, since it was being conducted in a subject that had not been taught at the university since before Roger's birth; but plainly the crowd had caught its import long before Roger had. As he reached his peroration, Roger faltered, trying to recall what he had said in his helplessly quick answers which might make grisly interesting reading for Bishop William, but it was all gone clean out of his head; it was all he could do to conclude the period he had going.

"*Sit thema*," Albert said instantly, and in the same grindingly monotonous voice: "Whether the world existed from all eternity, as Aristotle says; or whether it was created by God."

As Roger opened his mouth to answer, there was a roar from the hall; and that noise of amazement and delight saved him. Albert had almost achieved his effect: lulled by the long series of petty points as well known to him as breathing, Roger had been about to render a quick opinion on the most terrifying problem in the whole of Aristotle. But the mob had sensed the trap, and its baying cry of appreciation had sprung it prematurely.

Now the ordeal was at last begun again.

"The world," he said slowly, "was created by God, nor does the letter of Aristotle's argument deny this; it is Averroes who imposes this interpretation upon the text. *Non tamen recipitur, si factus est, in vacuum nec in plenum sed in nihil, et ideo mundus non est eternus secundum Aristotelem et veritatem.*"

"If God created the world, He had a sufficient reason, otherwise this detracts from His omnipotence."

"This I concede, Magister Albert."

"Therefore did not this reason exist before the world existed? Did it not in fact exist *ab eterno?*"

"I believe it did, and that this is the sense in which Aristotle must be read."

"Then," Albert said, "was not the Creation in fact *per accidens?*"

"No; because to deny God the power to create the world at some single time also detracts from His omnipotence."

"Oho," said somebody in the front rows. He was hissed at.

"Yet if sufficient reason for the world existed *ab eterno,* the Creation implies a failure on God's part to observe His own holy law."

"Not so," Roger said. "That law applies only in nature; *non valet in voluntariis, nec est querenda cause sue voluntatis.*"

Albert shuttered his eyes against a gentle murmur of laughter from the part of the hall where the faculty of theology had gathered. It could not have been pleasant for him to be reminded before an audience that even in the course of a formal heresy-hunt he must not question the causes of God's will.

"The moment of Creation," he said ponderously, "divided existence from nothingness, the one after the other, implying the existence of time *ab eterno.* Motion is the measure of time; therefore motion existed *ab eterno*; therefore the thing moved; therefore the world."

This fiendish argument left Roger floundering; though he thought at once of the "eternal now" of Paramedes, he could hardly be sure that it was relevant, let alone admissible. The hall held its breath in sympathy.

"Motion and nature are inseparable," he said at last. "Thus what came into being at the Creation were those things, which were to be measured, not measure itself. Time is of God, and eternal, but motion is of the world, and temporal."

"Then it follows that time will last to eternity, beyond the world and motion. If for this there is sufficient cause, why not also for the world?"

"Sufficient cause exists, but not sufficient virtue," Roger said. "Infinite virtue exists in the First Cause, which if He filled the world with virtue, could make it last forever; but He chooses to give the world finite virtue only, so that it may last a long time, but not forever, as He will last. Equally, He could end the world now, but has promised us He will not, till the number of the elect be made up."

"It is not reasonable to suppose that Aristotle knew the number of the elect," Albert said harshly.

"This I concede. Nevertheless he was divinely inspired and does not deny the faith. He says that without time there is no motion, implying that motion did not begin in time, which we have shown to be true; and in the *Metaphysics* he says that there are always first things, otherwise there would be no later things; hence even in Aristotle the world has a beginning, as all else."

"He says it will have no end; no time nor motion."

"Which any philosopher may say, Magister Albert; this lies not in the realm of the provable, since it lies in the future which is not knowable by argument; nor does a beginning assume an end. In the future all that is knowable is by revelation."

"I concede this," Albert said with a sour grin.

"Then it may be shown that this revelation was vouchsafed," Roger said evenly, "and that Aristotle knew that motion would end, though time might not. He has it in the *Ethics* that if man is to have happiness, it can only be after death. How can this be? Only after the resurrection of the body; and this will never happen until the number of the elect is filled, in Aristotle exactly as it is in *Revelation vii.*"

People were standing up now all over the hall, and there was a growing shuffle and drumming of feet. The students were beginning to demand that Albert concede; already the examination had set records for severity and for patience, and the long low sunbeams slanting over the benches from the mullioned windows were an unnecessary reminder that even the second meal of the day would be missed should Albert persist still longer. The German set his lips and glowered at his book.

"If the world is not *ab eterno* —" he said, and the hall shook with howls of protest. He straightened his back and stared over all their heads, waiting. It took a long time.

"If the world, nor motion, nor even time," he said, and though his face would never show itself shaken, the zigzag grammar betrayed him into Roger's hand as surely as a written surrender, "and the Word of God tells us that these three things are true, is it nevertheless *possible* that the world was and is eternal?"

"No, it is not," Roger said. "Since everything that is comes from something, all causes must regress indefinitely to that one thing which comes from nothing and was caused by nothing. That, being prime and perfect, can be God and none other; wherein lies the eternity of which Aristotle speaks, and not elsewhere."

The hall hung on the breathless verge of riot. Albert lowered his head, but he was still looking at Roger. In that look Roger knew that they were to be enemies forever, and was content.

"*Quod concedendum est,*" Albert said, and closed his book.

VI: THE CHARNWOOD HILLS

To Adam Marsh the abrupt disappearance from Oxford of Roger Bacon, that winter of 1237, without word or screed, was puzzling; surely the boy could not have imagined that Adam would hold against him a quarrel born from the twin agents of miasma and wine? Yet was it so Roger-like as to raise no eyebrow even among the boy's few acquaintances who soon forgot; but it remained on Adam's mind until word came that Roger was indeed in Paris. Then Adam's mind was freed for higher matters.

The world was moving, and be Adam never so agile, its heavy footfalls were thudding in his spoor. Frederick II had taken an Empress less than seven weeks after Grosseteste's consecration as Bishop of Lincoln. This Empress Isabel had seemed, at first, of little moment to him, especially compared to the letters that Pope Gregory had sent throughout Christendom on September fourth preaching a new crusade; but both meant heavier papal levies upon England, a matter about which Grosseteste

was already incensed and which hence could not but be of
moment to Adam whether he willed it or no. In his natural
mind, nothing would have moved him so much that same
year as the death of Michael Scot: for of kings and princes
there were, the groaning world well knew, far too many,
but of great scholars never more than a famine; but now it
was these very kings and princes who were to be Adam's
familiars, and this, mathinketh it hem with whatever saving irony he might, by his own devious intercession—there
being no pebble too small to lame the cloven hoof of the
world, and set it to limping ponderously at one's back
thenceforward.

Nevertheless it had somewhile seemed to him that his
cross might be lifted from him—grief though that lighten-
ing might be—and thus fit him to bear more gladly such
lesser burdens as kings and princes and offices. And in
truth the world seemed docile enough to his management
at first. In the stifling, unpromising calm of 1236 King
Henry had allowed Simon de Montfort sufficiently to
shake off the royal displeasure to attend, as lord high steward, his marriage to another Eleanor, daughter of Ramon
Berenger, count of Provence; and therefore to attend with
gradually increasing frequency such meetings of the royal
council as Henry could be persuaded to call. As spiritual
adviser to the new queen, as well as to de Montfort, and as
lawyer and theologian to Doillface-of Savoy, the queen's
uncle, Adam's excuses for avoiding the confessional of
Eleanor of Pembroke became more and more many-
coloured and plausible (though not without night-thoughts
of the state of sin in which he stood even now, through having heard her past confessions with emotions he himself
dared to confess to no one, at least not yet). Furthermore,
he was all the better placed to advance the one cause
which would divide him from Eleanor as cleanly and finally as the knife-stroke which split Hermaphrodite and
Salmacis into the two sexes in the Greek story: the marriage of Eleanor to Simon.

Confession, he thought hurriedly—yet again and
again—could follow. As deliberately he shied away from
imagining what Grosseteste would say when he heard it.
Grosseteste had himself urged Adam not to shun offices:
whence all else.

The marriage first, confession after, and abide the outcome. It was, he well knew, a poor formula for salvation;
but damnation spread its cold green talons wherever else
he might turn.

It was far from easy to predict with any confidence what
the king would make of such a marriage, but Adam haz-
arded that he would endorse it. It had been Henry who had
effectively delivered Leicester into Simon's hands, by forcing Amaury de Montfort either to concede to his brother or
become an Englishman; the loss of Normandy had taught
Henry, it seemed, the dangers of a divided allegiance. Was
not the next step obviously that of allying Leicester with
the Crown, as the other earldoms had already fallen? So
Adam conceived it.

And so indeed it fell out, with in fact more royal favour
than Adam had dared to pray for, with a ceremonial marriage at Westminster in 1238 on the day after Epiphany;
the king himself gave his sister away. The ceremony was
secret, on Henry's insistence; and as secretly Adam Marsh
crept away to savour in his wound the salt of his self-
congratulation, and repair if he could his soul for
confession.

Into which vigil without any pause came the grinning
mask of his folly, to remind him that even now, like that
hero of Horace, he trod on smothered fires, scarce
extinct—and that like any silly scholar he had trusted the
ambition of a king to be somewhit less fond than the follies
of churchmen and lovers.

For of course the secret could not be kept: Henry's very
reason for holding the wedding privately were warrants of
publication and torches to the faggots. Henry could hardly
have cared that the marriage of his sister to a foreigner
would be gravel in the craw of the common mob, no more
did this occur to Adam, so new was he to these high con-
cerns, until far too late; but the outcry of the barons, Adam
knew equally belatedly, could have been no surprise to
Henry. After all, the queen was still barren; were that
curse to persist Eleanor of Pembroke's child might one day
inherit the throne, and this a child by a man still no more
than an alien—no matter when, if ever, Henry chose to
confer Leicester formally upon Simon.

The uproar was terrifying even to Adam, and he could

imagine with anguish what ill it was working in his spiritual charge, who had trusted him utterly in the engineering of this very disaster. And between the mob and the barons the tinder of another rebellion seemed to await no more than the first spark.

"Which I would abide," Simon told him quietly, "did I think aught to be gained. But the barons are children to be rattling their swords against Henry over such a trifle, and did I let it proceed so far, I'd find myself on the wrong side to the offending of mine entire good sense. I'll not divide England for a marriage, even to Eleanor."

To this Adam for a while had no reply; but remained at gaze through a long low window, wherein was framed beyond a deep, gloomy sea of still forest, part of a low but rugged range: the Charnwood Hills, hazy in a pelting cold rain. It was here in the hunting lodge of Simon Iv. de Montfort, the dead earl Simon's father, some nine miles from Leicester near Hugglescote, that Simon had been accustomed these six years past to entertain Adam, and Adam's increasingly weed-choked rivulet of advice; but lately the Franciscan had become more and more a stranger in the lodge.

"And then?" Adam said at last, in a voice which sounded to himself as louring as the brow of Bardon Hill to the north. "Would you dissolve the marriage, then? The succession—"

"Nay, that I'll not—did I say that? The succession's a bauble against such a diamond as my lady, most gentle Adam; for that, as for much else, I'm in thine eternal debt. But who's to have it? Not Salisbury surely, and there's no earl of Chester now. Best to defer to Cornwall, as is meet for a brother-in-law."

"But how? Richard too is childless."

"Ah," Simon said, smiling, "there's an art to deference, most gentle Adam; I've explored the matter. Richard's the brand ready to be cast, that much is plain. Yet consider: Should he set England aflame like the earl-Marshal before him, it must be against the King his brother; and will some child of Richard's be king of England thereafter, canst thou conceive? Nay, not from this present quarrel, unless I'm fond altogether; the barons need the mob, and the mob's not so easily to be embroiled in more wars of succession, not so soon after King John, howsoe'er it mutter and mowe."

"I defer to thee," Adam said. "Lately I am affrighted by the ignorance from which I meddled. But doth Cornwall see tomorrow as thou dost?"

"I'm prepared to prove that question," Simon said, not smiling now. "I've sent him a letter, saying I will retire from the royal council. This will suffice, I am sure."

"But shall hardly morsel the King, Simon; it is as good as admission of wrong on his part, to have sponsored the marriage."

Simon shrugged. "I'll please the King again in some other season, so only it shall go on raining rain in this one, and not blood. Let's put it to the test, and make of Henry a second question, once he sees his realm subside. He'll love me less shall I pit him against his barons with his own brother bearing their pennons."

He paused and lowered his head until his long, hatchet-like face seemed about to split Adam's skull with the intensity of its closeness.

"My countess asks for thee, most Christian Adam," he said, "And thou hast absented thyself from me as well no little while. Bethink thee, while I repair my temporal faults, of those absolutions I'll have need of ere all this be ended; for I'll best be my own governor forenenst Richard Cornwall, but thou'rt my minister afore God to reckon it all up; otherwise I am done. With thine help I shall be God's instrument, Adam. I trust thee for this, wherein I am all otherways helpless; be not removed, I beg of thee."

Thus capped and shod with lead, Adam Marsh stumbled like an old man back to Oxford, and prematurely to his confession before Robert Grosseteste, Bishop of Lincoln; and got therefrom his early reward.

"These are sins grievous and multiple, yet am I confounded to condemn thee," Grosseteste said in a heavy voice. "I foresee many such I shall commit, and wonder what penances to give for sins I know to be grave, yet might enlist the princes of the earth in the army of God. These are the sins of prelates who serve princes, as thou and I must do, Adam; let us not be bewildered, but act as we are counselled to do in 1st Corinthians: *Let no tempta-tion take hold on you, but such as is human.*"

"A text without a gloss," Adam whispered. "Art not all human—or all demoniacal?"

"Adam," Grosseteste said, "despair thou not of God, which is verily a demoniacal temptation; or thou shall tempt me too, and I am as vulnerable as thou. We know well enough what 'human temptation' is. It is when one sees no escape from danger by man's help, and so suffers it humbly for God's sake, confiding in His help. Only thus could we trust ourselves to serve the princes of this world—even such as Henry, or Simon."

"Then is Simon so great a sinner? His heart is large, Capito, if I am any judge of men, and certes he means to serve God in every way a prince can. Nor loves England any the less, ne more than do thou and I. How shall I ab-solve him of sins lesser than mine—or thine, as thou wouldst have it?"

There was no answer for a long time. Grosseteste leaned his head into his hand, so that his eyes were covered; but Adam could see the corners of his mouth turning down and his lips firming, gently, but implacably. At last the bishop said:

"Simon's marriage is an abomination to the Church as well, Adam. I thought thou knew'st this, else why didst seek absolution for thyself, not first for him? Because in the matter of his wife, thine eye offended thee? In plucking out thine eye, thou hast fostered mortal sin among thy pa-rishioners; it is not thus that we are instructed to cure souls."

Stunned, Adam shook his head. His hope of being unburdened in this confession had never been great enough to help him toward it, but this blow was from the only quarter whence succor might have come. "Dear Christ forgive me; I did not know. Tell me, where doth the fault lie?"

"In thee, Adam; it was to this that I thought thee con-fessing, until now. Thou shouldst ken full as well as I that Eleanor vowed a chaste widowhood on the death of William Marshal—"

"Capito, Capito, dost think so little of thy student?"

Adam cried in anguish. "That's a very commonplace; couldst believe I'd ignore it? Eleanor herself hath assured me that there was no such vow, long ere I broached to her the first whisper of my brokerage."

"Women see the truth in strange lights when marriage is in question," Grosseteste said with a heavy frown, "and stranger still if the marriage be of great advantage. Hast no better warrant that no vow exists?"

"Nay, and ne more requireth I," Adam retorted. "The lady hath been my penitent these many years, and I say she hath it not in her to speak untruth to very strangers, namoe to kinrede."

"Let be; thy lauds become thee, Adam, but suffice not for the hour nor th'offence. Well, I must ponder this; let's to lighter business for the nonce. It was misfortunate that I could ne attend the ceremonies of thy brother's degree, most gentle Adam; but ordain him priest was I able, and have done, as thou asked me; I see he's told thee that. For now, I propose him to be of my *familias* under canon Robert of Cadney, who hath resigned his deaconry at Kelstern in suit for the rectory of Heckington, to which he'll sure be instituted be he not superseded. Be this stile o'er-passed, I've in mind to make Cadney precentor of Lincoln in due course; doth this make a suitable tutor for thy brother, think you?"

"That is most generously done," Adam said. "As always, thou givest with both hands, Capito. I am more than abashed, and pray thee use my brother henceforth on his merits, not as my kinsman."

"Assure thyself, ne more have I done algates. Now, as for Simon: Meseemeth this a matter for Rome, he being beyond my dispensation as the husband of a sister of the King; nought can serve here but papal absolution, and sanction of the marriage."

"Which he will but purchase, as thou knowest," Adam said hoarsely, breathing again the fumes of the pit reopening at his feet, "and it be worthless thereafter at Rome's whim."

"Nothing is more likely," Grosseteste agreed, but his voice was gentle, almost serene. "Yet there is but one Holy Father, most gentle Adam, and he is Gregory until God wills it otherwise. The corruption of the Lateran is a stench even in our northern nostrils; yet it is from thence that Simon's absolution must come. Naught else is possible, but that we must eat of the dish that is set before us, or starve. And this be thy special penance, Adam: That thou shalt bear this rede to Simon thyself, in thy proper person."

Adam swallowed. It was an irregular penance, reflecting Grosseteste's odd notion that atonements for sins ought also to do, when possible, some positive good; the bishop was famous for them. For an instant Adam was moved to protest that such an errand was in itself an occasion for sin in the present matter, but the words stuck in his throat, for-why he had failed even now to confess the root sin; that word he had been unable to utter even to himself, as though the very sound in the inner ear would crack all dams. Nothing would do now but that he help himself, wearing such armour as he could scavenge from the waste countryside of his own soul.

"That me regards," he said. "But I will bear it."

Though it was not the errand itself that Adam feared, but rather its certain consequences; which indeed followed with the implacable logic of evil, whose arrangement of events is without those catastrophic breaks with the past which, because they are unpredictable, men called Providence. In brief, Simon acquiesced to the pilgrimage on which he was bidden, as aforetime in draughty Beaumont he had indeed said he would do at the first necessity. He was embarked for Rome within the fortnight.

Thus when Adam found himself for the third time that year riding under Bardon Hill, it was with Eleanor and her retinue—and Simon in Italy. It had been from the need of any further such encounter that Adam had been seeking all along to withdraw, a fact which, he suspected with wretchedness, she had smelled out at long last. In consequence their conversation was very strange.

Simon characteristically had left almost all his knights at home, and they saw no reason to let autumn wither in neglect of the hunting; the undulating tablelands of the Montfort holdings were particularly rich at this season in stag and other game. Priests and women being wholly

unwelcome even as spectators at such work, Eleanor and
Adam were left to ride the more open aisles of Charnwood
forest near the lodge, with no company but that of her
ladies.

She rode looking straight forward, her eyes calm and
contemplative, her profile in an exquisite balance of
awareness and repose upon which Adam could hardly bear
to look. Off, there were sometimes the calls and cracklings
of the hunting, but they were muffled and carried no
meaning here. The day, too, was curiously muffled; for
though the sun was brilliant, in the tall Charnwood aisles
there was a diurnal dusk, paved with flickering many-
pointed little suns like a spatter of golden tears.

Their confession was already over. It had been brief, for
Adam had aforetime given Eleanor his last word of secular
counsel in the confessional—and this impasse was what it
had come to. As for Eleanor, such sins as she had to offer
were never very deadly, beyond perhaps a touch of pride
too pathetically close to trust in the goodness of others to
be censurable by anyone. He had tried to fatten somewhat
the unusual brevity of this confession with a special pleading, secular enough in intent to be sure, but bearing
closely enough upon the cure of souls to pass over the
sharpening edge of his scruples; but to this Eleanor had re-
sponded so little that he found himself unable to press it
further.

And now there was the rest of the day to pass, for Adam
could not leave for Oxford until the next noon, when some
of the knights would again be available to convey him, as
Simon had ordered. He would have been glad enough to
leave all by himself, but Simon would hear of it and Simon's household would suffer; in such matters the new
earl, like the old, was cold to anything but instant literal
obedience.

"Tell me of thy brother, Father Marsh," Eleanor said
after a while. "Is he as gentle as thou art?"

"That I hardly know how to answer, my lady. I'll bring
him thee, an thou'lt have it so, and thou canst examine
him at pleasure. Is a scholar of parts, so I think, and firm
in piety. Yet 'tis but a young man; I'll not abuse thee with
o'ermuch praise of what's unproven."

"Doth he favour thee?"

"Why, perhaps. None could deny us our father. Otherways the resemblance is not strong, I am persuaded—though the Bishop doth insist it is uncommon close for brothers with so many years between 'em. Again, be thou the judge; for I'm of such a mind as fails to recognize its very image, more than not."

"So do I mine," Eleanor said. "I'd not have it that there could be another such as I, nay not even in a glass. I think verily I'd not seek God Himself, did I believe his to be mine own image and likenesse, as is written; but I am wicked, I think that impossible entire, and that is my small salvation."

"Certes—He is not the image; we are. That 'wickedness' is but the glass between, which shows the left hand where the right should be—"

"I know these significations," Eleanor said. "Give me leave, Father, to be weary of them today. 'Twas I spoke of them first, but I was ambling. Thou shalt instruct me in them later, let me pray thee."

Adam bowed his head. "Command me."

"Tell me then of Robert of Cadney."

Now he could see where she was going: she had reversed him, and brought his last plea out of the confessional into the dappled secular day.

"Forgive me, my lady, but I do not know that priest. I've told thee all I know, which I have from the Bishop; all else in hearesay."

As she made to speak, there was a faraway shouting, and then just ahead something started up of a sudden, thrashing in the underbrush. Their horses balked, almost together, and peered about with bulging eyes, tossing their heads as if hoping to feel the reins go lax enough for a bolt. Adam pulled to, sharing their caution; were it a boar, there might be danger.

But it was only a sheep—a squat, short-legged ram of that immemorial race peculiar to dark Charnwood forest, which had probably stared up at the first Roman invaders of its aisles with this same expression of idiocy, blank, furious and sinister. For a moment it stood with its legs spread out, like a mis-made four-legged stool; then it spun, with astonishing swiftness for so clumsy-looking a beast, and disappeared with a scrambling bound.

"Belike he thought us alnagers, come to collect the wooltax," Eleanor said.

"Smalwe thought in that skull, I ween," Adam said. Something in the animal's face had shaken him, though he could not say what it was: as though all his life he had been reading in a *roman*, and closing the book, had looked up into the eyes of a headsman. "Yet I'm persuaded we should turn back, my lady. 'Tis clear we're verging on the marches of the hunt, and our next visitant may be not so benign—or so timid."

"An thou wouldst, Father," she said quietly.

As they turned about, Adam saw to his greater disquiet that they had somehow outstripped Eleanor's entourage, or lost it. He cast about distractedly, but nothing he saw reassured him; and now the forest sighed and the aisle ahead was suddenly a-twist with falling leaves: the winds of dusk were beginning to rise.

Yet instead of pressing forward, they seemed to move very slowly, and even slowlier; and at last their horses were standing stock still, side by side; and they two, the riders, stirrup to stirrup. Just as abruptly, the wind died, and the leaves came rocking silently down the still air, or spinning like children's boats in a whirlpool.

"Then I shall say what I have in me to say," Eleanor said quietly, as if there had been no interval at all, "which is for no other ears but thine; for soon there'll be overhearers aplenty. And bitterly it mathinketh me to say it . . . yet thou dost not know the despair thou'st cast me in with thy today's redes and purposals, nay not a tithe of it. And I know thou art not cruel."

"My lady—"

"Please . . . this our time is brief enough. And well I wis that any holy father in the Bishop's *familias* must be good and noble, and befitten for the cure of worthier souls than mine. Yet that's no balm to me that am nigh without a friend . . . my first lord dead; the justiciar my guardian still with charges of treason hanging o'er's head; my brother the King mad, as I can say, deny it who will; my lord that is may not be my lord tomorrow, maugre any pieces of silver he can offer the Vicar of Christ. And now, now thou wilt give me over to some good and noble priest whose very face I know not! Gentle Adam, I beg thee—if by the will of God I am to be tried again, I will have courage—yet must I go without friend either spiritual or temporal in such an hour? Doth God intend? Adam, hear thou me, desert me not for the love thou bearest me, that moved thee to bring me to my lord . . . that moved thee to offer for my soul thine own brother. I beg thee, let this cup pass from me."

Her voice failed, and there was silence, except for the wind; and then, an agitated feminine murmuring in the middle distance ahead. The horses' gait quickened a little; they knew the way now; and Adam could well imagine with what relief the ladies would welcome back their princess. He took a breath and brushed the leaves off his thighs.

There was now no time left for him to give Eleanor any reply, except cryptically; but no more was needed to convey his refusal, the only reply he could utter. The word had been spoken, that very word which he had prevented himself even from thinking for these many years, and it was a word of power.

No matter that on Eleanor's lips it might intend no more—as he would pray, if he could—than its Biblical meaning; for there it is also written that love suffereth long and is kind; and the species of love is not qualified.

And still he dared to hope for a respite, if not for a pardon. Simon returned in October. By his mien of cheerful cynicism, his ordinary humour in prosperous times, it was widely read that the papal Rota had not found his arguments unattractive; nor had Richard of Cornwall, which seemed to satisfy the King, at least outwardly. Perhaps, against all normal expectation, the matter of the marriage was now settled.

But Adam was not sanguine. And in fact on November first, All Saints Day, there was a new star born *in caudam Draconis*; and by the feast of St. Edmund it stood forth blazoned, baleful and anarchic across half the night sky, the greatest comet since Hastings.

Adam had no superstitious horror of comets; unlike the mob, he knew what they were, and their place in the scheme of things. They were simply bodies of earthly fire which, because of an affinity for one of the fixed stars, had been sublimated and drawn into the sublunar heavens, there to share the motion of the star that had called them up. But it followed from this that on the earth there would be an infirmity or corruption in the men, plants and animals over which that star principally ruled.

And the stars in the tail of the Dragon ruled those who ordered their lives by princes.

VII: THE CAMP OF PALLAS

Without any warning, there came swimming into Roger's head a memory of the green comet of 1238 so vivid that the low stone building above him almost dissolved, and with it all his new friends. Streaming with pale cold colours for which there were no names, the comet rode before his eyes in the darkness of Peter the Peregrine's most secret workshop, breathing its fumes and adding to them.

Surely it had a meaning; but what? That comet was three years gone and all its panics with it, yet there it was, flowing motionlessly through the black sky of Roger's bemused mind, like a reminder of worlds transmundane not vouched for nor even allowed in experience, in history, or in the Scriptures: an arch of light as demanding as a word from the mouth of a demon.

In the furnace-cluttered cellar the great smear of starlight, like an infernal rainbow, soaked gradually into the nitred vaulting. After a while it had vanished, merging into its own phantom in the light-generating eye, and thence back into the ghosts of memory. For a moment he was inclined to ascribe it to the caprices of whatever mephitic vapour Raimundo del Rey was elaborating, but a closer look showed that the young Spaniard was not yet through with his third distillation; the elaborate still, with its many-beaked "pelican" alembic, water bath and furnace (it was the athanor that he was using, despite Peter's protest that it was too hot for the work, because it also heated the damp cellar better) required constant tending. There was to be sure an alchemical smell in the air, but Roger, who had had a little prior experience with Raymond's concoctions, thought he recognized it; which meant that it could not be the totally new principle Raymond had promised.

"Now," Raymond said regretfully, "we'll need to put out the furnace. The distillate burns readily, and what I'm about to show you is even more inflammable. I'm drained; will anyone volunteer?"

After a moment's hesitation, young Julian de Randa arose from the opposite side of the circle and solemnly doused the coals by the usual method of urinating on to them. There was still some fire when he was finished, but shutting off the draught would smother that quickly enough. Up to this point Peter had simply watched and listened gravely, as was his custom, but now he interrupted.

"Raymond, we have one new *socium* tonight; it would be better were you to explain *ab initio.*"

"Certainly," Raymond said, with a wide gesture. "What I began with was ordinary aqua fortis; the kind brewed from corn is better than brandy for this purpose—the smell doesn't let the outside world know what you're doing so quickly, and it leaves less gummy residue in the alembic. This, one distills three times with quicklime, as I've just completed doing here." He lifted a shallow dish a third full of clear, colourless liquid, cautiously, using a rag to protect his hand from the residual heat, and showed it around. "The distillate is completely pure potable spirits, fire without water—or almost, for of course without a little water it would be flame. It burns on a surface without burning what's under it. Two or three swallows of this and Bacchus will envy you; four or five, and it will knock you down."

He grinned cheerfully at Roger. Their relationship was a peculiar one, very unlike the usual commerce of master and student. In fact, these roles were reversed, for in all things that mattered, Raymond was now the master.

This had happened most suddenly, and over a single word in the *De plantis* over which Roger had stumbled in class: *belenum.* The stumble had been followed by a roar of laughter from his Spanish students which had first baffled and then infuriated him; for it had turned out that the man who had put the Arabic version of the *De plantis* into Latin had simply left standing any Arabic word he did not know. Translations were full of strange words from the same source: alkali, zircon, sherbet, camphor, borax, elixir, talc, nadir, zenith, azure, zero, cipher, algebra, lute, artichoke, rebeck, jasmine, saffron.

This was no trouble to the Spaniards, who through long forced intimacy with the Moors knew from infancy that *belenum* was only *jusquiamus*, the common henbane; but their laughter had cut Roger to the liver. He had lost no time seeking among them for one to tutor him in Arabic, and Raymond had expressed the most quickly of all his interest in the small fees involved. Even more important, it had been Raymond who had introduced Roger into the clandestine circle of Peter the Peregrine.

"This much I have demonstrated before," Raymond was saying. "But this is not the end. Here in this flask I have vitriol. Now if one takes up the vitriol in a glass straw as you see me doing here, and adds it to the spirits drop by drop . . . you must be very careful, it may plash or sputter, not good for the eyes. . . . Now perhaps you will begin to smell it. This I call sweet vitriol and I warn you . . . it dizzies the mind as no wine could ever do. Also, it is highly volatile . . . in a little while it will be gone into the air. . . ."

"A very fearful apothecary you're likely to prove, Raimundo," de Randa said. "Each new principle's more potent than the last; and far more likely to bowl the patient over than to cure him."

Now Roger could in fact begin to smell it: an odour sweet indeed, and heavy, yet which penetrated into the brain with the directness of a driven spike. There was no odour in his experience with which he could compare it; it was closest, perhaps, to that of a corpse which has lain in the sun several days, and yet not like that at all. After a while, Roger tentatively decided that it was rather pleasant.

"I believe I've died already," someone else added.

Underneath the general laughter, however, there was a thorough-bass of grudging respect, which Roger could not help but share. Ungrounded though he was as yet in any but the very simplest elements of the arts alchemical and medical, he felt vaguely that any substance which affected the animal body, and indeed even the vegetative soul, as readily as did Raymond's essences must have some implications for physic, whatever its apparent inutility in the raw state; and utility, after all, was the test of knowledge. It required little imagination, for example, to conceive that in a case of brain fever, an electuary made with Raymond's sweet vitriol might go to the seat of the illness like dew rising to the sun.

Raymond, however, did not respond to these sallies. He was concentrating upon his drop-by-drop transfer of the vitriol to the spirits, his small lower lip caught between his teeth. The smell grew sweeter, and heavier.

"Roger," Peter said. "What have you this time to add to our knowledge? Rumour has it that you prosecute certain investigations on your own."

"Several such, though only the most minor," Roger said slowly. "I am only a beginner, Peter, as you well know; and began small, as is suitable, with certain superstitions."

"As?"

"As, it is generally believed that hot water freezes more quickly than cold water in vessels. The argument in support of this is advanced that contrary is excited by contrary, like enemies meeting each other. This I have tested, and it is not so. People attribute this to Aristotle in the second book of the Meterologics; but in fact he says no such thing, but only something like it that's been read carelessly—or worse, translated carelessly: that if cold water and hot water are poured on a cold place, as upon ice, the hot water freezes more quickly; and this is true, as experiment shows."

"Good; I wonder why?" Peter said. "Now there's a thing. But it's autumn now, and winter a long time gone when that test was made, surely. Have you aught else?"

"Mmmm . . . somewhat. This belief that diamonds cannot be broken except by goat's blood, which I believed since my childhood myself; it's false, whatever you may read to the contrary."

There was a snort from the other side of the circle.

"Whoever read that and believed it," a voice demanded, "except our Roger?" In the gloom, Roger could not decide who was speaking.

"Unfair," Peter said instantly. "A test is a test, whether the answer be No or Yes. What grounds of your own do you have, goat of Picardy, for believing that they *don't* dissolve?"

"I knew you'd say that. Very well. But what grounds, then, do we have for believing that the test has been made? To make such a test one must have (a), a goat, and (b), a diamond. I see nobody in our college who could pay the price of (a)."

And there was the money again, daily adding to an already intolerable burden of evasions, disguises, lies, betrayals. He was beginning to hate it, and hate most of all his inability to let go of it. But here, at least, he had been no more than foolish, in choosing unthinkingly so expensive an experiment.

"I had a little money," he said. "I have it no more. Now I have the diamond, and I was cheated, it's but a chip hardly big enough to see. If anyone would care to buy it from me . . . ? Or a goat with a rag tied around one foreleg? He has a kindly heart, but stinks, and munches the straw from my bed directly beside my ear while I'm trying to sleep."

There were no takers, at which he was just as well pleased; for the goat was in fact a nanny, which he was economically milking—with an occasional squirt from the teat for John of Livonia's friend, the dice-playing cat. He was not over-fond of goat's milk, but lately he had become used to the cat, which reminded him a little of that old Petronius of his Ilchester youth, and belike also of John himself. Yet that *vagus* had left behind in the room on Straw Street a memento of power which had changed Roger's life; he was in no danger of being forgotten for neglect of his cat. All the same, the cat was a companion in Roger's bosom, where John had gone away entire.

The fumes were now very thick, and Roger wondered that he had at first thought them pleasant. Now indeed they were reminding him of something, but groping through them for the memory proved almost impossible . . . nevertheless, he captured it at last. It was the thudding flocculent memory of the explosion at Westminster.

"It might be well," he said hesitantly, "to snuff the candles as well. There's enough light from the window."

"Why?" Peter said.

"Well, the fumes. . . . Substances as volatile and mephitic as this have an affinity for fire; Raymond so testified."

"Oh, it only burns if you touch flame to it," Raymond said. "Then goes up all in a puff, and ware eyebrows! But there's no danger from the candles."

He straightened uncertainly; and somehow dropped his pipette on his foot. It shattered promptly, but luckily there was no acid left in it.

"Tcha," he said. "Well, now I believe we are finished. If anyone would like to come up and inhale the vapour, let him come. But I will warn him, breathe shallow; this sweet vitriol of mine puts chickens to sleep for half a day."

As he spoke, he moved away from the beaker with caution; and Roger, observing more meaning in the movement than in the words, decided at once to remain where he was. Julian de Randa, however, came forward with customary brashness, and lowering his face over the quiet white liquid, sniffed sceptically.

He straightened as suddenly as if he had been kicked; but he did not quite stand erect, but rather at a slant, as though the whole room suddenly had been tilted by some silent earthquake. His hand groped for support, and came to rest flat on the top of the athanor, which had hardly cooled at all in this short time. Roger winced in anticipation of the inevitable scream.

It did not come. Julian walked crabwise back toward his seat in the circle. Before he got there, he had collided heavily with the sharp corner of a table; but this, too, he did not seem to feel. With the utmost care, as though climbing down the face of a precipice, he lowered himself into a sitting position; smiled a magnificently silly smile; and fell straight back, his head hitting the sod floor with a soft thump.

"Mother of God!" Peter cried.

"Never fear," Raymond said, in a slightly thickened

voice. "I warned him, anyhow, didn't I? He'll sleep a while,
and wake up none the worse."

"But his hand! It's seared, you can smell it, even
through your devil's vapour. There's lard in the kitchen,
someone fetch it—or no, I've sesame oil right here. And
lint, there in the cupboard with the funnels. Quick!"

He knelt beside de Randa, who was breathing most gently, his mouth wide open.

"That's a frightful burn," Peter whispered. "And look
you, he's sleeping—nor felt a pang when he leaned against
the furnace! Help me, del Rey; this is your fault, your experiment is a very qualified success at best. You *must*
learn to think twice. If he complains against us to the colleges, or dies, our circle is foredone."

The whole cellar was in an uproar now, but much of the
scurrying was not notably purposeful. Throughout it all,
Raymond's saucer of sweet vitriol sat neglected, continuing to sublime into the close air, to the subtle but marked
confusion of everyone in the room. It was now so strong
that it was making Roger sick. He arose quietly—and
slowly, after what he had seen—and took up the beaker.

This close, the odour was unbearable. Holding the
beaker at arm's length, he went up the stairs and out the
door, into a blast of sunlight which was stunningly unexpected: he had forgotten that the gathering had com-
menced before noon, for it was always the next thing to
night in Peter's cellar. After a moment's fuzzy thought, he
set the beaker down against the wall of the building, in the
direct sunlight.

A wandering, cruel-ribbed dog saw him put the dish
down and came trotting over, a little sidewise . . . and
then, as suddenly, it cringed away and ran upwind. A more
sensible nose than any down below stairs, obviously.
Roger moved upwind himself, and sat down on a sill to
clear his lungs; and instantly, like a stone dropping into a
well, he fell asleep.

He awoke in cool moonlight, still and stiff, and not yet
quite clear-headed. His first thought was of the comet; and
then, like the prompting of the self, but without its gnomic
directness, came another vision; that one needed no intoxi-
cation of any sort for hints of worlds transmundane . . . for

there was the spectre of the moon, riding overhead at any hour of any season, blotch-faced, corpse-like, keeping its own calendar, neither here nor there nor in Paradise.

He stirred tentatively, and found that his joints ached even more than he had thought; and further, he was feeling sick, as though he had eaten bad food; which disturbed him, for though his frame had always been gaunt, he had never been ill except transiently. It would be best, he thought, to sit still a while, and stretch out the stiffness gently. It was perhaps dangerous to sit on a sill by one's self at night in Paris, but the narrow alley here was deserted, and Peter's laboratory was in a part of the city so appallingly poor that footpads would not be likely to think it profitable browsing ground.

And all as well indeed, this obscurity, as it was deliberate and necessary; Roger himself would never had heard of Peter, being a faculty member at Paris, except by thilke design and plan—plus certain dissatisfactions which the Englishman Roger's self had poured out to Hispanic Raymond during an Arabic lesson. Not that heroes were hard to find; everyone in Paris worshipped them, as a matter of course, if only because there were so many. Each order had its own: the Franciscans' was Alexander of Hales, the author of the stupefying *Summa Theologica*; the Dominicans boasted first of all of their angelic doctor, Thomas Aquinas—a huge lard-tun of a man who was not above calling himself "the swine of Sicily," and wrote to Roger's furious annoyance in a script so tiny that even copyists could not read it exactly—and secondly, Albertus Magnus.

It had been toward Master Albert that Raymond, as an apprentice apothecary, was most naturally drawn. Just so had it been with Roger; and to see this history unfolding once more under his nose in the person of Raymond was more than he could bear, not only in the light of his own disastrous victory—as a result of which neither Albert nor any master beholden to him would now acknowledge Roger's mere existence, even to the extent of giving way to him in the street—but because of discoveries he had made since which had cast over the whole of his Parisian venture the shadow of grievous fraud. In particular, Albert claimed not to have entered into the Dominican order until the age of 28, yet it was inarguable that he had actually done so at a very early age; which he could hardly have done had his birth date not been falsified for the purpose; though Roger had been unable to find certain confirmation of this, he was here willing to trust a deduction which could lead no other where. It was certain enough, forsooth, that Albert had slipped, as handlessly as an eel, by the many years of philosophical disciplines which were invariably enforced upon the minnows like Roger Bacon . . . and most certain of all, because made certain by Roger's direct experience, that Albert today multiplied his learning—as when, belike, had he not?—by the mechanical grinding of the thumbscrews upon the advanced university students whose teacher he purported to be. Who could not wax fat, had he blood to drink?

Certes, Albert was brilliant. He worked diligently; he had read and observed much; he wrote fluently; he summarized wittily; he talked unceasingly; possibly, with God's help, he dreamed fruitfully. But all this was magpie labour without some organon of knowledge to which the nuggets and the digging could relate; and of this Albert was almost wholly innocent; he traded instead upon a mixed coinage of dogmatism and intuition. And this, in God's name, was a fraud; this, in the holy name of God, was sinful beyond all sins, though there was no name in the Scriptures which such a sin might wear with certainty as yet. In the meantime, *item*: Albert knew nothing but the rudiments of the *perspectiva*: yet he presumed to write of optics *de naturabilis,* almost as though a deaf man should lecture on music. *Item*: Albert was ignorant of speculative alchemy, which treats of the origin and generation of things. *Item*: languages—he was unable even to use a simple Greek word without defining it in a fashion which threw sense out of the window.

Currently it was being said in Paris that Albert was a magician; and that in fact he had built himself by arts magical a head made of brass, which could answer any questions proposed by man. Of course, the head was said to exist no longer; Thomas Aquinas had happened upon it, and finding himself unable to cope with its powers of reasoning, had broken it into a thousand pieces with his staff. It was a pretty fable, but for Roger it stood for everything that seemed to him to be urgently wrong with the University. That Albert could have built no such head was beyond dispute, for of the arts magical he was ignorant beyond all his other ignorances; and as for Thomas, a blow from a staff was an argument without standing in logic. Were heroes made of such clay? Or of such clay as Alexander of Hales was made, for that matter? Yet Albert, through a reputation as a teacher made elsewhere than Paris, was applauded by the whole city as the equal of Aristotle, Avicenna, Averroes—and as a scientist could have been put into Master Grosseteste's pocket without disturbing a fold of the Capito's gown. Was it for this that Roger had given up Grosseteste, and Oxford as well?

Raymond had listened to this jeremiad to the end with an expression peculiarly undisturbed. When it was over, he had said only:

"Master, I know nothing of all this against Albert, and in truth I'm sorry to hear of it. Yet it's all of a piece with Paris, that I'll agree; the natural sciences here are in so sorry a state that I'm afraid to tell my father how I'm wasting his money. But there is a remedy. Can I trust you?"

"Trust me?" The question was so unexpected that Roger did not have time to take offence at it. "In what?"

"In a secret, *idem est,* there are real scientists in Paris; but they are not at the University. I can introduce you to a whole circle of such, wherein you will learn more in a day than most masters have to teach in a lifetime. But this is no light matter, I'll need have oaths from you ere we seek it out; and should you refuse me such, our studies together must end, lest some lapse betray it to you."

"No, no, Raymond, I'll give you my word. But wherein lies the need for such ceremonies?"

"In more dangers than you know. It's true that Paris is full of little circles of students and masters where one might discuss a subject in an informal manner, without *Queritur* and *Quod sic videtur* and *Sed contra.* But the University frowns on them, as being 'colleges' unauthorized by the charter, and not under the control of the Chancellor. Ours is one such, and its purpose is the study of the natural sciences, and hence of Aristotle too where he applies. You can see how quickly the suspicion of magic, or heresy, or both, could become affixed to such a 'college'; wherefore I ask first your most holy and hermetic oaths of secrecy."

"Done! Let's go at once."

Thus, not at once, but not long thereafter, did Roger make the acquaintance of Pierre de Maricourt, that extraordinary son of minor Provençal nobility who called himself Peter the Peregrine because he had been to Palestine on Gregory's crusade. Tall, grave, reserved, judicious, and yet almost shaking just beneath his skin with the violence of his love for raw experience, Peter dominated his "college" like a bonfire inside a ring of candles, though every man in the circle was intellectually freakish and unique, a *lusus naturae,* a lapse of nature's attention to the forming of men's minds. By bent, in so far as he could be categorized at all, Peter was a mathematician; but even beyond figures, and relationships, and mensuration, he loved data—drawn nets flashing full of them, traps a-team with them, compost heaps a-squirm with them, skies a-boiling. At first, it appeared, he had been content with many small nets of his own devising: he walked in the fields, he collected specimens, he questioned travellers, he devoured the narratives and the opinions of laymen, old women, country bumpkins; he wanted to know about metals, mining, arms and armoury, surveying, the chase, earthworks, the devices of magicians, the tricks of jugglers—anything at all that an omnivorous soul could call knowledge. Where he could not go himself to find the facts he sent emissaries, trading first of all upon a small inheritance, and secondly upon his nobility, which he had used as a defence against becoming a religious of any sort, ne monk, friar nor clerk. How he had come to think at length of the still greater net of the "college" he had never said; but they were all his emissaries now.

Until now, in fact, there had been only three great sciences; but Peter, Roger thought, might be said to have found a fourth. It lacked only a name by which to hail it. The science of tests? No, that was too mean, it suggested uroscopy, or auspices. It was a science of the whole of experience, as distinguished from theory alone, theory superior, autonomous, empty: it was a *scientia experimentalis,* serving all other sciences and arts, yet somehow superior to all, out of which might come either confirmations of systems, or things as yet beyond systems. The notion was strange in his grasp; it conformed to nothing that he knew, and already was sliding evasively away in the deceptive colourless moonlight.

As he fought to hold it, someone directly beside him groaned most piteously. He straightened with a start and an almost universal twinge and cast about, one hand clapping his side for the sword of which stringent Paris had deprived him; but there was nobody in sight, not even at his elbow where the sound had seemed to well up.

Then there was a rustle and a grunt, and out of a thick black pool of shadow there rose into the moonlight the head of Raimundo del Rey, almost like the head of John the Baptist except that it was blinking rheumily. He looked at Roger for a moment without recognition, and Roger could smell traces of his sweet vitriol still freighting his breath. He licked his lips two or three times, rubbed his eyes, and looked about.

"Ah," he said at last. "So you're awake. That was a very shambles; I little suspected how far the fumes would penetrate in that stable of a cellar. And then, finding you here, Master, I feared I'd done you some ill too, and I sat me down to watch—"

"Nay, I was only asleep." Roger smiled into the darkness, visualizing Raymond himself nodding while on sick watch; he still had far to go to make an apothecary. Yet he forbore to loose the shaft, ready though it was at his lips. It had occurred to him lately that he had lost John of Livonia in part through some fault in himself, in that he had always been too little giving of himself no matter how innocently John might invite such confidence; so that with Raymond, he was resolved to be less cautious, wherever it might lead. But there was caution and caution; to allow his tongue to vent its mockery too readily would not be a valued gift for a poor young student.

"A strange business," Raymond said, getting up and looking about once more. "And do you know, Master, the very dish sublimed into the air after the sweet vitriol in it—a thing I never saw before. There was no man with us with the wit to steal it, that I'll certify."

"Oho, Raymond, there give I you the lie. I had, and I did. I set it here—no, a little to the left. . . ."

But of course it was gone, taken while Roger slept, nor could anyone honestly call the taker a thief. There it had sat on the open street, a perfectly useful dish of glazed clay with a fine pouring lip and not a crack in it, and how could the sleeping clerk six feet upwind of it be its owner?

"Nor were you," Raymond said ruefully. "Well reasoned all around; I'll just bake me another. And therefore, let's be off. By the look of the stars, real thieves aplenty are abroad by now, and I'm not steady enough for any sort of fight."

"Certes; lead on, for I've clean forgot the way back."

They moved slowly, feeling for the stepping-stones; this had been a Roman trackway with ruts for the wheels of carts cut into the roadbed. Several times in the cool moonlight Roger could see the forking of the ruts which indicated the start of a siding, where one cart might wait while another passed on the main track; but of course the sidings had long since been built over.

"And how like you our circle of real experimenters, Magister Roger?"

"More than well, Peter in particular."

"Peter of Picardy is the noblest intelligence of these degenerate times," Raymond said forcibly. After a moment's silence, he produced an apologetic cough. "Your pardon, Magister Roger, but when I think of all those tonsured donkeys sitting on their gilded chamber-pots at the University, while a mind like Peter's cannot draw a class except by some mean device as these our arcane trappings and oaths, I lose all my patience. You'll be well astonished when I tell you what he's launched on now—"

"I'm certain of it, Raymond, but say on more softly, else some cutthroat will be stalking us."

"Yes, certainly," Raymond said, in a voice perhaps a tithe softer. "He's preparing a treatise on the lodestone, and on all the species of magnetism. He does strange things with corks and bowls of water, and says that they *prove* that the world is a sphere. Not a new idea, certes; but to claim proof, that's a long bold leap upward from a floating cork."

"It's plain you're not from a seafaring people," Roger

said, "for there's proof aplenty of that in ordinary experience; otherwise how could a man on top of a mast see a port in the distance before his mates on deck can descry it? Were the world flat, those on deck would be closer to the port than the man on the mast is, and should see it better, not worse."

"How so?" Raymond said, scratching his head.

"Why, in accordance with the Elements—eighteenth and nineteenth propositions in Book One. The line from deck to port is one leg of a right triangle, while the line from mast to port is its hypotenuse, which is necessarily longer. But now our score is even, for no more can I see what lodestones have to do with the matter than you can."

"Hm. It's not the geometry that confuses me, but the instance. I don't think of the propagation of sight as Euclidean."

"It is totally Euclidean; I can show this; in fact I'm thinking of writing a book about it."

Raymond stopped so suddenly that Roger bumped into him.

"Another book? Master—again I ask your pardon, but I ask my question from love, and hence for forgiveness on that account. How long can you keep your health, working day and night in this kind? Small wonder that you fell asleep in the street—you the least affected of all the company by my sweet vitriol, as your light-fingered exit showed forth. But well I know that you are already working on some commentary, for I've seen the pages lying here and there when I've visited your room; and you've your classes; and the study of Arabic with me, a bad teacher in a difficult language; and your experiments, as with the goat, and the rates of freezing of ice; and then these night-wanderings to Peter's house, and perhaps to more such colleges unknown to me."

He turned left and a strange dim light fell across his face; then he vanished. Turning the corner after him, Roger saw that they had debouched into Straw Street. It was only slightly brighter than the rest of that part of Paris through which they had walked, but their eyes had become so used to the darkness that the difference was immediate. The noise, too, was much as usual; some part of the student nations was always awake.

"Fear not for me," Roger said gently. "I'm a wobbly spring lamb no more, nor yet the dotard of the flock; I know what I do. And do you persist, I'll put you that same question: for where I teach, there do you study; where I study, you teach; and prosecute experiments more dangerous than mine, by the look of that we've just but barely escaped; and sit at Peter's feet of nights, longer than I. All that needs be added is a book in the writing, and I'll give you a florin if you'll deny it exists."

Raymond stared at Roger for an instant, and then began to laugh helplessly. "Magister Roger, I fear me you are a magician before me, I that burn to master the art so that I can hardly sleep in the few hours I'm abed. Indeed there's to be a book, though as yet it's scarce more than a title, since I'm still striving to learn what it shall contain. And so I lose a florin. When I bring you your lesson tomorrow, I beg you let me bite it, for I think I've never seen a real one before."

It was only by biting his own cheek that Roger was able to prevent himself from offering the florin anyhow, and that only out of bitter memory of how divisive the money had already proven. The self, ordinarily so fuming with heady notions and the startling bubble-bursts of aphorisms unwritten, slept as quietly as a coiled snake at moments like this; though he was certain that, like the snake, its eyes were open, it remained as silent as it must have been at the dawn of the world, when then as now it saw everything, but then did not know what to think of it. Roger was by now quite certain that the thing was ignorant of morals, and therefore lived in some intermediary region between his highest faculties and his vegetative soul; yet all other attempts to assign it a sphere of action had failed—perhaps because it knew that when he found it, he would extirpate it, if he could.

"Certes I will, and my thanks, Raymond," he said before the door of his house. They shook hands, a little solemnly, for the custom was still new to Raymond; and then, with a more practised bow, the student-master was gone toward his own poor room.

Upstairs, the goat, on a short tether, was nevertheless chewing upon a book. She sprang sidewise with fear at Roger's sudden snatching of the manuscript, and hit the end of the tether so hard that she fell down all of a scramble. No real harm had been done, however; the book was only a copy of the simplistic *Sentences* of Peter Lombard, which Roger knew now by heart and despised with equal thoroughness. With a grimace, he threw the goat the rest of the despoiled pages and knelt to check the wound under the old rag knotted around her left forearm, just below the elbow next to her chest.

The wound was healing without incident. While he examined it, the goat butted at his neck and shoulder with such gentle solemn affection that he kissed the end of her nose before going back to his lectern. That version of the *Sentences* had been a fair copy, made at a cost of nearly three pounds from the original Lombard manuscript on the University shelves, and might have been sold—or better still, traded for a book of Seneca or something else worth reading; but never mind; it had found its ideal audience.

Waiting for him on the lectern was his own manuscript, a commentary, as Raymond had guessed easily enough—for almost all the new books produced in at least the past two centuries had been commentaries on older authors. But as Roger stood to it in the flickering light of the single candle at the head of the board, he found that his head was still too adrift with sweet vitriol, even after so long a walk, to permit him to write. Instead, he drew to him his older author: that book that John of Livonia had left behind as a gift, now for Roger Bacon the book of all books beyond every other in the world, save only the Word of God.

For on the morning after Roger had bested Albertus Magnus in full University, he had found that book to be *The Secret of Secrets*—a letter to Alexander the Great from his teacher, Aristotle.

Roger had never seen it before; he doubted that anyone else in Paris had; the very existence of such a document semed to be unknown. Yet no man who knew the style of the Stagarite could read this infinitely precious document and think it anything but authentic. Where John had come by it was a mystery, but that he had known or guessed at its value was suspect in the manner of its arrival: a gift to Roger, in return for Roger's gifts to John of books that John loved or might find useful. Or perhaps

John had not guessed, but had only recognized as any literate man would the name of Aristotle, and had bought the book in the hope that his difficult Aristotelian room-mate might be pleased.

Justice is Love, the self sang, and Roger nearly upset his high stool in the violence of his urge to kick out at that interior prompter. That the voice spoke the truth was undeniable, as any man could read in the Book of Job; but it was a less than welcome truth at this moment.

All the same, here was the great letter with its incalculable riches, the *Secretum secretorum* itself: wherein the secrets of the sciences were written, but not as on the skins of goats or sheep so that they might be discovered by the multitude, to the breaking of the celestial seal; from a hand that would rather love truth than be the friend of Plato. Here it was said that God revealed all wisdom to his holy patriarchs and prophets from the beginning of the world, and to just men and to certain others whom He chose beforehand, and endowed them with dowries of science; and this was the beginning and origin of philosophy, because in the writings of these men nothing false was to be found, nothing rejected by wise men, but only that which is approved. And yet on account of men's sins the study of philosophy vanished by degrees until Thales of Miletus took it up again, and Aristotle completed it, in so far as was possible for a man in a pre-Christian time.

Pope Gregory was dead, otherwise only a single section of the *Secretum secretorum* would force the complete revision of Roger's book on old age; this being a chapter called the Regimen of Life, wherein it appeareth that the inestimable glory of medicine, as being more necessary to men than many other sciences, was discovered to the sons of Adam and Noah, they being permitted to live so long for the sake of completing its study. Nor was the shortening of life from that time on due to the decay of the stars from their most favourable position at the moment of creation, as was commonly taught; but in part to the accumulated sins of men, which be remediable under Christ, and in part to accident, which is remediable by medicine; so that it is not in the stars that a man must pass a weakened constitution and a shorter lifespan to his sons, but a better path-

way there be if he but know how to take it; for God the
most high and glorious had prepared a means and remedy
for tempering the humours and preserving health, and for
acquiring many things with which to combat the ills of old
age and to retard them, and to mitigate such evils; and
there is a medicine called the ineffable glory and treasure
of philosophers, which completely rectifies the whole human body.

Of medicines for the spirit there was also God's plenty:
"Avoid the inclinations to bestial pleasures, for the carnal
appetites incline the mind to the corruptible pleasure of
the bestial soul if no discretion be used. Therefore the corruptible body will rejoice, and the corruptible intellect be
saddened. The inclination to carnal pleasure therefore
generates carnal love. But carnal love generates avarice;
avarice generates the desire of riches; the desire of riches
generates shamelessness; shamelessness generates presumption, and presumption generates infidelity . . ." a
strange catalogue of deadly sins to a Christian eye, both in
selection and in order, yet incredibly appropriate admoni-
tions for an Alexander; nor did Aristotle neglect medicines
for the body politic of his prince: "Take such a stone, and
every army will flee from you. . . . Give a hot drink from
the seed of a plant to whomsoever you wish, and he will
obey you for the rest of your life. . . . If you can alter the
air of those nations, permit them to live; if you cannot,
then kill them. . . ."

Yet these matters and the most secret of secrets of this
kind had always hidden from the rank and file of philosophers, and particularly so after men began to abuse science, turning to evil what God granted in full measure for
the safety and advantage of man; until he should strive
that the wonderful and ineffable utility and splendour of
experimental science may appear, and the pathway to a
scientia universalis be again opened.

And that by thee.

"Stand forth!" Roger shouted hoarsely. The goat leaped
to her feet and was again thrown by the tether. Roger
swallowed and resumed his perch.

"What art thou?" he said quietly. "I demand thou answer, in the name of Jesus Christ our Lord."

For a while there was no answer; and Roger noted that

in the darkness beyond the candle flame there were strange amorphous patches of colour, pulsing and elusive. Moreover, his giddiness was worse; was that still the sweet vitriol, or was he in truth working too long, as Raymond—

I am the raven of Elias.

"That is blasphemous and untrue. I charge thee, tell me who thou art!"

I am the man.

"What man is this? Tell me thy signification, else I'll exorcize thee straight!"

Thou art the man.

"Speak."

Thou art the man, shalt bring back into the world the scientia universalis. *Thou shalt make of it an edifice, unto the glory of thy Lord. All help I shall give thee, that thou requireth.*

"How?"

As food brought unto Elias in the desert. Thine edifice shall touch Heaven, and on its brow be written, Knowledge is power.

These cadences were putting him to sleep. Almost he failed to see the trap, that self-same trap into which the builders of Babel had fallen.

Nay. Moral philosophy is the pinnacle, otherways nothing can touch Heaven.

"How dost thou know?" Roger whispered.

Forbye the light of knowledge the Church of God is governed; the commonwealth of the faithful is regulated; the conversion of unbelievers is secured; and those who persist in their malice can be held in check by the excellence of knowledge, so that they may be driven off from the borders of the Church in a better way than by the shedding of Christian blood.

"And—this is the meaning of that saying, Knowledge is power?"

All matters requiring the guidance of knowledge are reduced to these four heads, and no more, the self sang sweetly. It was strange and horrifying to hear it discourse of these matters weighty and unusual in that same remote, bodiless, tuneless whine, as though it sang only to amuse itself.

The pages of the *Secret of Secrets* wavered and blurred before him, and he closed the book. He could think of nothing else to ask; he was suspended in an ecstasy of disbelief. In that emptiness, the self sang suddenly:

Time is.

"Yes," Roger said, wonderingly. "It is the subject of motion. But I don't—"

Time was, sang the self. *Time was.* Behind the voiceless music, Roger seemed to hear an endless mirroring of echoes.

"Is this the bread thou bring'st me, raven?" he said sternly, though the words came forth more than a little slurred. "Well I know that time is single and linear, and giveth up one age belonging to all ages. This is a necessary conclusion, and doubted by no one skilled in philosophy. Nor is it opposed to the sacred writers and principal doctors, but is in agreement with their view. Why triest thou this axiom with me?"

Fool!

The moment hung. The point of the candle-flame bobbed up and down, like a fisherman's float moored above ripples. When the self spoke again, its distant soundless voice was as terrible as the strokes of a gong of brass.

Time is past!

The candle went out.

Whence from the darkness there rose rank upon rank of armed men with Saracen faces, and the faces of sheep, and the faces of demons, too bright in their chains to look upon massed under the invisible sun, passing in their thousands as men who march to the last great engagement; and with them thousands on horseback, and more on animals not yet seen in the world; and many bearing strange engines; and at their head was Antichrist. Yet in a twinkling, all this terrible host shrank, so that each man was no bigger than a grain of millet; and then even this emmet army was turned out of sight, as an image vanishes when the glass is turned; and naught left behind but the whitecaps of some torrent, stretching to the far horizon, as if one looked in vain across a strait for the coming invader. Things moved, like Leviathan, beneath these waters, but they were engines, and there were men in them; and there were drag-

ons in the air like the dragons of the Aethiopians, yet there
were men in them; and there were moles under the earth,
and men rode them, all in mail, and with terrible counte-
nances. And one wearing a cowl came and stood upon the
headlands above the wide waters, and held up such glasses
and mirrors as were necessary to show forth these things.
And the mirrors turned, and there across the wide waters
was the self-same army brought close again, yet now every
man was as great as a giant across that distance, so that
every link of the mail could be counted. And the mirrors
moved, and the head of him in the cowl appeared in the air
above the army, greater than any of them, and burning as
it were of brass in a furnace, yet was not there; and many
of those giants threw down their engines of war and fled;
yet the host came on. And he made in the air certain com-
positions, which a man might know only by smelling them,
or not at all, but which were certainly fell, for the ranks
toppled in windrows; yet on came that inexhaustible host,
and at their head was Antichrist. And he in the cowl held
out his hand over the wide waters, and in the palm of it
were certain crystals like salt-petre from a dungheap; and
he wrapped the crystals in a scrap of parchment without
any writing on it, and cast it into the wind, crying,

LUPU LURU VOPO VIR CAN UTRIET VOARCHADUMIA
TRIPSARECOPSEM

whereat all that army was seen to fall in a single flash of
lightning, and with a roar of such sharp thunder that the
cowl flew from the skull of him that had cried out; and he
fell dwindling away to nothing, like an ever-burning lamp
cast into the sea.

After that for a long time there was darkness and silence. It was not the nothingness of sleep, in which the consciousness of time itself is obliterated, so that in an instant
the night is gone that wakeful men could vouch for. Time
passed, but what events marked it in that sable silence
could not be known, nor words spoken reach the ears, nor
any touch penetrate.

Then he moaned, and heard, and confused light passed
before his closed lids. In a while it was gone. In the new
darkness he almost awoke, drawing a breath only to dis-

cover that he could hardly breathe, and that he was soaked in sweat. Someone murmured near him, and there was an answer; he understood neither. Now, however, he could fall into true sleep.

In the early morning the world crept back into his room, grey and cautious as an old man. He turned his head exhaustedly. Raymond was lying in the straw beside his pallet, supine, his mouth open, snoring softly. The man at the lectern had his head buried in his arms, but while Roger watched with detached wonderment, he lifted heavy eyes and stared upward at the weak light coming in the window, as a man seeing somewhat unwelcome but beyond his powers to undo. It was Peter the Peregrine, his profile so gaunt and hungry that he looked like a beggared Simon de Montfort.

Then he was aloft, tottering toward the pallet on spider's feet.

"Roger! You're awake? Shh, don't speak, rest." He stirred Raymond with a toe; the boy only groaned. Peter nudged him harder.

"Be quiet, Roger; you're a sick man. Raymond, thou Spanish cow, get up and act the apothecary, in God's name! Julian, light the lamp and heat me some of that goat's milk; he's come around Gloria! But let's look lively"

Perhaps it was still only Tuesday, and time now for the Arabic lesson? But why were Peter and Julian here . . . and where were all those mailed glittering men? Then he remembered, seeing the cowl fly back from the skull in the instant of that enormous noise, and fainted.

Nearly the whole college was there, bustling and anxious, when he opened his eyes again. Hands lifted his head gently; other hands gave him something warm and sweet to drink; there was a cold wet cloth on his brow. Peter hovered over him like a man on stilts.

He felt weak, but curiously tranquil, as though he had just accomplished some great work. There were now so many things that he understood that it seemed to him that he had for the first time left his long childhood.

"How do you feel, Roger?" Peter said.

"Content. God bless you all."

"You were very ill. We did our poor best, but in sooth there was little enough to do but pray."

"I had the death," Roger said tranquilly. "I recognize it now. Perhaps it's been pursuing me all this time; but now I've slipped away."

Peter's face grew more worried; Roger shook his head.

"Nay, Peter, I'm not raving, only thinking back. I didn't mean to speak in riddles."

"I *told* you you were working too hard," Raymond said, appearing next to Peter. "Will you heed me now?"

"It's true you ought to rest," Peter said, "if you can, Roger. Is there no place you could go—perhaps to visit relatives in England, or in the mountains? Some place in the south would be the best of all, if that's even barely possible."

It was, of course, wholly possible; for now that he had decided, with an inspiration which had sprouted fantastically from the very heart of his delirium, what was to become of him, the problem of the money had solved itself; and a trip to the south would consume a substantial sum. It seemed so easy now that he knew, beyond all doubt, that he was to make of himself a scientist *instead of* a theologian; he had simply never thought of it in those terms before.

A rest in the sun . . . and leisure to read as much as he wished in the Vatican Library, greater even than the University's. And why not? The time had come to repudiate Paris in any event, it had given him all that it had for him, and were he to stay on much longer he too would harden into the same mould as those tonsured donkeys he and Raymond had been flyting just before the death had seized him in its fowl's claw. Toulouse did not attract him either; the last letter from Eugene reported that the university there had restricted the teaching of the *libri naturales* for the first time in its history—a long step backward into the darkness. The rest of the Latins would soon follow; for the first act of Innocent IV after his coronation (his first, that is, after his wild flight from the Emperor who had sponsored him) was to rescind Gregory's acts of absolution of the Paris masters who lectured on the books of nature. The fever was already festering in Paris itself: the Dominicans had promptly forbidden all members of their order the study of medicine and natural philosphy, Aristotelian or otherwise. The handwriting for Latin Christendom was on the wall; the darkness was coming back.

Yet it might not reach England, where Roger's friends were in the ascendancy in court and church alike, and where independence of the Pope would continue a long time after it had been snuffed out on the continent, despite Henry's proclaimed vassallage to Rome. Later, the continent, might change again, for letters from Adam Marsh intimated that Guy de Foulques, the papal legate whom Roger had met briefly at Westminster, might find himself in the apostolic succession—and Innocent, in revolting so instantly against Frederick II of Hohenstaufen, had not laid the best foundation for a long pontificate.

Oxford, then, was the place; Oxford, by way of Rome.

Someone coughed lightly. "Shh, he's asleep," Peter's voice said, in a whisper so intense that it was almost savage.

Roger opened his eyes at once. "Nay, I was but thinking of what I should do; and have concluded, I must leave off work and rest; wherefore I'll go to the Holy City for a time—perhaps as long as a year."

"Gloria!" Raymond crowed excitedly; and immediately his face turned sober. Roger wondered if he had suddenly thought of the loss of his Arabic tutoring fees; but never mind, all that would be well shortly.

"Most excellent wise," Peter said. "And now, we'll let you rest; and come bid you farewell when you're ready."

"No, Petrus Peregrinus, there's one more favour I've to ask of you. Help me up."

"You're mad," Peter said, horrified. "You must rest absolutely; though you know it not, a full week has passed while we watched you, and the better part of another. You are not ready for any sort of venture, but must rest, and eat."

"A brief venture only—nor will I be dissuaded, gentle Peter. First someone must open my chest and take out my money; someone strong in the thews, for there's a lot of it, and much adulterated with base metals. Raymond, do so. There's the chest, lift the lid, and there you see the bag; set it out."

The rest of the college gathered around curiously, except for Peter, who remained by the pallet, disapproving yet obviously without enough foreknowledge to raise any objection he could think reasonable.

"Now, Raymond: select what coins be most useful in Paris this year and count out five pounds all around, except to Peter—which I charge you all, use either in learning, or in such charity as your dear souls showed me in my illness. As for you, gentle Peter, well I know you're not without resources, but that's not the issue. You should be wealthy, too, but that's not within my power; I will you out of my little death fifty pounds, for your college and its master."

The bag slumped open on top of the chest. Peter might have been about to protest, but if so, the sudden small flood of coins out of the bag's mouth paralysed him with astonishment. Roger was filled with glee; how much more joyful a thing it was to spend money than to hide it! The coins chinked musically as Raymond, biting his lip and sweating, poured share after share into the hands of the fellows of Peter's college. Then he stood aside, and Peter approached the bag hesitantly. He looked down at it for a long time without moving; without, it seemed, even blinking.

"Peter, I beg you," Roger said. "Fifty pounds is but a fraction of the whole, your own eyes so testify. Take it; for there's much else yet to be done."

Peter nodded blindly, and reached into the bag. When he was finished counting, he discovered that he had no place about his person to put fifty pounds; one of the fellows tied it up for him.

"So. Now I require you all, help me up, as first I asked. Julian can carry the rest of the money; I once ran with it, when there was more, and he's far larger a carl than I."

"But, Roger," Peter said. "This wealth—what mean you to do now? Think me not ungrateful, but is not this wholesale generosity a little fond? Bear in mind, you're not wholly in your right humour, and. . . ."

". . . And was always a little strange," Roger said. "Never fear, Peter, these since yesterday are different times, and better. I'll not scatter the rest of my patrimony in the streets of Paris; I mean to keep it, until I may use it again in the study of the sciences. And this day or die I shall join the Franciscans who are rich in learned men, for only strict sanctity of life can foster true philosphy; thenceforward shall I be poor in Christ. Who will help me? Peter, Raymond, Julian, lift me up!"

And silently: Lift me; I must be in orders, before another voice say again to me: *Time is past.* I have seen the powers of the Antichrist.

They would have improvised a litter, but he would not have it; so they bore him downstairs in the cradle of their interlocking hands, and set him on his feet in the blinding sunlight; Raymond on one side, Peter on the other, and the rest of the college knotted around Julian and the bag, glowering at passersby. While they stood waiting for Roger's nausea to pass—for he was really as weak as death, and knew well that he was wood to insist upon today for so solemn a step, and so taxing—a voice came calling against them in the middle distance.

No one seemed to notice; they shifted Roger's weight, and the weight of the bag, preparing their first steps. After a while, a man in tatters came in sight at the intersection and began to cross it slowly, limping painfully and indistinguishable with dirt. That way led toward the English Nation, and he was crying in English as he stumped the street:

"An alms for John. . . . Only a penny to touch the bowl of Belisarius. . . . Only a sterling for John the Pilgrim. . . . An alms for John, who hath the very relict of Belisarius the Anointed. . . . Only a penny. . . ."

Then he stopped, and caught sight of the unusual still group in Straw Street. He swivelled around and came toward them, his gimpy leg making poor weather of the broken paving, holding out a wooden bowl with carven writing around its edge. He needed a crutch, that was plain, but he had none.

The fellows around Julian closed ranks and jostled forward, but the beggar went by without paying them any heed. His filthy hand, missing its middle finger, thrust the bowl toward Roger.

"An alms, clerkly sir, to thy better health. Only a penny."

For a moment the two haggard men looked each into the

eyes of the other. Why Roger was so moved he did not
know, but leaning for the moment more heavily upon
Raymond, he stretched his hand out to the bag and by the
feel of the metal fumbled out a penny. No more, no less;
this was what had been asked; he reached it out to touch
that most famous of all begging bowls, which had been
freighted once with tears from the blinded eyes of the last
general to defend Rome from the infidels. Surely he who
carried that bowl in the streets of modern Paris must be a
holy man.

"God bless thee, Daun Buranus, holy friar," the beggar
said. "I'll will thee my relict, an thou livest." He tasted the
penny, and put it away in his rags. "God bless thee, students. Alms, alms for John! Only a penny for John the
Pilgrim! . . . Only a sterling to touch the bowl of
Belisarius. . . . An alms for John. . . . Alms, an alms for
John. . . ."

Sweetly the cry died . . . *hyrca* . . . *hyrca* . . . *nazaza* . . .
trillirivos . . . and with a heart waiting to be filled, Roger
Bacon turned his burning face toward Rome.

VIII: KIRKBY-MUXLOE

The announcement of the King being even more weari-
somely held back than was usual at a commanded secret
audience, Adam March cleaved, perforce, to his room;
where, even after many prayers, he found ample time remaining in which to think of what he might say to Henry,
and Henry to him; and each of these imagined interviews
was more disquieting than the last.

The very walls and village were disturbing, not only because Adam had never been there before, but also that the
King himself was strange to them, as belike all of his line
had been. The castle at Kirkby-Muxloe, a property of Simon de Montfort's, was beyond being merely ancient. Regarding it, one could hardly bring one's self to guess at
who had built it, maugre what might have happened in its

narrow precincts since. In so rude and disproportioned a
keep might the Grendel-worm have been slain, that the
most brutish of the serfs used under their breaths to
frighten their children. The outer works might have been
more recent, but looked much older by fault of neglect; for
a work of Norman design cannot simply be maintained, it
must be constantly under construction, otherwise it falls
down almost at once.

Without a past, it frowned emptily upon the town from
its tonsured hill. Someone had been there, once, for torches
had smudged the ceilings inside; but who? No one could
say. This room and a few others had been hastily fur-
nished, but only because Henry had demanded of Simon a
place of meeting secret and unlikely enough to permit him
to pursue one single matter of state without interruption
until the King should in his own time have done with it.
Hence they were in Kirkby-Muxloe now, but neither wind
nor wall would grant that they occupied it. Here they were
less even than ghosts, for that nothing that had ever happened to their ancestors was more than a rumour of a rumour. It was not only for warmth and for the modesty of
his Order that Adam kept his hands inside his sleeves, and
not only from diligence that his thoughts pursued imaginary audiences with Henry which gave him no satisfaction
nor comfort.

About the Inquisition itself, he believed, he might with
confidence offer certain reassurances. The King necessarily still had vividly in his mind that series of Lateran
edicts against heresy by which the Emperor had bought
the favour of Honorius III for his coronation, and later, the
favour of the Church as a whole despite his break with
that Pope. In these Henry, a pious king, could hardly have
seen any real access of devotion on the part of the Emperor; it was very plain that Frederick was no friend of the
Church, nor in fact of any religion, true or heretical. No,
the real motives had to lie elsewhere, and where but in the
greater aggrandizement of the imperial power, over even
such lands as England? And if so, what could be more
alarming to a devout king with a heart of wax, than the joy
with which the Church itself had adopted these edicts as
its own?

This, Adam was almost convinced, was needless alarm.

It had to be granted that Gregory IX seemed also to have embraced the edicts; but Adam was wholly familiar with *Ille humani generis* and *Licet ad capiendos,* the two papal bulls involved, and it was quite clear from their texts that Gregory's intentions had been to limit the Emperor's statutes, not to extend them. The bulls did no more than invest all preachers of the Dominican Order with legantine authority to condemn heretics without appeal; and even this power he had at once further limited by placing the selection of the Preachers Inquisitors in the hands of the provincial prior involved. That so heavily qualified and cumbersome a procedure might represent any threat to Henry's throne or realm—that Frederick might reach through it and grasp the King—this was only a fancy.

But intentions are not the only forces that rule popes; and the first bull in question had been promulgated in 1233 on April 20, which was not a saint's day; the second on May 20, 1236, which was not a saint's day either; two days later in the one case, only a day later in the other, the Pope might have been vouchsafed better guidance. The fact, in any event, remained, that the Inquisition was *already* reaching into England—and not by the agency of the Friars Preachers either, but in the hands of a Franciscan: Robert Grosseteste.

In the face of this, how could Adam rationally assure the King of anything? It was even possible that the Capito had been prompted to this surprising new outburst of zeal by the urgings of some within his and Adam's own Order, discontent that only the black-robed Dominicans should be deemed worthy of the pursuit and punishment of heresy. Nor could it be said with any assurance that the English nation lacked the inquisitorial temperament—not here in Kirkby-Muxloe, inherited from the man who had extinguished the Albigensian heresy in the field in a torrent of blood.

And hindsight made it equally clear that what Grosseteste was doing was wholly consistent with his nature, his conscience and his history. The regularity and severity of his visitations to the deaneries, chapters and monasteries of Lincoln were already famous; he had long fought for the resumption of this right, which had fallen into disuse even in his own cathedral chapter, and had

been confirmed in it by the new Pope, Innocent IV, only
last year. He had proceeded to apply it with such vigour
that the religious houses were already wondering that
they had ever called his predecessor *omnium religiosorum
malleus,* "the Monastery-Hammer."

In this light, it might even be accounted remarkable
that Grosseteste had allowed nine years of his episcopate
to elapse—ten since Gregory had issued *Ille humani
generis*—before proclaiming throughout his diocese a syn-
odal witnessing. Yet this too was hindsight; for the *teste
synodale* was hardly comparable to the ordinary visitation, even of Grosseteste's drastic kind. In these the people
were only involved peripherally, being assembled to hear
the word of God, and bringing their children to be confirmed; inquiries into parish administration and correction of abuses came later, after the bishop had preached,
not to the people, but to the clergy.

The net of the *teste synodale* was drawn much wider. As
the bishop reached each parish, the whole body of the people was assembled in a local synod, from which Grosseteste
selected seven men of mature age and proven integrity.
These were sworn upon relics—of which there was never
any scarcity, though no doubt some were spurious—to reveal without fear or favour whatever they might know or
hear, then or susequently, of any offence against Christian
morals. The accused—noble or commoner, priest or
parishioner—were summoned before his archdeacons and
deans, and examined under oath.

Most of the abuses which came to light during a visitation were, alas, wholly ordinary: the holding of markets in
sacred places, which had been expressly forbidden by
Gregory ten years ago; the *scotales* or drinking bouts; the
open celebration of the pagan Feast of Fools, on the same
day as the Feast of the Circumcision, also proscribed for a
decade; the gaming in churchyards; the clandestine marriages in inns of youths no older than fifteen, valid to be
sure in canon law by vows *per os* alone, yet sinful without
the Church; the paying of milk-tithes not as cheese, but as
a pailful spilled on the floor before the altar; Sunday work;
the overlaying of children; the squabbles over precedence
in the Pentecostal processions to the cathedral . . . all familiar, all unlikely to be stamped out, few so horrible as to

justify the application of the law, and none, surely, heretical. For the people it were better to be fatherly, and seek to be loved, rather than merely to be obeyed. Nor did the visitations find much to write against the clergy: some slackness, some simony, some embezzlement, some collecting of moneys at Easter from those who came asking the sacrament, some exacting of corpse-presents from the dying, but again no sensible trace of heresy; nothing, indeed, but cupidity, for which preaching and correction might not suffice, but all the same would have to do. And nothing anywhere in all this could have reached the ears of Henry the King by ordinary, nor interested him if it had—forbye at his most watery, he knew well what ought and ought not to engage a king—had it not been for the *teste synodale* still blowing like a gale through the diocese of Lincoln.

With a start, Adam became aware that he had been staring for some moments at a small painted figure, at first seemingly on some flat surface near at hand, then suddenly far away at the base of what Robert Bacon—no, it had of course been Roger, not the stable, wise Dominican—had called "the cone of vision," and now plainly in motion toward him, its footsteps beginning to tick like dripping water in his ears. He stood up, feeling cold rills of sweat running down his ribs, trying to retake possession of the laws of perspective which the Capito had taught him, yet unable to focus his eyes beyond the walls of the cell in which he had been praying and hoping for all the seven hours of the ecclesiastical day; it was as though the distant marcher had indeed stepped down from the nearest wall, still clad in the indigo and madder and mosaic gold of a fresco, leaving behind a wall of Kirkby-Muxloe as dreadfully bare of any human touch as it had always been.

Yet the ticking went on; and in an instant the cell turned inside out to his eyes, and the reaches before him with it. At once he saw what he should at once have seen; and could not forbear to laugh. There were no doors in Kirkby-Muxloe, only low stone entrances which probably never had been curtained, and surely never had been closed. He had been sitting all this time looking down a passageway, down which the revenant was coming; had he not been pondering so earnestly what he could say to

Henry, he might have been spared these tapestried illusions, and apprehended instead only what there was to be seen and naught more: a familiar of Edmund Rich, his name unknown but his face comfortable to Adam, a mere piece of ecclesiastical furniture—not a ghost, but only a lawyer.

"Friar Marsh: I am bidden to summon you, and bring you to the Archbishop. And he bids me say: The King is with us."

Adam took a deep breath and covered his forehead with his wimple. "Bless you," he said, "and lead me; for the love of Christ our Lord."

"We thank you; enough," Henry said, resettling the silver clasp of his robes on his right shoulder with slender fingers. "We forgive you these ceremonies; there is work to be done, and quickly. Take your places."

Adam studied him as they all moved to the table. In this vein the King was sometimes at his most dangerous, because least like himself. His white hands were bare, and so were his robes; in fact he wore no ornament to body forth what he was except the workaday fleur-de-lis coronet. Beneath that circlet his handsome, long-nosed countenance with its delicious red mouth was both framed and softened by the curls of his hair, almost like those of a page, and of his short silky beard. By the many furrows between his brows, and the set of his lips, it might have been thought that the King was only troubled, or perhaps even sorrowful, but no more than that. His voice was even and reasonable.

It was when Adam looked into Henry's eyes that he knew he had reason to be frightened. He wondered, a little, why he was not.

"My lord King, an it please you," Edmund Rich said, and bowed his head. The iron fleur-de-lis tilted almost imperceptibly, as if in the gentlest of hot breezes, while the Archbishop made some brief benediction too much under his breath for Adam to catch. Possibly Henry could not hear much of it either, though Edmund stood immediately on his right hand. Then they were all seated around the table and Adam had a moment to tell over the beads of these his confreres in this hermetic conference.

To Henry's left, Simon de Montfort, in half mail. To Edmund's right, a thin sallow grey-haired man with a pointed nose, wearing a spotted pallium, with inkpot and quills before him; Adam remembered him without quite being able to name him. To Simon's left, Adam himself. Between Adam and the man in the pallium, a baron Adam had never seen before, and knew better than to heed: an abject thing created by Henry to honour the letter of the barons' demand that one of them be always in attendance in matters of state; if he held any castle, it was probably something like Pontrhydfendigaid or Biddenden the Less. He was magnificently attired, but might equally well have come in cap and bells.

A small company, in a small bare ancient hall; and the air as taut and full of incipient thunder as a drying drum-hide.

"We are not again to be menaced and forestalled by the Bishop of Lincoln," Henry said pleasantly. "We have called you here for your advice as to the means, but the end is already fixed in our heart. To wit, this *teste synodale* is pernicious, and must be ended."

"How, my lord King?" Edmund Rich said. "It is danger-ous, yes; pernicious, perhaps; but eke an established and ordered procedure of the Church. How prevent an ordained bishop from it?"

"This we have summoned you to ask," Henry said. "We are not ignorant in these matters. The great Grosseteste may use this procedure, or not use, according to his best judgment for the cure of souls. We do not hold his judg-ment in the highest regard today. We still bear in mind the congratulations he sent to us in Wales."

This reference baffled Adam entirely, as by their expres-sions it did also Simon and the counterfeit baron. Edmund only shrugged.

"You cannot choose not to understand us," Henry said, his eyes narrowing. "Matthew, enlighten them."

The narrow man in the pallium, whose pen had been squeaking and sticking away over a new parchment at al-most miraculous speed, dropped his quill on to the table, where it made a shiny irregular black clot. He bent out of sight, and materialized from between his feet a thick roll of manuscript. This, when he began to read from it, turned out to be part of a mensual of Henry's reign—an account so detailed and full of gossip that Adam was amazed to find the King even tolerating it, let alone sponsoring it.

Now he knew the man in the pallium: this was the clerk Matthew Paris, appointed by Henry to continue the history of the Plantagenet kingships begun by Roger of Wendover, and whom Adam had first seen at Beaumont, avidly recording Henry's strafing of Hubert de Burgh. Incredible! Henry was a notable patron of the secular arts, that was well known; but how could he stomach a historian so contemptuous, and not only between the lines, even of his good gifts? Like much else about the King, it passed understanding, or even the hope of understanding this side Jordan.

"Also in this month of 1236 was issued by the King to the Abbott of Ramsey a mandate requiring that he act as an itinerant judge in the counties of Buckingham and Bedford," Paris read in a sort of scornful gabble. "To this Grosseteste Bishop of Lincoln raised strong protests and asked recall of the mandate, declaring to all who would heed that canon law forbade all clerks below the rank of sub-deacon to become justiciars under princes; to which purpose he cited 2 Tim. ii. 4, *nemo militans Deo implicat se negotiis saecularibus,* and many other authorities both sacred and secular; among these being his contention that such a king treads on the verge of the sin of Uzzah, who usurped unto himself the office of priest—"

"My lord King, have we not laid this ghost these ten years bygonnen?" Edmund Rich broke in. "I see that this ill-favoured scribe hath been a-reading at my letters, and indeed intercepting them unless I doubt mine ears. Thereby he knows, and my lord should know, that neither I nor any other prelate of substance supported the Bishop of Lincoln's position on this question to such an extreme; finding which, he fell silent."

"We assure you that he was still sending us archdeacons to the very field of battle, a good four years later, to accuse us of violation of the liberties of the Church," Henry said. "This is the Welsh affair of which we spoke; had the preferment at issue not been resigned by him whom we had named, the Bishop'd be gnawing at our laces still."

"Sure not, my lord," Edmund Rich said, forcibly calm. "I deem we'll hear no more of it henceforth."

"Will we not?" the King said. "Matthew, read on."

Matthew Paris peeled off a great limp sheaf of pages, tucked the roll of them under the rungs of his stool, and resumed reading at once, as though he had targeted this next passage like a lancer aiming his point at his challenger's visor.

"And in this month of 1245—"

Adam stiffened; suddenly this was no longer a history. Whatever Paris was about to read had happened only last year.

". . . King Henry was much vexed to be told by the Bishop of Lincoln that he would not yield the church of St. Peter in Northampton to one Ralph Passelew, a forest judge deserving in the sight of the King. And to the King's vexation the Bishop replied, first, that he sought not to give offence but only to make composition of the difference, out of concern for the souls of the said parish, and out of zeal for the King's honour; second, that he begged the King's clemency for opposing him; third, that he hoped for an audience; and fourth, that he hoped that the King shared with the Bishop the desire that all things be directed to the glory of God, the salvation of souls, and the liberty of the Church. And fifth, that the Bishop was right, and the King wrong."

"But this should indeed all have been settled, my lord King!" Edmund Rich protested, his face white. "I wis nat how it came into your majesty's hands at all. Ralph Passelew himself never took it to the secular arm. He sued Archbishop Boniface under canon law for a mandate of institution in eight days, and won it; but I was forced to tell the most holy Boniface that such an appointment would bring scandal upon the Church, and also assuredly upon himself—"

" '. . . since thou wilt be acting not out of zeal to do what is right, but only out of fear of the King,' " Matthew Paris added from text, his forefinger following the contracted, unforgiving minuscules of the code on the page before him.

Edmund stared at the historian, and after a moment's thought, crossed himself. Adam did likewise, but only abstractedly, as a man who would do himself no harm but did not seek to ward off any positive ill. He had found himself wondering why Matthew Paris should have written of these matters with such malice, and why he was now contributing his most carefully selected arrows to the King's bow. It was plain that Paris did not love the King; nor could he have borne any grudge against the Capito for past visitations, for his own monastery at St. Albans was exempt and always had been. Could it be that he was a man compelled by his single gift of history to take no man's part but his own, or that of his words? If so, never mind that to declare any man surely damned was a sin; Matthew Paris was as damned as any living soul could conceivably be, and the *Logos* itself would forbear to pity him.

"And?" the King said.

"You have exhausted my knowledge of the matter, my lord King," Edmund Rich said. "But I had thought it composed; and well it should have been, long ere now."

Adam raised his hand. The circlet inclined toward him, and the eyes looked at him.

"Most Christian Adam: proceed."

"My lord King, I know of this tangle, and the ways of it, all too well. Ralph Passelew is an outworn story to me, and to all of us in the parish; was once much loved and honoured, and deservedly so by your majesty, as any wise and just master hunter should be honoured. But in his dotage he hath presumed upon the Crown to aspire to a prebend, that should have rested in gratitude in your majesty's bounties. Robert Grosseteste had warned him, long before his dotard's greed reached your majesty's ears, not to hope to exercise such an office, which if won would lead to imprisonment for all involved, clergy and laity alike. So the law runs; but he was senile, and would not listen.

"Only then was the Capito forced to appeal to Boniface, begging him not to allow this most dearly beloved old man to sue for any post in the Church. I myself helped to compose that letter, in which we said that such an installation would be to the detriment of Boniface his suffragens, whom it was his duty to protect. Boniface was ne more pleased by this our intercession than is your majesty, but he was forced to allow us our argument, seeing in the light of reason that it could hardly be gainsaid. Hence he proposed to us that he should instead institute in

Northampton in due course a Master John Houten, then currently archdeacon of the church; to which we of course consented, since pastoral care was our only object . . . not, not certainly, to thwart our King."

"Your King named Ralph Passelew," Henry said.

"He was very old, my lord King," Adam said steadily, "and though every man loved him, he was not even a clerk, let alone a prelate."

"Where is he now?"

"He died, my lord King, on the feast of St. Blase. That this petty broil still diverts the most high King of England from his affairs of state is not by the intention of Robert Grosseteste, Bishop of Lincoln. God and the King I beg give me leave to say that someone else is inflaming your majesty's good sense."

"Beware," Henry said, almost sleepily. Matthew Paris' quill squeaked and sputtered. Adam bent his head and fell silent. So did they all.

"But where are we now?" Simon de Montfort said at last. "We've argued ourselves into an ingle, and yet it has nothing to do with why we're here."

"Nothing, Simon?" Henry said.

"Very little, my lord King. We have been talking all along about his complaints against the Crown; but let us look for a moment at what the Capito doth to the realm now, and will do henceforth if we cannot say him, Stop! all in one voice. For look you, I am but a plain solider as God knoweth, yet it seemeth me that after contumacy the gravest of crimes for any monk is to publish the secrets of hall or chapter to the laity, whereby he becometh a fautor of popular scandal and bringeth holy Church herself into scorn and disrepute; which rule of sense hath mostly prevailed in the practice of visitation, to the protection of rude and ignorant men such as I am, in constant peril from the meanest of temptations. This rule the noble Robert of Lincoln hath now put into desuetude—in quest of perfection of spirit among his flock as I ne doubt, but to visible confusion and despair."

"We dare not hope," Edmund Rich said heavily, "that corruption shall put on incorruption in this life."

Adam was uncertain whether this was intended to be taken as agreement with Simon's proposition, which had

stricken Adam with certain doubts as to the purity of his
own attitudes which he had never entertained before. Simon, however, seemed to adopt the Archbishop's words as
though they had been his own.

"I thank you, my lord. Yet this is not yet all. These massive public examinations of the conscience of a whole cure
bring eke *in communis fama* the sins and purported crimes
of everyone drawn into the net, noble and commoner
alike—and so in the end, when the noble Robert hath withdrawn to his next county, wife will ne longer bow the neck
to her goodman, burgess hath no obedience from his citizens, no landholder buys and sells from any other, sheriffs
are scorned, serf thinketh his lord ne better nor worse than
himself, allegiances fall all awry, charters are turned into
scraps; fealty itself becometh naught but a word, and may
yet sink to less than a word, even to you, my lord King: to
the yelp of a kicked cur who kens the foot in his ribs and
licks it, sithen it belongeth to the only hand that will feed
him."

The counterfeit baron looked as though he were about to
cheer, but somebody must have trodden on his toe; he
looked glumly down again. The King, who had been
drumming his fingers upon the table-top, gradually
brought his tattoo to a stop. It had been slowing noticeably
during Simon's peroration.

"Both halves of this judgment be but simple sooth," he
said. "And so we will speak plainly. We doubt not any fraction of the fealty of Robert of Lincoln; but 'tis mortal clear
what dangers he is courting. The bondsmen hate the
clergy, we need not Grosseteste to be warranted of
that—out of that passion sprang the last insurrection,
which our barons were not loath to channel under the pillars of our throne. We do not wish these nobles afforded another such pretext: wherefrom, this meeting."

"The danger is clear," Edmund Rich admitted.
"Though, my lord King, when it hath passed away, I will
remind your majesty again that in the matter of the prerogatives of the Church against the Crown I will be as
strong a champion of Bishop Robert's views as ever I was
before. But let us put that to one side for this day. Frater
Marsh, thou art not without influence in the Bishop's
household. Canst not prevail upon him to be less drastic?

This is our quarrel too; and our just grievance with Rome
will hardly be mitigated if the Bishop himself, our
strongest spokesman, knows not that he promulgates in
England the newest and most perilous of Papal oppres-
sions."

"I sorely misdoubt me that the Capito can be influenced
of anyone in this," Adam said heavily. "His righteous
wrath is at its hottest, as indeed how could it not be, considering the magnitude of these evils he upturneth daily at
the synods? Nor would the rede of Earl Simon be calculated to moderate his holy fury. This is a saintly man, as
your lordship knows well, and as we all seek to be. He's nat
to be wooed by arguments from expediency; is from the
outset-far too great a logician, maugre the affront to
the moral laws he'd smell like brimstone smoking up from
the very first such word."

Henry was drumming on the table again.

"Thou wilt try this course, most Christian Adam," he
said.

"Certes, my lord King, I will. Lack of zeal be'eth not my
cross this day, but only misfaith in the efficacy of what's
commanded. Can all these wise heads here think of *nothing* better?"

Henry's fingertips beat a soft rataplan. "We will sit
here," he said, licking his moustache, "until they do."

This had been announced as a relatively ordinary midday meal, but nothing could be entirely ordinary in which
the King was involved. True, the gathering at the dais was
not large, consisting only of Henry, flanked by two
knights; Simon and a trusted captain of his father, his devotion formed during the Albigensian campaign; the
counterfeit baron, uncompanioned; Matthew Paris;
Edmund Rich and his lawyer-clerk; Eleanor of Leicester
and her handmaiden, and Adam Marsh. Only a dozen in
all; but this was reckoning without the entourages of the
King, Simon, the Archbishop and the baron all assembled
at the lower tables, their usual tumult of banging tan-
kards and bragging not greatly subdued by the royal presence. Add to these, too, the breadcutters and the water-
carriers, the squire at the hall dresser who poured the
wine and gave out the cups and spoons, the usher at the
door, the waiter and two servitors at the high table, and

even a clerk to count Simon's silverware on and off. It was not such a crush as Adam had survived at Beaumont, but in his present liverish spirits it was sufficient to threaten him with a headache.

And the food came on without let or respite; black puddings, roasts of venison, herrings in wine, trout with almonds, spiced pottages, ducklings in verjuice, vegetables in vinegar and fruits in wine sauces, turnip jam and pumpkin jam, sweetmeats, pastries, wafers and entremets, all sifted over with ginger, cinnamon, cloves, cardamom, pepper, galingale or sugar, even the meats; and more wine than Adam would otherwise consume or see consumed in a six-month.

Nor was this all of his trouble; for this was for Simon an occasion of state, and where by ordinary his lady would have sat by her lord, today he had found it more fitting that she should be attended by their joint confessor, at the other end of the table. It was of course unthinkable that Adam should not discourse with her at all; though this was his inclination now, neither the amenities nor his duty to her soul permitted that. Nevertheless, he was at a loss for words, and filled with a sudden, ill-defined resentment toward Robert Grosseteste.

She did not allow this long. Reaching out a narrow white hand, she plucked a sweetmeat from his neglected dish and nibbled it judiciously.

"The Father is contemplative today," she said without looking at him, licking her fingers daintily. "Whence this wintriness, most Christian Adam?"

Adam shrugged. "In sooth, I know not," he said uneasily. And in fact, he realized, though he was not without some skill and craft as a diplomat, he fathomed himself not half so well as he often understood others. He knew well, for instance, that Roger Bacon and many older men often had found him somewhat of an enigma; that was easy to read in their faces. He wondered if they would be amused to know that his soul baffled himself as much as it did them. "Belike 'tis this confrontation with thy royal brother."

"I sensed it was going ill, and much regret to have it so."

"There may be more. He is being white-faced and scrupulously polite."

Eleanor crossed herself. "Yet that's nat the all of it, I wis," she said. " 'Tis plain, that's but the rope that turns the windlass, by which we ken there's water in the bucket though it be never so far down in the well."

Adam was forced to smile by the outrageous trope; like many another noblewoman, Eleanor evidently could listen to minstrels more often than was good for her.

"Bail away, my lady," he said, "though I'll warrant thee, there's naught below but mud."

"Gems are born in that," she said, with some determination. "Well, then, I'll confess thee, good Father! Examine thy soul, and speak it."

This was probably safe ground. At the least, they were exchanging words, no matter how like they were to gibberish, which would look more in keeping to Simon than his former sullenness.

"I was thinking when first thou spakest, my lady, of the Bishop of Lincoln," he answered dutifully. "In this there's naught surprising, sithin we've talked with the King about naught else all day."

"True," she said, "And the noble Robert is thine oldest friend, thy teacher, thy spiritual father. How now this coldness?"

"Coldness?" Adam said, astonished.

"Certes; an thou hearest it not in thine own voice, remarkest thou on how thou spakest not of a man, but only of an office."

"Thine ears be sharp indeed, my lady. 'Tis true I feel a certain distance, though I wis nat why or wherefore. Again, belike 'tis only this foredoomed occasion; for he hath all unwittingly caused me to appear before the King to answer to him, and utterly without those recourses which the King ne'ertheless demands of me. But stop, these are the reasonings of a child, to hold the Bishop responsible for my small embarrassment, that he wots nat of, and never meant to cause. 'Tis all this wine that hath me by the wits."

"Fear not, I'll shrive thee for thy gluttony," she said, and lifted a goblet to her own lips with a smile. "I'll press thee more yet, Father, for now at least thou'rt plaudering with me. Art thou alone in this?"

"I fail to understand."

"What Henry wants, he would from thee alone?"

"Nay," he said slowly, "nay, nat so. He would have it from any man here, could any bring it him. But none can."

"Then still thy coolness is unplumbed, most Christian Adam, for e'en unwittingly the good Robert hath not singled thee out; yet speakest thou as if he had. Why is this so?"

These questions were verging upon impudence from a penitent; yet she was in her own house, as he was not. He must abide the course; indeed had consented to it. Perhaps it was indeed the wine, but for whatever reason he felt impelled to give her a little of the answer—not all, not all—as it began to appear to him. Though such a course was as hazardous as rope-dancing, that too seemed to urge him forward.

"No man can wholly love justice," he said slowly, "e'en from the mouth of his confessor and brother in Christ. I did confess to our saintly Robert; and until this day, I deemed I had done my penance in sufficiency. Mayhap my heart seeks now a drop of mercy, and findeth it not, and so blames Grosseteste."

"Now I'll not ask thee what that sin was, Father, for a game is but a game," she said, her face instantly grave. Surely she had no notion that it was in this cast of mind and countenance that she most wrung him. "I perceive I played at *bric* with fate-straws, and will cease; forgive me."

"Nay, I thank thee for thy goodness," Adam said. "Thine innocence is proof against offence; and truly, what transpireth here hath no connection with this expiation, a burden I wrought solely for myself. I told thee, there was naught down there but mud."

But at the same moment, the rope broke under his weight and, falling, he saw. With it his voice broke too, beyond all hazard of his mastering it, as he tried to cross over the last five words.

She turned her head and gazed at him, her delicate brows lifting slightly. He tried to look away, but could not. When at long last she spoke, it was in a whisper, so that he could not hear her over the noise in the hall; but he could read the movements of her lips.

"I know it," she said. "I know it. Otherwise how could it

matter here? It is I. I am the occasion of this sin. *It is I.*"

No power on Earth or under it could have prevailed upon him to peril her by the faintest sign of assent; but there came to him no Power from Heaven by which he might have summoned the strength to deny it. For a few falls of grains through the neck of the glass, there were no powers, and they two were the only living things in Kirkby-Muxloe, or in all the world.

Henry would have left by nightfall, but that no course forenenst Grosseteste had emerged which was agreeable to all; so that now he would have to stay another night in Kirkby-Muxloe.

"Very well," he said, arising at last from the table. "We will make our own composition of this matter, as time and again we are driven to do. We will have the sheriff of Lincoln serve a writ upon Grosseteste, requiring this Bishop to show forth upon what grounds lay persons of his diocese are forced to take oaths against their wills. And if that serveth not, we will direct our sheriffs in general to allow no layman to appear before this Bishop to answer any inquiries under oath—nay, even to give statements on other matters, maugre marriages and wills, against the customs of the realm and to the prejudice of the crown. That, we hazard, will put this *teste synodale* to the halt; think you not, gentlemen?"

He did not wait upon an answer.

After some while, there was the five-fold sound of breathing being resumed. At the sound they smiled at each other, tentatively, ruefully.

"Ne doubt it will," Simon said.

"Ne doubt it will," Edmund Rich agreed sadly. "And equally surely, will inflame anew the quarrel between Grosseteste and the King."

"Canst thou not forewarn him, holy Edmund?"

"Impossible. He's still afield with Roger de Raveningham and five other clerks, turning up fresh scandals. Nor could that help us now. These acts the King proposeth, he'll see as fresh interference with the rights and liberties of the Church, to the detriment of her disciplines. And he'll be right."

"Ne doubt the good Grosseteste hath justice on his side,"

Simon said gloomily. "Yet his case would be the more defensible, had he himself been less careless of the rights of his majesty. Witness the dischurching of the sheriff of Rutland."

"I am unfamiliar with the instance, my lord earl."

"I wis it well," Adam said. "A clerk, his name unknown to me, was deprived of his benefice for incontinence, during a visitation; but refused to surrender it, whereupon the Bishop excommunicated him, and ordered the sheriff to imprison him. But this sheriff of Rutland was a friend of the contumacious clerk and refused to act; whereat, Grosseteste excommunicated the sheriff as well. An arbitrary act, I thought then, and I think now; yet what else could the Bishop have done?"

"Why, simply what precedent would dictate," Simon said. "That is, a letter to the King, asking for royal assistance, and setting forth the cause. Henry then orders the chancery to issue a writ *de excommunicato capiendo,* ordering the sheriff to seize the clerk—"

"Would he in sooth have done so?" Adam asked.

"Henry? Why should he not? He would under those circumstances have had no cause for anger. You see him misfortunately, when he's most crossed, and then he's wood, I'll not deny what's writ on cedar; but grant him what's a king's, he can be reasonable then. And here, look you, the king's bailiff cannot be summoned before an ecclesiastical court in a secular matter, as in fact Innocent IV had to remind the Bishop in this very affair. And hear me, my lords, though canon law's a mystery to me, I ken the civil as well as I can find my own bum in the dark, and this testifying under oath we've been debating all day so fruitlessly is just as clearly illegal."

"My lord earl hath read this law aright," Matthew Paris said quietly.

"Be still, gossip; and leave us." Paris smiled and gathered up his quills and biblions. When he had gone, Adam said:

"And what of the King's appointing abbots as itinerant judges, withdrawing them from the cure of souls to collect money for the King's ever-empty purse? That in the long run is what led to that Passelew affair, as your grace doubtless knoweth."

Edmund nodded heavily. Simon sighed and said,

"We need better scholars on both sides, meseemeth; though none like that I put out the door, I'd trust him nat to sell me a dead horse. And I myself lack time to be a lawyer, and bear sword besides. Tell me, most Christian Adam: what hath been the fate of thine aforetime familiar, that Roger Bacon who put the tinder to the Poitevins? There perhaps was the ilk of sightly and forward student that we most lack for now; and 'twas not long years past I heard the papal legate say the same, that is a friend to all of us, no man may grant less."

"Forward and sightly and scholarly, that I ne gainsay," Adam said; but by now of this day his heart in his breast was hot and black as a lump of peat-coke. "And hath joined the Franciscans, as he writeth me, as a lay brother. Yet never have I seen any novice more unpromising for these our purposes, or e'en for those of Holy Church alone. If the King fears the Inquisition rightly, Roger's very presence would be a danger; he is arrogant, disputatious, impatient, cold of mein, condemnatory. . . . Not my first election for a man of God."

"Oh? Art aware, most Christian Adam, that thou art describing someone an enemy would say much favours thee?"

The peat-coke turned dull red and began to smoulder.

"Nay, my lord, I was not. But I'll abide it, and we shall shortly see. Roger returneth to Oxford as regent master in Aristotle, to second the learned Richard Cornwall, this next year."

"Surprising, in view of what you say. By whose appointment?"

"By whose . . . ?" Adam said, himself surprised. "Why, mine, of course."

Explicit secunda pars.

Sequitur pars tertia:

OF HEM THAT YAF HYM WHERWITH TO SCOLEYE

IX: VILLA PICCOLOMINI

And now, was it all over—or all but over? Strange it seemed to Roger, as he rode north with the post through Italy, toward the cold green sea and home, that an interlude which had begun so greyly could have ended in such a burst of colour; strangest of all, perhaps, that the beginning had seemed anything but grey, even in the midst of his illness.

In Rome the Franciscans had housed him, simply but comfortably, in a monastery in the Travestere, the arrowhead-shaped part of the city on the other side of the Tiber. From the campanile of the monastery, he could see the ruins of the Circus Maximus, if he cared to climb the tower. He often did, after his strength returned a little—not only to look at the Circus, but also to marvel at the sky, which was of an intense cobalt such as he had never imagined could have existed. If from that side he turned his back on Rome, he could see the hills of the Janiculum, thatched with the flat green domes of pines.

Below there was little to see but tenements, but it was simple enough to cross the Pons Aemilius—called by the unclassical citizens the Ponte Rotto—into the rest of the city. He did some sightseeing, helped more or less by an exceedingly worn copy of *Mirabilia urbis Romae,* a compilation lent him by the brothers; but he was bitterly disappointed to find that most of the ancient structures were little more than heaps of rubble, some of them so dispersed that it was impossible to visualize their original plans even with the help of the guide-book.

What was happening to the old monuments was painfully visible to him whenever he approached the bridge in the morning, where he passed a house of some size which seemed to be made entirely of marble fragments from the pillars of history. An inscription over the door said that the house belonged to Crescentius, son of Nikolaus, but there had been no Crescentius in it for over fifty years; otherwise Roger might well have gone on inside and kicked him.

For the most part, however, he simply wandered, looking for nothing in particular, ready to be astonished at whatever the next turn of the narrow, crooked streets might bring. Though modern Rome was far from being as populous as it had been during its great age—the brothers guessed that it might contain thirty thousand people, most of whom lived huddled together about the strongholds of the barons—it was always busy; and the yellow brick with which it seemed everywhere to be faced contrasted sharply with Roger's memory of Paris, giving the Eternal City an oddly incongruous air of gaiety. If Paris had been music, Roger thought, then Rome was light.

It was none the less somehow saddening to hear with his own ears that the language of the Romans was not Latin, though he had known in advance that it was not.

One major surprise was the discovery of the bookshops of the Via Lata, in the very shadow of the arch of Claudius—not just stalls, but full-fledged bookstores. The booksellers assured him that Rome had had bookstores even under the Republic, and moreover, each man insisted that his store had in fact been in its present location since before the birth of Augustus. To prove it, they offered to sell Roger original incunabula from such hands as Cleopatra's, forehandedly penned by that queen in a number of modern languages.

Such dubious wonders aside, however, the stocks of the stores did not prove to be nearly as various as those of the pedlars of Paris. On reflection, Roger decided that this was only to have been expected, since Rome had not the good fortune to be the home of a great university.

Nevertheless, he found enough of interest to lure him gradually back into the habit of study, and thence almost insensibly out of the Roman sun, back toward that darkness from which had issued,

LUPU LURU VOΓO VIR CAN UTRIET VOARCHADUMIA
TRIPSARECOPSEM

Of these words there could be no doubt whatsoever, nor had there been any when Roger had heard them uttered at the climax of his struggle with the death. He had seen them also; or, perhaps, he had only seen them and not heard them at all, for he could not remember the timbre of the voice he knew had spoken them. On the other side, he could ne more recall the size of the letters nor the hand they were written in, though his memory for such things was nigh on perfect; yet at the same time he knew that none of the message had been in minuscule, but rather throughout in Roman capitals like those he had seen only yesterday graven over the Forum.

Well, not all dreams are from God, just as Aristotle said, no matter what the nit-pickers of Paris made of the doctrine; and if some are from demons or the self or one of the souls, should any man be astonished that they were sometimes hard to riddle? What remained was what remained: here, that the spelling of these hard words in an unknown language was perfect, maugre the ambiguity of the senses by which they had reached him in the dream.

Nay, not an unknown language entirely, for it was this that had given him his first key. VIR was a Latin word, UTRIET favoured a Latin word in despite of the fact that it was free of sense, LUPU was Latin but for one missing character—which if supplied, however, would make VIR incorrect, or else *lupus* was, since both were grammatically uninflected. It was clear that the frightful meaningless pronouncement had to be an anagram, not a language, but the parent language had to be Latin.

At first there had seemed to be no way to establish this with certainty. The resemblances could be artificial, or indeed provoked, by some artificial breakage of the line which did not follow the real pauses between words at all. But the slippery certainties of the dream allowed him to think that the spacings were not wholly without meaning. Almost beyond doubt, neither VIR nor *lupus* were the words meant, but their separation into words that favoured Latin could not be an accident; there was Latin in it, that much the separations clearly intended to convey.

Was there also Greek? The fragment ARCH in VOARCHADUMIA suggested it. In a message containing fifty characters—or fifty-seven, if he were intended to count the breaks between the words—how likely was it that the four-letter form ARCH, almost diagnostic of Greek, could occur

even once? Roger did not know, and nothing in his mathematics suggested to him any way of finding out. There
were so many Greek words almost unchanged in Latin, for
that matter, that there might well be no Greek to be deduced from this single grouping, but instead further confirmation that the whole would be Latin when he had it in
his hand.

Thus slowly, slowly, and without real awareness of the
road, he began again to resume his night-time existence.
No one at the monastery took real heed of him or ever had,
even as a novelty, for pilgrims were common enough at all
seasons. As a visitor he was not so closely bound to the regimen as were the brothers, and when he first failed to appear from his cell for the better part of three days—he was
in fact asleep, utterly exhausted—it was assumed simply
that he was in retreat. Thereafter he rose famished, for-
aged briefly to break his fast, and then was back at the
task, filled with solemn high excitement verging once
more on delirium, hard put to it not to begrudge it even his
devotions. The friars, their just sleep warded by the mercy
of thick walls, neither saw his candle-flame nor heard him
coughing in the black chill of midnight.

Yet for all his labours the riddle remained as unbreakable as an Etruscan inscription. Increasingly he was
driven back out into the day, in a grim canvas of the bookstores for anything that might help him, did it have to be
Cleopatra her spurious self. The booksellers took to greet-
ing him with less and less eagerness or even patience, for
by now they knew that they had not what he asked for and
were without hope of finding it; which in turn only increased Roger's desperation. Forgetting to eat, marching
around and around the centre of the city in broken sandals, back and forth under the arch with its garret inscription DE BRITANIS, he at last heard one of the shopmen say,

"Him? That's the English ghost. They say he's come to
haunt Claudius for killing the Druids."

Roger turned. For a moment he was blinded by the sunlight, for in the past few weeks his eyes had begun to hurt
and water constantly. After a few moments of blinking,
however, he saw that he was being regarded steadily, and
had the instant impression that he too was being haunted.

The bookseller was leaning out of the wide window of his

shop, which like them all had a wooden front set in a
grooved travertine sill. In the narrow doorway stood a layman whom Roger had seen often before, though he had not
realized it until now: a thin swarthy man in good cloth,
perhaps a form of livery—though expensively cut, it was
not otherwise ostentatious, and bore no devices. On the instant of recognition, Roger knew that he had been being
followed.

As their eyes met, the man stepped at once into the
street and came toward him. Roger almost moved away,
but something held him: neither hope nor fear, but some
fascination which was neither, and perhaps no more than
hunger and weakness.

"Most Christian friar," the man said, in excellent Latin.
"I beg your blessing and indulgence. May I speak with
you?"

"Certes," Roger said. Then, in confusion: "Why have
you been trailing me?"

"Ah, you noticed! In truth, I didn't set out to do so, not at
first. Let me first name myself: Luca di Cosmati, secretary-
in-chief to Milord Lorenza Arnolfo Piccolomini, marquis of
Modena and senator of Rome under the Emperor and Jesus
Christ our Lord. And you, clerkly sir?"

"Roger Bacon, Franciscan and doctor of arts."

Luca smiled. It was a thin smile, but not unpleasant. "A
scholar, I knew it well! I said so myself! Your patience for
an explanation. It's one of my duties to seek books for the
marquis' library, the most notable in Rome; and well you
know, I observe, how many rounds of the stores must be
made on such an errand, and how barren they be by ordinary. Lately I was charged to find a book of Seneca—"

"Yes, Seneca! Have you seen any—"

"Nay, alas. But there you have it. Wherever I went,
there were you, seeking the same author, and often others
whom the marquis has, or would have if he could. An unusual circumstance, eminent doctor, for Rome is not these
days a bookish town; my lord is not its only bibliophile, but
the rest are possessors only, not students, and buy any
trash or forgery offered them."

Roger found himself returning the smile: "A man may
buy whatever he can pay for, but that kind of buying is
hard on poor scholars."

"And on wealthy ones, books of all kinds being rarer than riches. And so, good sir, I took to following you, to make certain I was right in taking you for a scholar; and when I was certain, I so reported you."

A chill struck in the small of Roger's back. The phrase was not a happy one. He made an abortive move of his hand toward his sword, but he had given it up over a year ago, on the day he had taken orders.

"Nay, be not alarmed, most Christian friar. Milord Modena welcomes scholars, whom he loves dearly. I am sent to beg you to be his guest at dinner."

Thus began Roger's association with the Piccolomini family, and the belated dawn of his Roman years.

The family was large in estates, but startlingly small in number. The marquis' villa at Tivoli, not far from the enormous reaches of the Emperor Hadrian's, had few but servants to walk its mosaic floors and silent gardens; the line was dying out. That first dinner was attended only by Piccolomini himself, a stringy man of fifty with the long nose, lean face and sparse hair of a Caesar off some worn silver coin; his daughter Olivia, a withdrawn, austerely beautiful woman, but taller than Roger and far into her twenties; and Luca, the secretary-in-chief who had recruited Roger, who was treated by the marquis, who was his patron, as a brother and confidant. It would have been an easy position to abuse, but Roger never saw Luca abuse it; in fact, he seemed to cherish it.

After only a few hours of Piccolomini's company, Roger could begin to see the sources of Luca's loyalty and affection. The marquis was the gentlest of men, but that was not all. Like Luca himself, he loved learning and beauty with a great and almost exclusive intensity.

"I am only officially a senator, you must understand," he told Roger. "Roman politics sicken me; I withdrew years ago. These barons! They may be noble in the sight of God, but I hope He does not need my help to love them, or I shall be damned. What think you, friar Bacon? Am I so obliged?"

"The Scriptures seem to say so," Roger said thoughtfully. "But the translations are so corrupt that it is often hard to choose between the Word and conscience."

"That would not be surprising after all these centuries," the marquis said. "But it might be difficult to prove. Is there then much textual criticism afoot in Paris these days?"

"Hardly any," Roger admitted. "The idea, such as it is, seems to be my own. I have been trying to learn some of the languages needed: Arabic in particular, but I mean to go on to Hebrew and Chaldean if I can find teachers—"

"Then you must of course use my library while you are here," Piccolomini said earnestly. "There must certainly be some works in it which are to the purpose. I no longer recall everything I have, the shelves have become so crowded in recent years, but Luca here can help you; he keeps the catalogue."

"There is, I believe, a Hebrew grammar," the secretary said. "I fear I can't vouch for its merits, if any. But it might serve as a beginning."

"There, you see?" the marquis said, his enthusiasm visibly mounting. "And of course you have other studies that you might be able to prosecute here."

"You would be doing Milord a favour," Livia said with a half smile. Her Latin was perfect to the point of elegance, a circumstance so incredible in a woman that Roger thus far had been unable to answer her directly except in monosyllables. "He seldom has anyone to talk to but Luca and me."

"Which is usually more than sufficient," the marquis retorted. "You will find Luca a man of parts, I assure you, friar Bacon. In fact the Cosmati are a gifted family, all artists of stature for three generations. Luca's brother Jacopo is even better than he is."

The secretary smiled without malice. Evidently he was used to this gibe. "Which is why you are my patron instead of his."

"Wait until the Church is through with him and then see how long you'll last! But no, he doesn't know where the books are. And, friar Bacon, you already know that the city is a desert where books are concerned. It's the greedy collectors who make it so, including of course myself. Our imperial ancestors invented few new vices, but private art collecting seems to have been their own authentic discovery. It would hardly have been possible to the Greeks."

"How so?" Roger said.

"Why, it was the old Romans who wrote into law the principle that the man who owned a painting, for example, was the man who owned the board it was painted on, not the artist; and the same with manuscripts. Private collecting really began with that, because it made it possible for a man to become wealthy without having done any of the work involved, simply by saving the board until the painting on it became valuable. And so you can't find a book today in Rome that isn't nailed down, and with a hugely unjust price on it. There are no libraries but private ones, and all of us scheming to unearth a new treasure and snatch it to our bosoms before somebody else happens upon it."

Roger laughed. "But this would seem to mean that there must be *some* men in Rome to whom you could talk of learning, Milord."

Piccolomini only shrugged; it was the girl who answered. "Father may be the only collector in the city who *reads* books."

Once more, Roger was shocked into silence. Though Luca had used almost the same words on the Via Lata, they had then seemed only banter.

"Then the matter is concluded," the marquis said. "You will live with us. I am sure nothing but good can come of it. As a beginning, let me show you the library now."

The library was in fact a marvel, second only to the University's own at Paris, and far superior to any Roger had seen at Oxford, even Grosseteste's. But it was only one marvel of many.

The beauty of the villa itself was of a nature wholly new to Roger. The omnipresent thatch-roofed pines under their multiple spindly trunks were no novelty, but he had never seen cypresses before; here they were everywhere, marching in straight lines right across the landscape to the horizon. Under his window, and in almost every other sheltered spot, grew low bushes with shiny dark green leaves which bore oranges—small ones, but to Roger marvellous enough, for until now the fruit had been only a name to him. Piccolomini's vineyards were familiar enough in principle, for Roger had seen grapes aplenty around Paris

and even at home; but his father had told him often
enough that the vineyards of Ilchester were the outcome of
an unprecedented century of fair weather, and that the
time would surely come again when there would be no
such tipple as British wine.

At Tivoli all this abundant natural beauty had been subdued into a kind of order, made to grow against and soften
a backdrop of marble arches and pillars, or taught to sweep
into exfoliative Euclidean curves and aisles. The Piccolomini gardens were not large by comparison with those of
many of the marquis' neighbours, but they had been laid
out by Lorenzo di Cosmati, grandfather of Luca, before
Roger had been born, and were such a work of art as
Hadrian's villa itself could not boast: a serene and ravish-
ing island in which to walk in the morning, amid a purity
of doves. And over it all was the Tyrrhenian sky, even
more intensely blue than it had seemed over the city
proper, out of which poured sunlight in overwhelming
profligacy.

And the food! Roger had never before dreamed that
there could be so many different kinds of things to eat.
Northern food repeated itself endlessly, disguised only by
its many sauces and spices. Here he seldom recognized
what was in his bowl, and on some occasions was sorry to
have asked; he was, *exempli gratia,* more than fortunate to
discover that squid was delicious before learning what he
was eating. But this passed quickly; there was too much of
moment on his mind to allow him a pause in which to become also the inventor of squeamishness.

The standards of cleanliness were equally new to him,
and had to be taught him, none too gently, by the attend-
ant assigned to him: a stout old housekeeper, once Livia's
nurse, who overcame with granite obduracy his initial
scandal at being tended by a woman, and saw to it that his
linens were fresh, his sandals mended, and his feet clean.
Piccolomini's estate made its own soap, a substance rarer
than diamonds; here it was largely *lapis Albanis,* a mixture of lava and ashes, which eventually wore down to a
central sliver abrasive enough to point nails, but the old
matron saw to it that he learned its use. He found himself
taking more baths in a month than he had formerly taken
in a year.

The housekeeper herself was harder to become accommodated to. *Pro forma* monasticism in this warm radiant air did not put up a serious battle, but his old bitter distrust yielded less easily. It was several months before he could bring himself to accept that her warm and rather quarrelsome concern with him was totally without predatory intent, and ran much deeper than he could in any justice have expected or asked. She had of course been assigned to him by the marquis; Roger was her task, like any other task; but beyond that, she worried actively and constantly about the pale English friar, often to a knife-edge beyond which he did not know whether he would shout with exasperation or burst into helpless laughter. She was the first woman of this kind that he had ever encountered; and he awoke one dew-cold morning to her morning scolding, after nearly half a year had gone by, with the realization that he liked it.

Livia was the second. It was through her that Roger first came to understand the essence of her father's loneliness, his generosity to a stranger, the curious tone of wistfulness that perpetually underlay even his most abstract and scholarly conversations. Most of the Piccolomini fortune was founded in lead mines—half the plumbing in modern Rome had come out of them—and no subject interested the marquis less than public works, except perhaps lead itself, or politics. Of his surviving children there were only two, and the other was the son of whom his wife had died in childbirth: Enea Silvio, who had fled the marquis' bewildered hostility the moment he had come into a marriage portion, and lived now in Siena, incommunicado and—Roger deduced—disinherited. No one was left the marquis but Livia, whom he had given at his own hands the broad humanistic education that Enea Silvio had sullenly refused to suffer, let alone absorb.

("That explains much," Roger said in the library, when they were alone together. "I have never heard a woman speaking Latin before. It surprised me."

("It explains more than I find comfortable," the marquis said. "That precisely is why Latin is only spuriously a universal language, friar Bacon. It is never spoken to women any more. Women are confined to the vernacular, whatever that may be. On this account alone, Latin is dying."

("Surely not! It is the language of scholars, everywhere; and the only written language of note. Under those circumstances, surely it can hardly matter whether or not it is spoken to women."

(Piccolomini had given him a long, slow look, and at last seemed to be about to comment; but instead, again, he only shrugged.)

Nevertheless, it was not too hard to see that Livia's learning had unfitted her as a woman, as witness her spinsterhood still persistent in her third decade, in despite of both her father's wealth and her dark personal beauty. Young Roman princes bored her, and she alarmed them; and now there was added the simple problem of age, itself a proof that there was something amiss with the girl, a proof that grew more convincing simply by itself growing older.

None of this could matter to Roger, who found himself able after only a few months to accept her presence in the library, and her knowledge of subjects in the scholarly province. To him, everything at Tivoli was strange and hence might well be usual; he had no touchstones. She was inarguably well read—no match for Luca, who seemed to have vast stretches of the library by rote, but on the other hand more than simply a reflection of her father. She not only knew the texts, but often saw into them in a way entirely her own. After a while, Roger was taking so little notice of her sex that he talked to her in much the same style he might have adopted with any fellow scholar, maugre the parcel of respect he owed his noble host, and was occasionally surprised to find that he had been assuming knowledge on her part that in fact she lacked. By ordinary, this amused her, though he could not imagine why.

She was also far more sympathetic to Roger's interest in engineering than was her father, who was actively depressed by the practicality of his imperial ancestors; the marquis was not precisely pleased that the Goths had cut the aqueducts nine centuries bygonnen, but there was something in the manner in which he had referred to the incident which suggested that he thought it had served the Romans right for being so in love with piling one stone on top of another. About this difference Roger and his host drew nigh to real disputatiousness until Livia stepped in, diverting Roger into daytime tours of the Roman public works and so freeing his mind for nocturnal conversations more to the Piccolomini taste. When the marquis was ill with the Roman fever, as he was with increasing frequency as the second summer wore on, Roger and Livia walked in the garden and talked—of the lost secret of mortar, of active geometry, of what the buried floor of the Forum might have looked like, of the crime of quarrying ancient monuments, and other suitable subjects, while the housekeeper, Roger's servant, kept to her marble bench and looked up at the stars, sighing resignedly.

But there was nothing to sigh about. Roger had never before felt so well, so young, so totally alive. The climate, the sunlight, the food, the beauty, the feast of reason, the antiquities, the friendships, the solicitude, all seemed conspiring to make him positively sleek. Sometimes in the fluttering evening in the Piccolomini gardens, listening to Livia's grave melodious voice and breathing draughts of citron and other perfumes, he would hear also through the doves' wings a long, long story being told by a nightingale; and with it came down around him such an imminence of the glory of God that he could not even give thanks silently, but only hold Livia's hand until some cough or stir from the marble bench brought back the lateness of the hour. Then they would part; there was always tomorrow; and besides, Roger was now required to wash his feet.

Above all there was the library, and the marquis of Modena himself. It was surprising how infrequently Roger could bring himself to think of the cipher, for all the wealth of help he now had; but somehow it never seemed to be a suitable subject for conversation. Piccolomini's enthusiasms lay elsewhere; he was a humanist, not a digger. Yet he would talk gladly of the sciences, so long as Roger cleaved to Nature as a source of correction for corrupt texts, and stayed clear of aqueducts and other plumbing. Moreover, they had early found in their joint admiration for Seneca—of whose works the marquis owned the most extensive collation Roger had ever seen, including portions of books previously quite unknown to him—a common ground in moral philosophy which widened and deepened with every evening's conversation, until Roger had to invoke a fortnight's retreat to assimilate all this magnificence, and make it his own.

It was difficult, in part because he had written nothing in nearly two years. It was, furthermore, not a formal book that was wanted here, but a schema, a hierarchy, which should of course be logical, but must in a sense be architectural as well, related in all its parts like the stones of an arch. He found himself spending almost as much time drawing diagrams as in penning argument. The struggle was protracted, for there were at least three grand elements struggling for mastery in his mind, each of which had somehow to be reconciled to the others: First, the vision of a universal science which had begun to haunt him ever since he had first read the *Secret of Secrets*; next, the domain of experiment versus revealed knowledge; and finally, the domain of the moral law, which could be allowed supremacy over the other two, but only in so far as it could be shown to derive from them.

At the end he was still unsatisfied, and gave over reworking the manuscript only out of regard for his host's patience. He did not read it that night, however, but instead used it only as in the past he had used lecture notes. The marquis listened attentively to the solemn friar who might have been his son; but he did not stint to ask questions.

"First of all, we have all the several separate sciences as they have come down to us, that is, imperfectly," Roger began. "I mean to include mathematics, and then medicine, alchemy, perspective, agriculture, all the sciences of natural philosophy. It is clear enough that they are all connected together and depend upon each other, as you can see most clearly in a science like medicine where the physician who knows neither alchemy nor astrology cannot be a scientist at all. He must know equally well the connections between these other sciences, as well as their relationships to his own."

"In what way? It seems a lot to ask. I can see that some knowledge of the patient's auspices might be useful, and that a knowledge of drugs is essential. But otherwise the connections are superficial, are they not?"

"By no means," Roger said warmly. "For example, what

might suffice against a disease of the kidneys, which are ruled by Venus? It would not be enough to know in what house Venus stood when the patient was born, which is astrology; or in what house she stands now, which is astronomy; or in what houses she will stand for the rest of the course of treatment, which is mathematics. There are likewise herbs that are governed by Venus, which is agriculture; and so is the element copper, which is alchemy. And the worst pitfall here is that the traditional medical texts say almost nothing of all this. I would rather not go into it now, but I have counted no fewer than thirty-six such grave defects in the classical teachings; I mean to write a book about it some time soon."

"Do so, I pray," the marquis said, blinking. "I did not mean to tempt you into a divagation."

"Then I mean to ask, How do we know what we know? These imperfections are rampant. They are even in Aristotle, partly because of the abominable translations we use, and partly because he concealed some knowledge for good reasons, as you can see in his book of secrets. Here we see the defect of revealed knowledge and belief, that again there is no certitude in it."

"Is this not a dangerous doctrine?"

"No. St. Augustine himself counsels us against making fools of ourselves by quoting the Word of God to deny some plain fact of nature, because when such an apparent conflict exists, it must mean that we have misunderstood the Word. People are constantly misunderstanding the Word—otherwise we should not be plagued by heretics. Now this brings me to my experimental science, which is not a part of the sciences of natural philosophy or mathematics, not a 'true' science in that sense, but nevertheless is superior to them all. It unites natural philosophy with revealed knowledge because it gives them both certitude; and imparts to each and all three dignities, which are its three prerogatives. I have written them down, thus:

"First, verification. Until you have this in your hand, anything you 'know' about natural philosophy, from revelation and authority, is simple credulity, which is only the first stage of knowledge."

"Even from Aristotle?" the marquis said. "Even from this mysterious book of secrets?"

"O, that is only the other side of the same coin. I will believe anything, no matter how apparently incredible, if it comes to me from a sufficient authority; but that means I must have faith that he has performed the experiments he says he has performed, and observed what he says he has observed. Aristotle passes this test—I have actually repeated some of his observations myself, and they were correct. And this is a necessary proviso, for no man can live long enough to repeat every experiment in history; perfect scepticism. Josephus says that the ancients lived long lives simply out of the necessity to *understand* what they had learned."

"I am answered. What is the second dignity?"

"The second is the one that we have already exposed, the drawing together of the separate sciences so as to see their relationships to each other, *quod in terminus aliarum explicat veritates quas tamen nulla earum potest intelligere nec investigare.* Again to cite an example, who has not seen sick dogs eat grass? Might not a man study the behaviour of animals to see how they prolong their lives, and thus recover knowledge of some healing herb long lost? Here would be a plain case of two sciences contributing to each other in a way that the man working only in one science could never hope to see. And here, most plainly, experiment is not a separate science in the usual sense, but a leaven of power at work throughout natural philosophy. And this represents the second stage of knowledge, which is simply experience.

"Now at last we come to the third dignity, again emerging from experiment: The use to which all this knowledge is to be put, for the protection of Christianity, the greater glory of God, and the greater welfare of man. And precisely here lie the greatest difficulties, because this is the domain of the third stage of knowledge, that is, reason, which must also decide to what uses knowledge *ought not* to be put. The man who sees the possibilities of the several sciences, and uses them as Archimedes did to make engines to defend Syracuse, is a man of power—of awful power if the book of secrets is correct, and I myself have had certain revelations . . . but of these I am still too uncertain to speak.

"Still it is clear, Milord, that the pinnacle of this schema must be an ethics. Moral philosophy is its outcome and its king. And it is here that I have made no progress at all. There is of course the ethics of Aristotle, but that emerges from natural philosophy, revelation and authority *as he knew them.* His knowledge is better than ours on most counts, but poorer on some crucial matters—most obviously, that he could not be a Christian, but there are others as well. And this is why our converse over Seneca impelled me to the impoliteness of all this scribbling."

"The study of nature is not my study," the marquis said gravely, "and on the whole I do not regret my incomprehension. But I have believed since the death of my wife that God meant my house to be the womb of something greater than the continuance of my line. And, praise Him, I have been allowed a glimpse of it. I might have been vouchsafed more had I not been jealous of it, for which I beg your forgiveness."

"Mine? Milord Modena, your kindnesses will be remembered in my prayers all my life long."

"Perhaps not," the marquis said. "You see, while you were in retreat, Luca brought me a letter for you. I kept it, not wanting to abort the work for which I might some day be remembered, if only in God's eye. I failed to think until too late of the injury I might be doing you, were it a letter of moment. With shame, I give it to you now."

He handed the packet across the table, and Roger broke the seal without haste; he had already recognized the hand, that of one of Adam Marsh's familiars. The message was brief—a mercy, since the candles were now burning very low.

"You have done me no harm at all, Milord. I am simply called home, and given new tasks I fear I ill deserve. It is good news, and in no wise urgent."

"I thank God," the marquis said. "Of course I knew it was to bring our visits to an end; that was fore-ordained and I must abide it. But I am emboldened to ask a favour."

"Anything in my power, Milord."

"Then . . . would you leave me the book you read from tonight?"

"Why, certainly. But, Milord, it is incomplete."

"I know," the marquis said, very quietly. "It is a child of this house. But I would have it if you could yield it up."

Silently, Roger laid the manuscript upon the table. Then he drew back the top leaf, and picking up a dripping quill, wrote across the top of it: *Communia naturalium—I.*

The marquis received it in a like silence, and held out his hand. As their fingers touched, a candle crackled and went out.

The housekeeper prophesied disasters as she packed him up, but he was used to that now. Why she should seem to be pitying him at the same time was impossible to guess; for he had never been happier in his life than in these two years.

He found the courage to tell Livia so when they parted . . . but that too ended in mystery, for as Luca and he rode companionably from the gate, he saw that she was silently weeping.

Going north, he had nothing left to think about but the cipher, which belatedly had almost solved itself, while he had been thinking about the recension of the *Communia* he had given to Piccolomini. In the midst of these labours he had been vouchsafed a revelation of a kind, though a difficult one and without any promise that he could trust. It had been simply a prompting from the long-silent self; and it said nothing, but, *Count.*

After pondering this word long and long, in some bafflement as to whether or not it was itself another word of the cipher, he had used his last days in the marquis' library to ferret out three long books to study—books on subjects of so little interest to him that they threatened to put him to sleep after the first chapter. (That in itself had proven unexpectedly hard; there was virtually nothing at all in this vast ranking of manuscripts which was not wholly fascinating, regardless of subject.) He counted every character in all three, and made up a table of how many times each letter occurred. He had intended to go on to make more tables, the next to tabulate how many times pairs of letters occurred, next triplets, the next fours, but he had utterly failed to anticipate how stupefying just the first task would be, and how long it would take him; and his time was running out. He would have liked, also, to make up a congruent table for three Greek books of similar length, and make allowances for the differences arising out of the relative shortness of the Greek alphabet, and the fact that one letter in Greek might often stand for groups of two or even three in the Latin; but there was no time.

But the Greek tables did not turn out to be pertinent. With incredible swiftness the unbreakable pronouncement began to rank itself into meaning, so fast indeed that he did not pause to consider it for sense until well past noon; it was enough to see the words surfacing, one by one, like a procession of dolphins each bulging at the forehead with patent wisdom yet seeming to the sailor on such seas as alike as pea-beans.

Then, famished once more without being aware of it, and almost mortally exhausted as well, he stopped and looked. He had supplied the wolf his serpentine tail or yard, and on that model given another to LURU as a word plainly encoded on the same model; but as he had expected, that wolf had vanished now. The man in the middle, the still unbroken VIR, now stood in the heart of an explosion, with saltpetre on the one shore and sulphur on the other. He had now: *Sed tam sa petr . . . e sulphur,* separated still by VOPO VIR VOARCUMIA RICO, but he was in no doubt that something enormous had already happened. Standing himself in the middle, Roger remembered the sharp crepitating crackle of the saltpetre crystals, salvaged from his father's dungheap, under the blow of a rock in a boy's hand when he tried to shape them into larger rhombs through which to look into the eyes of Beth or old Petronius or at blades of grass, and had got nothing but that noise and a puff of pepper-smelling air for his pains; and on the other bank, there thudded in his memory the exit of the demon from the window of his noisome room at Westminster. In the middle with him was the dream, in which these huge ciphered words had become an explosion like nothing so much as the earthquake which shall exhume the dead for the Last Judgment.

He began to tremble. These words were words of power. Even in the terror of the vision he had not dreamt of how much power there was in them, nor could he yet fathom why it was being put into his hands; for he knew well enough what it was. This was the *ignis volans,* the flying fire of the Hellenes which had been lost for all these many

centuries; and Roger Bacon had been told in one single
struggle with the death how it was to be made . . . and of
what horrors would follow. How could that be? In Simon de
Montfort's grave words, would God allow? Yet He had allowed it to the Hellenes; and now in this age it was almost,
almost come down to a simple piece of alchemy, about to
flow from the quivering tip of the quill in Roger's hand.

Yet not quite. The rest of the anagram, it seemed, would
not be broken. Again and again Roger rearranged the remaining characters, but nothing emerged but a Satanic
gabble, more impenetrable than the four remaining blocs
themselves. Yet it was as sure as death and resurrection
that this was alchemy entire, and nothing more. What
could be missing? Saltpetre and sulphur and . . . what?

Roger went back to the tables of numbers, though they
were now hard to read in the light of his candle. Wiping his
eyes and forehead, he tried again, counting, half asleep,
gradually losing once more his awareness of the meanings
of words, only seeking to see in the numbers some relationship which. . . .

And then, in a moment of whirling delirium, he had the
dream back, and with it the answer. That answer was
numbers. Why had he not seen before that all those U's
could not be told from V's in Roman capitals? There it all
was, the great fish at the bottom of a pellucid pool:

SED TAM SA PETR RC VII PART V CAROUM PV NOV
CORULI V E SULPHUR

It was painfully crabbed Latin, but certainly correct, for
it was in the style of his demon self, which spoke nothing
well but English and that not often; and its meaning was
totally beyond argument. With the elisions expanded, the
pronouncement said: *Sed Tamen salis petre recipe vii
partes, v carbonum pulvere novelle coruli, v et sulphuris.*

FOR THIS TAKE SEVEN PARTS OF SALTPETRE, FIVE PARTS OF
POWDERED CHARCOAL FROM YOUNG HAZELWOOD,
AND FIVE OF SULPHUR

He was versed enough in alchemy to know that nothing
useful could be expected unless one began with pure substances, he had absorbed that in Peter the Peregrine's college; but he knew well enough how to proceed. Alongside

his Arabic lessons he had learned the test for pure flowers
of sulphur, which should crackle faintly when rubbed between finger and thumb; he had known from boyhood how
to dig a pit in which fine charcoal is burned; and from boyhood too he remembered without irony that the most re-
fined of all saltpetre is to be found in a dungheap. Nothing
remained but to go forth and procure these things.

And this white flash of knowledge took him no longer to
encompass than would have sufficed him to write down the
shortest verse in Scripture; which reads, *Jesus wept.*

X: ST. EDMUND HALL

Much had changed at Oxford, as was only to have been expected; and yet in that special world which was called into
being by its very name, the University had not changed at
all; it was almost deceptively peaceful: the same streets,
the same customs, and above all the same faces, unchanged after so much had changed him. To be sure, Adam
Marsh had gone quite grey about the temples, but it did
not make him seem old. Grosseteste was only just as grave
and venerable as he had always been, no more; the Bishop
was properly beyond age, as though he had been canonized
at birth. If the King's aborting of his *teste synodale*—a con-
fusing story, of which Roger heard so many conflicting ver-
sions that he gave it up as little better than a
myth—disturbed him, he did not show it, nor did he speak
of it. Roger saw him but seldom, as before; and Adam,
more than ever preoccupied with the affairs of state which
he loathed and loved, was at court or at Leicester for much
of the year.

After the pleasures and explorations of reunions were
past, Roger rather welcomed the relative solitude of the
new life. He had much to do, beginning, appropriately, in
the a's, with alchemy. His lectures were time-consuming,
for he had discovered in himself a real passion to
teach—had, indeed, discovered it in Paris; but herein lay

the principal change since he was last at Oxford, in that he
was now a master, weighty with respect, and could to some
extent allot his own hours. He was somewhat at a loss to
account for the obvious tentativeness with which the other
masters treated him, however, until he discovered that
Richard of Cornwall had bruited it about the University
that this Roger Bacon was a dangerous sciolist: at Paris he
had attended other men's lectures and confounded them
before their students with questions they could not
answer.

Well, Roger had done that now and again, in particular
to a booby-headed master in Euclid's *Elements* who had
not actually known enough geometry to calculate the volume of a mousehole; and then there had been that lector on
the law of Moses, four out of five of whose statements
about the chirogrillus Roger had pointed out to be wrong;
that one could count himself fortunate, since the fifth
statement had been as wrong as the others. But it was a
custom in Paris; Albertus Magnus had done it to Roger
once, after his débâcle at Roger's examination, though
happily Albert had come out again the loser and had
immediately—and balefully—given up the sport as unprof-
itable.

As for Richard Rufus of Cornwall, rumour had it that he
would not be making mischief for long, for he had received
a permission—in essence, an order—from John of Parma,
Minister General of the Franciscans, to return to Paris to
lecture on Lombard's *Sentences*. From what Roger knew of
the man, it seemed a wholly appropriate assignment.

In the meantime, Roger contentedly made many bad
smells and burned himself repeatedly, to considerable
profit. Within a span of two years he had mastered most of
the appalling jargon of alchemy, designed not to communi-
cate but to conceal, and was able to record with satisfaction the discovery of methods for refining three metals to
the pure state. One of these—he had no names for them,
and the books did not know them—seemed to be a genuine
element, which when blended with iron made a mixture of
phenomenal hardness perhaps promising for arms and armour. Each of the other two exploded when dropped into
water, an observation which nearly cost him his eyesight,
and gave him a festering sore on one shoulder which took

three weeks to heal. Since nothing so fickle could be of any practical use, he dropped the matter there; if he needed a loud noise, he had the secret of the cipher—the first alchemical formula he had tried. It had worked awesomely well, particularly when, as in the vision, it was packed tightly into a parchment roll and lit with a spill at one end.

With the aid of the Arabs, whose language he now knew well enough to be able to distinguish a stylist from a plodder, he began himself to write on alchemy: in particular a new translation of excerpts from Avicenna, centred upon such passages as he had himself been able to test, or to enlarge upon. It did not greatly surprise him to find that knowing how the experiments went in practice was almost as corrective of bad translation as was a knowledge of Arabic grammar; the world, it was perfectly clear, was only the other form of the Word, and often much easier of access to its meaning. This work with the text of the great Islamic physician sent his pen scratching into several side excursions, wholly natural to his way of thinking now, into medicine. Among these was a revision of his first attempt at a book, made long ago at Oxford: *Liber de retardatione accidentium senectutis et de sensibus conservandis,* the book on old age, undertaken this time at the request of Piccolomini, marquis of Modena, brought to Roger in a letter from Tivoli as equally far away and long ago. It was a hair-raisingly bad book and probably could not be much improved, but this recension, at least, would have the benefit not only of Avicenna but of the book of secrets.

Richard Cornwall stubbornly refused to disappear. His health was uncertain, and the Paris appointment had not been to his taste. Misfortunately, Adam Marsh took his part. He wrote to the provincial minister, begging him to allow Cornwall to stay; Oxford, he said, would be delighted to keep him. Cornwall was now spreading the word that this Roger Bacon was obviously also a magician, in which he was aided more than a little by the notorious stinks, noises and oddly-coloured lights which emanated of nights from Roger's cell in St. Edmund Hall.

These sinister mutterings reached the students, as they were bound to do. The young men looked to Roger now not only for outrageous propositions—which taste was inevitably gratified, for Roger generated outrageous propositions

these days as naturally as other men breathed, and with
almost as little awareness of it—but also for miracles. He
was tempted, and after a while he fell: with the help of alchemy, small "miracles" were not hard to produce, and
Roger quickly discovered that they were dramatically useful as teaching aids.

Cornwall's sickly malice puzzled Adam sufficiently to
move him to question Roger about it, but Roger's
theory—that it derived from Albertus Magnus, whose familiar Cornwall had been for a time in Paris—would not
have sat well with the lector, and so instead he professed
ignorance. In the end, Adam contrived to set it down to ac-
ademic jealousy over the popularity of Roger's lectures on
the *libri naturales*; and these indeed were now more of a
success than ever, since Cornwall had indirectly led Roger
to exhibit experiments in the hall.

Nor were these the only good to emerge from that malice: for the provincial minister sent his clerk, one Thos.
Bungay, to Oxford in respose to Adam's letter, to investigate the merits of the case. Though he decided in
Cornwall's favour, that is, that he need not go to Paris, the
incessant chatter he had to endure about that sciolist and
magician Roger Bacon aroused his deepest curiosity.

Within half a day Bungay and Roger were fast friends.
Thomas was an astronomer, which happened to be the
next item but one in the a's, just after astrology. Within
six months he had applied for leave to study at Oxford;
within another month, they had together leased the massive eight-sided gatehouse across St. Aldate's Street in the
walls. This blocky structure, which was eighty-four feet
high, served them as observatory. In addition, Thomas
lived there; Roger, for the time at least, kept to his quarters at St. Edmund to be near his classes, but it was already evident that he and the University would probably
benefit alike were he to take his stenches elsewhere—regardless of the fact that he was already better than half
done with alchemy.

They were, they discovered, remarkably alike in some
ways. Thomas Bungay was plump and affable, but he was
in his heart a solitary man—and like all such, as ready to
cleave to another of his rare kind as one lorn Assyrian to
another. He had the love of knowledge, though with him it

looked mostly toward the stars (still, he had recently been
reader in theology at the nascent University in the distant
marsh town of Cambridge). And despite his higher rank in
the Order, he plainly regarded Roger as his teacher, deferentially playful though their manner was toward each
other. He had caught the vision, at least in part.

Also they quarrelled constantly; and drank more than
was good for them; and stayed up all night, studying the
stars; and planned to live forever. They were alike ridiculous in their tonsures, tunics and talk, middle-aged and
laden with learning, and all unaware in love; two men in a
desert.

"Tonight we shall have Venus and Jupiter in conjunc-
tion in Aquarius."

"Good for us. Where's the wine?"

Nothing disturbed them, though 1250 was a year of
overturns. The Emperor Frederick died; they said, *Requi-
escat in pace,* and watched the occultation of Vega by the
moon. To find a book for Thomas, Roger went briefly to
Paris, where with his own eyes he saw in the streets the
leader of the Pastoureaux rebels; the sight interested him
mildly, but he was in a hurry to return home. This year,
too, Adam Marsh left Oxford for good, forced to give up his
lectorship to the Franciscans by the pressure of his politi-
cal duties. Roger and Bungay attended his last lecture,
where he created a sensation by conferring upon a youngster named Thomas Docking—no older than Roger had
been when Grosseteste had plotted to send him to
Paris—the unprecedented honour of succeeding to the
readership (though not, since the rules forbade it, to the
title itself; this and its prerogatives would be held in abey-
ance until a formally qualified master could be chosen;
Docking's was an interim appointment, and even this did
not wholly please the University).

The departure of Adam cost Roger a pang, but its sting
too was solved by the new friendship with Bungay. Besides, the vison was growing clearer every year; he was
now occupied, as a work of preparation, with the writing of
a gloss for the *Secret of Secrets,* of which he had found at
Oxford four mutilated copies. Fortunately, the MS given
him in Paris by John Budrys of Livonia appeared to be
perfect—fortunately, because his money was now sensibly

diminished. One of the pre-conditions of the *scientia experimentalis*, it was beginning to appear, was a bottomless purse.

He was still incubating, too, that same treatise on the causes of the rainbow which he had conceived as a member of the Peregrine College; but no question of perspective he had ever encountered was so difficult as this. He could advance no farther than a plateau of theoretical nihilism, represented in manuscript by nearly a score of leaves demonstrating that all the existing explanations—even Grosseteste's, even Aristotle's—were inadequate. The road to a valid theory, however, remained invisible.

Cornwall was now lecturing on the *Sentences* in Oxford, instead of at Paris, and in his success seemed to tap a fresh well of slander. The new campaign finally succeeded in annoying, not Roger, who was too preoccupied to do more than take perfunctory notice, but Bungay.

"Thou should'st take steps against that man, Roger."

"O, I may at some time, meseemeth. But truly he's so stupid that I'd have scant use for his good opinion anyhow. In the meantime he is doing no particular harm."

"There thou'rt mistaken, I avow," Bungay said earnestly. "Thou hast not been in orders as long as I. He may well be damaging seriously thine hopes for advancement. He stands higher than thou dost, and ne matter how stupid he appeareth to thee, he hath a reputation for wisdom among the vulgar. Let me assure thee, politics among the Franciscans is quite as complex as it is at Westminster—though eke a measure quieter."

"Hmm." This put a somewhat new light on the matter. Roger could hardly afford not to think about his hopes for advancement in the Order, to which were tied his hopes of continuing his work; there was now no question but that the money would not last many more years. "What wouldst thou recommend me? The civil law? He doubtless knoweth far more about that than I—most of his ilk seem to think about very little else."

"I couldn't advise thee there myself; like thee, I would tend to avoid it. Nay, I was hoping thou might'st think of some way of pulling his teeth—perhaps by depriving his accusations of some of their force . . . ?"

"Nay, I'll not do that," Roger said firmly. "These little

shows of experiments are valuable to the students, and on the other side I'll not alter my teachings to what that ass thinketh the truth, for accommodation's sake or any other. But thou hast given me another notion."

"Good. What is it? Or canst thou say?"

"I think so. I am going to show him that in one respect, at the least, what he is saying about me is true and correct."

Bungay looked alarmed; but having started the juggernaut rolling, he knew better than to stand in its way.

Roger much begrudged the time he had to devote to thinking the idea through, but after a while he began to see a certain beauty in it. It emerged, first of all, from Richard's widely known and constantly reiterated views on the question of the plurality of forms: the same subject over which Roger had disputed with Albertus Magnus; and secondly from Richard's own peculiar method of disputation. He appeared to think that his position on the matter was substantially that of Albert, but in fact he had grossly oversimplified Albert's stand, if indeed he had ever understood it at all; the plurality of forms, Richard maintained, was contrary to the teachings of the saints. This was his way with the philosophers he expounded: mostly he simply denounced them, and when he did bother to explain their views, he did so in a form not likely to be recognized by the authors. All this had been true of him in Paris, and he had not changed.

On the doctrinal question, Richard's trimming of it to fit into the Procrustean bed of his understanding had led him straight into the theological position that Christ had become a man during the three days between His death and the resurrection. This view was no novelty—nothing new interested Cornwall—and hence failed to cause any real stir at the University, but it was ideal for Roger's purposes because it was logically absurd. In fact, it was incipiently heretical; a sound logician would need only a motive to transform it from a blunder into a scandal. Albert would never have fallen into such a trap—and Roger, having debated the plurality of forms with Albert to a standstill, did not anticipate that so weak a logician as Cornwall would be a serious adversary.

He was, in short, readying himself to demonstrate to

Cornwall, on Cornwall's person, that this Roger Bacon
was indeed and in fact a dangerous casuist.

Then Grosseteste died between the Feast of the Holy
Guardian Angels and the *Translatio Edwardi Confessoris;*
and for three days the bells boomed forth their grief from
every tower in Oxford, aye, and in England. He was
interred in an altar tomb of blue marble, with a border of
foliage around the table, which was supported at the corners by four pillars, in the south aisle of the church of Lincoln; and with him his ring and staff. There were reports of
miracles and nocturnal wonders, doubly marvellous in a
man once but a word away from imprisonment by papal order; and yet one manifested to no less a person than the
King, to whom in a vision a voice whispered, *Dilexit Dominus Edmundum in odorem benignitatis, et dilexit Dominus
Robertum in odorem fidelitatis.*

In the solemnity of this event, which drew together
Church and Court, Order and University in a common pag-
eant of mourning, and in the intensity—as always unreal-
ized until now—of his own loss, Roger almost forgot that
mannequin figure Richard Rufus of Cornwall; and when
he saw the man in the procession at Lincoln, again
through an air shivering with the mortuary words of the
bells, it was only with shame for the meanness of his own
scheming. This was the second death high in University
councils within a year, for the regent master, John of Garland, had preceded the Bishop of Lincoln into the shadow.
There was time to think, too, of what consequences the removal of Grosseteste's counsels might have on the King; a
matter necessarily of the most significance to Adam
Marsh, but Roger had seen quite enough of Henry to bring
him to speculating uneasily. The Bishop had been almost
the only strong palisade between the English Church and
the Crown—as well as between the English Church and
the Apostolic Camera; and, moreover, one of the principal
buttresses of Simon de Montfort's party.

But much though the death of Grosseteste signified to
Roger, it was apparently not enough to distract Cornwall
for long. The return of the faculty from Lincoln had not
been a week old when the campaign was resumed. Bungay
did not have to warn Roger a second time, for now he was
indeed in a white fury, less in his own behalf than for what

he took to be, for reasons obscure even to himself, a disrespect to the dead.

He promptly set his arrow and let fly. It was ridiculously easy, like shooting a popinjay from three feet away. It was also wondrous noisy: Roger's very appearance at Cornwall's lecture set the students to chattering so that the lecturer could scarce be heard. The argument with the master himself went so exactly as Roger had imagined it would that the older man might well have been reading lines from a written-out miracle-play. Some of the students, of course, took his part, and the result was something as much like a small riot as may be.

Bungay was appalled. "The University will send thee down," he said shakily. "If they do so, I will go too; I provoked thee."

"There's naught to fear, Thomas. A few cuffs given and taken in a lecture hall are commonplace. The University never pays the slightest attention."

"Oh, so?" Bungay said doubtfully. "Well, thou know'st them far better than I. But whatever they may do, I question that thou hast accomplished anything of value. At the very least, Cornwall will surely retaliate."

"Certes," Roger said. "Nothing is surer. Therefore the problem is, how to tempt him to retaliate in some way further disadvantageous to him. There too, meseemeth I have the answer."

"Roger, it seemeth *me* that thou shouldst give over. It mathinketh me that I ever tempted thee in the matter. This time it is certain to be still worse—thy methods are so drastic, Roger."

Roger smiled, a little grimly. "This will simply be the same allegory, played backwards, as it were. Dear friend, I will tell thee, I am going to announce a lecture on magic."

"O, suicide! Roger, Richard fancieth himself a student of that art, as am I a little, and I credit him. Thou wilt gain nothing of it—and Holy Church forbids it. Well it feared me thou wert setting thyself something foolish."

"All this is to the good," Roger said. "Each of these aspects will appear unto Richard—and he will appear unto me. The day will be Wednesday next. Bruit it about, Thomas; bruit it about."

* * *

The hall was of course more than packed, and there were many there who looked with curiosity at the apparatus on Roger's table—devices without which, by now, he would have looked near naked to his usual students. These last looked with indifference even at the caprice of a candle burning in the middle of the afternoon, knowing well that something would be done with it in due course.

Cornwall was there, with his faction of loyal students. Thus far, however, he had said almost nothing, for Roger had carefully left him few opportunities to object. Though Roger had published abroad the title, *On the nullity of magic and the usefulness of nature,* a paradox designed to start many an amateur metaphysician from his chair, in the main body of his exposition he had steered a middle course: explaining the major assumptions of magic briefly, and without details that a real student of the subject could find in fault; and showing that these were contrary to the teachings of the Church, a proposition to which no one would dare to dissent regardless of what he believed. The Cornwallians were having rather a dull time of it, and so, for that matter, were the students.

Never mind, affairs would become livelier in a moment; for Roger was about to expound the substance of his dream.

He said:

"Thus we dismiss speculative alchemy, since we see that metals cannot be transmuted *per speciem.* Aristotle in the *Meteors* means that only nature can transmute species. Art cannot *secundum speciem, et non negat quod non possit per naturam. In essentia et differentia specifica non potest transmutare,* as Aristotle says in the *De metallis.*

"But there is another alchemy, operative and practical, which teaches now to make the noble metals and colours and many other things better and more abundantly by art than they are made in nature. And science of this kind is greater than all those preceding because it produces greater utilities—not only wealth and many other things for the public welfare, but the discovery of methods for prolonging human life."

Cornwall coughed and subsided. Roger challenged him with a look, and the man bristled. He said:

"Certes a preachment of magic."

"Not so!" This was the beginning. "*Narrabo igitur nunc primo opera artis et naturae miranda, ut postea causas et modum assignem*—in which there is nothing magical, *ut videatur quod omnis magica potestas sit inferior his operibus et indigna.*"

There was a stir as he paused again, and his students grinned at each other: Roger was about to be outrageous again. Cornwall was smiling too, now crouched smugly beside his mousehole.

"Item," Roger said, "*nam instrumenta navigandi possunt fieri ut naves maximae ferantur uno solo homine regente, majori velocitate quam si plenae essent hominibus.*"

He paused yet again, but expected no objection, and got none; there were seafarers in the room who had talked of such things themselves, or dreamed of them; and surely there was nobody present who did not already know something of the lodestone.

"Item: *Currus possunt fieri ut sine animale moveantur cum impetu inestimabili.*"

"A wise man," Cornwall broke in with a snort, "would call such *auto*-*mobile* nothing but dreams."

"Except, perhaps, for the scythe-bearing chariots with which the men of old fought? But perhaps you are right, magister Cornwall. I proceed: Item, *possunt fieri instrumenta volandi ut homo sedeat in medio*—revolving some engine, necessarily, magister Cornwall—*alae artificialiter factae aera verberent modo avis volantis.*"

Cornwall seemed stunned. It was one of Roger's own students who said incredulously, "*Flying* machines, magister Bacon?"

"Flying machines," Roger said. "Item, *possunt fieri instrumentum, parva magnitudine, ad elevanda et deprimenda pondera paene infinita*—"

"O, certes," Cornwall said. "You could move the world with such a lever."

"No, it would not be long enough, magister Cornwall, as is plainly written in Archimedes. But nothing could be more useful in emergencies. By a machine three fingers high and wide, and of less size, a man could free himself of all dangers of prison, for instance. And his friends, if he had any."

There was some laughter, but it was uneasy. Even
Roger's own students, it seemed, did not entirely welcome
the admixture of flyting with true disputation; perhaps
they thought he did not need it. He went on: "*Potest etiam
facile fieri instrumentum quo unus traheret ad se mille
homines contra eorum voluntatem—*"

"I find it," Cornwall said, "rather crowded in this hall
already."

Another ripple of laughter. Flushing helplessly, Roger
ploughed ahead: "—and attract other things in like matter; for instance, thunderbolts."

Now the laughter was at full roar, and plainly at Roger's
expense. Even his own partisans could see that he had lost
his temper.

"I will go on. *Possunt etiam instrumenta fieri ambulandi
in mari vel fluminibus sine periculo*—even to the bottom
without danger, even as Alexander the Great explored the
secrets of the sea."

"According to what authority?"

"Ethicus the astronomer, as is well known," Roger said
with concentrated scorn. "*Haec autem facta sunt
antiquitus et nostris temporibus facta sunt, ut certum est;*
the same is true of the flying machine, though I have not
seen one and know of no man who has—"

"Nor has anyone else."

"—but I know an expert who has thought out the way to
make one."

"Ah, excellent," Cornwall said: "Let him then bring
home the bacon."

The hall skirled with a glee of catcalls. Roger said,
through his teeth: "*Et infinita quasi talia fieri possunt . . .
ut pontes super flumina sine columna . . . et machinationes
et ingenia inaudita—*"

"Belike," Cornwall said. "I hear nothing myself."

"Then I need a louder voice, magister Cornwall," Roger
said harshly. "Let me introduce you to a childhood friend
of mine, Sir Salis Petre. He has a small voice by usual; but
*per igneam coruscationem et combustionem ac per sonorem
horrorem possunt mira fieri, et in distantia qua volumus ut
homo mortalis sibi cavere non posset nec se sustinere.*"

Cornwall laughed, "*Quomodo?*" he demanded.

Roger picked up the tight roll of parchment and touched it to the flame of the candle. As soon as it was smouldering well, he threw it to the floor before the table. The nearest students drew back uneasily, but Cornwall only shrugged his shoulders.

"*Quomodo? Ecce!*"

The scroll exploded like two dozen thunderclaps, blowing out the candle and filling the hall with pungent grey smoke. With howls of panic, the students broke blindly for the door, striking out first with fists, and then with knives, to be first out. Cornwall, however, was closest and was first out by several rods—most fortunately for him, or they would have trampled him. Down the corridors they poured, cloaks flying, their cries echoing:

"Beware of the magician! Beware! Beware! Beware of the magician! Beware! . . . Beware. . . ."

Then Roger was alone, except for a few groaning wounded. Blind with triumph in the black powder-reeking air, he clung to the lectern with both hands, and shouted after them all at the top of his voice,

"TRIPSARECOPSEM!"

No plot in history, it seemed, had ever succeeded so well. From that day forward Oxford was unbearable for Cornwall; in his humiliation, he appealed to Adam Marsh to reverse himself on the matter of the Parisian post. With a sigh—for though he would still have preferred Cornwall to remain at Oxford, he was in truth becoming a little weary of the man—Adam again wrote the provincial minister, and shortly thereafter, Richard Rufus of Cornwall was no more to be seen. Roger and Bungay drank a toast to his departure, and went back to their more serious matters.

That would be, however, the last favour Adam would be able to do for anyone at Oxford, master or student, for his influence had evaporated. Earlier on, he had appointed Thomas of York as regent master, to fill the vacancy left by the death of John of Garland; and Thomas, wholly against the customs, was a man without a degree from the Faculty of Arts. It was recalled that Adam had done something like this before, in the case of Thomas Docking, but

this instance was far more serious. The outcome was a disastrous quarrel with the University.

Effectively, however, he had left Oxford three years before; to Roger the whole dispute, though it was common
gossip, seemed remote and unreal. He was now embarked
upon the composition of a *Metaphysica*, a heavy task to
which he had cheerfully allotted himself five years, allowing for other work to go on at the same time. There was
God's plenty of that, for about the University he was now
famous—or, he thought, perhaps infamous would be a better word. Though cries of "Beware of the magician!" still
sounded in the halls, they became more and more feeble
with the exile of Cornwall, and even while they were at
their loudest he had more students than he could comfortably handle. He was required by the Order, however, to
try.

Some of this weight was lifted within a year, fortunately, by a sudden increase in the popularity of theology
as a subject; for toward the end of 1254 there arrived at Oxford the first copy of the *Introduction to the Eternal Gospel*
of the Franciscan Gerard of San Borgo. Its reputation had
preceded it by months, for in fact the book was creating a
furor throughout Christendom—a fact Roger could well
understand after reading it himself.

The Eternal Gospel of the title was the work of one
Joachim of Flora, a Calabrian visionary who had predicted
that an Age of the Holy Spirit would begin in 1260, ush-
ered in by a new Order of monks headed by Merlin, and
heralded by the dissolution of all disciplinary institutions.
It was Gerard's contention that the Franciscans might become this new Order, provided that they return to the rule
of absolute poverty laid down by their founder.

Roger and Bungay discussed the work through many a
night, as did half of Oxford. To Roger, at least, there
seemed to be reason and justice in much of Gerard's
contentions.

"Including the prophecies, Roger?"

"They will have to wait upon events, of course. Yet the
imminent coming of the Antichrist hath also often been
prophesied; it seemeth me only reasonable that some great
spiritual leader might arise at the same time to combat
him. But thou kenst well that it is not the prophecies that

are creating all this dissension, but the doctrine of renunciation of worldly possessions."

"It hath put weapons into the hands of our enemies, that much is evident," Bungay said thoughtfully. "William of St. Amour in particular, an implacable man. He holds it as evidence against us from our own mouths."

"He will use it eke against the Dominicans if he can," Roger predicted. "Yet still I hold that Gerard's argument hath reason behind it. Consider, I urge thee, how St. Francis himself may look from Heaven upon the vast holdings of property we have accumulated in his name. Indeed, we should thank God that he was excepting Christ the mildest of men, or else we might find ourselves all barefoot in the road at this very moment."

"Many are saying what you say, Roger, yet withal I'd not proclaim it quite so loud. Joachimism is perilous close to becoming proclaimed a heresy; Innocent hath already called a special Council in Anagni to condemn the book—Gerard's, I mean, not the Eternal Gospel itself."

"And Gerard?" Roger said.

"Is in the hands of the Inquisition."

That ended the conversation for that evening. Yet for some months it appeared that Bungay's forebodings had not been fated to be borne out, for in Anagni matters had gone somewhat askew. The proximate cause, apparently, had been that same William of St. Amour, who had rushed to Rome to denounce the orders root and branch, and found a sympathetic ear—or a malleable mind—in Innocent IV. The result, whatever the cause, was a bull, *Etsi animarum,* seriously curtailing the privileges of the orders; not a victory for the Joachimites, but not a rebuff either.

The next act of Innocent IV was to die, to be succeeded by Alexander IV, who promptly repudiated *Etsi animarum,* fanning the flames higher once more. William of St. Amour, frustrated and furious, left Rome as hurriedly as he had entered it—he was a man who did everything in great haste, including thinking—and dispatched over Europe a polemic, *De periculis novissimorum temporum,* in which the orders were depicted as themselves inviting the advent of Antichrist. Gerard of San Borgo remained in his dungeon, the first to reap his own whirlwind.

(*Milord Modena: I send herewith for your kind attention
the book* De erroribus medicorum *which I promised you in
Tivoli. Ad majorem gloria Dei, R. Bacon.*)

There was a diversion: the killing in Lincoln of a boy
named Hugh, widely described as a ritual murder by
Jews—a story which grew as it travelled until the poets
took it up, after which all possibility of learning the truth
disappeared forever. There were miracles, and proposals of
canonization, and Hugh was buried next to Grosseteste in
the hope of speeding the lad's Elevation; but the campaign
to canonize the Capito had itself bogged down. In the
meantime, Hugh's enthusiasts pressed his cause with
Heaven by putting to the torch such houses in various
Jeweryes as seemed worth looting.

The Joachimite furor went on, until it had forced out of
office the very general of the Franciscans himself, John of
Parma, for pronounced Joachimite leanings. His successor
was Bonaventura, a dour and energetic theologian whose
closest friend was the Dominican Albertus Magnus: a
friendship bodying forth the inexorable enmity felt by
both men toward anything which stirred up trouble between the orders, in especial Joachimism with its grandi-
ose claims for the Franciscans as the coming Order of
Merlin.

"I told thee, Roger, politics is no whit less complicated
here than at the Court!"

"Brother, I believed thee then."

But Roger had almost given up following these coils; two
years of them had exhausted his attention for such theological hair-splitting; though he was still troubled by a suspicion that Gerard had been right, and that the mounting
troubles between the orders might well presage the coming of the Antichrist, voicing this opinion won him nothing
but dark intimations that he must be a heretic and a disci-
ple of the Antichrist himself. Bungay had called that tune
rightly enough. Besides, the *Metaphysica* was still far from
finished, and now there was a-borning a work on weights
and measures, the *Reprobationes.* Politicking could go on
without him.

"An alms, an alms for John! An alms for John, who hath
the very begging bowl of Belisarius! Only a penny to touch
the bowl of Belisarius!"

"Hark. What's that? Listen!"

"To what? What is it, Roger?"

"Below—that cry in the street. Listen."

"An alms for John! Only a penny! An alms, an alms for John. . . ."

". . . I hear nothing, Roger. Art well?"

Politicking went on without him, and reached to him. In 1256 Bonaventura voided the appointment of Thomas Docking, despite his new degree, and named a new lector to the Franciscans at Oxford, and regent master to boot. The successor to Adam Marsh's chair, and Grosseteste's before him, was Richard Rufus of Cornwall.

One month later, Bonaventura interdicted Roger's lectures at Oxford for suspected irregularities, namely, Joachimism and magic, and recalled him to Paris.

Cornwall had paid his debt, however belatedly.

Parting once more from Oxford, and now also from Bungay, was bitter; but the sharpest pang, which did not strike until Roger was better than half across the Dover Strait, was also the least expected: to realize only now that in all this time, he had never once visited Ilchester, nor even thought to do so.

The cold winds blew him on regardless.

XI: ST. CATHERINE'S CHAPEL

On the road to London yet another time, yet another wearisome time, Adam Marsh took thought most conscientiously of those high matters which awaited him at the end; but only, as it were, within his intellectual soul, that raven of Elias. If long practice in manoeuvres he abhorred had given him nothing else, it had trained him to reflect simultaneously upon two wholly different sets of circumstances, with the set he loved less relegated to the outermost regions of his mind, where it ticked away like a water-clock without the necessity of paying it much heed: *will, guilt, will, guilt.* . . .

Today, in his sensitive soul, that ticking went endlessly toward reminding him that he was fifty-seven years old. No! Yet it was most certainly correct; his age was always one year less than the last two digits of the year; and this was certainly 1258, and the dregs of it at that. It had been almost two years since Roger Bacon had ruined himself at Oxford with his arrogance, as Adam long ago at Kirkby-Maxloe had greatly feared that he would, and been re-called to Paris . . . and it had been almost ten years, nay eleven, since he had seen Eleanor of Leicester.

For that punishment—for he could not but regard it as such—high matters were at least in part responsible, and could not be kept as far from his heart as his will would bid them stay. It had been eleven years ago that Henry, no doubt with a view to removing from England a continuing well-spring of defiance, had named Simon de Montfort his *locum-tenens* or Seneschal in Gascony, and had kept him there for six years; would indeed have kept him there for-ever had it not been for the stupid zeal of Henry's friends, who stirred the Gascons to so many complaints of cruelty and injustice—plausible enough, if one recalled the Albigensians—that the earl was provoked to come home and demand trial. He had been acquitted, but was still af-fronted and had demanded reparations, thus leading to still another quarrel with his liege which could surely have been avoided had Simon's enemies simply left well enough alone.

Henry knew this; last year he had sent Simon abroad again as one of his ambassadors to France. Beyond doubt there had been other reasons as well, for the reparations had not been the only cause of the broil in 1255. That had also been the year when the King, at the behest of the Pope, had allowed his second son Edmund of Lancaster to claim the Crown of Sicily, with the clear expectation that the realm was to pay for a war of succession on Edmund's behalf over that much-disputed Kingdom; and Simon was scarce in France again before Henry's brother Richard earl of Cornwall—that same earl to whom the King had earlier mortgaged sole right to extort money from the Jews—sued for the Imperial throne, his election bribery again to be paid from English taxes.

Remote, remote—yet painfully close to the heart. Surely

it was but natural in the earl of Leicester to take his lady
wife with him to his estates in Gascony, no man could dispute that. He was not even depriving her of a confessor, for
she still had Adam's brother Robert, now Dean of Lincoln
and a strong clerical partisan of Simon's cause against the
King. Yet that argument cut two ways: for by the same
reasoning could it be called natural to leave her there for
three years more, while he fought at home with the King?
Certes, for all of England was a-shimmer with rebellion,
and a man with a Gascon sanctuary for his lady could not
but count himself fortunate. The fact that, once more back
in England, he was still without Eleanor was amenable to
the same explanation.

There was without doubt a curse upon the land, and that
not only the burden of Henry's and Rome's rapacious
greed; for the harvests this year had been the worst in
memory, and famine was everywhere. Thousands had
starved to death in London alone. No one who loved her
could wish Eleanor anywhere but where she was.

Yet the thorns of guilt steadily poisoned Adam's blood,
and in his soul there whispered constantly another explanation. That voiceless whisper was abetted by additional
circumstances: for though the insurgent barons claimed
St. Robert of Lincoln as their chiefest patron (notwithstanding that the Capito had yet to be canonized),
Simon himself no longer spoke more than perfunctorily to
Grosseteste's only spiritual heir, regardless of opportunity.

Did the earl know? But what was there to know? There
had been no sin committed, nay nor ever would be. But to
this objection there was an inexorable reply in Scripture.
Eleanor was surely guiltless; but this could not be said of
Adam, in his heart nor in Heaven.

He had been tempted eke to think that Heaven had a
little conspired to help him in these outward events, keeping Eleanor in Gascony the while his old age crept toward
him. Too, his services as mediator were still in demand at
court, maugre Simon's absences and his coldness, for the
primate, Boniface of Savoy, made no secret of his admiration for Adam as an expert lawyer and theologian; and the
primate was also a member of Simon's party. Two years
ago Boniface had even tried to win Adam the see of Ely, an

attempt abetted by the King, who perhaps saw in this a way to placate two clerical opponents at once. Doubtless Henry was unaware of the gulf that Adam sensed between himself and Simon; yet even if he had, Henry knew also that Adam confessed his Queen. The see, however, was refused, for the Lateran still remembered Grosseteste with little love, and would not advance his most favoured familiar even at the petition of Rome's most obedient secular prince.

Heaven's help or no, Adam's essay to pluck out his offending eye also had failed.

Simon's return had been stormy beyond all imagining, and though the King had prepared for it, he had not thought far enough ahead. At the April parliament in the Great Hall at Westminster, the barons, at Simon's advice, had arrived in complete armour. They stood as silent as statues while the King's half-brother, William de Valence, denounced the earls of Gloucester and Leicester as the sources of every evil under which England was suffering. Even de Valence's rather shaky denunciation of Simon as "an old traitor and a liar" went by in a silence so complete that Adam had been able to hear clearly the scratch and sputter of old Matthew Paris' goose-quill.

Evidently de Valence had misinterpreted that silence, for his next words to fall upon Adam's incredulous ears had been a demand for more money. After a moment, Simon had wordlessly deferred to Gloucester.

"Nay," earl Bigod said. "More money paid to the Pope, on behalf of the King's son and his Sicilian Crown? Not a mark!"

"It lieth nat with thee to refuse us, my lord Gloucester. An ye be mutinous, we shall send thee reapers and reap thy fields for thee."

"And I will send ye back the heads of your reapers," Bigod said evenly.

The King had entered as he was speaking, and for the first time there was movement: there swept through the statues a threatening clatter of swords. Whatever Henry had anticipated, it had not been this, but he was far quicker to see what was under his nose than his half-brother had been. He said at last:

"Am I then a prisoner?"

"Nay, sire," earl Bigod said, but his voice had been most grim. "But we must have reform."

"Reform, Gloucester?"

"Yes, sire. Know ye that all here are sworn to die, rather than that England be ruined by the Romans."

There had seemed to be no immediate danger of death to the full-armed barons, but the King had been reduced rapidly to a stuttering transport of terror. It had not proven an onerous task to extort from him the appointment of a Council of twenty-four lordships, to meet at Oxford in October and draw up a table of reforms.

That meeting Henry's partisans had promptly dubbed the Mad Parliament, but none them took heed of that to their hurt. One of its earliest acts was to invest Simon, first, with the post of military commander-in-chief for the seigniorial forces, and second, with the custody of the castle of Winchester—whence, to guard against any surprise, the Mad Parliament at once removed itself before completing its table of wrongs to be righted. The table itself was nevertheless titled the Provisions of Oxford, to ensure the preservation of the letters patent under which the twenty-four had begun their labours.

Ere that work was through, Henry's power—or at the very least, his power to make mischief—had been wrenched from his hands; the Mad Parliament had given over the taxing of the realm, and much else, to three committees of its own. Little could have galled Henry more than to assent to such Provisions, but assent he must, albeit they were capped by the boldest insult offered to the Angevin crown since 1215: the demand that he reaffirm, on holy ground, the Great Charter which his father had so unwillingly signed that June 15th at Runnymede.

It was to this high and ominous ceremony that Adam was riding now, in the greyness of his old age and the shadow of his guilt.

It had pleased the Mad Parliament to give Henry his choice of holy ground, and he had chosen a ruin: the Westminster Abbey of Edward the Confessor, which that saint had spent most of his life a-building, and which Henry himself had pulled down in order to erect something even greater to the Confessor's memory. Nothing of the original was left now but Edward's high-raised shrine, and the new minster, though it had already cost a vast sum, was still radically incomplete.

Nevertheless Adam could bring himself to admire it; the King as a patron of the arts was not an inconsiderable man, whatever his other weaknesses, and it was already plain to see that this church—of which Henry was in part also the architect—would be nobly beautiful, could it be finished before the money ran out. In the meantime, the conclave forgathered in St. Catherine's Chapel, one of the few chambers which was whole.

No arms nor armour now, but instead crimson, gold and vair, all new, without so much as a grease-spot: all the chief lords of England, each with a lighted taper in his hand; Henry the King, his face white as milk, the shadows on it deeply cut by the upcasting light of the candle in his own hand, slightly a-tremble; the princes, Edward wearing the dark brow of suppressed mutiny; the bishops, the primate, even the papal legate, Guy de Foulques, Archbishop of Sabina himself; and from somewhere in the darkness the cat-purr of the aged Matthew Paris, *scribble . . . scribble. . . .*

They had already begun when Adam entered, and he was far from the centre of the conclave. Much indeed had changed since he had stood at Grosseteste's elbow in the Great Hall and heard not only the public words but the private consultations. Yet from scraps of murmurs Adam quickly divined where they were at: earl Bigod was reading, in a monotonous, rapid drone-bass, the articles of the Great Charter, and had already reached the twelfth.

"No scutage or aid shall be imposed on our kingdom, unless by the Common Council of the realm . . . and in like manner it shall be done concerning aids from the City of London. . . . The King binds himself to summon the Common Council of the realm respecting the assessing of an aid (except as provided in XII) or a scutage. . . ."

And to each of these Henry the King said, through nearly motionless lips, "We so swear," and signed himself.

". . . to be proportionate to the offence, and imposed according to the oath of honest men in the neighbourhood. No amercement to touch the necessary means of subsistence of a free man, the merchandise of a merchant, or the farming tools of a villein . . . earls and barons to be amerced by their equals. . . ."

"We so swear. . . . We so swear. . . ."

". . . nothing shall be taken or given, for the future, for the Writ of Inquisition of life or limb, but it shall be freely granted, and not denied. . . . No freeman shall be taken or imprisoned or disseised or exiled or in any way destroyed, nor will we go upon him nor will we send upon him except by the lawful judgment of his peers and/or the law of the land. . . . We will sell to no man, we will not deny to any man, either justice or right. . . ."

"We so swear. . . . We so swear. . . ."

". . . reaffirm Article I that the Church of England shall be free, and have her whole rights, and her liberties inviolable. . . ."

The tapers burned lower; the chapel was reeking of sweat and tallow; but at last the earl put aside his parchments.

"We so swear."

The King let the words fall almost in a whisper, and then stood frozen for what seemed a long fall of sand. Then he dashed his taper to the stones, and cried out thinly:

"So go out with smoke and stench the accursed souls of those who break or pervert this Charter!"

By the breathless pause which followed, Adam knew that this oath had not been prescribed by the bishops for this occasion. Then Simon de Montfort's own taper struck the pavement, and the chapel rang with his voice, repeating the words.

The barons followed his lead, in a ragged chorus. Within no longer than it took to say a Paternoster, the chapel was plunged into blackness, choking with wick-fumes . . . and then, it was a-shuffle with men edging cautiously, blindly toward the doorway each remembered as being the nearest.

Adam pressed stumblingly through the slow-milling shapes, making haste slowly lest he jostle someone with hand on dagger, toward where he had last seen earl Simon, guiding himself by the one remaining, distant star of Matthew Paris' candle-flame. It was slow work, against the main current; and by the time he had reached his goal, the smoky chapel was empty of all but himself and the nodding, grinning historian.

Thus, Simon de Montfort's farewell to his confessor; for he was at once to go on an embassy to Scotland. There was naught left Adam Marsh now, *nec spe nec metu*, but his judgment, which was not to be found in this world. In greyness and in shadow, he rode without haste toward Oxford to await it.

XII. THE CONVENT

And this, then, was the first year of the Age of the Holy Spirit! Small cause 1260 had given Roger Bacon for joy; and though what he had been able to learn about the world outside the convent walls was little, he saw small hope for that world either, except it rejoice in the imminence of Antichrist.

Within the convent, each day of this putatively great year dripped away exactly as had each day of the preceding three, worn down under the corrosion of his "corrective discipline"—changing straw; sweeping out cells; carrying slops and night-soil; teaching a few young apprentices to the Order; copying Psalms; dipping candles; washing bottles; mending sandals; and praying for deliverance. He could look forward now to naught else.

In the dragging-past of these lifetimes of days, but little study was possible, and less work; yet for a while he had refused to be defeated. The *Reprobationes* was finished; and an introduction to a new subject, *De laudibus mathematicae,* and even the work itself, a *Communia mathematica,* although only in first recension. But nothing was so time-consuming as computation; and in especial one needed tables, which he had neither the leisure to search out nor the money to buy.

The money was gone, all gone, leaving behind only a sort of lightness in the head, as that of a man but recently delivered of a fever; or, more to the purpose, of a man in the

aftermath of far too much wine, miserable in the knowledge that the only cure is more, and that not to be had.

Nor was there any help for him from his brothers and superiors. In Oxford he had been at the least a resident master; here, he was nothing. Early on, he had proposed to
them that for the fame of the convent, in Paris where
scholarship was everything, he should write for them a
summary of everything that he had read or found in the
natural sciences from the beginning, a *Communia
naturalium*, to be published on to the shelves of the University; surely a better use for a scholar than setting him
to changing beds. He had shown them the preface for such
a work; they had laughed at it. He did not speak to them
now unless spoken to, and that was seldom.

A few threads to the outside still were allowed him.
Eugene wrote to him: outraged at still another prohibition
of Aristotle at Toulouse, the younger brother had at last
come home to Ilchester and taken up the galling burden of
the damaged estate—a victory for Robert which Roger seldom cared to think about. Belatedly, because he had been
so long out of England, Eugene had discovered the great-
ness of Grosseteste, and was buying copies of his works as
he could. Unable to share in the problems of the estate,
Roger could at least feel with Eugene the poignancy of the
murder of the younger man's studies, and wrote for him a
summary of the Capito's teachings on time and motion,
with a commentary; Eugene drank it down like water in a
desert and prayed urgently for more, but from the fastness
of the convent there was little more to give.

Too, there were letters from Bungay, who had left Oxford in disgust at Roger's exile and returned to his post as
the vicar of the provincial minister. But they were seldom
heartening:

I must tell thee that the turmoil is in no wise lessened
and that most of what was gained in St. Catherine's chapel
hath since been lost, an I understand it aright. No sooner
did earl Simon return from his embassy to Scotland than
the King charged him with fixing the particulars of the
peace with France, a matter which kept him away most of
this year; and in the meantime the "bachelors," as they
now call those knights and gentry created out of incomes of

fifteen pounds a year, those that were formerly contented
to be no more than coroners and jurymen, have had a Mad
Parliament of their own. Now they demand that the barons concede to them as vassals and tenants those same
privileges wrung by the baronage from the supreme landlord the King, and being rebuffed, do repair increasingly to
the royal above the seigniorial justice. In this matter earl
Bigod appeareth helpless, referring to it as a disturbance
in the commonalty, which is in no wise the case, but
serveth all the same to drive many a weaker baron to the
King also, in hope of better arms against this mythical in-
surgency. This division Prince Edward hath been quick to
exploit, and it feareth me that earl Simon's return from
France hath not been speedy enough to compose it. Thou
wilt recall how at the birth of Edward our Henry was so
eager to receive gifts of congratulation that it was said at
the Court, *Heaven gives us this child, but the King sells
him to us:* I fear that we shall suffer much more at the
hands of this prince before we suffer less. Remind thyself
however how much of what I say needs must be rumour;
for that chatterer Matthew Paris the King's historian is
dead, and his thousands of leaves of gossip are shut up by
the monk's of St. Alban's; and this year hath died also the
most Christian and most noble Adam Marsh, the last of
our Order who might have known the truth.—*Thos.*

Here indeed was cause for sorrow, and for despair. Who
now was left to him but Eugene, and Bungay? There still
existed the small circle of the Peregrine College, but he
had been able to visit that only the once since his exile, and
had found all there strangers to him but Peter de
Maricourt himself. Moreover, it was dangeous to keep
such arcane company, never for Roger more so than now.

He moved about through his galling chores in a mist of
lassitude and weariness. The days went by. Were it not for
the frequent Holy Days, he would have lost all track of
them. Listlessly, he recast his notes from his lecture-battle
with Richard of Cornwall into a small volume, but even
the panoplies of that demonic vision had lost all power to
move him now; the words came as slowly from the clotting
quilltip as those of a neophyte, and the temptation to write
"Finis" at the bottom of each new page was almost irre-

sistible. In the end, he dispatched it as a letter to Eugene, who was baffled by it, particularly by the passage on black-powder, which Roger in a moment of prudence had partially re-encyphered.

It was well that he had not published it. But a month after, there was read forth to the brothers of the convent at early Mass, by order of Bonaventura, the new Constitutions of the Chapter of Narbonne:

"Let no one glory in the possession of virtue in his heart if he puts no guard on his conversation. If anyone thinks that he is religious and does not curb his tongue, but only allows his heart to lead him astray, then his religion is vain. It is therefore necessary that an honourable fence should surround the mouth and other senses and acts, deeds and morals, that the statutes of the regulars may not be destroyed by perfect men, but kept intact, lest they should be bitten by a snake when they let down the barrier. . . .

"Let the brothers carry nothing in words or in writing which could conduce to the scandal of anyone. . . .

"Let no brother go to the court of the Lord Pope, or send a brother, without the permission of the Minister-General. Let them, if they have gone otherwise, be at once expelled from the Curia by the procurators of the Order. And let no one apply to the Minister-General for permission unless serious cause or urgent necessity demand it.

"We prohibit any new writing from being published outside the Order, unless it shall first have been examined carefully by the Minister-General or Provincial, and the visitants in the provincial chapter. . . . Anyone who contravenes this shall be kept at least three days on bread and water, and lose his writing. . . .

"Let no brother write books, or cause them to be written for sale, and let the Provincial Minister not dare to have or keep any books without the licence of the Minister-General, or let any brothers have or keep them without the permission of the provincial ministers. . . .

"We lay under a perpetual curse anyone who presumes either by word or by deed in any way to work for the division of our Order. If anyone contravenes this prohibition, he shall be considered as an excommunicate and schismatic and destroyer of our Order . . . brothers incorrigible in this shall be imprisoned or expelled from the Order. . . .

"If anyone think that the penalty for the breach of statutes of this kind is severe, let him reflect that, according to
the Apostle, all discipline in the present life is not a matter
for rejoicing, but for sorrow; yet through it, it will bear for
the future the most peaceful fruit of justice for those who
have endured it."

It was an immense document, the proclamation of which
consumed most of the morning, but the sense of these ru-
brics was all too clear: for the defence of the orders against
the seculars, and the defence of the Order against itself,
the Minister-General had instituted a censorship.

His friends dead, or beyond his reach; himself forbidden
to publish; the vision a vapour. Wherein lay the usefulness
of labour, if nothing was to come of it? Wherein the beauty,
where there were none to see it? Why write at all, if there
were to be none to read? He prayed for guidance; but the
silence flowed on, unresponsive.

Another year. Silence, and apathy.

And then, abruptly, he was awake; it was as though he
had been plunged into icy water. The convent had a
visitor—not in itself unusual, nor that Roger should know
the man, albeit but slightly. His name was Raymond of
Laon, but it was what he was that mattered: he was a clerk
in the suite of Guy de Foulques.

A friend alive—never mind how remote a friend—and a
Cardinal! There was help here, could he but engineer it;
why had he not thought of this expedient before?

Moreover, it required scarcely any engineering, for
Raymond himself asked to see Roger, and permission was
granted.

"The Cardinal charged me to make certain of your
whereabouts, Master Roger," Raymond said nervously.
Obviously he had been warned that the case confronting
him now had been one of peculiar fractiousness, and still
full of potentialities for schism.

"Make him aware, I beg of you, Raymond. There was a
time when he spoke with interest of my studies in the sciences, and asked for writings. Tell him I would make him a
book of these, were it not for the decrees of Narbonne."

"He has no power to exempt anyone from those,"

Raymond objected. "True that he's a Cardinal, but also a secular; durst not interfere with the rules of the Orders."

"Of course; but surely he might relieve me of my burdens in some way?-As matters stand today, I am forbidden to keep books, let alone write them—I have preserved all my manuscripts only by keeping them circulating among certain friends here in Paris, and even this may be 'publication' within the meaning of the sixth rubric of the Narbonne Constitutions."

Raymond was thoughtful. "I will tell him what you say," he declared at last. "I know of no prohibition against it, though belike he may. And the very worst he can say in reply, to me or thee, is, No."

"God bless you, Raymond. I shall pray for you all my days."

The dirt flew under Roger's besom that afternoon, albeit he was otherwise careful to show the brothers no elation after the interview; neither, however, did he satisfy their curiosity—seen solely in their glances, for they would have scorned to speak it—as to the business of a Cardinal's household with an inconsequential friar under corrective discipline. Nor did he reveal the secret elsewhere as yet, so that Eugene must have been baffled all over again to receive of a sudden this from his exiled brother:

Man, in so far as he is man, has two things, bodily strength and virtues, and in these he can be forced in many things; but he has also strength and virtues of soul, that is, of the intellectual soul. In these he can be neither led nor forced, but only hindered. And so, if a thousand times he is cast into prison, never can he go against his will unless the will succumbs.

But there was much preparation to be done while Guy's reply was awaited; and this Roger prosecuted with a cunning which surprised even himself. It could not be concealed that he was suddenly and furiously writing again—in fact his best pupil Joannes, a brilliant thirteen-year-old who worshipped his Master, was under orders to report such an event at once—but to the expected prompt question Roger was able to proffer nothing more incendiary than a set of fearsomely complex tables of numbers.

"To what purpose?"

"These are notes toward a better calendar, Father. Doth
it not seem ridiculous that with the one we have, we cannot even say with certainty what is the veritable date of
Easter? That can hardly be pleasing to Our Lord, that we
must celebrate His resurrection on the wrong day, more
often than not."

This was unexceptionable; in due course the censors,
though uncertain whether to be suspicious or to rejoice in
the reclamation of an erring brother, even allowed *De
termine Paschali* to be copied and published. By that time,
Roger was deep into the composition of a *Computus,* which
on early inspection by the brothers proved to be even more
technical—so much so, as Roger had foreseen, that nobody
else in the convent but young Joannes could have even a
hope of understanding it.

Thereafter, when they saw him drawing geometrical diagrams, the brothers avoided asking questions which
might prove embarrassing to themselves. Thus they also
successfully avoided discovering that these were not part
of the incomplete *Computus* at all, but instead were the
visible signs of a process destined to reduce the very Ark of
the Covenant to naught more than the passage of sunlight
through raindrops.

In all this, young Joannes was a willing conspirator. He
was a black-haired, hollow-eyed youngster, painfully thin
and awkward, of no known family—a charge of the
Church. He was eager and quick, despite his talent for
knocking things over when he was excited, and was filled
with delight at being made privy to the secret. He was
even more delighted to realize that he and he alone, of all
the learned minds in the convent, was capable of following
the racing of his Master's thought; and in sober truth, at
Roger's hands he already knew more of the laws of optics
than had the great Grosseteste himself, as Grosseteste had
known more than Alhazen.

Even Joannes, however, despite the most careful and
elaborate instruction, was left gasping at the next leap,
which went soaring directly from the propagation of vision
into the propagation of force:

Every efficient cause acts by its own force which it produces on the matter subject to it, as the light of the sun produces its own action in the air, and this action is light diffused through the whole world from the solar light. This force is called likeness, image, species and by many other names, and it is produced by substance as well as accident and by spiritual substance as well as corporeal. Substance is more productive of it than accident, and spiritual substance than corporeal. This force produces every action in this world, for it acts on sense, intellect and all the matter in the world for the production of things, because one and the same thing is done by a natural agent on whatsoever it acts, because it has no freedom of choice; and therefore it performs the same act on whatever it meets. . . . Forces of this kind, belonging to agents, produce every action in this world. But there are two things now to be noted respecting these forces; one is the propagation itself of the action and of force from the place of its production; and the other is the varied action in this world due to the production and destruction of things. The second cannot be known without the first. Therefore it is necessary that the propagation itself be first described.

. . . But when they say that force has a spiritual existence in the medium, this use of the word "spiritual" is not in accordance with its proper and primary meaning, from "spirit" as we say that God and angel and soul are spiritual things; because it is plain that the forces of corporeal things are not thus spiritual. Therefore of necessity they will have a corporeal existence, because body and soul are opposed without an intermediate. And if they have a corporeal existence, they also have a material one, and therefore they must obey the laws of material and corporeal things, and therefore they must mix when they are contrary, and become one when they are of the same category of forces. And this is again apparent, since force is the product of a corporeal thing, and not of a spiritual; therefore it will have a corporeal existence. Likewise it is in a corporeal and material medium, and everything that is received in another is modified by the condition of the recipient. . . . When, therefore, Aristotle and Averroes say that force has a spiritual existence in the medium and in the senses, it is evident that "spiritual" is not taken from "spirit" nor is the word used in its proper sense. Therefore it is used equivocally and improperly, for it is taken in the sense of "inperceptible"; since everything really spiritual . . . is imperceptible and does not affect the senses, we therefore convert the terms and call that which is imperceptible spiritual. But this is homonymous and outside the true and proper meaning of a spiritual thing. . . . Moreover, it produces a corporeal result, as, for example, the action of heat warms bodies and dries them out, and causes them to putrefy, and the same is true of other forces. Therefore, since this produces heat, properly speaking, and through the medium of heat produces other results, force must be a corporeal thing, because a spiritual thing does not cause a corporeal action. And in particular there is the additional reason that the force is of the same essence as the complete effect of the producer, and it becomes that when the producer affects strongly the thing acted upon.

. . . Since, therefore, the action of a corporeal thing has a really corporeal existence in a medium, and is a real corporeal thing, as was previously shown, it must of necessity be dimensional, and therefore fitted to the dimensions of the medium. . . . If, therefore, the propagation of light is instantaneous, and not in time, there will be an instant without time; because time does not exist without motion. But it is impossible that there should be an instant without time, just as there cannot be a point without a line. It remains, then, that light is propagated in time, and likewise all forces of a visible thing and of vision. . . .

The poor youngster was not to be censured for his incomprehension; for Roger, as he himself well knew, was reinventing physics, an endeavour in which he had had no predecessors since Aristotle himself. The existence of this seminal document, like that of the *Perspectiva*, was hidden with Joannes' aid as runner by putting it into circulation in the Peregrine College, which now as before did not care to reveal its own existence, let alone what it was reading. Peter, Joannes reported, said of it only:

"Were this from any other hand, I would have called it gibberish."

No matter; as an experimenter first and foremost, Peter could not be expected to have much knowledge of or pa-

tience with the ancient problem of the multiplication of
species—as Aristotle and the Arabs had called the propagation of action; and besides, the work would in the end be
only a part of that *Communia naturalium* the proposal of
which the convent brothers had so scorned. Its comprehension could likewise wait; for the ignorance of the times
there were sufficient causes—not alone the coming of Antichrist foreshadowed in the strife of which Bungay wrote
anxiously:

Civil war hath broken out anew, and no man may say
from one day to the next how he views his expectations.
Henry the King hath repudiated the Provisions of Oxford,
and the barons, led by earl Simon, have taken to the field.
Of late they have made several victories in the West and
South, and have taken London with the greatest fanfare of
welcome from the stinking populace. Yet methinks our
Henry is but temporarily cowed, for it is most clear that
Leicester's support is still much divided. Give thanks to
God that thou art where thou art.

—but, also, as Roger saw upon one false dawn among
many, the whole failure of any scholar in history to divine
how knowledge (it mattered not what knowledge) might be
made trustworthy.

Since the days of revelation, in fact, the same four cor-
rupting errors had been made over and over again: submission to faulty and unworthy authority; submission to what
it was customary to believe; submission to the prejudices of
the mob; and worst of all, concealment of ignorance by a
false show of unheld knowledge, for no better reason than
pride.

"I had better get this out of the house right
away," Joannes said, when he had caught his breath.

"Memorize it first, while the ink dries. If the College
loses it, we will need to write it again."

"I don't even want to think of it again, Master. Uhm . . .
it lacks a title."

"So it does," Roger said. "Very well. Write at the top, *De
signis et causis ignorantiae modernae.* . . . It is dry? Then,
run."

Joannes ran like a deer; but no industry of his could take

that explosive doctrine away. Within a week, Roger was
writing it again: the *scientia experimentalis*, that knowledge from experience of which even Ptolemy had spoken
and henceforth had ignored, had found its method and its
sieve, by the mercy of God, the negative fervour of
Socrates, and the voiceless, pervasive whisper of Roger
Bacon's imprisoned demon Self.

Thereafter, he was ready to go back to the *Computus*;
but he was interrupted by Joannes, in a transport of excitement. After two whole years and more, the letter from Guy
de Foulques had arrived.

It was on first reading all that Roger could possibly have
wished it to be: a mandate from Guy de Foulques,
Cardinal-Bishop of Sabina and papal legate in England, to
send him forthwith, and notwithstanding any prohibitions
to the contrary of Roger's Order, the *scriptum principale*
which Roger had offered on the natural sciences. But
Roger's elation was short-lived; for on the very next reading of the letter, it became apparent that something had
gone seriously awry.

Only to begin with, this prince required that there be
sent to him forthwith the long-promised synthesis of
knowledge, of the completion of which, after so many
years, he was delighted to hear—but there was no such
book, nor indeed more than the shadow of one. How had
this happened? Roger could but speculate; yet it seemed to
him that the fault must lie with Raymond of Laon, or in
the caution which had led Roger to send Guy only a verbal
entreaty. Perhaps Raymond had taken Roger's reference
to those manuscripts in the hands of the Peregrine circle to
be chapters of some large work and had so informed the
Cardinal; whereas they were of course only isolated
opusculi, now on this science and now on that, and some
not formal works at all, but only letters. Of those two
major works with which Roger had meant all along to
crown his life, the *Communia naturalium* and a *Summa
salvationis per scientiam*, only the first existed, as a few
scraps; the second he had not even begun to think about.

Moreover, the charge that Roger was to send this work
notwithstanding any prohibitions of his order to the contrary was followed by the stunning words, "in secret."

Guy's letter provided no way around even the most minor of the prohibitions of Narbonne; nor even any direction to Roger's superiors at the convent for the easement of his menial duties; on the contrary, Roger was specifically forbidden to speak at all to the brothers of the very existence of the mandate.

Furthermore, the Cardinal-Bishop of Sabina and papal legate in England had sent no money. Perhaps, out of older memories of England, he had thought that a scholar-son of Christopher Bacon of Yeo Manse would hardly be in need of it.

Yet withal, this was the mandate that Roger had sought; and, being a mandate, that he must obey.

The absolute overriding need was money—first of all for books, particularly the *De ira* and *Ad Helviam* of Seneca which Piccolomini had shown him at Tivoli, and Cicero's *De republica*. Also he was still lacking essential astronomical and mathematical tables. All these he could probably set one or another of the students in the Peregrine circle to searching out, but he would have to stand ready to pay for them. It would be useful to have an astrolabe, too, and a new set of magnifying glasses—most of his present ones were badly chipped.

And the greatest expenditure inevitably would be for the writing of the book itself. His usual failure to be satisfied with any manuscript until he had revised it four or five times consumed huge amounts of parchment, but there was no help for that; indeed for this labour he must be more scrupulous than ever before. The MS. completed, there would then be the copyists to pay, since the injunction to secrecy and the censorship alike would make it impossible to have the work copied inside the convent.

There was no one to turn to but Eugene, harassed though the boy already was. The only deference Roger could show toward his younger brother's burden was to ask for the smallest possible sum compatible with the work to be done; after some calculation, Roger fixed that, not without misgivings, at one hundred pounds. He took no pleasure in the writing of that letter.

That much passed over, the next question was, what kind of a work should it be? There was only one possible answer, grim though it was: nothing less would be suitable

for Guy than the *Communia naturalium* itself. Finishing
that under the restrictions and distractions of this confinement, he realized glumly, would probably take five years.

The sooner begun, the sooner ended; and there were, he
realized, certain expedients that might shorten the labour.
As a second move, he dispatched Joannes to recover everything that was in the keeping of the Peregrine College.
Much of it, he hoped, might go almost verbatim into the
final document, thus sparing him the recomposition of
many whole chapters.

While he waited, he proceeded with the *Computus,* con-
spicuously strewing its pages about his cell. Its value as a
mask was now even greater; and besides, it too could go
into the final document when it was completed—which, in
view of its complexity, might take almost as long as the
Communia itself. Well, durability is a virtue in a mask.

Slowly, the scattered manuscripts came back. He was
astonished at their bulk; this was the first time he had
seen them *en masse;* there were no less than eight books
here, all but two begun since his exile, all but one completed since then. That one, the *Metaphysica,* was not suitable for the major task; in fact, reading it now, ten years
after its inception, he was strongly tempted to destroy it;
but the others would almost surely fall into place as he
proceeded.

Only then did he become aware that, despite the impres-
sive mass of leaves now stored in his chest, there were at
least four smaller works missing. The *De secretis operibus
naturae* and the letter on time and motion could doubtless
be recovered from Eugene, but that still left the alchemical
summary, which had cost him so much in apparatus in noble metals and in rare drugs, and the book on astronomy.
Repeated inquiries by Joannes produced no results; somehow, the College had indeed lost them.

That had, certes, always been a part of the risk; and
since the *Summa alchemica* had been published, it might
be possible to have it copied from the shelves at Oxford;
but for the astronomical work there was no recourse but to
write it all over again when the appropriate point in the
Communia was reached. Now unquestionably he would
have to have that astrolabe, and an armillary sphere, and
starcharts . . . more expenditures to contemplate.

"How long is it since you've been outside of nights, Master?"

"Eh? Truly, I don't know. Perhaps months. Two months, at the least, I believe."

"Then you haven't see the comet. It's a monster—covers almost half the sky. You've never seen anything like it."

"*You* have never seen anything like it." Roger corrected him, remembeing with a chill the cold glare in the Dragon of his first Paris days, an incredible twenty years ago. Naytheless, he took himself outside to look at it, and found that Joannes had been right: this one was much greater. Such an apparition could not have been vouchsafed for any mean mischance, but Roger could not spare the hours needed to riddle out its astrological import; if the thing had, as it appeared, been generated under the influence of Mars, its portent was bloody; but he contented himself with thinking, uneasily, that a disaster requiring so terrific a prognostick would be unlikely to have much bearing on his personal problems.

And perhaps it did not; for what astrologer could say with confidence that the ill foretold might not be some plague or war far in the East, of which the Latins would never hear? Yet for Roger the word he heard was disastrous enough. Bungay wrote:

Earl Simon hath been excommunicated by the papal Curia, but it doth not appear to have depressed his secular fortunes overmuch. He hath behind him the reformers among the barons; many of the knights and gentry; all of Oxford, eke including the students; and much of the commonalty, to which the Dominicans are appealing on behalf of the poor, with the preachment that Pope and King is an unnatural marriage. There hath been a pitched battle on the heights above Lewes in Sussex—scarce twenty miles west of where Hastings was fought under another such comet—and with an equally strange outcome. Earl Simon's forces appeared on the field at the head of some fifteen thousands of citizens of London, marching to the tunc,

Nam rex omnis regitur legibus quas legit
Rex Saul repellatur, quia leges fregit.
* * *

On May fourteenth they joined, and Prince Edward was
lured into breaking and chasing the rabble, while earl Simon and the barons devoted themselves to smashing
the main body of the King's army like a nut beneath a
hammer. Both Henry and Edward are prisoners, and
Simon hath gone to London, where on St. John's Day
he summoned a parliament and proclaimed his purpose
to draw a new constitution. I know no more this day,
dear brother, and for fear of interception offer thee no comment, but only this story as I have it, I think, reliably.
—*Thos.*

And on the same ship, apparently, had travelled the reply from Ilchester:

Alas Roger I can be of no help to thee and may never see
so much money as 100 pounds again. This our South is
overrun with rebels and Yeo Manse having once been held
by de Burgh was ruled to be King's land and taken from
us; with what little I myself was allowed to keep have had
to ransom myself, and may yet be in such a toil again. Our
brother Robert is reported slain, having taken the field
with the Londoners at Lewes all unaware that his own side
was doing this ill work at home; and so are the fortunes of
the Bacon name and family at an end. Pray for me, as I for
thee.—*E.*

All this news was nearly a year old, but it was final
enough; it contained no cause for hope that any later word
would be better. For this conclusion came verification at
first hand from Sir William Bonecor, a knightly neighbour
and friend of Christopher Bacon.

"Eugene hath told me how to find thee," he said in English, a language Roger had not heard spoken in a decade;
"and as I am carrying letters from Henry to the new Pope,
I paused to see thee. But 'tis true, what thy brother writ
thee: the Manse is bankrupt. Of Robert there is no certain
word, but belike he's dead; Edward's slaughter of the Londoners was fearsome, and many died of panic."

"God rest Robert, alive or dead," Roger said dully. "But
Sir William, what's this of the King? Wast not taken prisoner last May?"

"Aye, but not for long. It happened early this year, after earl Simon's second parliament—a vast muddle of boots, and bare feet, including not only the barons, but two citizens from each city, two townsmen from each borough, two knights from each county, and two witches from each coven for all I ken. But it was scarce concluded ere Prince Edward escaped and put himself at the head of a royalist army; and King's man though I be myself, little to the credit of the barons is it that so many then defected from Leicester, who had given them naught but devotion. He was returning from the field in the west, marching to join his son at Kenilworth and thence home, when he was surprised two days after Lammas by Edward at Evesham; and comported himself most knightly, as the tale runs; sent his barber to the top of a church tower to read the 'scutcheons as they forgathered below, and noted down his rude descriptions of these blazons and assigned them names, till 'twas plain that even Gloucester and Roger Mortimer had gone over to the King; whereupon went out among his army and quoth, 'Commend your souls to God, my beloved; for our bodies are the foe's.' For nigh half the afternoon the battle was in doubt, but in the end 'twas the King's, and earl Simon slain."

And yet another death of the most beautiful and noble. It no longer bore thinking about.

"God grant that will be the end of all this strife. Tell me, an thou canst, what manner of man is this Clement the Fourth? Here we've heard naught but the bare word of his election."

"Why, Roger, thou know'st him as well as I, it seemeth me. Clement is he that was our jolly-solemn legate, Guy de Foulques—or Foulquois, as the Frenchmen call him."

Roger could not find a word to say. The white-haired knight nodded sympathetically.

"Strange, is it not? Never did I dream he had the makings of a Pope; indeed I thought his Cardinal's hat sat ne so up-and-down as was seemly. But 'tis His will."

"Sir William," Roger said with all the intensity he could muster; "wilt thou do the Bacons, who owe thee so much already, one last service?"

"Why, certes, am I able. How wild thine aspect, Roger!"

"Your pardon, but it means much to me, much perhaps

to us all. I must write a letter to this Pope, at once. Wilt
carry it for me?"

"An it's nat too wearisome long in the writing. I must
leave within the week."

"I'll give it thee tomorrow, promptly after lauds. And
charge thee too with a verbal message, an I may; that will
be brief."

The old man smiled. "Lay on, boy, and I'll be thy post."

XIII: THE BOWL OF BELISARIUS

Never was there a more delicate task of composition than
the making of that letter. What was to be gained was enormous: freedom from the censorship; freedom from his
chores; freedom from money; perhaps even freedom itself,
pure, unqualified and complete. Yet there stood in the way
his failure to reply to the first mandate, now a good two
years old; this would have to be explained, yet not at such
length as to appear that he was seeking redress of a grievance. It would be best simply to touch upon the difficulties
of writing anything at all inside the convent; to suggest
that there existed remedies for the evils—all the evils—be-
setting the Latin Church; and to leave the matter of money
for Sir William to broach *viva voce*, should the Pope show
interest in these propositions.

After the letter, he was left with naught to do but to continue with the *Communia:* but this went badly. In part, he
was beginning to realize reluctantly, the difficulty lay in
his own limitations, in that he was now attempting to deal
with a science of which he had had no personal experience.
The attempt to apply the sieve of the causes of error to the
writings of other men sometimes left him with no statement that he trusted, and at others with an account of the
subject so confused as to be unworthy of its valuable
parchment.

In addition, the daily difficulties were mounting once

more. No matter that he stood under no accusation, and that the work he was doing was officially understood to be blameless; the disguise was wearing thin; these comings and goings of minor eminences inevitably aroused the suspicions of the brothers once more, and coupled with Roger's visible industry, convinced them that something was afoot. They did not need to know what it was to conclude that Roger had best be hindered in its prosecution.

Nothing, overtly, was changed, but his chores were enforced with great strictness, and Joannes was expressly forbidden to go outside the convent walls without permission from above—a permission Roger knew better than to ask. In the *longueurs* of scrubbing and sweeping, and in the hours of despair over the blotted, scratched-out, interlined and cut-apart leaves of the *Communia*, there was ample time to reflect upon the temerity of what he had done, and on the magnificent unlikelihood of its coming to any good end, or indeed to any outcome at all.

This cloud grew month by month—irrationally, for well Roger knew that two years might pass before a busy Pope might reply to a letter of no official urgency—no matter how urgently the writer had put his case—and the reply could find its way from Rome to Paris. By spring he had convinced himself that Clement, had he read the letter at all, had called to mind Roger's failure to respond to his first mandate—which, after all, had also been solicited—and had dismissed the matter out of hand.

And indeed the reply was very late; it arrived on the Feast of St Ursula and Her Companions, and was dated June; had at the best spent a long summer among the avalanches:

Dilecto filio, Fratri Rogerio dicto Bacon, Ordinis Fratrum Minorum.
Tuae devotionis litteras gratantes recepimus: sed at verba notarimus diligenter quae ad explanationem earum dilectus filius G. dictus Bonecor, Miles, viva voce nobis proposuit, tam fideliter quam prudenter.

Sane et medius nobis liqueat quid intendas, volumus, et tibi per Apostolica scripta praecipiendo mandamus, quatenus, non obstante praecepto praelati cujuscunque contrario, vel tui Ordinis constitutione quacunque, opus

illud, quod te dilecto filio Raymundo de Laonuno
communicare rogarimus in minore officio constituti,
scriptum de bona littera nobis mittere quam citissime
poteris quae tibi videntur adhibenda remedia circa illa,
quae nuper occasione tanti discriminis intimasti: et hoc
quanto secretius poteris facias indilate.

Datum Viterbii, x. Cal. Julii, anno II.

CLEMENT IV.

DEO GRATIAS. AMEN. AMEN. AMEN.

Oh, Deo gratias, amen! His day was come: Friar Bacon,
the obscure, the rebellious, the exiled, the scorned and despised, had indeed become that Magister Roger of whom he
had dreamed before he had ever left home: Magister
Roger, whose works were writ for Popes!

He studied the miraculous document long and long, not
only for the fiercely solemn delight with which it filled
him, but also because he was determined, equally fiercely,
that it should be put to the best possible use. It was enough
like the first mandate—indeed, some of their phrases were
identical—to contain many of the same traps. Clement had
not only remembered the first mandate, as was clear, but
had come very close to repeating it. There was the same requirement that Roger's writings be sent to him "in good
letters," which of course meant that copyists would be required; the same requirement that the work be sent regardless of any provisions to the contrary in the constitutions of the Order; the same corollary failure to include
any instructions to the brothers for the mitigation of
Roger's menial duties; and above all, the same injunction
that all this be done in secret. Furthermore, there was
again no money—either Sir William Bonecor had failed to
carry that part of the message, or he had not put the case
strongly enough.

What, then, was he to do? On the face of it, a mandate
from the spiritual emperor of all Christendom should be
the most powerful of instruments; yet in point of fact, it
seemed to leave him very much where he had been before.
He could still proceed no further without making a thorough, indeed a drastic attempt to raise money; for this he
needed time, and the whole purpose of corrective disci-

pline, no matter who was corrected, was to fill up time which might otherwise be used for thinking or some other mischief.

Roger sloshed his mop thoughtfully into a corner. It had not occurred to him until now, but under circumstances of this kind the injunction to secrecy would be impossible to fulfil, no matter how faithfully he himself obeyed it. The use of outside copyists would defeat it. If they did not pirate the work itself as it passed through their hands—the usual practice in a university town if the work in question appeared to be of some substance, likely sooner or later to be saleable to students—one or another of the scribes, sooner or later, would be sure to whisper to Roger's superiors the work which would undo his triumph, branch and root. Then he would have no choice but to show the brothers his letter from the Pope, and secrecy of any sort would be at an end.

But there were, to be sure, different kinds and degrees of secrecy; and it might be possible, by forfeiting the lesser, to preserve the greater. The question was: since secrecy *in toto* was impossible, what aspect of it would be the greater in Clement's eyes? To answer that, one would have to know why Guy had enjoined it in the first place, and not even a hint of such a reason appeared in either this or the earlier mandate. It would have to be a reason which would be as compelling to Pope Clement IV as it had been to the Cardinal-Bishop of Sabina, a reason which did not change and might indeed loom even larger with the donning of the Tiara.

One such which might have bulked large to a Cardinal, a reluctance to interfere with the internal discipline of the Orders, could hardly crouch so obstinately in the way of a Pope, on whose sufferance both Orders—both founded within the lifetimes of living men—depended for their existence. Yet young though they were, and corrupt though they were even in their youth, the Orders had proven their value to Christendom, and no Pope could now want to see them disrupted, let alone dissolved; so it might well be assumed that Clement, like his predecessors, would wish to avoid any move which might promote dissension between them—such as permitting an errant Franciscan to publish in despite of the direct prohibition of his Minister General;

and publish, furthermore an extensive work in the natural
sciences which the Dominicans were forbidden to study at
all.

In so far as Roger could determine, the reasoning was
sound, but the conjecture upon which it ultimately stood
was a shaky one indeed upon which to build in addition a
course of action. Nevertheless, he had no better foundation; and its consequences were that, first, what Clement
would most desire would be the concealment of the nature
and content of the work, not only from the world, but from
the Franciscans themselves; and, second, that in defence of
this the larger secrecy, the smaller secret of the existence
of the mandate might in middling-good conscience be sac-
rificed. Were the conjecture to be true, then it would follow
that while the first mandate—from the Cardinal—might or
might not specifically identify the work to be prepared as
dealing with the natural sciences (as in fact, of course, it
did), the second—from the Pope—would not; and this indeed was one of the major differences between these otherwise so similiar documents. The logician in Roger shuddered at the prospect of launching into these unknowable
seas aboard the keelless, sailless, rudderless fallacy of af-
firming the consequent; but the self whispered, *What
choice?* And answered, *None, none.*

He sought out the Father Superior, and showed him the
letter. The consternation it produced was gratifying, but
dangerous as well; to the demand that Roger surrender it
for an examination in council and by the provincial minister, Roger refused on the grounds that it was addressed to
him and was his property, which was inarguable except
on the rarefied theological ground that as a Franciscan
he had no property—an argument too tainted with
Joachimism to be usable here. After three days the provincial minister was called in, to see whether by the plea to
the Pope on Roger's part of which Clement's letter plainly
gave evidence, Roger had transgressed the fifth rubric of
the Constitutions of Narbonne, which forbade any Franciscan to approach the Pontiff without many specific permis-
sions; but the mandate, whose authenticity could hardly
be doubted, was a white-hot iron to be thrust into the
placid, indeed stagnant waters of a Parisian convent of no
other account, and the charge was dismissed on the techni-

cality that the text of Clement betrayed no intention on Roger's part to pass over his superiors to the Holy Father simply to prosecute a grievance, the main act the fifth rubric had been inscribed to prevent. In this much, *Deo gratias,* the discretion he had exercised in casting the plea had been paid back.

Suspicion, jealousy, envy, all these remained; to which was added even a certain savagery in the enforcement of his daily tasks; but the words and the signature of the Pope could in no wise be contraverted, nor could the brothers deny him time to go forth into the city to raise money for copyists—they being no better able than he had been to interpret otherwise Clement's command to secrecy.

For the rest of their malice, he had a sufficient remedy, in his heart. He wrote to Eugene, without exposing the subject: "It is the vice by which man loses himself, his neighbour, and God, which forces him to break peace with all, even with his dearest friends. He disparages everyone with insults, and assails everyone with injuries; he does not omit to expose himself to all perils, and is not afraid to blaspheme God."

He had none to say to him, "Art aware, most Christian Roger, that thou are describing someone an enemy would say much favours thee?" That man was dead.

Thus armed, he went forth into the city, which he had not seen since before Rome. By the river there was a ruin which he studied silently for a long time before his memories of both towns combined to give him understanding of what had happened: the Parisians had clumsily piled a third course atop the aqueduct, and the whole long structure had come pouring down in a rain of ill-cut stones, leaving behind naught but a few arches and a parade of jagged stumps, like a burlesque of cypresses. There was a monument to ignorance that would stub toes and bark shins for centuries to come; but he had no time now to brood over it any further, let alone teach simple Roman engineering to the rough-dressed heads of Paris. His present errand was to Louis IX, King of France.

There was no one to tell him that this were madness, since he had broached it to no one but himself. It seemed to him to be a simple and sensible project: it was the best visi-

ble use to which one could put a letter from the curator-
princeps of the next world to a prince of this, and Louis was
the best kind to read the message, as Henry III would
doubtless have been the worst. Louis loved knowledge, and
had been for a long time the patron of Vincent of Beauvais,
a Dominican who had written in the domain of theology
just such a work as Roger was now asked to write in the
sciences; had in fact not only made Vincent his librarian,
as Luca di Cosmatí had been made the librarian of
Piccolomini, Marquis of Modena, but had made him
teacher and guide to his royal children.

The letter, indeed, did bring him to the king; but it also
struck him dumb. Louis was remotely kind, as well as
amused, but would know what business it was of the
Pope's that demanded so much money; and seeing from the
letter that this could not be told, and from the shabbiness
of the emissary, of whom he had never heard, that it could
hardly be a matter of state, dismissed Roger with such a
purse as he might give to any other mendicant and turned
his mind to the next petitioner.

The purse was full of clipped trash, worth perhaps two
pounds after the counterfeits were shaken out: a magnificent gift for a beggar, but a day wasted for Roger; he retreated at dusk to the convent, gloomily biting the ragged
coins and spitting them out on to the cobbles.

It seemed reasonable, nay inevitable, that the response
of any other high personage who did not know Roger would
be the same, or perhaps much less gracious than that of
the Saint-King had been. Such remaining quality as did
know who Roger was, was in England, effectively beyond
his reach for the indefinite future; and, of course, in Rome,
which was no aid either. But wait: there was the Marquis
of Modena.

But the more he considered the matter, the more reluc-
tant he was to ask the grave scholar of Tivoli for money.
Roger had not written to Piccolomini in a dozen years; and
though there were assuredly many good and sufficient reasons for this, to break such a silence with a series of excuses directly followed by an appeal for funds would hardly
sit well with the Roman aristocrat. Yet Roger was on the
Pope's business, and durst not let any field lie fallow that
he knew might bear.

In the end, he wrote to Livia instead, explaining the circumstances frankly in so far as the mandate permitted him to do under his interpretation of it. Then he promptly forgot about this essay, for nothing was surer than that any response would be much delayed. If any money did indeed arrive from that source, it would not do so until he was in the concluding days of the work; and that would be just as well, for it would be then that the copyists' bills would be falling due one after the other.

His next port of call was the laboratory of Peter the Peregrine.

"Roger, you know well that I am cut off from my family as of old," the experimenter said when he was finished. "Yet you gave me money when you had it, and I'd not be such a poor Christian as to refuse you now. What to do? Well, here's two pounds, as a beginning—a most poor beginning, but I am a poor man."

"Believe me, Peter, I take it as gratefully as if it were riches; as from you it is. Could you, perhaps, suggest where else I might go? I have already tried the King."

"You have? Well, you were always bold. Belike I'd have gone to him myself, had I a mandate from the Pope in my scrip . . . but I doubt it. Now let's see. . . . It would be easier, had we still the same circle of students as in the old days, to whom you gave your money; then we could simply pass a bowl around. Well, I can do that anyhow; I'll tell those present that it's a special assessment, and either they pay up or school's out. But it'll not produce so much as it would have did they know you and I could explain."

"Would it do any good, do you think," Roger suggested tentatively, "to explain it all the same, and tell them that I am the author of all those inflammatory books they've been reading?"

"No, probably not," Peter said, frowning. "They're an anti-clerical lot; what care they for the Pope's business, especially since I cannot say to them what precisely it is? Yet it might be as well to tell them that I am collecting the money for you. After all, they did lose four or five of your books, the young noodles; had those parchments belonged to the University library, the fines would have stings in them for fair; I'll sting 'em too."

"I am more grateful to you than I can say, Peter."

"I have my reasons," Peter said, smiling. "Say me neither yea nor nay, but you prosecuting a business of the Pope's must concern some work of knowledge, and you being who you are, it is bound to be knowledge in the natural sciences. I can think of nothing more worthy to be pressed upon a Pope; I have given my own life to them—what's a few pounds?"

That interview cheered Roger for the remainder of the week; and at the outcome, he had six pounds, counting the two from the King. Yet there was no objective reason for cheerfulness—six pounds was almost as little use as no money at all; and he had exhausted his roster of noblemen, major and minor alike. Well then, merchants.

Here again, he knew of none but William Busshe, an Englishman; but that limitation was not without hope. It was true that the rebels had controlled the Cinque Ports—it was at Dover that they had met Guy de Foulques on his landing as mediator from the then Pope, and had torn the proposals he carried into a thousand bits and cast them into the sea—but they might not control them now, after Evesham; and in any event they had wanted the ports for the revenues, to help keep their armies in the field, and so would have had their own interest in the maintenance of shipping. What cost Roger more worry than this theory of strategy was winning from his superiors permission to make the long trip to Wissant; he won it at last not by an exercise of subtlety, but by flourishing the papal mandate at them like a bludgeon.

He had no hope of finding Busshe himself, for this was not the season for it, nor had he learned to know the family of Busshe's hosts, during the three days that he had convalesced in their house, well enough to ask money of them. But he had with great care prepared a letter to William to be placed in their hands against the time when the *Maudelayne* should again be in port with its packs of fells. He knew the host at least well enough, he believed, to charge him most urgently with its cherishing, and most prompt delivery.

But Busshe was there. After some hesitation, and much whispering up and down stairs, the eldest daughter of his

Flemish partner brought Roger to him, with her finger laid to her lips.

Busshe lay in that same great bed in which Roger had once recovered from his sea-sickness. His hands, that had hauled cordage in Channel storms, were crossed impotently in his lap, and beneath the linens lay the shadow of a torso as narrow and as lax as a length of tarred rope. His hair, totally white, was spread out on the bolster; and in all of him there was no colour, save for a bright-busked patch of red on each cheekbone, and the blue shadows under the closed eyes.

Below, there continued the muffled sounds of comings and goings: the host's family, physicians, solicitors, agents, creditors, even sailors; Roger had seen, however, no ecclesiastics as yet. After a while, without opening his eyes, Busshe whispered:

"The plate . . . the plate. . . ."

Roger understood very well; there had been just such a vigil of kites at his father's last illness, and Robert, who had scattered it with brutal efficacy, had not then been too self-removed from his next-youngest brother to explain it. Roger bent and touched Busshe's hand gently with two fingers.

"Dear friend," he said, and then was forced to swallow. "They cannot seize thy plate for thy debts. Thou'rt not at home."

The dying man's eyes opened at the touch, looking steadfastly at the ceiling. Nevertheless, he said:

" 'Tis Roger of Ilchester. Hast come to pray for William Busshe? I am thy debtor."

There was no answer to be given; the question was as good as an indictment. The feathery voice said on:

"I have many such. The horsemen . . . at Dover . . . took away my sarplers. Bare 'scaped I with my ship. . . ."

"Rest, William, I entreat thee."

The hands stirred, fruitlessly. "Nay, no need. Well wis I . . . I be not long on live. . . . Thou'rt older too, Roger."

"Rest thee, in God's name. How may I help thee?"

At that, William Busshe's head turned on the bolster. His eyes glittered, but did not seem to see; it was the look of a limed bird. "Pray," he whispered; "pray. We will

foredo them, thou and I, Roger. Ever scrupulously fair and
honest was I with them; and now . . . they're below dividing me, like . . . the cloak of . . . many colours. Seek in my
chest, Roger."

Roger looked about. "Good William, for what?"

"The *Maudelayne*. The title's there. Nay, first the key
. . . 'tis under this pillow."

Gently, Roger extracted it, and opened the chest. In it
there seemed to be nothing but a jumble of clothing.

"The jerkin . . . 'tis sewn flat into the right-hand corner.
Thou art tonsured; say that I gave it thee to be shriven."
He gasped, and his eyes closed.

Roger hastened to him. The sweat-beads on the white
forehead were cold under his palm. But once more,
Busshe's lips moved.

"Now . . . do I thank God . . . that one came to see me
. . . in mine extremity. . . . Roger . . . what dost do?"

Through his tears, Roger croaked forth the best half-
truth of his life.

"I am an adviser to the Pope."

"Ahhhh. . . ."

The wrinkled mouth failed to close. Roger knelt; and remained kneeling for a long time.

When he was able, he closed the blind eyes with two
groats, and locked the chest; and then folded the papery
hands about the key. Then he signed himself; and laying
the leather jerkin over his left forearm, quitted the cold
room.

The kestrels were gathered just outside, and all up and
down the staircase. Roger closed the door softly, and
turned upon them a stare all the more terrible for its blind-
ness. He said: "It is ended."

There was a ragged susurrus of breath. "Good friar, we
thank thee," a heavy male voice said unctuously. "Wilt
come below, we'll sign the book; and raise a goblet for the
soul of the departed; and give thee somewhat for thine office, and thine holy Order."

"I have this for charity, and require naught else," Roger
said harshly, showing the jerkin, all Channel-weathered
as it was. "Show me thy document, and I'll leave thee
straight to thy mourning."

Forever after, he would remember Wissant not for the

rumble of its trade or the slapping of its waves, but as the dry sound of hands being rubbed together.

Out of this revulsion and guilt he lost much, forbye he could not bring himself to pause in Wissant to sell the title of the *Maudelayne,* nor even to engage an agent, but waited for this until he was back in Paris; and so for the beaten ship realized but six pounds—three times what Busshe had paid for her in his unrecoverable youth, but that had been before the wars, when the pound had been the hardest coin in all of Christendom; and the journey to and from the *Maudelayne*'s master had itself cost Roger nearly a pound. The net was ten pounds.

Tragic though it had been—and selling the *Maudelayne* had been more than a little like selling one of his sisters—the success of the trip, thus qualified, led him to thinking farther afield. Not to Rome, naturally, and certainly not to England; but since the brothers had let him go as far as Wissant, then most of the Gallic nations should be open to him. For example (though it was the only example that occurred to him): it had been Simon de Montfort who had brought Roger to the attention of Guy de Foulques, thus in a sense beginning all this; or it had begun even before, when, as Eleanor's Confessor, Adam Marsh had arranged that marriage. And Simon's widow was now in exile in Gascony. Why not?

The brothers produced reasons like virtuosi; Roger demolished them. The demolition would have accomplished nothing had it not been for the precedent of the journey to Wissant, which had weakened their logic as the mandate of Clement had weakened their authority. Roger handed his mop to Joannes, who flourished it like a banner, and set forth.

The castle in Labourd was not yet ruinous, but it had not far to go; and it was almost empty; if the man-at-arms who took Roger to Eleanor was not the same, without his mail, who later served as her footman, they were at the very least fraternal twins. The footman had first to drag off an enormous slavering mastiff which snarled and roared at Roger till the bare hall rang shatteringly; the footman would have taken the beast entirely away, but at a motion from Eleanor, he instead chained it to a ring in the near wall, where it stood straining, its snarls as steady and unsettling as the noise of an anchor-hawser running out.

Though the clamour distracted him, Roger somewhat welcomed it too; for many years had passed since he had seen Eleanor last—never, he recalled slowly, since Beaùmont, for despite their propinquity at Westminster their paths had not crossed there. And he had never noticed then that she was beautiful; he saw it now for the first time, as, *But she is still beautiful.*

He could hardly interpret what he meant by this, except that he knew vaguely that she was older, somewhat, than he was; which meant that she was more than fifty *ae.* How much more mattered not in the least, for to Roger's eyes she had not changed: tall and slender she stood as before, eyes the colour of sheet lightning under the broad brow, hands white, tapered and smooth as an eidolon of Mercy, issuing from the sorrowing sleeves. Looking at her, Roger's demon self said to him, also for—alas!—the first time: *Livia too was beautiful.*

"My Lady," he said above the growls of the animal. "I . . . presume upon your mourning, and ask your pardon. I am about a business for his highness the Lord Pope, otherwise—"

"Most Christian Roger, thou'rt welcome." Roger took a step forward; the dog leapt against the chain, shouting. Like a girl, Eleanor clapped her hands to her ears. "Oh, we shall never hear each other! Hanno, I'll switch thee!"

She smote her hands together, once. "Bring him his bed—else will I never hear the friar's holy rede!"

The footman silently brought a circular rag carpet of no particular colour and far gone in dog hairs, and threw it cautiously against the wall under the ring. Hanno stepped on to it one vast pad at a time, and then turned on it as if making up his nest, until he had created a grey lump of cloth far too small to sleep a puppy upon. On this he sat, regarding his mistress with patient reproach, and growled thereafter only faintly, deep in his chest, when Roger raised a hand, or breathed.

With one eye nevertheless upon Hanno, Roger tumbled forth his errand. As Eleanor listened, her eyes closed slowly, until at the end her spare strange beauty was not that of a woman, nor even of a statue, but that of the Platonic absolute of which all beauty is but a shadow in a cave, cast by the Fire beyond fire. Hanno grumbled and lay down; Roger faltered; beyond the embrasures, the sweet birds of Gascony faltered too.

Then her lids flew open. "Oh," she said, putting her hands to her throat; "oh. Sweet Roger Bacon, I am old. Oh, an I could give thee what thou need'st! But I am not what I was—and though so praydeth I to the Virgin, nay never could I give, but only take. I think I must be damned."

"Good my Lady! . . . None can know that to be true. Thou art noble surely, and wise; why dost despair of God? Hast not courage? I know thou hast."

"But have not love?" Eleanor said. "Not that? I prayed for it when I was married to Pembroke, as a little girl; prayed to give it, that I might be worthy of receiving. And oh in what perfect measure my lords gave it me, and so also my sons—and they are gone, all gone from me who failed them. I loved them. I loved them, oh Mother and Bride; but it was not enough. They were all taken away."

"My lady. . . . We shall all be taken away."

But she was already kneeling, her tears coursing over the backs of her hands. The monster coughed, but made no objection when he knelt with her, though its eyes were smoky as obsidian.

After a while, she stood, and it was almost as though they had only just met.

"Forgive me, Friar Bacon. I am not myself today. Now let us see what I can do for mine enemy the Pope."

With a subdued shock, Roger realized what she meant, and raised a hand to halt her, but she would not be halted.

"Once had I hope of those high designs of my lord of Leicester, those Mad Parliaments and new charters, those forays of peoples against princes," she said somnolently. "I little thought the King my brother capable of withstanding Simon, strange though the Earl's purposes oft struck me. But the King's course was also the Pope's, and mayhap God's—I took that too little into mine accountings, and so am bereft, as now you see me; that course prospers, while my lord's is dead with him; as you here and now remind me in heaven's own good time."

"Not I!" Roger cried. "I am on no business of King

Henry, good my lady." But the words sounded thin in his own ears. The Pope had been, and was still, Henry the King's ally . . . and for her, the civil war had been, literally, husband against brother.

"Nay, nor did I mean my words to be taken so. In thee, I see only the prospering of God's business in Rome, through its best English instrument; we French are near outworn. So taught me my lord to think of thee, Friar Bacon, when I knew thee not; my lord, and eke one other."

"One other? Forgive me, my lady—I ask it not in vanity, but for the judgment of mine own soul in hope of heaven: who was that one?"

Her eyes closed again for a moment. "I cannot speak for him."

"Well wis I. Yet was it—was that one Friar Marsh?"

There was no answer. After a while, she clasped her hands and walked slowly to a near window.

"Let us speak no more of all those that are dead . . . no more of these, but only on thine errand. How may I help? The way is far from clear. I am in perpetual exile, a widow, and without arms. Were this fief threatened, I could not protect it; were the castle besieged, I could not hold it; nor have I men to collect my taxes, so that I cannot even keep my fortifications in repair. Of late, some worthy franklins have remembered who was my lord, and his strange doctrines; and thus emboldened, have banded together, against some future war, to buy the castle from me, with myself as . . . caretaker. Though I have refused, I shall not be able to refuse a second time, and will instead betake myself to Montargis; but I have not these monies yet."

"Good my Lady. I should have anticipated of this some substantial part. Give me but a shilling for mine Order, and I shall not trouble thee more."

She swung quickly upon him. "This to me, Roger Bacon? I am Eleanor of Pembroke and Leicester, and sister to a king! Shall it be said that she gave the Vicar of God a shilling? Wait."

She left the hall, supple as an elm, and seemingly as tall. Roger was left alone with Hanno, who had risen, and blinked at him with slow implacability. A sweet smell of apple-blossoms drifted in through the window she had quitted. Suddenly, as though he had come to some dim conclusion, the huge dog lay down once more and put his head on his paws.

When Eleanor returned, she bore in her hands a small casket of boxwood, with iron clasps: a mean thing, and crudely carved, yet she held it before her as though it were more costly and more fragile than a crystal egg.

"When I was but a princess five years old," she said quietly, "Hubert de Burgh that was my guardian gave this to me. I wore it round my wimple, and feigned to be a queen; and, as so feigned I, so was I. I kept 't for mine own daughter; but now I shall have none. See."

She lifted the lid and held out the rude jewel-box. Within, upon a fold of worn damask, lay a child-size coronet of gold filigree, set with pearls and fronted by a cool amethyst about the size of a millet. The woven gold was much dulled by time, but glowed slowly with a reddish light, as if in the sleep of Charlemagne. Roger lifted his eyes and tried to see her as a child with this above her brows, and for an instant did so; then the pain in the present eyes, womanly beyond all compare since the orange gardens of Tivoli, sponged away the vision and left him empty.

"My Lady . . . it may be that I do not understand. Is this—? I dare not think it."

Her eyes shuttered. "Were you to refuse me, I would take it ill. Here, please, Friar Bacon. Take it. I have held it far too long; that child is dead."

Numbly, Roger took the boxwood chest. How had he come to this? Surely he had never been formed to be a beggar; for the wounds were dreadful.

The coronet did not prove to be as valuable as he had hoped, but nevertheless it brought him by far the largest fruit of his beggary yet: thirty-five pounds, bringing his total to forty-four. And unexpectedly, while he was in Gascony, there had arrived for him a letter from Rome.

It read very brief:

My daughter Olivia whom you address is gone into a convent. I send you herewith ten ducats. Had you written to me I would have sent more.

MODENA

And so, another friendship spoiled by his gracelessness; it was easy to see, now that it was too late, wherein the affront had lain. And the price of his friendship was ten ducats, or approximately three pounds.

His time was virtually run out. The new year was upon him, and the brothers were demanding that he return to his duties. There was nothing left to do but go to the usurers; a step that was anathema to him, but all other possibilities were exhausted. He was forced to visit three of them, for no one would give him any substantial sum, because of his visible lack of good security; it was only upon his promise to send an expense account to the Pope that they would give him anything at all.

Even this petty scrabbling was brought to an abrupt end upon the arrival of four more pounds from Peter Peregrine—not by the sum itself, but Roger's discovery that Peter, having gotten wind of Roger's dealings with the usurers, had mortgaged his house for the money. This was truly the final humiliation; the firm sign to stand fast with what he had.

As early as Epiphany it became clear to him that the *Communia naturalium* would have to be abandoned. It could no doubt be finished at a later date, when he had had more time for study and for consultation with other experimenters and philosophers, but he could not encompass all of the natural sciences for the Pope in his present state of ignorance and confinement. There could be no *scriptum principale*; the best he could hope to achieve would be a *persuasio* of some length, an attempt to convince the Pontiff of the value of natural knowledge, and the importance of supporting its investigation.

Nevertheless even this would have to be most carefully planned. After a week, he had an outline which seemed satisfactory as a start. The letter would be divided into seven parts: The first would expose and analyse the four causes of human error, and here he could use a great part of the *De erroribus* verbatim; next would come the relationship between natural philosophy and theology, with special attention to the problem posed by the knowledge of the pagan philosophers and poets, and its solution as revealed in the *Secret of Secrets*; third, the beauty and utility of the study of tongues, with brief discussions of Hebrew,

Chaldean and Greek, and a commentary on the evils of faulty translation; fourth, a demonstration that mathematics is the key to all other sciences, beginning with *De laudibus mathematicae*, and drawing examples from astrology, astronomy, calendar reform, chronology, geography and optics; fifth would follow the *Perspectiva*, covering the general principles of vision, direct vision, reflection and refraction, with an analysis of the anatomy of the animal eye, and in addition enough of *De multiplicatione specierum* as was needful to show that the propagation of light was only a special case of a universal property of space and time; sixth, an exposition of the virtues and methods of experimental science, with a demonstration of its powers provided by the treatise on the rainbow; and finally, moral philosophy, the crown and seal of the whole, the science of the salvation of man. It would be no small task in itself; but unlike the *Communia*, at least it looked practicable.

And thus it began:

A thorough consideration of knowledge consists of two things, perception of what is necessary to obtain it, and then of the method of applying it to all matters that they may be directed by its means in the proper way. For by the light of knowledge the Church of God is governed, the commonwealth of the faithful is regulated, the conversion of unbelievers is secured, and those who persist in their malice can be held in check by the excellence of knowledge, so that they may be driven off from the borders of the Church in a better way than by the shedding of Christian blood. Now all matters requiring the guidance of knowledge are reduced to these four heads and no more. Therefore, I shall now try to present to your Holiness the subject of the attainment of this knowledge, not only relatively but absolutely, according to the tenor of my former letter, as best I can at the present time, in the form of a plea that will win your support until my fuller and more definite statement is completed. Since, moreover, the subjects in question are weighty and unusual, they stand in need of the grace and favour accorded to human frailty. . . .

Now there are four chief obstacles in grasping truth, which hinder every man, however learned, and scarcely allow anyone to win a clear title to learning, namely, submission to faulty and unworthy authority, influence of custom, popular prejudice, and concealment of our own ignorance accompanied by an ostentatious display of our knowledge. Every man is entangled in these difficulties, every rank is beset, for people without distinction draw the same conclusion from three arguments, than which none could be worse, namely, for this the authority of our predecessors is adduced, this is the custom, this is the common belief; hence correct. An opposite conclusion and a far better one should be drawn from the premises, as I shall abundantly show by authority, experience and reason. Should, however, these three errors be refuted by the convincing force of reason, the fourth is always ready and on everyone's lips for the excuse of his own ignorance, and although he has no knowledge worthy of the name, he may yet shamelessly magnify it, so that at least to the wretched satisfaction of his own folly he suppresses and evades the truth. Moreover, from these deadly banes come all the evils of the human race; for the most useful, the greatest, and most beautiful lessons of knowledge, as well as the secrets of all science and art, are unknown. But, still worse, men blinded in the fog of these four errors do not perceive their own ignorance, but with ever precaution cloak and defend it so as not to find a remedy; and worst of all, although they are in the densest shadows of error, they think they are in the full light of truth. For these reasons they reckon that truths most firmly established are at the extreme limits of falsehood, that our greatest blessings are of no moment, and our chief interests possess neither weight nor value. On the contrary, they proclaim what is most false, praise what is worst, extol what is most vile, blind to every gleam of wisdom and scorning what they can obtain with great ease. In the excess of their folly they expend their utmost efforts, consume much time, pour out large expenditures on matters of little or no use and of no merit in the judgment of a wise man. Hence it is necessary that the violence and banefulness of these four causes of all evils should be recognized in the beginning and rebuked and banished from the consideration of science. For where these bear sway, no reason influences, no right decides, no law binds, religion has no domain, nature's mandate fails, the complexion of things is changed, their order is confounded, vice prevails, virtue is extinguished, falsehood reigns, truth is hissed off the scene.

And with this, he launched upon such a fury of composition as he had never known before in his life; nor, in fact, had ever been known in the history of the phenomenal world.

The letter grew and grew, and the months went by: the Purification of the Virgin, St. David, St. Richard, Inventio Sanctae Crucis, St. Barnabas. By June, a year after Clement had sat down to write to Roger, he had gotten only as far as the analysis of the rainbow, and here he was forced to stop by the discovery that, of the nineteen experiments by which he proposed to demonstrate the nature of the bow, he himself had not performed three, and that they did indeed require an astrolabe; and in addition, he needed to observe a lunar rainbow, which stubbornly failed to appear for nearly a month. Only then could the writing be resumed.

The feasts marched by: Visitatio Mariae, Lammas, St. Giles, the Holy Guardian Angels. At last he was launched into the section on moral philosphy; he knew as he worked that the pressure of time was coming between him and the subject, but for time there was no remedy but eternity.

The letter was finished on All Saints' Day, almost precisely ten months after he had begun it. It would take more months to copy, for its length was almost half a million words.

While he waited on the copyists, he began the composition of an introductory letter for this huge mass of leaves. He was by no means through; for as he worked, he was dogged both day and night, labouring and resting, by the whispering of his demon self, tormenting him constantly with the thought that the large work might well be lost amidst the perils of the road, and never reach Clement at all. At the very least, the introductory letter should contain a summary of the plan of the work, and of its major conclusions; this would be useful as well, were the Pope to be too busy to read the large work, as was also wholly possible.

But the self did not let him rest even there. There were sections of the large work that were inexcusably badly argued, particularly the discussion of the seven sins of theology; the analysis of astrology was scrappy and inconclusive; and although Roger had discussed medicine at some length, he had said almost nothing about alchemy, that most useful of the ancillary sciences, and the one in which—though for the wrong reasons—any prince would be most likely to be interested.

All these matters went in, and more besides, until what had been meant to be but an introductory letter had become a treatise in itself; by no means so formidable as the first, but still a good thirty thousand words long. More expenditures! But there was no question but that it, too, would have to go to the Pope; he dispatched it to the copyists, and began all all over again to write an introductory letter, this time for both works.

Though he had not spoken of it as yet in the convent, Roger had already conceived the scheme of sending his *persuasio* across the Alps in the hands of Joannes. There was probably no wise man in Paris who would be as able as the boy to explain to Clement the difficult passages in the work, should the Pope require it; and for Joannes, the opportunity to exhibit his understanding before the Supreme Pontiff was such a one as no apprentice would dare aspire to in his usual life, nay not even in his dreams. Roger had allotted the boy some mention in the large work, but a more elaborate introduction might not be amiss—especially in view of the possibility that Clement might not read the large work at all.

Then the large work came back from the copyists. Roger was appalled. It was an even poorer performance than he had realized; it would have to be extensively revised, especially the first three parts. As for the seventh part, it was hopeless; no amount of revision would rescue it in the time he had available.

While he wrote, the small work also came back; and with it, the bills. They took the remainder of the sixty pounds cleanly away, leaving behind only the small sum Roger had set aside for Joannes for the journey to Rome. Yet the large work was now so heavily marked that much of it would have to be copied over again.

From this dilemma there was only one way out, regardless of the Pope's command: he would have to show the large work—but certainly not the small, for that contained a passage on the spectacular stupidities of Alexander of Hales which might well be judged to be in violation of the provisions of Narbonne, as tending toward the division of the Order—to his superiors, and appeal to have it copied in the convent. It was risky; and Clement could not be told of it; but all the money was gone, and so naught else would serve.

In the meantime, he still needed to write an introductory letter to both works, for he had cannibalized the second such for the revision of the large work so heavily that hardly anything was left of it. Best to abandon that for the time being, and make still a third introduction —this time strictly confined to its purpose; if the second introduction were on the verge of becoming another volume of Roger Bacon his universal encyclopedia of all that was known or knowable in the world, it would not suffer for being held back a while; nor would Clement suffer the lack of it, or know that he so suffered until he saw it; after which, if God allowed him wisdom, he could not but forgive, and learn; or else, what was knowledge for?

The response of the Father Superior to the large work was unexpected, and more than welcome: he not only found it unobjectionable—though there were some harsh words in the first section, they were not applied to anyone by name—but admirable. Though he did not say so outright, the notion seemed to have occurred to him that perhaps there was after all some fame to come to his convent through the activities of this obscure but obviously learned friar—exactly as the exasperating man had claimed all along.

Regardless of what he thought, what he did was gratifying. Not only did he authorize the copying of the large work inside the convent, but also relieved Roger of his corrective discipline until the labour for the Pope should be completed. In casting his ruling in this form, he inadvertently put himself into Roger's hands; for both the third work—as Roger was now coming to think of it—and the *Communia naturalium* were for the Pope, as he could abundantly prove, and not even he could say how long it would take to complete them both. It would be a matter of years, without doubt.

The brothers, by dividing the task among themselves, speedily finished the copying of the revised large work; and the almost intolerably excited Joannes, with many protestations of his undying love and gratitude, and attended by many prayers for his safety, was sent forth into the city to seek out and join a party ready to journey over the Alps.

With a sigh, and an additional prayer for the safety of his fifteen months of unremitting labour, Roger returned to his writing. To be able to study and compose once more without distraction or impediment was a blessing; he felt, indeed, like Cicero recalled from exile. And there was still much to be done: in addition to writing a discussion of the nature of a vacuum, and many other matters not covered in either of the two departed works, he had now to consider what his course was to be were the response of the Pope to be favourable.

For this he had already developed a plan, which he had outlined briefly in the final introductory letter; namely, that the Pope—and other princes too, if necessary—sponsor a true compendium of all knowledge of the natural sciences, for the edification of laymen, each section on a special science to be written by a man learned in it. It was now time to develop the proposition and think it through.

Obviously the book must be true throughout, and its truth proven as far as possible by trustworthy experience. The contents would have to be chosen carefully and in a systematic way, so as to avoid the manifold confusions between metaphysics and the natural sciences which were the bane of the universities. Brevity too would be a virtue in a work for laymen, and this might well be difficult to achieve, not only an account of the well-known tendency of even the best scholars to be as pompous as possible, but in addition because there would surely be areas of study where brevity would prove to be incompatible with clarity. The work would need as its director something more than a mere commentator and guide: he would have to be someone skilled in a special science, as yet uninvented, which would examine the findings of each of the other sciences as given, and draw them together into a meaningful whole.

Roger set himself now to the creation of that new science, so that if word should reach him that the Pope looked upon the initial effort with approval, he should not be found unready, as he had been found before. And then too, would be the time to present to the Pope his tally of the expenses he had incurred on behalf of the Curia.

He worked with great care now, since the need for haste had disappeared, making every argument as closely reasoned and perfect as was in his power. That some of these were consequently extremely difficult and dense of texture he was well aware, but after all, Joannes would still be in Rome to explain the hard parts if Clement required it.

He had begun in mid-April; by August he had a work of some sixty thousand words, with which he was thus far reasonably well pleased; and he paused to consider what should be done with it. Though it was unfinished, it might be as well to offer what he had to the brothers, for copying while he worked on the remainder; this would save much time when the next papal mandate arrived. But after long thought, Roger reluctantly decided against it. The difficulty lay in the fact that the new work opened with a long account of the difficulties he had undergone in writing the first two; and though it was all only too true, assuredly the brothers would take it ill. He was equally determined not to remove the passage, for it was the very heart of his case to Clement that his expenses should be repaid. He would have to copy it himself; and that being the case, it were sensible to finish it first.

But he had gone little farther ere he was called before the Father Superior.

"Friar Bacon, it is ordered that thou art released from all discipline, and permission is granted thee to return to thy parent house of our Order at Oxford."

Roger's heart nearly stopped. Surely, surely this was a sign of favour from on high!

"For what reason, Father, I beg thee? And who hath so ordered?"

"No reason is given. The order cometh from the provincial minister; and could not have been issued, of course, without the knowledge and consent of the Minister-General. Beyond that, we know nothing."

"But my works for Pope Clement! Is there no word from His Holiness at all?"

"No word," the Father Superior said, signing himself. "His Holiness is dead."

XIV: THE MINISTRY

Too numb to feel despair, Roger returned to his old eyrie in the gatehouse. He had not even Bungay to share it with him now, for Thomas was still the vicar of the provincial minister of the Franciscan order in England. He was quite alone; and the great work of his life was gone as well, dropped into a vacuum; *nihil ex nihil fit.*

He never found out why it was that he had been sent home, nor whether Clement had read any part of his letters, or ever had received them. He wrote to the papal secretary and got no answer, which did not surprise him; that beleaguered man had matters of more moment to think about. The death of Clement had thrown all of Christendom into confusion. The disorders between the regulars and the seculars had broken out anew, and with more virulence; and so had the rivalries between the two Orders, thereby further worsening the situation. Polemics accusing the Orders of dreadful sins and excesses, very reminiscent of William of St. Amour—who had himself indeed returned to the offensive—again abounded, and both Bonaventura and Thomas Aquinas found themselves occupied almost full time in composing answers to them.

The centre of the storm was in Paris, where the polemics flew like snowflakes; but no centre of learning and piety was immune. Roger arrived back in Oxford, in 1269, just in time to be a witness to a scarifying dispute between the Dominicans and the Franciscans, on the virtues of poverty versus the Franciscans' practice of it, held in public before the entire Faculty of the University. The throne of the emperor, too, was vacant and in dispute, and in the Italian peninsula, now almost wholly in the hands of Charles of Anjou, there was civil war. Even after five years, the bale and woe distilled by the great comet through the ambient air was implacably at work.

Roger was not greatly surprised. He had told the Lord Pope himself that the Joachite prophecies, and those that warned of the imminence of Antichrist, were worthy of being credited, though with due caution as to the date they gave; these disorders were but further evidence to the same effect; but Clement had been taken, and there was now no Pope to hear such counsel, let alone heed it. Nor was Roger disposed to give it; caution was not in him, but his taste for Church politics of this kind had never been great, and the long grinding of the years of corrective discipline in the convent had worn even that little down to nothing, as, he realized dully, it had from the outset been intended to do.

He had before him, too, another example, should he thus far have failed to draw the moral. There was now being circulated among the Faculty of Arts—and throughout Europe, apparently—a letter on the theory and the uses of magnetism, from the hand of Peter the Peregrine. The circumstances of its writing were curious: somehow, as a Picard, or perhaps even by choice, Peter had been caught up in the army of Charles of Anjou, and on the eighth of August, while sitting out the siege of Lucera, he had decided to summarize his twenty years of study of the problem, and put it into the hands of a countryman, lest the knowledge die with him. He began:

You must realize, dearest friend, that the investigator in this subject must know the nature of things, and not be ignorant of the celestial motions; and he must also make ready use of his own hands, so that through the operation of this stone he may show remarkable effects. For by his carefulness he will then in a short time be able to correct an error which by means of natural philosophy and mathematics alone he would never do in eternity, if he did not carefully use his hands. For in hidden operations we greatly need manual industry, without which we can usually accomplish nothing perfectly. Yet there are many things subject to the rule of reason which cannot be completely investigated by the hands.

It was all reasoned with the most admirable rigour, and buttressed everywhere with experiments with lodestones of all kinds, including spherical ones, and with both pivoted and floating needles, the latter collimated against a reference scale divided in the Babylonian manner into 360 degrees.

It was a monument to what could be accomplished by a carefully planned programme of study, from which, until this mysterious adventure with the army of Anjou, Peter had not deviated in all those twenty years; and thus the virtue of silence and study, as opposed to the search for fame and position. For those same twenty years what had Roger to show, but two inordinately swollen manuscripts which now were lost, and an incomplete third impotently addressed to a prelate already dead? nay, his rule would be silence and study from this day hence; naught but silence and study.

Nor did it fail to occur to Roger that between Peter's presence outside the walls of a town in southern Italy, and the mortgaging of his house to raise money for Roger, there might be some causal connection. Toward the usurers which Roger had visited, he felt neither obligation nor compassion; usury was a sin, for which they would yet pay more dearly than by the loss of the paltry sums they had lent him; and besides, they were of course only Jews, since no Christian could engage in such commerce. But Peter, should he survive, must have back every penny.

The most obvious route to this goal was to write and publish books, from the sale of which the Order would profit, and would allow him a tithe. Though the censorship of Narbonne was still fully in effect, he was now more sophisticated in the various ways of coping with it, and he had several new advantages. Chief among these was the presence of Thomas Bungay in the office of the provincial minister, from whence permission to publish a work by Roger Bacon might be much more easily won than had ever been possible in Paris. Furthermore, there was no real impediment to the publication of works which obviously could add no faggots to the fires of controversy now raging within the bosom of the Church.

Roger tested this hypothesis with a Greek grammar. It was published without question, and widely copied; in the first year of its existence, it brought in as his share almost a pound. For a subsequent Hebrew grammar there proved to be much less demand, as he had anticipated, but again its publication had been brought about as easily as though there had been no censorship at all. Encouraged, he set himself next to finishing the *Communia mathematica.*

In the meantime, necessarily, he had also resumed lecturing. It swiftly developed that he was widely remembered at Oxford, and though he was now less bold than he had been with his physical demonstrations, he still found a lively audience. He initiated a class in astronomy; and because this had to meet at night, discovered also that his reputation as a magician had not only survived, but grown, fed apparently by his Parisian incarceration, for which no reason had ever been made public at Oxford. In default of such a reason, there was a saying about—"There is no smoke without fire"—which he admired almost as much for its elegance as he despised it for its injustice. Against these rumours, in any event, there was no remedy but circumspection, an art he set himself to practising with all the fervent clumsiness of any neophyte with neither experience nor talent.

The *Communia mathematica*, finished at long last, was published without incident; it proved popular; the account for Peter was growing, minutely but perceptibly. Now seemed to be the logical time to finish the *Communia naturalium*; though it was not without elements of controversy, it was probably not too highly spiced a dish to be inedible by Bungay, who had now succeeded to the provincial ministership itself; and so sizeable a viand would surely fatten the Peregrine fund considerably.

Silence and study; and let the world wag. It was managing that task, on the whole, little more badly than usual. The papal interregnum had ended, after three years, with the election of Gregory X; the event undammed a tremendous outpouring of prophecy, most especially from the Joachites, who saw in Gregory the Ultimate Pope predicted aforetime in the *Introduction to the Eternal Gospel.* Roger was hopeful, but reserved judgment. Richard of St. Amour was no longer alive to dispute it; and the death of

Gerard of San Borgo, in the eighteenth year of his imprisonment, raised his partisans to new frenzies.

These half-thought-through prophecies and polemics filled Roger now with nothing but cold disgust, but he was most highly resolved to stay aloof. Still he could hardly argue, even with himself, that these coils and toils could not have been avoided years ago by application of but a little knowledge; and he permitted himself the most oblique of public comments, by making his perfect copy of the *Secret of Secrets* available to the University, and with it an introduction explaining its significance. Both Bungay and Oxford were stunned and delighted, and the work did not go back on the shelves for more than a day before it was out to be copied again; but the time for it was past—or perhaps not now to come for a century. Aristotle's advice to the godking Alexander served, in the meantime, to swell the Peregrine account.

Yet it did appear that Gregory X was not entirely comfortable at finding himself depicted by the Merlins and others as a fractional messiah, or anti-Antichrist. In the second year of his episcopate, he called a Council at Lyons, to discuss all the troubles of Christendom, spurious and real; but he had no proper appreciation of which was which, and the Council's decisions could not have made matters worse had they been deliberately calculated to do so. At the death, before the Council had even met, of Bonaventura, it was nothing short of inevitable that the new Franciscan Minister-General should be the dour Jerome di Ascoli, the bitterest enemy the Joachites had in all the Latin world. Nor did Jerome lack for new reasons. He was barely installed before being called back from a mission to the Greek emperor by the first real outbreak of Joachite violence, in a small central Italian seaport called Ancona; the brothers had taken a decree of the Council to be an endorsement, and rebelled when their Order failed to take the same view. Jerome retaliated by casting all the dissidents into prison for life, and on the spot.

Deeper and deeper all these holy men went into the mire; it was as though the guidance of God had been withdrawn from the world until the end should come. How to keep silent now, on the very verge of Armageddon? Knowl-

edge should be useful! and for the lack of it these devout
knaves were stumbling to and fro as blindly as sheep in a
burning fold. *Speak,* the self insisted, almost as though it
were pleading with him. *Speak!*

But speak in what voice? None listened to Roger now,
beyond the confines of his special competencies. Daring to
attack these follies he had, and bitterness enough as well;
but he had no audience that might effect the changes that
were most needed in the world. Suppose that he were to
undertake at last that compendium of philosophy which he
had so often projected, and from which he had so often been
turned away—how would he finish it in time to reach those
who would need to read it, and how shoulder aside all ob-
structions vehemently enough to cast sulphur into the
eyes of the Antichrist before it was too late?

These questions allowed him no recourse. He must try to
write that work, though he had never been less ready. And
it must begin with a frontal attack, for the time for prudence was run out.

As he wrote, the memory of his slights began to rise and
rise in him, until in his throat he could taste nothing but
bile all the day long, and all the night too; until the very
ink that dripped from his quill was greenish with it, until
his every word was engorged with it. Now was the time,
not only to name errors, but to name names:

For nearly forty years the University of Paris has been
dominated by some who have made themselves into masters and teachers of the subject of philosophy, though they
have never learned anything of it worth while, and either
will not or cannot, being utterly without training. These
are brothers who entered the two Orders as boys, such as
Albert and Thomas and others who in so many cases enter
the Orders when they are twenty years of age or less. They
are not proficient because they are not instructed in philosophy by others after they enter, because within their Order they have presumed to investigate philosophy without
a teacher. So they become masters in philosophy before
they are disciples, and so infinite error reigns, and the
study of theology is brought to ruination, and with it the
conduct of the Church.

The work went quickly; though long, it took him less than a year; but after he sent it to Bungay, the silence was protracted, while the world decayed apace. He sent a query, but no answer came back; and then, much later, a brief word that the provincial minister was John Peckham, Friar Bungay having been called to other tasks, and could Friar Bacon somewhat better describe the MS. in question, of which there seemed to be no record?

The first inkling of the truth reached him when the lector to the Oxford house, the Dominican Robert Kilwardby, called together all members of the Order in the city to hear the condemnation, by Bishop Tempier of Paris, of no fewer than two hundred and nineteen "erroneous theories" now rife in Christendom, and in Paris in particular; to which Kilwardby added some of his own. Roger had been present at such a reading before, when the constitutions of Narbonne had been proclaimed, but that had been a short proclamation and a mild one compared to this. Bungay had yielded up his ministership to suppress the *Compendium studii philosophiae*, and indeed seemed to have run away with the MS. for none knew now where he was, solely to protect his friend of old—thus perilling, for love, his immortal soul.

That mortal kindness, however, did not avail; Thomas had thought only of what might happen in England, but it was the responsibility of the Minister-General's office to think of all Christendom. Within the month, that office had called in all suspect members of the Order, to present themselves in Paris, and give an account of their teachings and writings on these errors. At the head of those called from Oxford, despite all Bungay's good and desperate offices, was the name of Roger Bacon.

The office of Jerome di Ascoli at the Ministry was windowless, and bare but for a long massive table. Behind this sat Jerome himself, flanked by two brothers who seemed to be lawyers; with him too were the Parisian provincial minister and a secretary. Before the table stood Roger; but it was not he whom Jerome first addressed.

"I am no little irritated," he said slowly, but in rather a pleasant tenor voice, "that this case should have come before me. These extremists are constantly distracting me

from the serious business of the Church. Why could not it
have been dealt with locally, as I have frequently ruled?"

One of the lawyers stirred uneasily. "It was called to
Your Eminence's attention *de multorum fratrum
concilio.*"

"Because of the negligence and sloth of the provincial
minister in England. I will write to Friar Peckham of this.
It is my main duty to prevent schism in the Order, not to
question brothers on such petty offences as I see here written down. Astrology! Magic!"

"The man is also charged as a schismatic, Your
Eminence."

Jerome looked down the parchment before him, and
then nodded curtly. "I see. Then I am forced to conclude
that neither of you yet knows how to draw up an indictment. You civil lawyers will be the bane of the Church. Let
us dispose of these pins and needles." He turned to Roger a
face like a rusty hatchet. "Prisoner, do you practise the art
of astrology?"

The word of address shocked him, though he had expected naught else; but Roger was not afraid of the question. "No, Your Eminence; but I am a student of it."

"Precisely," said Jerome, looking back at the lawyers;
"and so are Thomas Aquinas, and the Bishop of Ratisbon,
and half of the scholars in Christendom."

"But, Your Eminence, the astrological doctrines of
Albertus Magnus have been specifically condemned by
Bishop Tempier!"

"Since this man has not taught them at Paris, that is
quite beside the point, and ought not to be in the indictment at all."

"Nor would I ever have been guilty of such, Your Eminence," Roger said. "I do not subscribe to the doctrines of
the *Speculum Astronomiae.*"

"There, you see?" Jerome waved the subject away.
"Now, magic. Let me see—night walking; a brass head;
raising demons; what alewives' tales! As a student of astrology, naturally the man must look at the stars, now and
again. But here's somewhat of substance: a defence, in
writing, of the books of magic condemned at Paris. Prisoner, do you acknowledge this?"

"Yes, Your Eminence. But I am and have been all my

life an opponent of magic, and have written a book to prove its nullity."

"Then what's this document?" Jerome demanded.

"Your Eminence, the books are largely nonsense, but they contain nothing that is contrary to the Christian religion. It seemed to me to be unjust that they should be condemned by men who had not even read them. So said I in that writing."

Jerome looked at him narrowly. "That was contumacious. And this on raising fiends—it is sworn to by a number, including our learned brother Richard of Cornwall."

"Your Eminence, I but demonstrated in a lecture how one can make a loud noise with a composition of saltpetre. Richard Rufus was—disconcerted."

Jerome suppressed a slight smile. "Can you show it me?"

"Certes, Your Eminence, with proper materials, as many times as you wish. You could do it yourself."

"Nay, I dislike noise as much as Cornwall. Let us press on. You are alleged to hold to Averroeist beliefs on the unity of the *intellectus agens.*"

"Your Eminence, if your clerk will bring you the record of my reading for my secular mastership, which I took here in Paris, you will find that I specifically and successfully argued against that view with Albertus Magnus himself."

Jerome swung on the lawyers once more. "But this is the document adduced in evidence! What does this mean?"

"Your Eminence—we took the argument to tend the other way."

"Then why would the prisoner adduce it himself? Let me see it."

The fascicle of the transcript was handed to the Minister-General in silence. He studied it, frowning. Roger found that he was beginning to become tired with standing; it occurred to him, with some surprise, that he was sixty-three years old. But he knew that he would remain standing for a long time yet.

"You gentle scholars," di Ascoli said finally, "cannot read, either. This is admirable disputation, and to the complete refutation of Averroes on this subject. Your incompetence leaves me no choice: all these charges are dismissed, categorically and completely."

"Your Eminence," Roger said huskily. "You are as just as you are merciful."

"Rejoice not yet, Friar Bacon. The remaining charges are of the utmost gravity. For the safety of your body, and the salvation of your soul, I bid you answer me thoughtfully. You are accused of having published forth, not once but many times, a belief in the prophecies of Joachim of Calabria; of Merlin; of the Sybil; of Sesto; and of others whose names are unknown. Do you deny any part of this?"

"I do not believe that they can all have been wrong," Roger said steadily. "The ultimate source of all knowledge is revelation, which is given, according to Scripture, to those who lead perfect lives. Can there have been none such in our time?"

"That is not for me to say, nor for any man. I speak now only of Joachim, putting these others aside. You are aware that the doctrine of the Eternal Gospel is adjudged schismatic?"

"Yes, Your Eminence. But it is not yet proclaimed a heresy."

"True," Jerome said grimly, "else would you be in the hands of the Inquisition, and not here. You have written that this doctrine in particular is worthy to be believed. Do you cling to this rede? Beware what you say!"

"I believe it to be true," Roger said. "I writ His Holiness Clement IV, of glorious memory, that I so believed. Shall I deny it to any other?"

"Then we are done," Jerome said heavily. "What matters the rest of this tally? Impudence to superiors; public attacks on eminent Dominicans, leading to strife among the regulars; infractions of the discipline of the Order, such as publishing letters to the Pope; provocation of dissension—all beside the point. Yet stay, these are also heavy charges. For the record, Friar Bacon, do you deny them?"

Roger stood silent.

"Shall it be said that you offered no defence? The Lord God seeth into thine heart, Roger. Testify, I beg thee."

"I do not deny these last," Roger said, wringing his hands, "They are true. I have been frail and contumacious indeed, and ask your mercy; and the mercy of Jesus Christ our Lord. In His name I ask it."

"In His name thou shalt be given it, in every possible measure," Jerome said, holding out his hands across the table. "These other charges are but internal matters of the Order, for which punishments are prescribed; for example, for publishing without permission letters to the Pope, three days of bread and water, and the loss of the writing. But, Roger, for the schismatic, repentance is not enough; thou must recant, else thou are still lost. What thinkest thou, in this thine extremity, of the doctrines of the Eternal Gospel?"

Roger said stonily: "Your Eminence, I believe what I have thought for twenty years. I believe them to be true."

Jerome sank back in his chair. The lawyers were congratulating each other with their eyes; but the provincial minister said:

"Your Eminence—on this matter of publishing to the Pope: The record will show, and I so testify, that I gave the learned friar the necessary permission."

Jerome looked at him for the first time. "Yes. I will deal with you later."

"But I submit, most humbly, to Your Eminence that these letters were commanded by the Holy Pope himself."

"It shall be so regarded; but what does that matter now? There is only one charge of substance here, and of this, the prisoner is guilty. He has spoken, published and acted in support of a doctrine leading toward the division of our holy Order; in plain controversion to many prohibitions thereof; and in the confessed knowledge that this was being furthered by his every word and deed."

The Minister-General stood up, resting his fingertips upon the table. His eyes were hooded and dark.

"Friar Roger Bacon is remanded to the company of his fellow schismatics, in the March of Ancona, there to be kept in hobble-gyves, with none to speak to him, for all the rest of his natural life; and on his deathbed, he shall be deprived of the sacraments of holy Church, and buried in a common grave; and his writings are forbidden all men from this time forth.

"This inquiry is now declared closed. Martin, have chains brought."

Explicit tertia pars.

Sequitur pars quarta:
HOW THAT WE BAREN US THAT ILKE NYGHT

XV: THE MARCH OF ANCONA

In the wall opposite the black iron door there was a curious
niche or alcove, whose original function was wholly
puzzling. Two stone steps led into it, and within there was
a single block of granite so placed that a man might sit
there, sidewise; but to what purpose was impossible to
fathom. Overhead in this alcove was a breach in the wall
which went to the outside, but it was so high that, even
standing on the block, Roger could barely touch it—nor
could he have seen through it had it been placed lower, for
his fingers told him that it slanted downward from the inside; so that it could not have been placed there for an arch-
er's convenience. By the rime of seepage around the sides
of the cell, it was plain that a third of the chamber was below the water line; so that the exit of that small rectangu-
lar hole, no bigger than the end of a book, could not be
more than four feet above the ground; perhaps less.

Each day, from that slanting, recondite embrasure, a
beam of dim yellow light made a blurred patch on the ceiling of the cell, coming gradually into being long after
dawn; it was brightest and had the sharpest edges at noon,
and then faded again. Otherwise it did not change; certainly it never moved.

But it was the only source of light that he had. Early and
late in the day there was a little glow in the alcove from
the downslanting hole, but only when the sun was directly
on the ground on which it looked, would it make that
blurred rectangle on the ceiling. On rainy days, there was
no light at all, and the floor of the cell became an even sea
of thick mud, through which his hobble-chain dragged the
decaying strips of old rushes, and his privy-hole filled to

the brim. On such days he sat on the stone block in the
niche, huddled away from the dripping walls and listened
to the endless hollow sighing of the Adriatic; that sea was,
he knew, very near, though he had not been permitted to
observe just where in Ancona his prison was.

On bright days he tended his calendar, though after only
a few months he no longer had any confidence in it; nor
had he from the beginning any belief that it was going
anywhere but toward his death; it had simply been something to do. He made it by lifting the centre link of his
chain, which would reach about a foot up the wall from the
dirt, and making a scratch with it in the nitre. The early
scratches, however, already were tending to fill with a stiff
gluey stuff, vaguely blue-green when the light was brightest, though they were almost surely not much more than a
year old. By summer, they would be unreadable, indeed
obliterated.

Once a day, also, he took up his vigil by the slit in the
iron door, ready to thrust out his bowl as soon as the hinges
at the end of the corridor screamed and the horses began to
trample and snort expectantly. After the horses were fed,
Otto would dump into Roger's bowl, as into everyone's as
long as it lasted, some of the gelid, mouldy mash from yesterday's trough. On holy days, if Otto was not too drunk,
there was also a sprouted onion, often less than half soft.
You withdrew the bowl quickly, because Otto would knock
it out of your hand if you appeared to him to be begging for
more, and might not give it back to you for days; and you
ate quickly, so as to hold the bowl out again for water. Occasionally, for a joke, you got horse-piss; but usually it was
water.

During these transactions, Otto could often be heard
swearing at the horses, especially when he was leading
them in or out, or when one of them trod on his foot; but he
never spoke to a prisoner. That was forbidden. Nor did
they talk to each other any more; that had been difficult
from the outset because the cells were so far apart, and
there were many echoes; but also it disturbed the horses,
and betrayed the attempt to the gaoler. Now no one spoke,
except those who were too sick or daft to know that they
were speaking, and none answered them. Occasionally, on
the hottest days when the ground was almost dry, there

came the brief musical rustle of a chain, and then another; that was their conversation.

Some sounds besides those of the sea came into Roger's cell from outside. There was obviously a road not far away—close enough to allow him to hear, now and then, the bray of a donkey, a clanking of pots, the bell and cry of a leper, or even indistinct human voices, sometimes of children—and, daily, Otto hitching two of his animals to the wagon, to go buy in the market for the brothers far above. To hearken to these, Roger came more and more to spend even fair days in the alcove, where, furthermore, he now and again was vouchsafed a vagrant current of sweet air. But this was impossible to do in the winter; though there was no part of the cell that was not cold then, the niche seared the skin even through the rags, and the wind made a prolonged dismal fluting over the lip of the mysterious embrasure, as it did also during storms.

Then, too, there were the animals. Nothing could be done with the rats; sporadically, Otto tried to trap them, and in consequence they were unapproachable. But Roger found that mice made pleasant companions. They were exceeding shy; yet by long patience he trained several to trust him, and one would even sit on his palm, grooming its fur like a cat but with much quicker strokes—there was something almost bird-like in the movement. He had little to give them for a reward, but that little seemed to be more than they were accustomed to. For some reason, it never occurred to him to give them names.

The cockroaches, like the rats, were invincibly self-centred and vicious, and horribly stupid, too; Roger learned to loathe them. But he also learned to his astonishment that spiders, for all their cruelty, love music. There was one near the door which would invariably let itself down on its cable if he whistled. It did not seem to be able to hear the voice, which was fortunate; for the second time Roger tried it with a fragment of plainsong, several other prisoners took up the tune, the horses panicked and kicked each other, and then there was no food for three days. In Roger's nightmares, all the fiends had horses' heads.

And for more than a year—or was it two?—he tried to compose in his mind the *Summa salvatione per scientiam*; not that there was any hope of committing it to writing, but only to see how it would go; and perhaps to memorize it then, to have it in his soul for the Judgment. Thinking without parchment and quill was not so impossible as he had always before supposed, and for a while he fancied that he was making a little progress; until he realized that for the want of authorities to quote, he had been for months inventing them; one, a St. Robert of Lincoln, had even somehow in his mind acquired a life history, although he knew well enough that there was no such saint.

Hunger impeded him as well, and cold; even the stench, though he was no longer more than intermittently conscious of that; and the constant galling of the gyves; and the swollen bleeding gums of the scurvy; and then, the gradual, inexorable dementia of pellagra, until he sometimes could not tell the imaginary vermin which gnawed him from the real. Now when he sat all day in the niche, he thought more and more of less and less: over and over again, one sun-ripe day in the gardens at Tivoli would pass through his memory, and then again, and again, like the combers of the unseen Adriatic; or he would dwell helplessly upon some line of Boethius, whom as a boy he had so meanly despised . . . the little lambs, frisking their tails in spring . . . the little lambs.

One year as he sat, it seemed to him that he heard someone breathing. He made nothing of it, for he often heard such things; they were only sent to torment him; often he had been promised even death and it had been snatched away. Yet the sound was very loud, and ragged, and after a while began to turn into sobbing. It was the voice of a child; and real or unreal, Roger was of a sudden distressed with God for the sorrows of His children.

He tried to speak, but could not; it had been too long. The second time, some words emerged, though in no voice he recognized as human:

Demon, do not weep.

The sound choked off abruptly; and then there was the faint drumming of running footsteps; and that was all. Yet some days later, Roger again heard the sound of breathing—now rapid, but somehow no longer sorrowful.

"Who is there?" he whispered.

The breathing quickened further, but there was no other

reply. Perhaps it was an Italian demon, and did not understand good Latin. He had a little Roman, remembered from—he did not know when; he tried that.

"Who is there?"

"Are you real?" a child's voice came back to him, tremulous, in that language. It came, like the sun, through the brick-shaped hole. He had not expected so hard a question, and tried to think of an answer; and when he had given it up, the light was gone and so was the voice.

Nevertheless it was back the next day. "Who are you in the hole?" it said directly.

That was easier. "I am called Roger Bacon, the schismatic."

"Are you in prison?"

"Yes . . . yes, I am."

"Everyone says the March is a prison. But the friars say it is only an old monastery. Were you a grave sinner?"

"Very grave. . . ."

"Then I shouldn't talk to you."

"That is also true."

"How did it happen? Was it *very* grave?"

"I do not know any longer how it happened. Why were you weeping, when I first heard you?"

"Was I? I don't remember. I sit here all the time, in this little niche in the wall, when I'm thinking. Maybe they'd punished me. But it never spoke to me before. Can you see through that black place?"

"No."

"Can you see my hand?" There was a faint sound of scrabbling, very like a rat's, and then the tips of four small fingers wove like seaweed over Roger's head.

"Yes. I could even touch it."

The fingers were snatched back. For a while there was silence. Then:

"Do you know any stories?" Far off, in Ancona, a bell began to toll. "O, I have to go. Will you be here tomorrow?"

There was a long hiatus, until Roger became sure that it had been only another hallucination. But finally the voice came back, again demanding a story, and during their exchange, Roger learned that he was talking to a boy of six *ae*, the youngest son of an olive merchant. Roger told him the story of Thomas Aquinas' encounter with the brazen head of Albertus Magnus, but he did not much care for it; the story of how the mighty Gerbert rode the eagle was better received.

Each day, Roger ransacked his memory for legends; and in the meantime, he was gradually building up a picture of how they sat together. It seemed evident that this twin alcove had originally been nothing but a priest's hole, which meant that his wall had once not been on the outside of the fortress; the structure must have been centuries old to have required such thick inner walls.

There came a day when the boy came into earshot already babbling excitedly, of what, Roger could not tell; and then, there was the slow, also indecipherable rumbling of an adult male voice. Then, came the usual gambit: "Here I am today, Roger. Tell me another story."

Roger was ready, for having run out of folk-tales, he had been for some weeks steadily working his way through the *Aeneid*; though puzzled, he proceeded as well as he was able. The preceding night had been unusually wretched, and his voice often broke, but he managed to finish without other incident.

The boy's voice said clearly: "See? What did I tell you!" And then again there was the slow rumble of the adult voice. Now it was all over, and Roger would have to go back into the silence; obviously the boy told his father or some elder brother of the delightful mystery of the talking wall, and he would be forbidden to come again; no one of mature years in Ancona could fail to know what the March was.

The deep voice stopped. The boy said, all in a rush: "My father says you are a learned man and very kind and is there anything you need?"

He seemed thoroughly delighted with himself. But how to answer the question? There was nothing that Roger did not need. After a while, he said, slowly, "I thank your knightly father. What I most need is better food. But I fear me it will never pass through that stone rat-hole."

The boy reported this. Then he said, "My father says if you had a bit of money could you put it to any use?"

"I do not know. I would have to try."

Now there came the scrabbling sound of the boy's hand,

and then the pursed fingers were above him, like a closed
anemone, precariously pinching a coin. As Roger took it,
the hand was hastily withdrawn, as though the flesh behind the voice were still more than the boy could bear.
Roger stood shakily on the stone block and looked at the
chip of metal in the scant light. As nearly as he could tell,
it was a ducat, not much clipped.

"God bless you both. I would my blessings were of some
avail. I . . . can say naught else."

A silence. The sea moaned.

"My father says that Virgil is said to be a waste of time
except in Latin. Can you teach me that?"

Roger put out a hand for support against the wet stone.
"I can teach you better Latin in a week than any other
master could teach you in a year."

"He says I will be back tomorrow. O Roger, I wish I
hadn't. Now it will be more like school."

"Oh, no. You will see. We will go right on telling
stories."

On the next morning, Roger left his bowl on the stone
seat, and instead held out into the corridor his open palm
with the ducat in it. Such was the gloom out there that
Otto, seeing nothing but the hand, passed by with a snort;
but at the end of his rounds he was back again, peering
more closely first at the outstretched palm, and then bending to glare through the slit. Finally, he took the money.
Roger left his hand where it was.

"Where'd you get that?" Otto growled. Though it was
difficult for him, he was obviously trying to be as quiet as
possible. It was the first time he had spoken to a prisoner
since Roger had come to the March—somewhere between
four and six years. Roger remained motionless, and said
nothing.

"Somebody's talking to you through some hole, eh? I can
seal that up in a hurry."

Roger withdrew his hand. "They give me money every
day," he said.

"Much good it'll do you." But Otto did not go away. Finally he said: "What do you want?"

"Some fruit. A bit of fish. Even a little meat. Clean
water."

Otto laughed. "How about a stoup of wine, Your Lordship? Go back and rot."

The next morning, there was nothing put into Roger's bowl. Otto came to him after the rounds and said, deep in his throat: "Where is it? Hand it out."

"I have nothing yet."

"So you get nothing. Hand out the ducat."

"No."

Otto went away. After three days, Roger had two coins to chink together in his cupped palms as Otto went by; and on the fourth morning, his bowl held not only the usual mash, but also a decayed orange and the head of a herring. He gave back one ducat; and after thinking the matter over for a short while, Otto silently took it.

The feast was more than Roger's body could bear: he lost it all into the privy-hole. The next, however, he kept down; and although there were other bad days, he began gradually to feel stronger. Having someone to talk to was almost more healing than the food.

In this most curious of all schools the boy, whose name was Adrian, learned in fair weather his Latin and his Greek and his logic, and even other subjects that could not ordinarily be taught through a hole, such as the Elements of Euclid and descriptive astronomy. Roger saved his ducats as he was able, and in turn learned the unspoken art of mutual blackmail, at which, though the advantage lay sometimes on this side and sometimes on that, he found himself to be a better practitioner than Otto; for in the majority of their conflicts, Otto was faced with the ultimate resource of the condemned man, *nec spe nec metu*—no hope can have no fear. Nor had the gaoler any real cause for complaint, for even the most that he gave for the money would buy a score of times as much in the outside world where he moved free.

On one fine spring morning Roger was ready for the most bold of all his undertakings. Though he had been unable to win himself new rags or new rushes, because Otto would not enter the cell for any amount of money, so that no betterment could be gained that would not pass through the slit in the iron door, he felt well and cheerful; and he had hidden in the privy-hole—for there was no other place to hide it—no less a sum than twenty-seven ducats, hoarded over three years. For this wealth he meant to demand nothing smaller than the removal of the horses from the corridor. He did not think that Otto would try to take it away from him, not after having been three years sole owner of the golden goose.

But Adrian did not come that morning; nor ever came again. While Roger waited in the alcove, the ducats in the privy were given out one by one, for nothing but food; and the moment Roger began to try to conserve them, Otto sensed that there were soon to be no more. For the last few he gave nothing but the old slops from the horsetrough, and for the last one, he gave nothing at all, but simply starved it out of Roger's hands.

A fuzzy square of light on the ceiling, motionless. No, it was raining. A wailing in the night; someone was dying. A wrinkled scum of ice over the privy. Blood in his mouth, and livid spots under his filth. Horses with rats' heads. Rain. An incessant hammering. The little lambs in spring. The structure of the eye. As I shall prove to Your Holiness by many examples. Look in the mirror, Beth, just for a moment. Would God allow? If you have no time to examine these difficulties, Joannes is more capable than anyone. I gave him thirty pieces of silver. I have these smaller manuscripts, *aliqua capitula.* Here, Petronius, here, puss. Why don't they stop that hammering? Virtue, therefore, clarifies the mind so that a man may comprehend more easily not only moral but scientific truths. Is it today that He gives us the onion? *Forsan et haec olim meminisse juvabit.* Tonight we shall see Mars and Jupiter in trine. Sit here, Livia. Is that rain again? I will explain everything. Silence and study. If I were not so cold, I could explain it all. Mother of God, sit here. I can explain it all.

One morning there was a commotion in the corridor after the horses were taken out, an angry shouting, and the flaring of torches. It went on all day, and in the evening the horses were not brought back. When the noise resumed the next morning, he crawled to the slit to watch.

The trough too had been removed. Otto was directing some three or four men with spades; they seemed to be attempting to clear the corridor out, a truly Augean task. From this activity as much as from their talk, which Roger could hardly understand, he deduced painfully that some important personage was coming, to see that the remnants of the schismatics were still properly imprisoned.

This could be of no moment to him. None the less he watched; for any change, however trifling, in the routines of the March helped to pass the iron days. The shovelling and cursing went on all week, and now that the horses were gone there was also a change in the food—lumps of bread instead of congealed mash. At the end of the week, it might have been said that the corridor was a little cleaner.

On Sunday morning—easily indentifiable by its bells—the visitor came. Roger could not see him, but he heard the door open, and then a strange voice:

"Are these the spirituals, the disciples of Joachim?"

Its tone seemed angry, perhaps even incredulous. Otto's reply was in so unusually low a voice that Roger could not make it out.

"Would that all of us and the whole Order were guilty of such a charge as this! Gaoler, release them."

"Release them? But, Your Eminence, my most clear instructions from Your Eminence's predecessor—"

"He is no longer responsible for the Order. I am. Let them out, I say!"

One by one, the black doors were opened, protesting blindly for that they had not been stirred in more than a decade. Several of them required the combined strengths of Otto and all his crew. At each cell, the ritual was the same:

"I am Raymond de Gaufredi, Minister-General to the Franciscans. Who art thou, holy friar?"

"I am called Angelo of Clareno, Your Eminence."

"Go thou with God, where thou willst. Strike off his chains." And then there was the sound of a hammer.

But not after all at every cell, for there were several of those wretches who could neither reply nor come forth, but needed to be led out, or in one instance, carried; and there were some doors which no longer needed to be opened. Roger watched and listened with only the barest comprehension of what was happening, and that little not to be believed, until the slit that fed him was jerked away from his face with a mighty squeal.

"Who are thou, holy friar?"

"I . . . am called Roger Bacon, Your Eminence."

"Go thou with God, where thou willst." At Roger's feet, Otto knelt with the hammer.

"Your Eminence . . . your pardon, if I . . . would you tell me . . . what year is this?"

"The one thousand two hundred and ninetieth of Christ our Lord."

The hammer fell, and thus he was answered. It had been thirteen years.

XVI: FOLLY BRIDGE

Blind as moles they blundered about in the even lemon glare of the sunlight, all those that survived, as confused and full of wonder as men just expelled from a garden. For the serious business of convalescing, Raymond di Gaufredi gave them three whole months, and they all went about it with the high seriousness of scholars; though there were some hurts no herbs nor unguent nor hour could heal, especially in that fortress in whose dungeons they had so long groaned and heard no other voice.

For Roger, it was overwhelming. He could assimilate it only a little at a time, beginning with such small matters as he had become accustomed to seeing at the boudaries of the universe: cracks in the wall, the taste of salt, the touch of water, the shape of his shadow; and then, gradually, the sound of voices; and then, the movement of their sense.

While he was working at it, one came to visit him, from the village—not Adrian, but some merchant, of whom he had never heard, and whom he had sent away. He was not ready for worldly converse yet; he had talked too long to himself. And he was only confirmed in this when they told him—everyone was still "they"; he was not yet able to tell one face from another—that the visitor had left him a purse. With horror, he sent it to di Gaufredi, without stopping even to look at it.

Gradually, too, and then voraciously, he won back the

knack of reading, though it gave him blinding headaches; and through this began once more to grant the world a population, with names and actions to which the minuscules testified. The written words could not give him back his thirteen years, but they could in part give them back to the world, prove that it had had a history even when he had not been watching. Through the words of the play, he was able to see the possibility of actors.

Among these he was at first more interested in the dead, as least likely to have changed; but even this was not always true. While Roger Bacon, living, had gone down into his long defeat, the dead Simon de Montfort had clothed his memory in triumph. Edward the King—who had in fact been wholly in control of England ever since Evesham, though he had not been crowned until late in 1274—had had the excellent good sense to adopt the parliamentary revolutions of his slain antagonist, and in addition, to act at once to restrain the exactions of Rome—a victory for another corpse militant, Robert Grosseteste. These moves won back Edward Longshanks both barons and rabble, as well as ample time for hunting and jousting, and the wrestling of North Wales from the hands of Llewellyn (although there were said to be some signs that that conquest was in danger of slipping away).

As for the living, Jerome di Ascoli had become Pope Nicholas IV; and he had small reason to be pleased with the new English King. Moreover, he had neither anticipated nor desired that his vacated office over the Franciscan Order would be filled by Raymond de Gaufredi; for Raymond, though wholly free of any actionable taint of Joachimism himself, could never believe that there was any heresy in its doctrines nor any evil in its adherents. What Raymond had done in the March of Ancona would be even less to the new Pope's liking, yet Raymond was far from finished. He now proposed to send all those he had delivered, when their health permitted it, as missionaries to Armenia.

This mission, Roger was permitted to decline—not only by virtue of his age, which was now seventy-six, but also because upon examination it appeared that he had never been a missionary Joachite, and that the reasons for his punishment had been much more complex than were those

that had been applied to Angelo and his brothers in the
March. There was still extant a prohibition, obtained by
Jerome from the then Pope by special letter, ruling that
the dangerous doctrines of Roger Bacon be totally suppressed. Without knowing or wanting to know what these
dangerous doctrines might be, Raymond nevertheless had
no desire to turn them loose among the schismatic Armeni-
ans. It were more prudent to let Roger go back to Oxford,
where among the sophistications of a great University his
mysterious teachings might not lack for refutation.

In addition, this disposed of the purse, the mere existence of which troubled Raymond sorely, and which Roger
could no more explain than he: the money could be used to
cherish the frail scholar on the long journey, surely a small
enough gesture from the Order at whose hands he had
undergone so much that was evil.

And thus did Roger Bacon return at last to that gatehouse above Folly Bridge, in which he and Thomas
Bungay had once studied the stars.

Here, all alone, he began once more to write, slowly,
painfully, but with an iron determination, that great work
with which he had wrestled so vainly in his first years in
the pit in Ancona: the final statement of the case for salvation through science, to be awakened gently from slumber
under a title that suggested nothing so explosive: *Compendium studii theologiae*. While he could hold a pen, the living might yet outrun the dead; Simon de Montfort might
rule a nation—though hardly more than one, for only the
English were so phlegmatic of humour as to make practicable the admission of so many plebeian voices into the
high art of government—but what if Roger Bacon established domain in the minds of men?

The dream kept him alive, and kept him company. None
asked him to lecture now, nor required aught of him at the
house of the Franciscans. He was forgotton: a ghost, scribbling away in a tower, sometimes wondered at by late-
walking students when they looked up and saw his flickering window.

So, after a year, did Bungay find him, when after this
kind old man heard in his hermitage that among those released from the March of Ancona had been one man called
Bacon. He brought back with him that manuscript of the

Compendium studii philosophiae for which he had imposed his own exile, and they kissed each other. Roger forbore to ask what pain Thomas had suffered in his behalf,
and Thomas forbore to say, for they understood one another, and that were pain enough.

Now it was almost as it had been of old. They talked far
into the nights, though their voices were very reedy;
Thomas did what little housework there was to do; and
Roger wrote. Late in autumn, there came to the gatehouse
an absurdly young olive-skinned yellowbeak, already
slightly a-shiver with the first intimations of the English
weather, who gave his name as Adrian something and desired to study with Magister Bacon, but Thomas turned
him gently away. The time for that had passed; now all
possible protections must be raised about the book.

Word by word, leaf by leaf, the great work evolved, and
Bungay read it as it came from Roger's squeaking pen, as
it could have from no other. It began quietly enough, with
a note that until now, Roger had been prevented from writing certain useful things, but had made all haste to remedy the matter. There followed the outline of the four
causes of error; the indictment, though a most gentle one it
was in the eyes of the man who had lived in hiding for fourteen years with the *Compendium studii philosophiae* for a
pillow, of the errors of men considered wise by the world;
the statement of how the argument to follow would be
conducted. . . .

All the purest Roger Bacon; and yet Bungay, as page followed page, refrained from weeping only by a pure and ag-
onizing act of will.

Roger's memory had failed. Not his memory of his reading or of his past, nay, that was there written down in vivid
detail, but his memory of what he was doing from minute
to minute. There were four causes of error, he wrote; but
on the next page were given only three; he had forgotten
not only the nature of the fourth, but that he had promised
four at all.

And yet neither elegance nor eloquence had failed him.
The reasoning was superbly close; the writing sometimes
crisply brilliant, sometimes wryly humorous, sometimes
filled with visionary beauty. But no mercy could blind
Bungay to the central chasm: Roger was arguing now only

with the shadows of his old subjects. The great work had all the apparatus of mastery, but it was not about anything. It had nothing at all to say.

Spring came; the leaves emerged, one after another, covered with delicate writing, dedicate with traceries to the sweet glory and love of God, words and works at once. On the last day of May, Roger cried out, and made a great blot; and had Bungay not been by chance at his elbow, would have toppled to the rushes.

Thereafter he did not speak or move, though his eyes were open. Bungay composed him tenderly, and then could naught but wait, and pray. He prayed for eleven days; and on the Feast of St. Barnabas, he heard below a cry on the bridge, most dim and distant, but approaching.

"An alms for John! An alms, an alms for John! Only a sterling to touch the bowl of Belisarius! Only a penny for John!"

Rising stiffly, Bungay went to the broad window, in his mind some vague memory of a street-cry that only Roger had then heard; vague, but as disquieting as a badly remembered oracle. The limping beggar crossing Folly Bridge was old, as old as Bungay himself, and as weathered as a seaman; but he looked up into Thomas's face with eyes of brilliant blue, and in that moment did not seem to be old at all. Taken aback, Thomas quit the window, but an almost inaudible bubble of breath behind him made him ashamed, and he returned. He called down:

"Boy, is that—is that indeed that ancient relic?"

"Indeed, lofty friar. Only a penny."

"Wilt swear to it, on peril of thy soul?"

"I durst not, Franciscan father. Well know you how many frauds be sold to such as I. Yet long hath it kept me on live, in all the countries of the world; and thus hath performed at least one miracle."

"Much need have I here of another. I pray thee, bring it up."

The beggar bent his head, and disappeared; but was heard almost at once upon the stairs. When he entered the tower room, he offered the bowl, but Bungay shook his head, and pointed silently.

Roger had not moved; he lay with his ankles crossed, like the effigy of one who had been to Palestine. His nose was transparent and fleshless, and his temples drawn into his skull, as were his ears, so that the ear-lobes stood out. Above black sockets his taut forehead was rough and parched; and his face was the colour of lead.

"Dear Christ!" the beggar said; and the craggy cheerful face coursed suddenly with a torrent of tears. "Friar or fiend, is this my last trap in the world? Oh, shame, oh shame, I never did any man harm—Lord God, why this to me?"

"What?" Bungay said, alarmed. "Peace, man, or thou'lt do him injury. Art so compassionate toward every stranger? If so, God bless thee; but it were better to be quiet; else take thy relic to some lesser pallet. Heed me, beggar; and mine every word; and hush!"

"No stranger to me," the beggar said, choking. "This is my *doctor mirabilis* that was; my master in Paris. Oh Christ, his ankles, his eyes—they have tortured him!"

"Nay; he was but imprisoned. Didst truly know him?"

The beggar stood to the pallet, and gently set the bowl against the sunken cheek. "Certes. 'Tis Roger Bacon."

Bungay signed himself; for this were a palpable miracle in its very flesh. "Now surely thou wert sent. What is thy name?"

"I was Johann Budrys, of Livonia; which means, John the Free. But long and long have I been only, John the Beggar."

"Beg thou with me."

They knelt together. Neither could think of anything to say. Heaven heard them, belike; but there was silence after.

"This was a holy man," Bungay whispered at last. "None credited him his piety and kindness, for that he was so perverse . . . forever at hares and hounds after matters men are forbidden to know."

John the Free looked up.

"Pious?" he said slowly; "yes, he was often pious. And kind, too, when it occurred to him; but that was not often. But there can be nothing that is forbidden man to know since we ate of that Apple; for it states in the Proverbs that knowledge is good and beautiful for its own sake. Nay—they that did this know he was a wiser man than any of his persecutors."

"The Order and the Church," Bungay said indignantly, "would never persecute—"

"Hist! Listen, holy friar!"

Roger's breathing had changed. His eyes moved.

"Roger . . . rest thee easy. Friends are nigh."

Roger sighed. They bent closer.

"Thomas?" The word barely stirred his lips.

"Yes. Rest, Roger."

"I . . . shall rest . . . after a while. It is time."

He stirred again; and then, was almost up on both elbows.

He said clearly:

"Bitterly it mathinketh me, that I spent mine wholle lyf in the lists against the ignorant. Enough! Lord Christ, enough!"

"Roger! Roger—"

But now at long last he saw, for a moment; and cried out again for love of vision, its usefulness and beauty; and for the loss of it; and reached for his pen; and went whirling down into silence and study; silence, silence and study.

Explicit Liber Fratris Rogeri Baconis.

DOMINUS ILLUMINATIO MEA

NOTES

Almost everyone mentioned in this book was a real person. The invented characters, such as Tibb, are usually obviously that, but there are some borderline cases. One of these is Raimundo del Rey, who appears both as one of the Spanish students who laughed at Roger's ignorance of Arabic (we know none of their names, but the incident is frequently mentioned in Roger's writings) and for that unknown alchemist to whose works the name of Ramon Lull was later signed (we do not know his name either, but we can be quite sure that the author in question was not the

NOTES 267

historical Ramon Lull, who was an unusually wild breed of
mystic innocent of any interest in the sciences). About
Roger's apprentice in Paris we know only what Roger tells
the Pope, which is obviously exaggerated, and what the
legend says, which is pure fantasy. The members of
Roger's family, similarly, are either real or unreal according to your preference; in my account they conform to what
little he tells us of them, but he gives no names and in
other respects as well I was free to exercise considerable
invention. (On this part of the subject invention is rife
even among historians; for instance, the flat untruth that
the Dominican Robert Bacon was the scholar-brother of
whom Roger speaks has been demolished again and again,
yet it crops up once more in Sir Winston Churchill.) The
Marquis of Modena and his daughter sprang into being out
of the opening line of the autobiography of Pope Pius II, a
Piccolomini, in which he states that his family came from
Rome—a statement most scholars consider doubtful; but
the Marquis's runaway son was certainly real, and I presume I do not need to vouch for Luca di Cosmati. William
Busshe is, of course, a pure invention, as are Wulf, Otto
and Johann Budrys of Livonia; but Raymond of Laon and
Sir William Bonecor were real, spear-carriers though they
are in this text. As for Friar Bungay, his association with
Roger is wholly legendary, but since virtually nothing is
known about him except that he existed, I felt free to accept it.

One example will suffice to show what use I made of the
Bacon legend. The incident in which Roger dispenses
learning through a hole in his prison wall is as completely
mythical as the brazen head; we know nothing at all about
those silent thirteen years. It is a charming story, however, and I adopted it because it seemed to me that if Roger
were imprisoned incommunicado, as the other Joachites
were, it offers an explanation of how this compulsive
teacher and propagandist was able to retain his sanity as
well as he did. The reader ought to be told, however, that
some Bacon scholars think he was never imprisoned at all.
This notion I judged to be nonsense—or at the best, Church
apologetics, in which this subject abounds. All the pertinent documents say that he was; the best the apologists
have been able to do is to point out that the documents, all

dated after his death, are not entirely reliable; but of what medieval document might this *not* be said?

One of the most curious quirks in the history of science is the relative weighting of two Englishmen whose names, entirely by accident, are easily confused: Roger Bacon, and Sir Francis Bacon. Both wrote enormous studies of the sciences of their times; both advocated experiment about theory; and both were masters of language, which guaranteed that they would be widely read. It is Sir Francis who is generally credited with being the philosopher who acted as midwife to the birth of modern science, particularly because he wrote and published in the seventeenth century when modern science was visibly a-stir; Roger's efforts, on the other hand, were ignored in his own time and for centuries thereafter, and lately historians of science (a relatively new discipline) have tended to dismiss him as a mere encyclopedist who contributed nothing new.

It is a pity that no major theoretical physicist or mathematician of our time has read either man. My own firm opinion is that Sir Francis Bacon's scheme for the elaboration of the sciences is purely the work of a literary genius, marvellously gratifying to read, but without the slightest demonstrable influence upon the history of science; in fact, had the scheme ever been realized, it would almost surely have set the sciences back a century or more, for Sir Francis, though surrounded by scientists of the first order, never had the slightest insight into how a scientist must necessarily think if his work is to come to any fruit whatsoever. The test of this judgment is that it is impossible to show *any* line of scientific thought after Sir Francis that is indebted to the *Novum Organum*.

Roger Bacon, though in his maturity an elegant stylist, was never even at his best an artist; but he was a scientist in the primary sense of that word—he thought like one, and indeed defined this kind of thinking as we now understand it. It is of no importance that the long list of "inventions" attributed to him by the legend—spectacles, the telescope, the diving bell, and half a hundred others—cannot be supported; this part of the legend, which is quite recent, evolves out of the notion that Roger could be made to seem more wonderful if he could be shown to be a thirteenth-century Edison or Luther Burbank, holding a flask up to the light and crying, "Eureka!" This is precisely what he was not. Though he performed thousands of experiments, most of which he describes in detail, hardly any of them were original, and so far as we know he never invented a single gadget; his experiments were tests of principles, and as such were almost maddeningly repetitious, as significant experiments remain to this day—a fact always glossed over by popularizations of scientific method, in which the experiments, miraculously, always work the first time, and the importance of negative results is never even mentioned. There is, alas, nothing dramatic about patience, but it was Roger, not Sir Francis, who erected it into a principle: "Neither the voice of authority, nor the weight of reason and argument are as significant as experiments for thence comes quiet to the mind." (*De erroribus medicorum.*)

It would be hard to find any branch of modern science which was *not* influenced by Roger's theoretical scheme; yet by the same token this leaven was so slow-working that I could do little justice to it in the course of a novel. Where I could legitimately do so, I have offered hints; but I could not, for instance, say anywhere but here that:

—a passage printed from Bacon provided Columbus with one of his chiefest theoretical props in presenting his case to the Spanish court;

—Peter the Peregrine's MS. *De magnete* greatly influenced the epoch-making treatise of Sir Francis Bacon's contemporary William Gilbert on the same subject, because Gilbert—as he says in explanation in his first chapter—attributed Peter's conclusions to Roger Bacon;

—the whole tissue of the space-time continuum of general relativity is a direct descendant of Roger's assumption, in *De multiplicatione specierum* and elsewhere, that the universe has a metrical frame, and that mathematics thus is in some important sense real, and not just a useful exercise.[1]

[1] I have quoted part of Roger's reasoning on this point in Chapter XII, but there is really no way short of another book to convey the flamboyancy of this logical jump, which spans seven centuries without the faintest sign of effort. The most astonishing thing

In some small instances, the work of lesser men did not prove to be easy to explain in fiction, either; for example, that the curious "sweet vitriol" discovered by the alchemist I have dubbed Raimundo del Rey was what we now know as ether (the anaesthetic, not the substrate). For this dilemma of historical fiction about science, I have found no workable solution but this long apology.

Roger's argument from Josephus in Chapter IX is a misquotation. What Josephus actually said was that the ancients were given long lives because they could not otherwise have made accurate astronomical observations. This may seem even more preposterous than what Roger makes Josephus say, but at least it is Josephus's own opinion, whereas the other is only Roger's. He often misquoted his authorities, even his revered Seneca, whom he misquoted at great length. It is of course entirely possible (especially when he is quoting Seneca on ethics) that he had hold of an edition now lost, which might or might not have been closer to the original than the one now extant; and quite often the variations must have been simply copyists' errors and/or mistranslations, against both of which Roger rails in work after work.[1] On the other hand, he may have introduced at least some of these distortions himself, for fo-

about it, perhaps, is its casualness; what Roger begins to talk about is the continuum of action, an Aristotelian commonplace in his own time, but within a few sentences he has invented—purely for the sake of argument—the luminiferous ether which so embroiled the physics of the nineteenth centruty, and only a moment later throws the notion out in favour of the Einsteinean metrical frame, having in the process completely skipped over Galilean relativity and the inertial frames of Newton. Nothing in the tone of the discussion entitles the reader to imagine that Roger was here aware that he was making a revolution—or in fact creating a series of them; the whole performance is even-handed and sober, just one more logical outcome of the way he customarily thought. It was that way of thinking, not any specific theory, that he invented; the theory of theories as tools.

[1] Roger's own scribes for the *Op. Tert.,* which includes a diatribe against the dog-orthography of his times, delivered the text back to him faithfully corrected into the *mumpsimus* it denounced.

rensic effect, which would have been entirely in character. Since we are dealing here with an age prior to the invention of printing, the more charitable interpretations cannot, at the very least, be disproven.

Money in the thirteenth century was scarce and its value in modern terms is difficult to estimate, since so many payments—expecially to the Church—were made in kind, and because there were then so few things to buy. It is probably conservative to reckon the English pound of the period—which was then a real pound of English pennies, the most stable coin of commerece throughout the century—at about forty-five 1960 U.S. dollars. Since the income of the average parishioner was about ten pounds a year, it can be seen that Christopher Bacon, who was able to bury two thousand pounds without even knowing (because of his ignorance of foreign exchange) the exact worth of the hoard, must have been a wealthy man indeed.

The best scholarly study of this subject known to me is Stewart C. Easton's *Roger Bacon and his search for a universal science* (Columbia, 1952), a warm, witty and elegant book. I am enormously indebted to it, particularly to its critical bibliography, which is a guide to everything about Roger Bacon which pretends to be factual, even encyclopedia articles and the scrappiest of pamphlets. Where my interpretations differ from Easton's, he is more likely to be right than I. The *Britannica* article's bibliography, however, also refers the reader to the Bacon legend; Easton studiously ignores this, but it is one of the reasons why Bacon is still a seminal figure in the Western world.